Rebecca Toueg is an Israeli citizen born in Shanghai, China, of Iraqi-Jewish parentage, and educated in British schools. After completing her B.A. degree in English literature at the Hebrew University of Jerusalem, she spent three years in England and two years in France as a foreign student. She then returned to a teaching position at Tel Aviv University in the English Department where she obtained her M.A. degree. On her retirement from teaching, she began working as a translator and editor and acquired a Ph.D. in Philosophy at Haifa University with a thesis on R.G. Collingwood. Her late husband, Ezra Toueg, was born in Cairo, Egypt. She has one son and three grandchildren.

For Arthur

Amicis semper fidelis

Rebecca Toueg

THE NEW COVENANTERS – PART I

The Rising Tide

AUSTIN MACAULEY PUBLISHERS™

LONDON • CAMBRIDGE • NEW YORK • SHARJAH

A CIP catalogue record for this title is available from the British Library.

Cover illustration: Painting of Jerusalem by the 19th century Scottish painter, David Roberts.

ISBN 9781398483514 (Paperback)
ISBN 9781398483521 (ePub e-book)

www.austinmacauley.com

First Published 2023
Austin Macauley Publishers Ltd®
1 Canada Square
Canary Wharf
London
E14 5AA

I am deeply grateful to Professor Arthur Segal, Emeritus Professor of the Department of Archaeology, Haifa University, for his unfailing support and encouragement, for his careful reading of the text, and for the corrections and critical comments that he has made throughout the course of my writing. He has been more than generous with his time and attention, and provided me with the benefit of his scholarly and extensive knowledge of Roman history, archaeology, architecture and general information about the period covered by the novel. It is therefore dedicated to him with appreciation, affection and gratitude.

I am also greatly indebted to many authors of books and articles for their historical research and reconstruction of past events. Among the more important ones are the following:

Steve Mason, *A History of the Jewish War, AD 66–74.*
Neil Faulkner, *Apocalypse: The Great Jewish Revolt Against Rome, AD 66–73.*
James Bloom, *The Jewish Revolt Against Rome, AD 66–135: A Military Analysis.*
Mireille Hadas-Lebel, *Jerusalem Against Rome.*
Martin Goodman, *Rome and Jerusalem.*
Joachim Jeremias, *Jerusalem in the Time of Jesus.*
David Flusser, *Judaism and the Origins of Christianity.*
Geza Vermes, *Jesus the Jew.*

Preface

This is a historical novel written as a trilogy: I. *The Rising Tide; II. The Approaching Storm*; III. *Apocalypse and Aftermath*. It begins with the death of Herod the Great in 4 BCE and covers the events in Judaea and Rome during the course of the 1st century CE. The main characters are Nicodemus ben Gorion, Joseph of Arimathea, Jeshua (Jesus), James the Just, Agrippa I, Agrippa II, Berenice, Johanan Ben Zakkai, Philo of Alexandria, Tiberius Alexander. The central figure is Josephus Flavius, his early childhood and youth, his mission to Rome, his appointment as general in the Galilee during the Great Revolt, his defeat and his transfer of loyalty to Rome.

Chapter 1 (4 BCE–14 CE)

It was the end of an era. King Herod, who had ruled the country for thirty-three years, lay dead in his winter palace in Jericho, diseased in body and mind. The funeral procession would set out from there towards the southwest, a long journey of more than 25 miles through the hot desert-like countryside to his palatial fortress Herodium where they would bury him. A phalanx of soldiers surrounded the golden bier on which he lay with precious stones embroidering it and a purple sheet covered the body. He had a golden crown on his head and a sceptre in his right hand. Herod's sons and members of his family followed the bier, and behind them came his guards, a regiment of Thracians, Germans and Gauls, as well as hundreds of his domestic servants and freedmen.

With the sound of clanking armour and booted feet, they slowly moved out. A large group of Sanhedrin elders stood by silently, watching the procession as it left. During their long imprisonment in the hippodrome by order of Herod, they had suffered extreme heat and exhaustion, and at last could leave it. A crowd of anxious Jerusalemites that had waited outside all this time rushed towards them. Among them was the Jerusalem magistrate Hananel Gorion and his son Nicodemus, as well as his cousin Joseph from Ramatayim, usually called Arimathea, who had recently arrived for the Passover holiday. Gorion was the chief magistrate of Jerusalem and had come to oversee the process of release for the Sanhedrin elders. After seeing them to the waiting carriages and making sure they had enough food and drink for the journey back to Jerusalem, Gorion turned to Joseph and shook his head.

"That bastard Herod, he could not go without one final terrible deed. These elders were going be executed as soon as he died. The old fox knew the people would be glad at his death and celebrate in the streets, so he wanted them to be in mourning instead. Fortunately, his sister Salome wisely countermanded Herod's order today."

"You know what they will say about him?" Joseph told him. "That he stole the throne like a fox, ruled like a tiger, and died like a dog. What a horrible end he had, diseased in mind and body, with his tumours, gangrene, intestinal cramps, and his paranoid fears and suspicions which must have driven him mad, even madder than he already was from the start. And they say his diseases worsened and his sores began to fester just after those two rabbis and some their followers were burnt alive for cutting down the golden eagle on one of the Temple gates."

"And now his son and heir, Archelaus, will follow in his footsteps."

"Archelaus? I thought it would be his eldest son, Antipater!"

"No, Joseph, you were still in Ramatayim at the time. About five days ago his father had him executed for plotting against him. What a fool that fellow was. He could have waited a while longer before trying to take over too soon, and would have gained the crown."

"You know what Augustus said about Herod?" Joseph said, remembering the execution of his other sons, those of Mariamne who had also been executed by him. "It would be better to be Herod's pig than his son."

Nicodemus, or Nikki as he was called, was listening to their conversation and turned to Joseph in surprise. "How could Herod have pigs which are *terefah* and forbidden for Jews to eat."

Joseph laughed. "What Augustus meant was that if he had them, they would have been quite safe from execution since it was unlikely that he would want to eat them."

Gorion said he liked Augustus. There was a great ruler! He was so unlike Herod. Rational, generous, seeing the best in everyone and trying to do the best for everyone. He had consolidated the empire, halted its expansion, and introduced the excellent concept of *Pax Romana*, which should really be called the *Pax Augusta*, marking a period of relative peace throughout the empire which he hoped would last for a long time. He also tried to keep the peace within the ruling families of his kingdom. When Herod first began to suspect his sons of plotting against him, those born to his second wife Mariamne whom he later executed for her supposed treason, Augustus reconciled fathers and sons, but this only delayed the tragedy of their deaths.

They entered their carriage to join the convoy taking the Sanhedrin elders back to Jerusalem. Gorion stretched his burly frame against the cushions, trying to relax his muscles. He was nearly sixty, so it was already becoming difficult for him to stand out for so long in the hot sun, and he was furious that those older men should have had to suffer under it for so long. He would demand legal redress although there was no one now to grant it. Like many other legal claims he had tried to make on behalf of the citizens of Jerusalem, it was always a case in frustration.

He looked affectionately at Joseph, leaning back with his eyes shut. Tall, slim-built, his black hair was only just showing a few white hairs over the ears. He was now a widower, about forty or so, with an only son, Marcus, and living in his estate in Ramatayim-Zofim in the hills of Ephraim north of Jerusalem. The family, descendants of the prophet Samuel whose tomb could be seen on a high promontory, had remained on their land there for centuries. Gorion's mother was the sister of Joseph's father, and the two families had close ties with each other. Marcus had stayed with him and his wife Rachela in Jerusalem after his mother died, and was like a son for them.

The carriage soon crossed the bridge spanning the broad river bed still flowing with the winter rains, and then began the 18 miles of a steep uphill climb, the Adumim Ascent, leading through the mountainous pass and into the area of Jerusalem. Adumim, which means red, was named for the red rock of the pass, but it was better known as the 'Way of the Blood' for the victims robbed and killed by roaming bandits. The Romans posted a few sentry outposts along the road but it made little difference. The attackers struck and then disappeared into the desert caves that bordered the road. This road also served as the main pilgrimage route to the Temple Mount. At least during the pilgrimage festival period it was safer with so many people travelling together, often escorted by soldiers. Gorion recalled to mind some famous lines about Jerusalem from the fifteen Songs of Ascent in the Book of Psalms:

> *Let us go into the house of the Lord ...Our feet shall stand within thy gates of Jerusalem ...Pray for the peace of Jerusalem ...*
> *As the mountains are round about Jerusalem, so the Lord is around his people, from henceforth and evermore.*

The going was slow, but Nikki was enjoying it. He loved the long walks he had taken in the Judaean desert, especially in the early springtime when the whole area was green and red with poppies and other flowers! Now that he was already sixteen years old, he often went on long explorations with his friends through it.

Their convoy of carriages passed through Bethany on the eastern slopes of the Mount of Olives. Bethany was the house of the poor, *Beth Ani*, as a refuge for beggars and lepers. A noisy crowd of ragged men from the alms-houses came out into the road begging for money. They threw some coins into the road and Gorion then pulled down the shades on the side of their carriage.

"There are some lazar houses ahead where the Essenes take care of the lepers they are trying to heal," he said. "It is a very infectious disease."

"Then how is it the Essenes don't get infected?" asked Nikki.

"They are very careful to keep their hands and face covered with linens soaked in vinegar which is quite an effective protection. They also wash all the vessels in boiling water and bathe themselves regularly every day. You must have noticed them living just below our house near the Essene gate. All those ritual baths and their clean quarters."

"Yes, I saw them and tried talking to them, but they don't like to talk. They dress in white clothes, live together in groups, but have no families or children."

"They are the best kind of Jews with very high moral standards. You could learn a lot from them, Nikki. By living simply and eating only what is necessary to keep healthy, they often live a very long life."

"And they know a lot about medicine and cures," added Joseph. "Herod favoured them and had Essenes taking care of him while he was ill. It was he who gave them the Essene quarter in Jerusalem and built their alms-houses and the leper colony in Bethany."

Their carriage was now pulling through the Dung Gate in the south-eastern corner of the city and turning left towards Mount Zion leaving the other carriages of the convoy that were moving towards the northern part of the city. As soon as they entered the Gorion home, Nikki leapt out and rushed through the forecourt into the house.

His mother, Rachela, heard him enter and called out "Buni? Is that you? Come here!" She was in the kitchen with the cook, Martha. How he hated his Aramaic childhood name, Buni, which meant 'my son'. His mother spoke to him only in Aramaic, the language she knew best from her younger days in Babylonia. Gorion had gone there to study at the famous academies of Torah study and brought her back with him as his wife. They always spoke together in

Aramaic, which Nikki could easily understand. It was a softer language than Hebrew, much more musical.

"Yes, it's me," he told her, entering the kitchen. "I'm hungry. Just want a few dates and some bread before I go upstairs."

"The table is already laid for everyone. Your father and Joseph, and some of his friends have come here to meet him. You are old enough to sit with your elders, not a boy anymore."

"So, if I am not a boy any more, you must stop calling me Buni. My name is Nicodemus, Nikki!" His shook his long hair out of his dark eyes and looked at her accusingly. But she only smiled and ruffled his russet hair.

"You will always be my Buni, my little son."

That was the trouble, being the youngest in the family. His two older brothers had already grown up, married and gone away. He was looking forward to the time he could finish his schooling and go to Alexandria to study there.

Jerusalem was much cooler after Jericho, almost cold now that the evening was approaching. It was still March, and it could rain again as it did the day before. The streets outside were still wet. As the sun went down in the west, the wind blew in from the distant Mediterranean bringing the fresh scent of pine trees.

After they had washed and changed, they sat down together with the friends of Joseph in the enclosed porch on the first floor facing the gardens behind the house. This was where they usually had their family meals. It was a leisurely dinner, the table laid with bread and wine and the servants bringing in the various dishes one by one. The meal ended with bowls of fruits and nuts.

"What excellent figs these are, Hananel," one of the friends exclaimed. "Are they imported?"

Gorion said they were from his orchards on the Mount of Olives.

"We have grapevines there and other fruit trees, and of course, olives. They are the best kind of olives except for those in the Upper Galilee, and we have a large olive press on the mountain, a *gat shemen*. The oil from our press, known as the Oil of Gethsemane, is used exclusively for the Menorah in the Temple."

Rachela was looking elegant in her green robes, with her long reddish hair caught up in a jewelled comb, and talking animatedly the women around her. Gorion began discussing the political situation with Joseph and his friends and also about his business ventures with Greek merchants plying the trade routes along the coast. Nikki felt a little left out, but was interested in the stories about

15

the shipping of goods from the port of Joppa to various ports in the Mediterranean, especially to the northern ones as far as Massalia in the west.

He was sixteen and when he finished school he would love to travel, to see the world but did not want to become involved in business. He only wanted to learn about other people, other cultures, other ways of living. If he had been born a Roman he would now, at his age, be going through the ceremony of wearing the *toga virilis*, the robe worn by adult men recognised as Roman citizens belonging to their gens, their family clan. Here in Jerusalem, when boys reached maturity at the age of thirteen, they had to go to the Temple where the priests and rabbis questioned them for their knowledge of the Bible and the laws of Moses.

Joseph was now talking about a possible venture as far as Britannia to import tin from the mines there. Phoenician boats had been plying this trade for years and years, and there were enormous profits he could gain from it. Where was Britannia, Nikki wondered? Somewhere far in the north but he was not sure exactly where. He had read some of Caesar's account of Britannia in his Gallic Wars. There was so much to learn, to discover. Reading about people and places was not enough, he thought, one had to travel. Perhaps he could ask Joseph to take him on one of his expeditions.

All he wanted to do now was to escape and go to the upper chamber at the top of the house where he loved to sit and read. The chamber extended over the entire length and breadth of the house with arched openings in the eastern wall through which he could see the Temple Mount. There were rows and rows of shelves on the walls full of scrolls and beautiful objects his father had collected over the years—Grecian vases, paintings, a few small statuettes of satyrs and nymphs. Most of the scrolls were of the biblical texts, the five books of Moses, the Prophets, the Psalms and Proverbs, Job, Jonah, Ruth, Esther. Some were in Greek or Latin which he could already read, although not very fluently. Many more were in Hebrew or Aramaic in a narrative style such as the story of the Maccabees, and those about various characters not accepted as part of the Bible. He especially liked the one of Bel and the Dragon. His hero was Daniel in the lion's den. That was real bravery and faith in God.

The men were now rising, and the guests began saying goodbye, promising to meet again during the coming festival period as Joseph escorted them outside. After they left, Nikki saw his father take Joseph aside to discuss something that seemed important. He saw their troubled looks and was curious to know what they were saying, so he remained unnoticed in a corner armchair almost hidden by drapes.

"You cannot leave them there," his father was saying. "Archelaus has his spies, and if he found out there was still another potential Hasmonean heir in this country he would have him killed. There is also some strange rumour that Alexander is still alive. I received a report about it, which I will read tonight in case of trouble here. I get these reports regularly from our network of agents around the country."

"I think they are quite safe with Elizabeth and Zacharias in Ein Karem, far out of the city among retired people living in their villas. Maryam is very happy there, and the child is thriving. Where else could they be sent?"

"They should be sent out of the country altogether. Send them to Alexandria, to Philo and his brother Alexander who are wealthy enough and have always supported the Hasmoneans. In fact, I am thinking of sending Nikki there in a year or two when he finishes his schooling here to study more Greek and Latin and mix with the cultured elite in that city."

"How can she go alone there with a two-year old boy?" Joseph asked.

"Find someone to take her, some old widower who will agree to marry her and give her protection. You can send them in one of your caravans going down to Egypt."

"Alright Hananel," Joseph said. "We have to go and visit her, to see if she will agree to this. I know she is quite happy where she is, but if there is any danger to her son she will accept our suggestion."

"We will take the carriage and go there tomorrow morning. I have the day free from my duties at the magistrates court. It will be less than an hour's drive."

Nikki sat still, wondering what they were talking about and who were the mother and child in dire danger. How could there still be a Hasmonean heir in the country? He knew that Herod had sent them all to Rome to prevent any possible treachery on their part or an uprising against him in their support. He thought he would hear more about it but his father and Joseph had gone upstairs to bed. It would be better to remain where he was for a while so that they would not know he had heard them.

He closed his eyes, and a few minutes later fell asleep. He must have slept for nearly half the night when he awoke to hear the heavy rain beating down on the forecourt outside. Sheets of lightning lit up the long room and then it thundered loudly enough to waken the dead. He stood up shakily, still half-asleep, and tottered towards the door just as his father was entering. They looked at each other for a long moment.

"It's the *malkosh*," said Nikki.

"Yes, the last rain of the winter season," Gorion said. "But what are you doing here?"

"I must have fallen asleep in the armchair after dinner," Nikki said with a gesture of apology, sensing anxiety in his father's voice.

"Did you hear what Joseph and I were talking about?" Gorion asked him.

"Yes, Father," he admitted "but I did not understand much of it."

Gorion was relieved at first, and then decided to tell him the story, but gave him only an abbreviated version of the facts. He sat his son down in the armchair again and pulled a chair in front of it for himself. He told him that the young woman was Maryam, the orphan daughter of a priest. She had been living in a special wing of the Temple as one the young virgin daughters of priests, weaving curtains and draperies, and doing other kinds of service for the Temple staff. Three years ago she secretly married Prince Alexander, the eldest son of Queen Mariamne and King Herod. That is another story which I cannot tell you now. After Alexander was executed she went back to live in Ein Karem with her uncle and guardian, Zacharias and his wife Elizabeth, who is Maryam's aunt on her mother's side, and gave birth to a son, Jeshua.

"You mean Jeshua is a prince, a royal heir to the throne?" Nikki asked in amazement.

"Hush, you must not mention this ever to anyone. It must remain our secret."

"But what have you or Uncle Joseph got to do with this?"

"Joseph had been arranging for the betrothal of his son, Marcus, to Maryam. He was in Jerusalem when he found out what had happened. He saved Maryam from the soldiers who arrested Alexander and took her to her uncle."

"I want to go with you and Joseph when you go there today," Nikki begged him.

Gorion nodded. "Let's hope the rain stops by morning. Go back to bed now."

****

It was much later in the day when they finally set out. The sun shone weakly through a clouded sky, and there were large puddles of rainwater in the streets. They mounted the carriage waiting in the forecourt and drove out towards the western gate leading to Joppa, passing by the huge palace of Herod on the left and the towers along the city walls. Ein Karem was to the west of the city, high up on a hillside, covered with pine trees and grassy slopes. The air was fresh after the rain, and the horses trotted briskly along the footpaths leading to it.

Nikki enjoyed the ride as he had rarely been out to these suburbs of the city. They passed through open fields and the vineyards in Beth Hakerem. Ein Karem was further on and higher up.

Gorion was seated opposite Joseph, and looking grimly at him. He knew that Joseph had invested largely in the caravan trade from east to west.

"Do you have a caravan going to Egypt soon?" Gorion asked him.

"Yes, there is one coming from across the Jordan which will meet up in Bethlehem with another coming down from the Galilee. Both caravans will go on towards the coast and follow the Via Maris, the sea route along the northern coast of Sinai to Pelusium, and then across the Nile delta to Alexandria."

"How are you going to find someone to marry her and take her to Egypt?" Gorion questioned him again.

Joseph told him that Zacharias would find someone working in the Temple, one of the older builders or carpenters. These men were mostly from the Galilee, hardworking, honest, reliable people not like workers from this area.

"She may not have to marry him, and just pretend that they are married. Once they are in Egypt the man can come back to Jerusalem. He will be well paid for his trouble."

Gorion felt reassured. "Best they go before the hot weather comes otherwise it will be a hard journey for the young girl and her child."

They remained silent for the rest of the way. Nikki thought about going to Alexandria in another year or two. It would be very hot and humid there, and the native Egyptian population as well as the Greeks were always so hostile to the Jews. Yet it would be interesting and challenging. He loved challenges.

Ein Karem soon came into view around the bend. A series of villas and gardens rising up the slopes, glistening in the morning sunshine, and raindrops pearling on the leaves of the trees along the road. The villa of Zacharias was at the end of the road where it rose up a steep incline. On the slope below, the grassy expanse ended in a stream where two women sat with their children playing around them.

"Elizabeth, Maryam!" Joseph called out to them.

He jumped off the carriage followed by Nikki and Gorion and told the driver to lead the horses to the barn behind the house. The women waved in greeting and the little ones began running towards Joseph, remembering the sweetmeats he always brought them on his monthly visits. Little Johanan was the first to reach him, and Jeshua toddled behind. Joseph crouched down and took out a bag of sweetmeats, offering one apiece to the children.

"How are you Maryam?" he asked her gently as she came up to them. She smiled shyly, but her eyes still seemed grave and sad.

"It is always good to see you, Joseph."

She glanced up as Gorion and Nikki were approaching and went to welcome them.

"Maryam, I am Hananel Gorion, Joseph's cousin. And this is my son Nicodemus."

"Nikki!" the boy said.

"Nikki it is," Maryam smiled at him, and pointed to the two children near Joseph. "These are Johanan and Jeshua."

The children had their mouths full and only stared at him. Johanan was black-haired, black-eyed and sturdy looking, while Jeshua was fair-haired, blue-eyed with fine, delicate features, his hair hanging in long blond locks around his shoulders. Johanan retreated towards his mother, but Jeshua came towards Nikki, holding out his arms to him to be picked up. Then they all went up towards the house together, mounting the steps to the open porch where Zacharias was sitting.

"Zacharias, old friend," said Gorion. "How are you?"

"Getting old, Gorion, as you can see. I miss the Temple and the city life, but Elizabeth is happy here."

They sat down around a low table piled with various kinds of fruit and a bottle of wine. The conversation was general, about the weather the day before, about Herod, about the imminent troubles that were expected. Elizabeth and Maryam went indoors with the children to feed them, and then to prepare a meal for the guests. The conversation turned inevitably to the political situation in the country.

"With Archelaus in power, it will be Herod all over again," said Joseph. "These are dangerous times and I am afraid for Maryam. She will not be safe here any longer. Gorion heard in court some talk about a man who pretends to be Prince Alexander, a look-alike it seems. The people are getting excited. He was always their favourite prince as you know."

"Who is this man, Gorion?" asked Zacharias fearfully.

"A Jew by birth, but brought up by a Roman freedman in Sidon. He looks almost exactly like Alexander in every way. He claims that his friends had hidden him and substituted a dead body for his burial. The pretender is now in Crete, collecting money from supporters, and is planning to go to Rome where he expects to be received royally by the Jews there."

"He will be exposed, I am sure," said Zacharias. "Once he comes before Augustus to claim the throne, the emperor will know he is lying. You can't fool Augustus."

"Perhaps," said Joseph. "But this may bring out what happened between Alexander and Maryam in the Temple. When I came to save her while they were arresting Alexander, some priests appeared and saw her clinging to him. She had hidden him for nearly two weeks in her quarters. Questions may now arise and it might all come out. She may be identified and they know where to find her— with you of course, her uncle and guardian."

They sat there in silence until Elizabeth called them into the house for the hastily prepared meal of mushroom soup, fresh lettuce and cucumbers, roasted chicken and rice mixed with lentils. The local wine was very good, Gorion thought. He noticed that Nikki was enjoying the good food as well. Perhaps they should stay there for a while until they could make the necessary arrangements for Maryam. Almost reading his thoughts, Zacharias suddenly suggested that they remain as his guests for a few days. Joseph and Gorion instantly agreed with thanks.

"There's plenty of room," Elizabeth told them with a lovely smile. "We built a large extension at the back, mainly to give the children more space to play indoors during the winter. There are several couches there and a washroom at the far end. You will also find an opening at the back that leads into the orchard and vegetable garden we planted and where we have our permanent Succah booth."

Nikki was delighted that they would remain in this lovely place for a few days. He wanted to explore the valley and the hills around it. He also wanted the chance to play with the children. He always wished he could have had some younger brothers or sisters.

It was an enjoyable week for them, but overshadowed by the preparations for Maryam and Jeshua. As a retired Temple priest, Zacharias knew many of the men working in it and thought of a certain carpenter of Nazareth, a good man, poor but well educated, whose wife had died several years ago. This man was going to retire very soon because he was getting too old for the job. He had four or five grown sons who were now managing the carpentry business in Nazareth. A large sum of money and further continual support would certainly persuade him to offer his services.

****

Nikki spent the early spring days in the countryside, happily swimming in the stream, climbing the steep incline to the top of the ridge from where he could see the city of Jerusalem on the eastern horizon. He also played with the two children. Johanan was a rough and tumble child who liked to run and jump, splashing his feet in the stream, trying to climb up a tree. Jeshua was gentler, kneeling to spread his palms on the grass, to look into a flower, to roll laughingly down a slope. Nikki loved to catch and toss him into the air until he shouted with glee.

Gorion sat near Elizabeth listening to a more detailed account of what had happened to Maryam. Three years ago, when she was sixteen, Zacharias placed her with the Temple virgins until her betrothal to Marcus, Joseph's son. When Herod's son, Alexander, fled to the Temple to escape the guards coming to arrest him and his brother Aristobulus, he decided to hide in the women's quarters. He found the door of Maryam's chamber open, entered it, and after her initial shock and fear, he persuaded her to hide him for a while until his friends could arrange for his escape.

During the time he was there with her, he told her why his father had ordered the arrest. His mother, Mariamne, was the granddaughter of the Hasmonean king and High Priest, Hyrcanus, supplanted by Herod. After her young brother, Aristobulus, was 'accidently' drowned in a swimming pool in Jericho, most probably by Herod's instigation, she became withdrawn and was under suspicion of plotting against her husband.

Although Herod loved her very much, he had her executed. This was nearly twenty years ago, when Alexander and his younger brother Aristobulus, were still very young. His father sent them to Rome to be educated there and they returned to Jerusalem when they had grown up. Antipater, Herod's eldest son, fearing that they would be the heirs of their father's kingdom, made Herod suspect them of hatred for their mother's death and of treachery against him. Herod then sent guards to arrest them, to bring them to trial, and sentenced them to be executed for treason.

When Alexander took refuge in Maryam's room, she brought him food and drink, and took care that no one would know of his presence there. He was with her for more than two weeks, and they fell in love with each other. He gave her his signet ring, and in the presence of a friendly priest and two others as witnesses, pronounced the words: "You are hereby sanctified unto me."

But one of the matrons in charge of the girls must have noticed Maryam's frequent comings and goings. She questioned her severely, had her room thoroughly examined, and Alexander was finally discovered. She alerted the Temple guards and called Zacharias her uncle to come to the Temple. Joseph happened to be with him at the time, and they found Maryam crying and clinging to Alexander as they led him away. The guards wanted to arrest her as well for hiding him, but Joseph rescued her and Zacharias took her home to avoid the crowds that had gathered at the scene.

The rest Gorion already knew, that in the winter, during the Hannukah festival, the Festival of Lights, celebrating the victory of the Hasmoneans, she gave birth to Alexander's son and named him Jeshua, which means 'God is my salvation', and she dedicated him as a Nazirite, which meant that he could not cut his hair or drink wine. Alexander's signet ring was kept on a chain around her neck, hidden under her dress. Since there was still talk about the affair at the Temple, Zacharias decided to retire from his duties there. He cared for Maryam and her child and devoted himself to bringing up his own child, Johanan, God's gift to him in his old age. He and Elizabeth had been married for over thirty years and the boy was his first and only child.

Joseph sent a servant to find Josiah the carpenter at the Temple and deliver a letter to him. He knew this man to be an honest, trustworthy person who had worked for him years ago on his estate in Ramatayim. They would only tell him that Maryam was a widow, that they had executed her husband for political reasons soon after they were married, and that she was in danger of arrest by the ruling authorities. If he accepted their proposal, they would take Maryam and her child to Jerusalem and hire a covered donkey cart for the journey padded with strong, soft beddings and pillows and a cot for the child to sleep in. No more than a day's journey was necessary for them to reach Bethlehem from Jerusalem. From there, a caravan of his passing through the town would pick them up and take them to Alexandria.

The answer soon arrived from the Temple. Josiah insisted on marrying the girl before taking her under his care. It would be against the law to be in her company otherwise. He was ready to go as soon as they wished.

****

It took them less than an hour to return to the Gorion mansion. They were warmly welcomed by Rachela and by Marcus, Joseph's son. He had just returned from his visit to Caesarea where he had spent an enjoyable week at the home of his Roman friend Gaius, the son of Joseph's business partner in that city. Marcus watched gravely as Joseph helped Maryam down from the carriage, thinking of how his father had nearly betrothed him to this beautiful girl. She did not notice him, and hurried into the house with her child in her arms. Rachela took her immediately to the room prepared for her.

"Marcus," Joseph called to him. "You have come for the Passover in good time."

"Yes, and I had a good time in Caesarea with Gaius. We went to the races in the hippodrome and then to the theatre. It was grand!"

Gorion turned to shake his hand. "What a smart young man you have become, Marcus. You are now the perfect Roman nobleman."

Marcus smiled. "That's what they tell me, and not only because of my name. But I know the difference very well between us and the Romans. There is that very subtle sneer when I am in their company."

Nikki was looking admiringly at him, and Marcus circled an arm over his shoulders.

"So how is our little Nikki, nowadays? You look all sunburned and grown so tall already."

"Not so little any more Marcus. I'm only five years younger than you."

They went in and saw a tall, very dignified elderly man, dressed in simple robes, standing alone by the fireside. Gorion went up to him with a welcoming smile to greet him.

"You are Josiah, then? Come to accompany the woman Maryam and her son to Egypt?"

24

"Yes, your honour," was the reply. He apparently recognised Gorion as the chief magistrate of the city. "But I will not just accompany her. I can take her to Egypt only as my legally wedded wife."

"Of course, of course, it will be arranged tomorrow morning," Gorion told him as he led him into the large living room. "You are welcome to stay here overnight and dine with us this evening."

Nikki invited Marcus to the upper chamber to show him the new scrolls and other art objects that had been acquired since the previous year. Up there, they heard loud sounds and noisy shouting from outside and went up onto the roof. Crowds of people were streaming through the streets in the direction of Herod's palace and trumpets were being blown announcing the arrival of a royal entourage.

"It must be Archelaus coming back to Jerusalem after the seven days of mourning," said Marcus. "Go and tell your father. He will be expected there to welcome him."

Nikki rushed downstairs and burst into the living room.

"Come quickly Father! Archelaus has returned to the palace. There are crowds of people going there."

Gorion and Joseph hurried out and walked as fast as they could through the streams of people. He had to be there as one of the city dignitaries together with the court officials to keep the people in order. How often it was necessary to do this! The citizens of Jerusalem were a volatile lot, easily roused and prone to be violent at times. Arriving at the palace gates, he saw the soldiers drawn up inside them to prevent anyone from entering. Archelaus was on the balcony above seated on a high golden chair, dressed in regal robes and surrounded by courtiers and his father's chief adviser, Nicholaus of Damascus.

"Of course," Gorion told Joseph. "He was the most trusted of Herod's supporters, the historian of his reign and of his dynasty. A real sycophant, but a gifted writer I am told! He should know that Archelaus has no right to assume royalty until Augustus invests him as king. He has to go to Rome first."

There were shouts from the people outside the gates, calling for justice for the eminent rabbis and their disciples executed by Herod for having taken down the golden eagle he set up on a gate of the Temple in honour of Augustus. They also called for reduced taxation, relief from debts, and demanded that he depose the hated high priest. Archelaus waved for silence and then shouted down to the mob that he was not yet empowered to do anything until he became king. He promised them that he would do whatever he could once he had the power.

"Good excuse," said Gorion sarcastically, "although he is already behaving like a king. The latest report is that even during the days of mourning he has been feasting with his friends late at night. His brother Antipas will challenge the will made at the last minute and claim that he was the one named in an earlier will. I think Salome and many others will support Antipas as the better option."

Gorion turned to go back home and Joseph followed him. People were still streaming the opposite way from the lower city. Angry faces, loudmouth curses, some with sticks and stones in their hands. All around them stood soldiers, the foreign mercenaries of Herod, standing guard on every side prepared for any dangerous rioting. Joseph pulled Gorion to one side to avoid the crowds that might crush him.

"Herod's rule, however bad, at least gave us some stability. He left a mess behind him."

On their way, they saw the High Priest, Joezer of the detested Boethus family, dressed in his priestly vestments coming out of his house with a large retinue. The Boethus family members were Hellenised Alexandrian Jews and were always high-handed in their dealings with the local priesthood and the Pharisee leadership. Herod gave them preference as high priests because they were Sadducees who promoted Hellenism in the country in opposition to the Pharisaic views of the general population.

Joseph and Gorion avoided the oncoming group by turning into an alley to let them pass. They could see the haughty look and complacent satisfaction on Joezer's face, so sure of his position in the kingdom. Gorion told Joseph that Herod had elected Joezer's father Simon to the high priesthood before he married Simon's young daughter, also named Mariamne. They had a son, first named Herod II as the most likely heir until Herod divorced her for implication in a plot against him. Herod II then became known as Herod Philip, and both mother and child went into exile in Alexandria. Nevertheless, the Boethus family retained their right to the high priesthood and Herod continued to prefer them over other priestly families.

"They will never resign their power and hold over the Temple administration," said Gorion. "They've grown rich with their corrupt dealings, and with their ties with wealthy Alexandrians. The people hate them for their cruelty and wicked behaviour towards the poorer classes, for their extortion of tithes and tributes."

By the time they arrived back at the house preparations were underway for an early supper. They went down to the bathhouse in the basement for a good wash and fresh clothing. A ritual bath had also been built on one side. On a lower level there was a wine cellar, storage jars for oil, casks of salted fish and meat, and a cool room to keep milk, butter and cheese from spoiling.

In the meanwhile Maryam had also rested, and came downstairs in her embroidered robes. She entered the dining room shyly, a little afraid, waiting to be introduced to Josiah. He was already seated at the table next to Nikki and Marcus, and she went to sit opposite them near Rachela. Gorion was at the head of the table, and Joseph came in last, to sit at the other end. He introduced Maryam, and Josiah bowed his head respectfully.

Nothing was said about the plans for the next day. They only talked about what was happening now at Herod's palace and the dangerous political situation, and of the bitter rivalry among Herod's sons over the kingdom.

"They will all be going to Caesarea soon after the festival and sail for Rome," Joseph said. "I intend to go there also and see what is happening. There are some ships due to arrive at Ostia with imported goods. Marcus, you will come with me and from now on you can remain in Rome to manage our trade office in the city."

Marcus was delighted. "Thanks, Father, I would like to live in Rome. Gaius is going back there very soon, so it will be great!"

Gorion smiled at him. "You will like it there; it is very different from our provincial Judaea. It will be a real change for you and will most probably change you as well. You may not want to come back here."

"I shall always come back to Jerusalem for the three festivals" Marcus promised him. "I especially enjoy the Passover in Jerusalem with you and the family."

"Passover will not be a festival this time" Joseph told him. "It will be full of disturbances, rioting, and violent protests against the Roman presence in the city and near the Temple. Not the pleasant, harmonious kind we had until now."

Gorion agreed and said they should avoid the Temple during the festival. One of the reports says Archelaus will appoint his half-brother Philip to take charge in the interim while he is away in Rome. But he will not be able to keep the people quiet. It was as if Herod's death has lifted the lid on a box of old trials and torments suppressed and silenced until now.

"Then it is good that Maryam will be leaving before the festival," Joseph told him. "The weather is favourable now. You will be going to Bethlehem first, Josiah. A caravan will be coming very soon from Persia in the east, traveling along the Nabataean route and crossing over the Jordan. Another one will be coming down from the Upper Galilee. When you get to Bethlehem, you can stay overnight at the inn for a while until they arrive. I will give you a large sum of money for the journey, and you will have all you need in Egypt from my agents in Alexandria. The caravan drivers may be expecting me, so perhaps they will think you are Joseph of Ramatayim. Josiah, Joseph, what is the difference to them anyhow. Show them my order which I will give you for the journey. They will be glad to take you and Maryam with them if they are paid well."

Josiah smiled. "My father's name was Joseph. And Bethlehem is where I was born. My family belongs to the Davidic lineage, but only very distantly. My parents died soon after I was married. I went to live in Nazareth because my wife was from there and had inherited a large carpentry workshop from her father."

"Well, Bethlehem is no place to make a good livelihood, just a lot of shepherds and their flocks of sheep and goats. They supply the Temple with sacrificial lambs, wool, and sheepskins."

"How long will the journey take? Is it a safe one?" asked Gorion.

Joseph shrugged. "It will take about two weeks I think, three at the most, along the Via Maris. They will stop along the way to rest themselves and the animals. But they will be well protected by Bedouin guards on horses. I have not lost a caravan so far."

"It must be a very profitable business, supplying all those goods to the Alexandrians with their taste for oriental luxuries."

"They can well afford it, Hananel, far more than the wealthy families of Jerusalem. No comparison at all."

****

They were all up before dawn and ready for the departure of Maryam by sunrise. The city was quiet, even though it was getting filled up with the pilgrims arriving for the festival. The sun gleamed golden on the walls of the buildings around, as they came out into the street. Joseph accompanied Maryam down to the Essene gate to see that she and Josiah left together with other carts and wagons traveling towards the south. He was sure they would reach Bethlehem before nightfall.

Joseph had thought at first to accompany them to Bethlehem until Gorion reminded him of the urgent business meetings with his partners in Jerusalem before the Passover festival began. Gorion also held long talks with Maryam, telling her what to expect in Alexandria, about Philo and his family where she would be staying. He also told her about the recent appearance of the spurious Alexander whom he was sure would soon be revealed as an imposter.

Tearful at leaving her uncle and Elizabeth, but smiling bravely, Maryam kissed them goodbye. Zacharias placed one hand on her head and the other on the child, as he recited the priestly blessing:

> *May the Lord bless you and keep you.*
> *May the Lord make his face shine upon you, and be gracious to you.*
> *May the lord lift up his countenance upon you, and give you peace.*

Maryam lay in the cart with Jeshua still asleep in her arms. She was warmly dressed and covered with her blue woollen cloak. Josiah sat up near the driver and she heard him reciting the psalm she knew so well: *The Lord in my shepherd I shall not want ...though I walk in the valley of the shadow of death I will fear no evil ...*

For all the reassurances of her faith, she was still afraid of the future for herself and for her child. She was going to a strange land, to live among strangers. Joseph had promised to bring them back as soon as it was safe, but he did not know when that might be. As long as Herod's sons were in power in Judaea, the danger remained.

It was dark when they arrived at last in Bethlehem. The driver let them off at the inn, and turned around to go back to Jerusalem. They entered the inn to ask for a room but the innkeeper said he had none to give them.

"We are full house with all the pilgrims going to Jerusalem. But you can stay in one of the stables. It is warm and the hay is soft enough to sleep on. You can put the child to bed in a manger. I have just put some strange old travellers from the east in another stable and they seem to be quite comfortable there."

They went out wearily, Josiah carrying Jeshua, since Maryam was too tired to hold him. A boy from the inn carried their belongings for them. It was a starry night, and in the distance they could hear the bells of sheep and goats being led back to their pens by the shepherds.

Three old men were standing outside the other stable looking up at the sky and talking together.

"There it is! That star you see coming up in the east. I told you it would appear tonight. It is an omen!"

"An omen of what do you think, of life or death?"

"Of both," said the third. "But not of now, perhaps in another thirty years' time."

"How can you see so far ahead?" the second one asked.

"It is a passing star which will flame across the sky till it burns out and dies as it goes behind the sun."

"Perhaps it is the lost star of Orion, the constellation from which it fell to earth in ancient days and brought the Nephilim, the fallen sons of the gods, the giants of old."

"We Chaldeans call Orion the 'heavenly shepherd' or the 'messenger of the gods."

"The Romans call it Sagittarius and the Jews call it 'Kesil' which in Hebrew means 'the fool'. But it is also their name for the month Kislev—the first winter month—when God's messenger will be born."

Josiah gazed wonderingly from one to the other. He recognised them as Chaldean or Sabian necromancers, known as 'star-gazers' or 'star-worshippers' from that faraway land beyond the mountains of Persia. They had large thick-lashed eyes and long hair, and were richly dressed in long padded robes and embroidered jackets. Some called them Magi or Wise Men of the East, who presumably could tell the future, but he suspected they practiced witchcraft.

They bowed when they saw him and Maryam, and smiled benignly at the little boy, now wide awake. One of them held out a small orb with a cross-shaped nob and small silver bells attached to it. "A plaything for the child," he said graciously, shaking it over the child till the bells chimed. Joseph did not like this and wanted to refuse the gift, but Maryam took it and thanked the old man. It would keep the little boy occupied till he slept again.

She entered the stable, placed Jeshua in one of the mangers lined with hay, spread her cloak nearby, and prepared to go to sleep. Joseph went to the other end of the stable, took off his sandals, and lay down on the hay. He was there to guard her against strangers and suspicious persons. She was still very young and impressionable, and he had to protect her against her own open and generous nature.

The caravans arrived early the next morning. Josiah went out to one of the Arab drivers and handed him the order for their passage to Egypt. Joseph had written his own name next to that of Maryam so that no questions would be asked. Josiah was glad to see that the three Magi were joining the other caravan. Maryam and Jeshua would travel in a large howdah on the back of a camel while he was given a place in one of the covered wagons being pulled by mules.

It was a slow journey, but fairly comfortable. They stopped very frequently to eat, drink and rest. Josiah wondered at the idea of actually going down to Egypt, the way that Jacob once took with the seventy members of his family to join his newly found son Joseph. And four hundred years later, a nation of six hundred thousand came out of Egypt to go the Promised Land. The Bible had commanded: *You shall never return that way again*. But here he was going back there the way that the Ishmaelites had taken Joseph after his brothers had sold him to them. Of all things, to celebrate the Passover in that country, the festival that marked the coming out of Egypt!

From what he had heard, there were now nearly two hundred thousand Jews living in Alexandria. Most of the poorer ones were crowded into a special quarter of the city in the north-eastern area, apart from the Macedonian Greeks and the native Egyptians who hated them. Continual tension existed between Greek and Jew, each vying for the favour of the Romans. But many of the wealthier Jews did not care about the tension, and built their homes and synagogues within the central area, the Brucheon, where the famous Musaeum of Alexandria and the Serapeum were located. Philo's family lived in that area.

The caravan reached the coast, passed through Gaza, and then drove along the highway, the Via Maris. There was a fresh breeze from the sea carrying the tangy scent of salt. The sand along the shore was fine and whenever they stopped they could refresh themselves with a dip in the shallow waters.

When they reached Pelusium, the site of so many famous battles, they were in the midst of thick traffic from the many roads and highways crossing through it. Moving on through the marshy delta area with its lush vegetation and the tall papyrus reeds, they finally arrived in the city of Alexandria two days before the Passover festival.

It was late evening when the caravans entered through the Canopian Gate and moved northwards in the direction of the Jewish quarter. While they were unloading the caravan, Josiah went to arrange for transportation to the western quarter. He could hardly understand the local Greek dialect spoken among the Jews, the *koine*, used by the Alexandrian population. This would be just one more barrier to overcome if they had to live here for long. He soon managed to find some sedan chair carriers to take them to the home of Philo.

They received a warm welcome by Philo and his brother Alexander, and spent the eve of Passover Seder and the festival week with them, resting in the large, luxurious villa surrounded by palm trees and exotic flowers and plants. The weather was pleasant in the early spring, but the hot, sultry days were not far off. Still, the rooms were cool and indoor pools kept them fresh. Most of the time they had the house to themselves and Nubian slaves supplied them with every comfort.

Philo spent nearly all day in the library of the Musaeum, and Alexander was always busy with his duties as a prominent member of the *gerousia*, the Jewish political council reconstituted by Augustus. When they were young, their parents were among those to whom Julius Caesar had granted citizenship while he was in Egypt. Their family gained great wealth in the export of grain and other goods to Rome. There was a third brother, Lysimachus, who handled their trading business at the port, and lived in the Rakhotis quarter, on the west side of the city.

It was only later in the day, after the evening meal, that they could question the two brothers and learn something about life in Alexandria. Most of the Jews were Hellenised and hardly knew how to speak or read Hebrew. The Bible was studied in its Greek translation, the Septuagint. After the Roman conquest of Egypt, many of the wealthier families adopted a Roman style of living, gave their children Roman names, as did the wealthy Jews of Jerusalem. But they retained their religious loyalties and were faithful supporters of their Judaean brothers. They faithfully sent the annual Temple tax to Jerusalem, and made donations of gold and silver for its adornment and generous contributions for its upkeep.

It would take a lot of time to adapt to the way of life here among Alexandrian Jewry, Josiah thought. They should find themselves a small house in the Jewish quarter and he would try to find some work or occupation although Joseph had promised to send them enough money to live well without worry. Maryam would manage the house and take care of the child with the help of a few servants. He wondered how long they had to remain here. Perhaps it would be only for a few years.

With Philo's help, they found a house in the Jewish quarter not far from the sea front. A month later, it was harvest time for the wheat crop, and Josiah easily found work supervising the transport of the grain to the ships carrying it to Rome. The workers were friendly, helping him to understand the Greek dialect of the city, calling him with the familiar name of 'Yossi' instead of Josiah, and interested to hear about his life in the 'old country'. 'Yossi' was also the diminutive for Joseph, and when Jeshua begin to attend the school for young children they registered him as Jeshua son of Joseph.

Josiah settled down in the city, making friends with neighbours, getting a better command of the language, and slowly adjusting to the new ways of living. Maryam made use of the knowledge she had received from her mother about the use of herbs and various plants with healing qualities to help sick people. She soon became well known in the neighbourhood for her curative skills and her kindness to the poor.

A year later Jeshua began attending the school for young children. He was a happy child, curious about everything, talking to everyone he met, gentle with animals, taking long walks with Josiah who was so kind and fatherly to him. Maryam was grateful for his faithful and loving care of them, although they were not living as man and wife. All she wanted was to keep her son safe and well. They did not hear very often from Jerusalem. Travellers between the two cities were frequent but they did not bring much news. Archelaus was still in power in Jerusalem and Judaea, which meant that they could not yet return there.

When Joseph arrived in Alexandria to visit them, Josiah and Maryam heard from him what had happened in Jerusalem. After dinner, they sat outside in the garden of their house and listened to a long and terrifying story. The Passover festival had not been a peaceful one. A large group of angry, seditious men bent on revenge for Herod's massacre of the two rabbis and their disciples had gathered during the festival week near the Temple. Together with the thousands of pilgrims in Jerusalem they threatened to kill Archelaus if he did not arrest and punish the men who had carried out the massacre.

Archelaus first sent some people to placate them, and when they failed, he sent a regiment of soldiers to prevent the sedition from spreading. The crowds assaulted the soldiers, pelting them with stones, wounding many of them and making them flee for their lives. Archelaus then sent his whole army and cavalry force against the rioters, killing three thousand people and chasing several thousand more into the mountains. The rest of the pilgrims left the festival and went back to their homes. It was a complete disaster, and he was glad that he and Gorions had not gone to the Temple at that time.

Soon afterwards Archelaus went down to Caesarea with his family and friends to sail for Rome. His brother, Antipas also set sail for Rome to claim his rights by a previous will of Herod. At the same time, the treasurer of Augustus, Sabinus, the treasurer of Augustus in Syria, arrived in Caesarea to make an inventory of Herod's property and effects and to keep them safe. Varus, the governor of Syria, was also there and told Sabinus not to touch anything and to wait until Archelaus returned from Rome. He also sent one of his three legions in Syria to Jerusalem to keep order in case of further rioting.

Archelaus left Caesarea, and Varus returned to Antioch. The Festival of Weeks, the Pentecost, was approaching. Sabinus hurried to Jerusalem and seized control of Herod's palace and his garrisons. It was clear to everyone that he intended to take a good share of Herod's treasures for himself. Bands of people who had arrived for the festival gathered to attack him and besiege him in Herod's palace. Sabinus quickly sent a letter to Varus to come to his assistance. He then went up to the highest tower, the Phasael, on the city ramparts overlooking the palace, and signalled the Roman soldiers to attack the besiegers. A battle raged between the forces, and when the Jews retreated towards the Temple, the Romans set fire to the cloisters, entered the Temple, and seized a great deal of money from the treasury.

The whole country was in uproar, and some of the Zealots in the Galilee region set fire to various royal properties. Two or three leaders of robber bands declared themselves king, placing diadems on their heads. Roman troops were under attack in various places, and Jews attacked and tried to rob other Jews. Varus immediately set out with two legions to quell the disturbances and marched to Jerusalem. Sabinus heard of his arrival and quickly escaped to Caesarea to return to Rome, knowing that he would be blamed for instigating the conflict.

Two thousand people were crucified by order of Varus for sedition and revolt. His cruelty only aroused thousands more against him, but some of the leading Jewish authorities and Sanhedrin elders in Jerusalem intervened to prevent further disaster. Among them was Menahem the Essene, a highly respected figure, loved by all the people and thought to have prophetic foresight. He told the Sanhedrin elders that Varus would meet his end in disgrace at the end of thirteen years. His prophecy came true later when Varus led three legions into a trap by German tribes in the dark forests of their country and they were decimated. Varus committed suicide and Augustus wept and cried out: "Quintilius Varus, give me back my legions!"

Joseph said that a few days after the riots ended he went to Rome with Marcus and was there when Archelaus and the other sons of Herod arrived to submit their claims to the throne of Herod.

"So what did Augustus decide about the succession?" Josiah asked him.

"The decision is not yet final, pending appeals against it," Joseph told him. "But from what I heard, Archelaus will not be appointed king, but only as Ethnarch over Judaea, Samaria and Idumaea. His brothers, Antipas and Philip will be tetrarchs. Antipas will have Galilee and Peraea, Philip takes Iturea, Trachonitis, Batanaea, and Auranitis. Interestingly enough, Lysanias, the nephew of Antigonus, the last Hasmonean ruler, will be given Abila and Chalcis which had belonged before to his father Ptolemy."

"And what happened with the man who claimed to be Alexander?" Maryam asked.

Joseph laughed. "When he came before Augustus, the first thing the Caesar noticed was the man's hands, rough and calloused. They were not the hands of a prince who had lived in luxury all his life. His voice was not the same, and his manner of speaking not as refined as that of Alexander whom the emperor had known very well since he was a young boy at court."

They asked Joseph what had happened to the children of Alexander and Aristobulus and he told them that Glaphyra, Alexander's widow had taken her two sons, Tigranes and Alexander back to Cappadocia and the king, her father. Glaphyra was very attractive and dynamic, and the rumour was that Herod himself fancied her, so he kept custody of the children in order to prevent her from leaving after her husband was executed. As for Aristobulus, who had married Berenice, the daughter of Herod's sister Salome, they had five children, Herod, Mariamne, Herodias, Agrippa, and Aristobulus Minor. Berenice was now living in Rome and had become a close friend of Antonia Minor, the widow of Drusus, younger brother of Tiberius.

It was getting late, and they retired for the night. Joseph was going to return with one of his ships to Joppa and from there back to Jerusalem. He spoke aside to Josiah and assured him of continued support for Maryam and the child. He was glad to hear they had settled down and felt contented with their lives. Jeshua was being well educated, and he would appoint a special tutor for him when he was a little older. Joseph felt reluctant to tell Josiah the truth about the child's Hasmonean descent. It was best to keep this secret for the present. He left early the next morning, a little before dawn. The city lay quiet under the moon and stars. It would be a pleasant sailing of a few days and would give him time to recover his spirits. The situation in Jerusalem was troubling, and he doubted it would improve in time.

****

Gorion returned on foot from the Temple Mount. He crossed the bridge over the valley, passing in front of the Council House where the Magistrates Court was located, and walking through the colonnaded plaza of the Xystus until he passed the Archives building on the other side of it. He then followed the road along the northern wall of the Hasmonean Palace and turned left into the street leading into the Upper City. It was a long way to Mount Zion and his home, but he needed to stretch his legs after sitting for so long in the Chamber of Hewn Stones, commonly known as the Hewn Chamber, where the Sanhedrin always met.

It had been a very long session, and he was not there as a Sanhedrin elder but to provide the official information about the events that had taken place. Still, he was also a well-respected person among them as the grandson of the famous scholar and mystic, Hananiah ben Hezekiah ben Garon. When Gorion's grandfather died, Gorion, who had been named after him, changed his name to Hananel and Garon to Gorion to avoid confusion with him.

He was already familiar with disputes in that chamber between the two schools, the House of Hillel and the House of Shammai. Some were serious and others absurd. There was the serious one about which students should be admitted to the study of the Torah. The school of Shammai thought only worthy students should be admitted, but the Hillelites believed it could be taught to anyone. The absurd one was whether an ugly bride should be told she was beautiful. Shammai said it was wrong to lie, but Hillel disagreed and said that all brides are beautiful on their wedding day. There were hundreds of issues on which they differed. Generally speaking, the Shammaite positions were more stringent than those of Hillel. But the vote nearly always went in favour of Hillel.

How admirable this old man was! He was already more than a hundred years old and still strong and able. His eyes were a brilliant blue and often twinkled with humour. And so much loved! Affectionately called Hillel ha-Zaken, the old man of the Sanhedrin. He remained an active participant and would most likely continue to live until he was a hundred and twenty, the age of Moses when he died.

The debate this time was focused on the terrible events that had occurred from Passover to Pentecost. Shammai proposed a special fast day to be held each year in memory of the two thousand who had died on the cross. Hillel said they had enough fast days for past sorrows, the fast of Tammuz for the siege of Jerusalem by Nebuchadnezzar, and the fast of Av for the destruction of the Temple, and the fast of Esther for threat of annihilation by Haman the adviser of the Persian King. Some people fasted for personal reasons, and pious people fasted regularly every Monday and Thursday. One of the Sanhedrin members called for a national and religious uprising against the Romans, but the idea was quickly suppressed. This was no time to bring on more calamities. Alternately, it was suggested that a delegation be sent to Augustus asking that Rome rule the province directly instead of through Herod's son.

This idea was debated with much heat as it meant giving up a measure of independence. The argument in favour of Roman rule said that in any case it was Rome that ruled, and that Archelaus was simply a puppet ruler. But others objected saying that direct Roman rule was sure to lead to public opposition and even revolt. A Roman governor would extort the people, raid the Temple treasure, introduce more pagan practices into the city. As it is they now had a theatre, a hippodrome, a gymnasium, and a lot of foreign residents and the youth were being corrupted by Roman customs and way of life.

They left the matter, and went on to discuss ritual matters in the Temple. Gorion felt bored by all these questions about purity and impurity, and when this or that sacrifice should be made, or what amount of a certain spice should be included in the incense. Why did they not discuss more important matters, something that would improve social relations, morality, living conditions, education, and many other things of greater urgency?

He had given his report so he felt he could go without anyone objecting, and slipped out quickly, unnoticed. He missed Joseph and the chance to talk things over with him. He valued his views and his broad knowledge of the political world and of Roman ways of thinking. He hoped he would soon return from Alexandria and they could discuss the situation and future prospects. When he reached his home, he went straight down into the basement to bathe and relax in the cool waters of the pool.

An hour later he was up in his room, dressed in his house robes and drinking some wine. Rachela came upstairs and was surprised to see him. Nikki followed her close behind, curious to know what had happened.

"You came back early, Hananel! Did everything go well at the Sanhedrin meeting in the Hewn Chamber?"

"Yes and no. A lot of empty talk as usual and nothing decided. But at least this means nothing dangerous will be done for the present."

"Why is it called the Hewn Chamber?" asked Nikki.

"Leave your father alone, Nikki," said Rachela reprovingly. "He is too tired now and has no time for your questions."

"It is alright, Rachela. The boy should ask questions otherwise he will never learn anything. I wish more people would ask more questions instead of just acting on the first thought in their bloody minds without thinking."

"Hananel" Rachela cried, shocked at his language. But Gorion did not apologise. He told Nikki that the Hall of Hewn Stones, the *Lishkat Hagazit*, has walls of hewn stones, *gazit*, unlike the stones of the altar in the Temple which must not be hewn.

"You remember the passage in the Book of Exodus, a few verses after the Ten Commandments. It says there: *And if you make me an altar of stone, you shall not build it of hewn stone, for if you raise your blade upon it you will pollute it*. No axe or chisel must be laid on the stones of the Temple altar which is a symbol of peace."

"Yes, I remember this," Nikki said. "David wanted to build the Temple, but God told him he could not because had killed people. It was his son Solomon who built the Temple because in the time of Solomon there was peace. The name Solomon means peace, and the name Jerusalem also means that it is the city of peace."

"In the time of Abraham it was simply called Shalem," Gorion told him. "And its king was called Melchizedek, which means the Righteous King. Do you remember the story of five kings who fought against the four kings in Canaan?"

"Yes, yes," said Nikki eagerly. "I know the story in the Book of Genesis. The five kings of cities in the Jordan area including Sodom and Gomorrah were conquered by the King of Elam, Chedorlaomer and three other kings who were his allies. They took many captives and all the treasures of the cities."

"Good," said Gorion, smiling at his clever son. "And what happened next?"
Nikki did not hesitate for a moment before answering.

"Abraham heard that the cities had been attacked and that his nephew, Lot, who was living in Sodom, was taken captive. Abraham took his servants and shepherds, chased the attackers, and brought back all the captives and the treasure. The King of Sodom wanted to give Abraham a tenth of the goods he had saved but he refused."

"Go on. Why did he refuse?" Gorion asked him.

"Abraham said: I will not take a thread or even a shoelace of anything that belongs to you, so that you will not say I have made Abraham rich. Only give the men who went with me some portion of the goods. Then Melchizedek, the king of Shalem, came out to greet Abraham and blessed him."

Proud man, Abraham, thought Gorion. He lived in absolute trust in God to provide for him. Shalem which was originally called Ur-Salim, later became Yeru-Shalem, which means 'We will see peace' Will we see peace in our time, I wonder! They would need to pray very hard for it.

He recalled the prayer of Solomon at the dedication of the First Temple: *Hear the supplication of your servant and of your people Israel when they pray towards this place ...whatever prayer and supplication be made by any man ...a stranger that is not of your people Israel.* This means anyone who came to the Temple to pray would be admitted. The same idea is expressed by Isaiah the prophet: *Also the sons of the stranger, that join themselves to the Lord, to serve him and to love the name of the Lord ...Even them I will bring to my holy mountain, and make them joyful in my house of prayer; their burnt offerings and their sacrifices shall be accepted on my altar; for my house shall be called a house of prayer for all people.* Could anything be more beautifully said, more inspiring!

Late that evening an unexpected visitor arrived. It was Hillel's favourite pupil, Johanan the son of Zakkai. Supper had been over for some hours, but Rachela immediately brought him something to eat and drink, since he seemed very tired and distraught. Nikki had gone to bed and Rachela withdrew to let them talk privately.

"My master, Hillel, requested me to ask you for a favour. He believes that the discussions in the Sanhedrin are becoming too political and can easily be overheard by someone who would report it to Archelaus or the Roman authorities."

"I noticed this today and it seemed like seditious talk," said Gorion. "But what can we do about it?"

"Hillel thinks that the small Sanhedrin, the executive committee of twenty-three senior members who are the real decision-makers there, should meet privately somewhere else. He wanted to ask you if they could meet in your upper chamber."

"Here, in my house!" exclaimed Gorion. "Mustn't the Sanhedrin meet in a sacred place? The two small Sanhedrins of twenty-three members meet at the entrances to the Temple, and one of them also meets occasionally in the house of the High Priest."

"Yes, I know," said Johanan. "But the High Priest has no love for the Sanhedrin, especially for Shammai and his disciples who now have a stronger voice after the recent crucifixions."

"I realise that," Gorion agreed. "But surely there is some other sacred place. The Torah study halls, for example."

Johanan shook his head. "Much too public, there is need for privacy, even secrecy. For once, Shammai agrees with Hillel."

Gorion looked at him thoughtfully. He seemed very anxious, almost desperate for an answer. There must be another reason for this urgency but he could not put his finger on what it was.

"If Hillel wishes it, I will gladly agree," he said. "Yet there is something else that troubles you. What is it Johanan?"

"There was talk of assassinations. By zealots and messianic fanatics among the people who were attending the Sanhedrin session today. It is no longer safe for public discussions either in the Hewn Chamber or in the High Priest's house."

"You are especially worried for your master, Hillel. Aren't you Johanan?"

"Yes, I am. He is the one that they think will stand in their way of revolt, not Shammai."

"Well, tell him I accept. It will be an honour. But the elders must come singly, or in pairs, at different times and from different directions so that people do not notice they are gathering here."

They mounted the stairs to the upper chamber. There was a large, round table at one end and sufficient space for chairs in front of it. He could remove all the art objects, and put curtains over the shelves to hide the scrolls. It was well lighted from the large window openings and there was a skylight as well.

"You know, this chamber was once a closed attic, dark, without windows. There was just the skylight. Until I had it renovated and designed as it is now. My grandfather, Hananiah, sat up here day in and day out for nearly forty years studying the Book of Ezekiel with only an oil lamp for reading. He kept a large barrel of oil up here to keep it going."

"I never heard this before," said Johanan. "What was his purpose in doing so?"

"The problem was that the rabbis did not want to accept the book as part of the biblical canon. They found it had some passages that did not seem to be in accord with the accepted views of Judaism. So my grandfather, who believed this book to contain divine prophecy and religious truth, wrote a complete treatise to interpret the meaning of every passage that would make it acceptable."

"So this room is sacred enough. The Book of Ezekiel is one of the three great books of prophecy in the Bible: Isaiah, Jeremiah and Ezekiel. Of these three, I think Ezekiel is the greatest."

"You know it then? I remember much of it by heart from the frequent readings I had with Grandfather."

"Most probably the visions he had, especially the first one of the heavenly wheels and the throne of sapphire, and the appearance of God in the likeness of a man. What we call 'Ma'ase Merkava', the mystic form of the Heavenly Chariot. It sounded too pagan for them."

"And the repeated phrase 'Son of Man' which God uses repeatedly to speak to Ezekiel. He also had a completely different description of the future temple to be built from Temple of Solomon that had been destroyed. That was a major problem. But it could all be interpreted symbolically as my grandfather thought, as for example, the vision of the valley of dry bones."

"That may have been the source for our belief in resurrection and in the afterlife."

"The Essenes believe in this, but the Sadducees do not. I think they are justified, at least as far as the Bible says. The dead are mentioned there as 'going down to Sheol', to the underworld which is very much like what the pagans believe. Though there are the stories of Elijah and Elisha who could magically revive the dead."

Johanan looked at him sceptically. "So, you do not believe in the resurrection or the afterlife. And talking about Sheol, you are of course thinking of the spirit

41

of Samuel brought up from the underworld by the Witch of Endor. After death, only the spirit can be resurrected, not the body."

"I don't think Samuel's spirit was literally resurrected. I think Saul saw him only in his mind, in his imagination. The witch put him into a dream-like state."

They went downstairs again, and Gorion suggested that, since it was already very late, Johanan should sleep in one of the guest rooms. He gladly accepted. He could help with arranging the upper chamber the next day for the first meeting.

****

The Sanhedrin, the Council of Elders, had been established soon after the victory of the Maccabees over the Seleucid tyrants, and it derived its authority from the earlier Great Assembly, the *Knesset Hagdola*, instituted by Ezra the scribe. It then had 120 members, and their main task was to formulate the rituals, prayers, and benedictions, to decide on the books to be included in the biblical canon, to establish courts of law, and to provide the day to day rulings of religious practice.

According to Johanan, the Great Sanhedrin, the full number of 70 members and its President, held their meetings in the Chamber of Hewn Stones. The meetings at the Gorion house were intended as preparations for the larger meetings, to present the issues to them in an organised way. The sessions could then be more manageable, although there were bound to be members challenging decisions and making counter-arguments, besides those who simply liked to disrupt the sessions. They used to have the power to try people for capital offences and to order executions, but this authority had been taken away from them by the Roman conquerors.

Hillel the Elder, now a hundred years old, was the *Nasi*, the President of the Great Sanhedrin, and his colleague, Shammai, who was nearly half his age, was the *Av Beth-Din*, the Head of the Law Court. Two smaller Sanhedrin courts of 23 members were established in Jerusalem and in a few other cities to deal with general matters of religious or criminal offence, but final decisions remained with the greater assembly. The High Priest was technically subject to the Sanhedrin, but sometimes acted independently of it when it affected Temple matters by convening his own court of Sanhedrin members.

Gorion and Johanan began arranging the chamber the next day. Nikki was excited at the idea of the Sanhedrin meeting in the upper chamber. Even though it meant that he would not be able to go up there as long as the meetings continued. Besides the meetings, some of the members would stay on to discuss matters in smaller groups, or to receive various kinds of reports through their disciples. It would be a busy place with people coming and going at different times so as not to be noticed. Rachela would also be busy supplying them with refreshments, and perhaps even with the occasional meal after a long session. There were also the scribes who recorded all the main arguments and final decisions of the rabbis. Scrolls and ink were set out for them with the writing implements, the reed pens.

The first meeting began in the early afternoon. Everyone there seemed to be at ease in this pleasant and informal venue. Hillel, Shammai and the leading members were seated around the table and the rest sat on chairs or couches ranged in front of them. Both Hillel and Shammai agreed that disputes would be conducted quietly and civilly. No shouting or loud arguments. The main subject to be discussed that day was the political one concerning the delegation that should be sent to Rome and what they should say there when they stood before Augustus. But they also wanted to discuss the internal situation, the volatile relations between the various populations in the country.

Hillel began with a soft-spoken introduction, thanking Gorion for his hospitality. He then gave his view of the present situation: "Our country is a patchwork of peoples—Jews, Greeks, Romans, Samaritans, Idumeans, Arabs, and many small groups from various countries, either converts or for personal reasons. We cannot afford to be in a permanent state of conflict with each other, or with our own internal factions and divisions—the Galileans in the north, the Essenes in the east. We must teach our people to love their neighbours like themselves, to offer them the hand of friendship and ask for their cooperation in maintaining the peace. And we must submit with patience to Roman rule and the domination of the Herodians otherwise we will be heading down the years to war and revolution, and the ultimate destruction of our nation."

Shammai interrupted him with his own view of the situation: "This patchwork of peoples is because we have become weak, we have allowed too many people to intrude into our country and to desecrate it with their alien culture. We are a people that will always 'dwell alone' according to Balaam's prophecy, 'they shall not be reckoned among the nations.' We have to separate

43

ourselves from other peoples. Our ways are not theirs, and they will never understand our ways or accept them. They think of us as inferior in culture, that we mutilate our children, we restrict our diet, wear strange tassels, do not work one day a week, perversely and obstinately refuse to intermarry with them. But this is the will of God, to keep us apart, the chosen few, as his people. He will protect us from destruction if we keep his laws—and keep them strictly."

The assembled elders sat in silent contemplation for a while. The choice was clear, social integration or social separation. Could the Jews retain their identity while intermingling socially with their neighbours? Or would it lead to assimilation and loss of identity? Could they not have the best of both worlds?

"As for submission to Rome and to Archelaus," Shammai continued, "we must bide our time and wait for the first opportunity to revolt against them. The Jews of Babylonian and Egypt will come to our aid. The Parthians will be our allies in any war against Rome, and so will Armenia and perhaps other nations in those Roman protectorates in the north who are tired of Roman rule."

The thought of war and armed conflict was terrifying to many of those present. And revolt was unthinkable with the wealthy and influential Pro-Roman priestly families and a general population that was sedentary in character and mainly rural in nature. True, they were oppressed with heavy taxes and often cruel discrimination. Herod had always favoured the Grecian population with their Hellenic culture. The Jews were like second-class citizens in their own country.

The old, blind sage, Baba ben Buta, a Shammai follower, supported the view for eventual revolt: "We must oppose evil whenever we see it. He who does not do so, will suffer from it. All the Roman rulers are wicked men who only seek greater power and riches. They have conquered half the world and desire the other half. There is no end to their greed and rapacious nature. Rome is the seat of corruption and licentious practices. It is Sodom and Gomorrah all over again. God will rain down fire and brimstone over it one day."

Gorion had heard how this man became blind. Herod, in his rage against the sages opposed to his rule, had ordered many of them executed. But he only blinded this sage because he had always valued his wisdom and advice. Some years later he came to visit him and ask for his pardon. The sage told that he would be forgiven if he rebuilt the old Temple and gave it greater splendour.

The assembled members sat in shocked silence at this heated diatribe of Baba ben Buta. Nehunia ben Ha-Kanah, a brilliant scholar and an expert in hermeneutics and the mystical interpretation of the Bible, then spoke in gentler tones.

"You overlook the benefits of Roman civilisation, Baba. They have brought us good roads, aqueducts to bring water from afar, organised administration, and protection from neighbouring countries. We are a richer country now, healthier, more enterprising, and more progressive. Herod knew this and allied himself with them. And we now have the grandest and the most beautiful temple in the world."

Gorion silently agreed, but said nothing. He was sitting at the back and did not want to interfere with the proceedings. A few more of the Sanhedrin members spoke, some siding with the views of Hillel and some with Shammai. Their voices droned on for a while until a gavel was struck on the table to halt the discussion.

It was time for a short recess, Gorion called down for refreshments to be brought up by Rachela and Nikki. Many people stood up, some going to the arched openings in the wall facing the Temple Mount, while others went up to the roof to get some fresh air. Nikki felt honoured to serve old Hillel personally, attracted to his kind face and smiling eyes. Hillel patted him on the shoulder and thanked him.

They soon reconvened, and Hillel presented them with the proposal of sending a delegation to Rome. It would have to be composed of three or four people only, and they had to submit a very clear and concise request to Augustus that would be both respectful and resolute. The problem was who to send and what exactly they wished to say. The request would have to be drawn up in writing and then read out at the imperial court.

They decided to send two members from each opposing faction. And the request that was formulated after much earnest debate and dispute read as follows:

As members of the Sanhedrin, the highest religious and legal authority in our country, we request that his highness, Augustus Caesar, will reconsider his appointment of Herod Archelaus as Ethnarch of Judaea, and appoint one of Herod's Hasmonean grandsons now in Rome to succeed him. And that this new ruler of Judaea will be guided by a council of ten elders from among the Sanhedrin to assist and advise him in governing the people and in carrying out his obligations as ruler of the country.

It was now getting late, and it was time to recite the afternoon prayers before the sun went down. The men rose and turned in the direction of the Temple Mount. Nikki stood looking at the bowed heads, listening to the low murmur of voices, and heard outside the cooing of doves settling on the roof. And then everyone filed out of the chamber, followed by his father, and he was left there alone.

****

Joseph arrived back in Jerusalem the next morning looking tanned and rested after his sea voyage from Alexandria. He was anxious for news about recent developments and Gorion told about the Sanhedrin assembly at the Chamber of Hewn Stones and the meeting of the previous day by the executive committee in the upper chamber. The delegation of four members was preparing to leave for Caesarea within a few days and Gorion suggested that Joseph go to Rome with them to assist them in gaining audience with Augustus. Marcus was staying with Gaius, and he would also be glad to see his father.

"It is not going to be an easy venture, this Sanhedrin delegation," Joseph warned him. "I have a few contacts at the imperial court, and may be able to quicken the process for their petition before Augustus. He usually has several of them a day and there is bound to be a long list of people waiting for an audience. But I have my doubts that he will listen to what they request. He will choose Archelaus because it was legally correct to do so and will not change his mind unless there are some serious allegations against him."

"Actually, I have been receiving many bad reports about Archelaus," said Gorion. "He recently went to Samaria and treated the Samaritans barbarously. They are also planning to send a delegation to Augustus Caesar, and I don't blame them."

"This might tip the balance then in favour of the Sanhedrin delegation. Perhaps they should join up with the Samaritan delegation."

"Samaritans and Jews join together? Not till the Messiah arrives!"

Joseph laughed. "You know what I heard on board ship? One of the seamen told me a story about some Chaldean astrologers that Archelaus sent for to interpret a dream that he had. Like the story of Pharaoh's dreams which were interpreted by Joseph, Archelaus dreamed that he saw nine large ears of corn being devoured by oxen. One astrologer said one thing and the other said something else, until he was exasperated and sent them away. He then he asked Simon, one of the Essenes who had been for many years at his father's court. Simon told him that the ears of corn were the years he would reign, and then he would fall from power and die in a foreign country."

"The man must be in a constant state of fear and anxiety. He will see usurpers at every turn and will become even harsher in his dealings with everyone. Good that Maryam and Jeshua are safe in Alexandria."

"Speaking of messiahs," Joseph added. "Did you hear about some characters in the Galilee presuming to be the promised messiah? Some fellow called Judas, a Zealot, the son of the robber chieftain Ezekias who had been caught many years ago and was killed by Herod."

"Yes, I had a report about him and also about a former slave of Herod, Simon of Peraea. He was bold enough to put a diadem on his head and declare himself king. He plundered the king's palace in Jericho and burnt it, and also burnt other houses of the king around the country. Gratus, the Roman infantry commander, set out to find him and when Simon tried to flee across the Jordan, he caught up with him and cut off his head. People always get attracted to such tall, handsome, charismatic figures. There was also another fellow, a shepherd called Athronges, one of five brothers, each with his own band of men. They attacked Roman soldiers until they were finally captured."

Joseph was astounded. This was anarchy and would lead to utter political chaos. He was afraid, not only because of the effects on his business enterprises but also for his personal safety. These crazy fanatics would soon begin to attack Jews who were seen to have personal dealings with Romans. He had many dealings with Romans, and even had one personal client and friend in Jerusalem.

"Hananel, how about coming with me now to visit a friend, Rufus Gratianus, a high-born Roman living near the king's palace? He is one of the agents that Augustus sent to Jerusalem to send him weekly reports on the situation here. He can be of great help with getting an early audience for the delegation in Rome."

Gorion gladly agreed, and they went out together. On the way, they met Nikki coming home from school, and they decided to take him along as well. They turned in the direction of Herod's palace. At its northern end, near the junction of the first and second walls of the city, they entered the courtyard of the Mariamne Tower overlooking the main gate of the city facing the highway to Joppa.

The Mariamne Tower was the smallest of the three towers along the walls and the most beautiful and luxuriously furnished one. It was used to house royal or important visitors from abroad, while the other two were held by the officers and guards of the palace. Grecian statues lined the courtyard and a fountain gushed high in the centre. An attendant led them up to the suite of rooms on the first floor and announced their arrival. Gratianus was delighted to see Joseph. They clasped each other's forearms in the comradely manner.

"You have not been to see me for a long while, my friend," he said, shaking his finger at him. "Too busy I warrant with all your many business concerns."

"I apologise, Rufus! These bad times have kept me from pleasant social visits."

Joseph then introduced Gorion and Nikki to him. Rufus bowed and saluted them in the Roman style, standing erect and placing his right fist over his heart. He was tall, with short, grizzled hair and he had a scar on his left cheek. Probably from one of the battles in which he had fought, Gorion assumed.

Rufus' wife, Fulvia approached and greeted them as well. They were taken into the spacious living room and seated on couches facing the balcony overlooking the courtyard. Gorion refused the wine offered him and Joseph suggested that they have some grape juice instead. Nikki remembered why they could not drink wine at the home of non-Jewish people. It was the forbidden *nesech* wine because Romans used wine for libations to their gods.

While the men talked among themselves, Fulvia came to sit near him and asked him a few questions in Latin about himself. He did his best to answer her correctly. He could read Latin very well, but did not have much practice speaking it. And then her young daughter, Aurelia, came in and greeted them shyly. She was Nikki's age, and he thought she was lovely, with her golden hair and blue eyes.

"Aurelia will soon return to Rome," Rufus told them as he rose to put his arm around his daughter. "She will be staying with my brother's family till we return there next year. We feel it would be safer for her to be in Rome after the recent events here."

To continue their discussion Joseph and Gorion retired with Rufus to his study and began drawing up the letter to Augustus. Fulvia was called by one of the servants to decide on some matter, and Aurelia and Nikki went out together onto the balcony. Below them, a group of soldiers were marching past the city gate in the direction of the palace. To the east they could see the Temple Mount with golden roof of the Temple reflecting the sunlight. All seemed peaceful, and the streets were almost empty but there was a feeling that this was quiet before the storm.

They did not say much to each other at first. But it was a friendly silence.

"I do not remember much of Rome," Aurelia said. "I was only six when I came here ten years ago. And I do not really want to leave Jerusalem."

"I would like to go and see Rome one day," Nikki responded. "I have never been away from Jerusalem, except to visit my cousin's house up north."

"If you come to Rome, I hope you will visit us there. My uncle lives on the Esquiline Hill, near the gardens of Maecenas and we have our own house nearby, though it is now closed up."

"My cousin, Marcus, Joseph's son, has just gone to live in Rome. I am not sure exactly where. He mentioned being in the Subura neighbourhood."

"Yes, that is where many Jews now live, mainly in the tall insula buildings. Julius Caesar was born and grew up there. His mother, Aurelia, owned one of these insulae. You know, I was named after her because my grandmother knew her well and admired her very much."

Nikki heard his father calling him in. Gorion and Joseph were preparing to leave and they parted with warm farewells. They walked slowly towards Mount Zion, the two men talking about the imminent departure of the delegation to Rome. Joseph would prepare to leave with them for Caesarea, and Gorion wanted to speak to the delegates before they left for Rome. Nikki trailed behind them, thinking of Aurelia and wishing he could go to Rome as well. Perhaps his father would let him go with Joseph for a brief visit.

When they reached the house, they saw a cart outside, and a strange woman standing near it looking very tired and harassed. A young girl was crying in the hallway and Rachela was trying to calm her down while some of the servants were clustered around them.

"What's the matter?" shouted Gorion. "Who is that woman outside?"

Rachela turned and held up her hand to silence him. She then lifted up the girl in her arms and took her towards the kitchen.

"Give her something to eat and drink," she told a servant-girl. "And then take her up to one of the bedrooms. Stay with her till she calms down and falls asleep. She is hot and exhausted from the journey."

"What journey?" Gorion asked. "Where did they come from?"

Rachela took him by the hand and led him back to the hallway and into the living room. Joseph and Nikki were already there resting on the soft couches.

"They came from Babylonia. The girl is Ruhama, the daughter of my younger sister Ruth," she said. "Her mother died a week ago in childbirth, and her father is too distraught to care for the girl. He thought it best to send her here to me for a while till he recovered from his loss."

"And who is the woman outside?"

"She was traveling to Jerusalem to visit her son, and agreed to bring the girl with her. She will be leaving as soon as she is paid for her trouble."

Gorion went out to pay the woman and thank her for bringing the young girl. She told him it was very difficult to handle the six-year old child who wailed continually for her mother and would not eat. Nothing she did could calm her.

"Well, we will see what we can do for her," Gorion assured her. "My wife will know how to calm the child and will be her second mother."

But it was only in the evening, after Joseph had left, that Rachela finally brought Ruhama down to have supper with them. Nikki looked at her dark brown face, her large brown eyes, and her long black hair flowing down all around her shoulders. What a difference from the lovely Aurelia he thought. He found her rather ugly, and as he looked at her she gazed back at him with fierce, angry eyes. She ate very little, and kept silent all the time, responding only to Rachela who tried to make her feel at home.

He hated the thought of her being in the house with him. Why couldn't she have been a boy? He would have liked to have a young brother to play with. Girls were no use as playmates. They were too fussy about being treated properly, and were bad sports when they lost a game. And this girl looked as if she would be troublesome, unfriendly. He wondered if she spoke Hebrew or only Aramaic. He heard his mother speaking to her in Aramaic as she often did to him. She was smiling at the girl now, and he had a sudden feeling of jealousy. Would she now give more of her love to Ruhama than to him?

Joseph had already left a few hours earlier, and after supper, Gorion went into his study, while Rachela went upstairs with Ruhama. Nikki felt alone and rather bored. The school year was ending soon and he did not know what he could do during the holiday interval. His father had rejected his pleadings to go to Rome with Joseph. It was an important journey and he would be too busy with the delegates to pay attention to Nikki. Marcus was also extremely busy with the trading business and would prefer to spend his free time with his friend Gaius.

Morosely, he climbed the stairs to his room. At least, the upper chamber would not be needed by the Sanhedrin elders for a while until the delegates returned. He could go there tomorrow after school and spend the afternoon looking through the scrolls and reading. The chairs were set around the table and the shelves were open. It would be the ideal place to avoid seeing the girl except at meal times.

In the morning when he came down, he heard her crying again, this time because they were trying to make her take a bath. She did not want anyone to undress her, and he could hear the servant girl pleading with her without success. What a nuisance she was going to be! His mother finally managed to persuade her, letting her undress herself and bathe without the servant girl standing by.

He had his breakfast and rushed off to school. He might have to endure her presence at least until the New Year in September when her father would probably come to Jerusalem to take her back. As soon as he came home he could just eat and then go straight to the upper chamber to be alone. His mother would surely not expect him to pay attention to the girl. The servant girl can keep her occupied with something or other. She had the garden to play in if she wanted.

When he returned after school, he did not see her downstairs in the living room or the dining room. Perhaps she was in the garden or in her bedroom. His meal was on the table and he ate hastily and went upstairs. After a brief rest, he washed and changed his clothes for a simple belted tunic and padded barefoot up the stairs to the attic chamber. And there, in a corner, he saw her sitting with her knees drawn up and holding one of the nymph statuettes. She was crooning some song to it, as if it were a doll.

"What are you doing here," he shouted at her. "Put that thing down, you mustn't play with it. It is not a toy!"

Ruhama jumped up in terror. She looked at him in fright which soon turned to anger. Lifting her arm she threw the statuette at him and it smashed against the doorway. He was furious, and caught her up as she tried to run out of the chamber, shaking her violently while she screamed in fear.

"Let me go you horrid boy," she cried. She said the words in Hebrew, with perfect enunciation. He was so surprised that he dropped her and she fled down the stairs in tears. Rachela came out on the lower landing and Ruhama ran into her arms sobbing.

"What have you done to her, Nikki," she called up to him.

"She was here in the corner with one of the nymph statuettes, playing with it or singing to it. And then she threw it at me and it smashed against the doorway."

Rachela realised Ruhama was simply imagining her mother singing to her in the evening before she slept. She took the girl down and comforted her. She would find some materials and make her a doll to play with. The servant girl she had assigned for her should have been taking better care of her. She must not be allowed to go to the upper chamber. Perhaps some small room behind the kitchen near the back garden could be made into her playroom.

****

Gorion was at the magistrates' court. He had been there since the morning and he would not be able to get away till much later in the afternoon. As the chief magistrate, only the major cases were sent to him, but it appeared that there were now many major cases. Two murdered men by armed robbers at the home of the rich trader from Adiabene, three violent demonstrators at the Temple who had set fire to one corner of an outbuilding where wood was stored. The worst was an attack at the royal palace where soldiers had fought with some Zealots throwing fireballs into the central courtyard and burning a memorial stand set up for Herod. They were arrested and almost executed on the spot until some elderly rabbis intervened and insisted that they be brought to trial first.

He was tired and hungry, but stayed on doggedly to see that everything was done for the sake of justice. *Zion will be redeemed by justice* as the Bible says. In biblical times, Zion was simply another name for Jerusalem itself, the City of David. Mount Zion was probably so-called because it was the higher, western hill that overlooked Zion, David's city.

Justice in Jerusalem was a Sisyphean task, an exercise in frustration when most of the people could no longer keep the peace. But they should not be blamed with such leaders as the king, the priests, and the wealthy, arrogant aristocratic courtiers. Although he was also wealthy he did not display it, and he contributed regularly to charitable institutions. Joseph was also generous to a fault. He had funded old age homes for his workers, saw to it that no man was in want for food or clothing, was open handed to anyone who turned to him in distress.

As he finally turned to leave the courtroom he was accosted by a palace official with the insignia of Herodian house on his sleeve.

"You are Gorion the Chief Magistrate?"

"Yes, I am."

"I have been sent by the Ethnarch Archelaus to request you to come to the palace as he wishes to speak to you."

"Is this an urgent matter? I am on my way home after a long day in the courtroom. Can it not wait until tomorrow?"

"I do not know, sir. But I was told to bring you immediately."

"Well, there is no help for it. I will follow you to the palace."

Arriving at Herod's palace, he was taken up to the royal suite and then into the room where Archelaus sat with his wife, Mariamne. She was the eldest daughter of his Hasmonean half-brother Aristobulus and his wife Berenice, the daughter of Salome, Herod's sister. After greeting him, Archelaus asked him about his experience as a magistrate and about his legal qualifications. Gorion set out all the details of his education and of career, first as a lawyer and then as a judge covering a period of nearly forty years.

Satisfied, Archelaus said that he would like to give him the position of personal legal adviser to him and grant him the title of Chancellor of the Court. He was in urgent need of legal advice concerning a number of matters, both public and private, and Gorion had been recommended to him as person most highly suited to the task.

Gorion was dumbfounded at first, not knowing how to reply. He looked at Archelaus with his haughty expression of condescension and found it difficult to conceal his aversion to him. After acknowledging the high honour, he was given, he began to make his excuses without causing any ill will by his rejection. He saw the surprise on the face of the Ethnarch, and then anger. But Archelaus restrained himself and said that perhaps Gorion would need some time to make his final decision and requested that he seriously reconsider accepting the high honour offered to him.

Bowing his head respectfully, Gorion saw Archelaus rise, give his hand to his wife, and retire into his bedchamber. He was glad to leave as quickly as possible. He asked at the gate to find him a litter to take him home as it was late and he was very tired. It was a worrying situation and he wished Joseph was in Jerusalem to advise him what to do. And then he thought of Rufus Gratianus and decided it was a good idea to consult him. He knew Archelaus well, was on good terms with him and could find some solution to the dilemma.

When he arrived home, Rachela did not mention the late hour or question why he was delayed. He would need a wash and some food first. While he bathed, she prepared a tray of food and a glass of wine and took it into the living room. He soon came in and sat on the couch as she placed the tray on a low table in front of him. Ruhama was playing on the floor nearby with her new doll and some other old toys that had once belonged to Nikki. Rachela sat by quietly while her husband ate and drank, and then she took the tray away to the kitchen.

Gorion lay back and relaxed on the couch. He looked down at Ruhama and she smiled up at him. It was the first time he saw her smile. He closed his eyes, thinking just to rest a little before going up to bed. His mind wandered over his past, the long process that had led from poorer beginnings to his present state of wealth and comfort. But then quite suddenly he fell asleep.

About an hour later Rachela came to take Ruhama to bed and found Gorion fast asleep with the girl curled up beside him on the couch, her head on his arm and her doll on his chest. She looked at them for a long while. It was such a lovely scene. And she knew now that the little girl had finally gotten over her grief and would be happy again.

****

Gorion went to see Rufus the next day in the afternoon. Nikki went with him because he wanted to see Aurelia before she left for Rome. After Rufus heard what had happened the day before with Archelaus, he sat thinking for a while and then came to some conclusion.

"I think if you wait awhile, he will choose someone else, or his friends will propose another lawyer or judge to be his chancellor. He will have forgotten you by then. But to make sure, I will inquire quietly among his courtiers and see if he is in any way angered or vindictive at your refusal."

"Thank you, Rufus. I am in your debt. It had me very worried both for myself and for my family."

"Yes, the man is quite unbalanced and ruled by his emotions, even irrational at times. But then it is easier to manipulate him if one knows him well. I have been able to deflect his anger by simply giving him something else to be angry at, something more trivial and less dangerous for the people he rules."

"The last thing I want is to be a member of his court. He will use my good name to cover up a multitude of his sins and leave me with a bad one."

Nikki was talking animatedly with Aurelia, his face alight with pleasure. Gorion looked at him and saw how glad the boy was to see her again. Nikki had not found many of his age that he liked and could call a friend. And never before did he show any liking for girls. In fact, he often disparaged them, saying they were silly creatures and even stupid. It was a pity Aurelia had to leave so soon. But then he thought it would be better if Nikki fell in love and married a Jewish girl. Some of the younger generation, those born in Rome or in Alexandria, were marrying outside the faith, slowly assimilating into Roman or Greek culture, and forgetting their heritage.

Their visit was prolonged since Rufus and Gorion had continued talking together about the delegation that had gone to Rome and the prospects of its success. And they went on to discuss the general relations between Rome and Jerusalem, the perpetual tensions and misunderstandings between them that could be avoided with a little good will on both sides. But the time came to leave and get back before sunset. Rachela would be expecting them for supper very soon.

On the way back, Nikki asked whether he could not go to Rome instead of Alexandria after he finish his schooling next year. He could study there just as well, and he could stay with Marcus. Gorion tried to explain to him that Alexandria was the better choice. He would have Philo to guide him in his higher studies and there was the wonderful library of Alexandria, a major centre of scholarship with its huge collection of works, large lecture halls, and gardens with long covered walks. There was even a zoo of exotic animals. The whole atmosphere there was ideal for study and research. Rome had too many distractions for the student.

Besides, he told Nikki, it had all been arranged in advance and Philo would be expecting him as his special student and protégé. He would be happier there in that environment of intellectual achievement among scholars who came from around the world to study there. Rome could come later, after he had spent a sufficient number of years at Alexandria and Philo was satisfied that he had gained a solid academic grounding.

That evening, after supper, a letter arrived by special courier from Joseph. He wrote that the delegates had been well received at the court of Augustus and were given an early audience with him. Their appeal was even supported by a large contingent from the Jewish community in Rome. The delegates spoke well and Augustus was impressed with their dignity and honourable bearing. He listened courteously to their words and questioned them briefly. But he said that it was too early to pass judgment on Archelaus who was still trying to consolidate his rule against his opponents and in time, with greater control and confidence, he would relax his harsh treatment of his people. Nevertheless, Rome would keep a close eye on his behaviour and reconsider the petition presented to him.

It was disappointing but perhaps only to be expected. Augustus regarded the matter very differently from the perspective of those living here in Jerusalem. They would have to be patient and see how matters turned out in the next few years. Personally, Joseph thought Archelaus would only become worse than he was now, more despotic, more paranoid, and even more extreme in his cruel behaviour.

Gorion expected Joseph to return within a week or so and was looking forward to consulting him about a plan to provide greater protection from abuse for the citizens of Jerusalem. He wanted to set up a special court to handle cases of unjust exploitation and summary judgments by the Ethnarch and the royal court. Rulers must be made subject to the law rather than have the law subject to their own interests. The Sanhedrin would have to vote on setting up such a court as an emergency measure. He would use all the influence he had to persuade them to do so. It was time for all good men to stand up and be counted.

He sat down in his study to write down his ideas and proposals while they were still fresh in his mind. The oil lamp had almost burnt down before he finished and went to bed. But even there, he tossed and turned with his thoughts on the subject and on what else could be done. Sleep did not come until many hours later, and when he woke the next morning he found he had overslept.

He would now be too late for the morning sessions at court. Rachela must have already gone about her household matters, and he heard Nikki running past the door and rushing downstairs. Then there was the patter of little feet, and Ruhama entered the room as she did every morning. She came up to the bed and said, "Good morning baba." And he answered, "Good morning Ruhama." He was now her 'baba', which meant father in Aramaic. They understood each other completely and she regarded him and Rachela as her parents. They in turn saw her as the daughter they had always wanted and wished they could to keep her with them in Jerusalem.

****

Joseph returned to Caesarea, bringing the Sanhedrin delegates back on one of his own ships. Marcus came with him for a brief holiday and left Gaius, who was now his partner in the Rome branch of their business, in charge of the trading office. As they approached the city he was amazed once again at the magnificence of the Sebastos harbour, which he thought rivalled the harbour in Alexandria.

What an enormous project it must have been for Herod who began building it sometime in the middle of his reign and probably took years to construct. It was an artificial harbour because the coast line was not naturally suitable for it. He had massive quantities of pozzolana imported from Italy, and used tons of kurkar, a chalky kind of sandstone quarried to make rubble, and also slaked lime to mix with the pozzolana. There was the long breakwater on the south side and a shorter one on the north enclosed a vast expanse of the sea. Architects had to devise ingenious ways to lay an underwater foundation directly on the sea bed, using divers to go down or sinking barges filled with sandstone rubble.

He could see the docks now, teeming with people, jostling each other, carts, wagons, wheelbarrows filled with bales of cotton, or wine jars, or vats of salted fish. A few young Greeks, half drunk, strolled along a narrow pathway, knocking aside some elderly Jews carrying small oil vessels. One of the vessels fell to the ground and cracked, spilling the oil. One of the young men laughed to see how the old men almost slipped on the greasy path. Had he been there he would have knocked them down. Arrogant fellows! There was always this kind of burning antagonism between the Greeks and the Jews living in Caesarea. One day it would cause a conflagration.

Marcus said he wanted to stay on in Caesarea to see some of the races in the hippodrome and meet some of his former Roman companions in the city. He had often gone there with Gaius and his friends whenever he visited Caesarea and stayed with him at his home. They would be glad to see him again after so long. Joseph also decided that he should remain there for some time to dispose of the goods he had just brought with him on the ship. As they descended from the ship he noticed people boarding another one drawn up alongside his own, and then saw his friend Rufus on the dock with his wife and daughter. They were too far away to be hailed, so he sent Marcus across to speak to them. He remembered that Aurelia was to be sent back to Rome and that they must have come to accompany her to the ship.

He saw Marcus approach them and stand talking to them for a long while, and especially to Aurelia. He saw her smiling at him and then laughing at some jest or other. Marcus always liked to joke, and also to tease. When he was living with the Gorion family, he teased Nikki mercilessly. Luckily, Nikki adored him and never resented it. Most people found him charming and personable. And he was doing very well with his position in Rome, bringing in many good clients for the trade. Gaius was also an asset to the business.

Impatient at Marcus and the delay, Joseph set about dispatching the delegates to Jerusalem on wagons going in that direction, and then saw to the unloading of the cargo. He knew that after Aurelia boarded the ship, Rufus and his wife would come back with Marcus to meet him. He would invite them aboard his own ship to rest for a while in the captain's cabin. He had some good wine to offer them and some luxury items from Rome that Fulvia would be pleased to have.

They came quite a long while later, after having stood on the docks and waited till the ship departed. Fulvia still had tears in her eyes and Rufus was trying to comfort and reassure her. By the time they were seated in the cabin of his ship, Joseph saw she had recovered, and they sat and talked, refreshed by the chilled wine and some cold fruit dessert.

"Till we return to Rome, Aurelia will be staying at the home of my brother and his wife," Rufus explained. "Their children are married and no longer live with them, so she will be rather alone until she can renew contacts with old friends."

Fulvia added that she was glad Marcus was now living in Rome, and that he kindly promised to take Aurelia out occasionally. She loves the theatre and musical performances. Also sporting activities such as race competitions.

"Only don't take her to any of those barbarous gladiatorial combats," she told Marcus.

"Gaius and I especially enjoy the chariot races in the Circus Maximus. She would like that I am sure," said Marcus.

"Quite the Roman already," Rufus laughed.

"It's a dangerous sport," Joseph said angrily. "I once saw a chariot smashed to pieces and the driver killed on the spot at the turning post. It was deliberately caused by a rival charioteer. I wouldn't take her to see that."

Fulvia nodded in agreement. "Sheer murderous sport I would say."

They talked on for a while and when they parted, Marcus accompanied them to their carriage waiting some distance away from the docks. Joseph saw that he had been attracted to the girl and might even begin courting her when he returned to Rome. He was not opposed to Marcus marrying a Roman girl. Although he remained loyal to his Jewish heritage, and enjoyed participating in the festivals held in Jerusalem, Marcus no longer observed the religious rituals of his faith and had adopted a freer style of life. Joseph had also begun to neglect many of these rituals since he became a widower and his parents had passed away. They seemed almost meaningless to him now, even though he observed them whenever he was in the company of his fellow Jews.

They remained in Caesarea for nearly a week, and then Marcus left for Rome and Joseph returned to his home in Ramatayim. The house felt empty now, although he would be glad of a little solitude after the weeks he had spent in Jerusalem, Alexandria and Rome. But he knew that he could not stay there long. He had a restless mind and a constant need to find new ventures, to travel to distant countries, to explore the world beyond the places he had already visited.

He decided that his next venture was Britannia and the tin mines of Cornwall. It was an ambitious project, though it was just what he needed now to get away from the tensions and troubles of his own country. He might even stay there for a while to establish a foothold on that island. It was a pleasant country, and the climate was mild except during the stormy winter season. He would go there in the springtime and stay till the autumn winds began to blow.

****

A year went by and it was now Nikki's final year at school. He had to pass several examinations held by the scholars of the Jerusalem Academy on the various fields of study. All twenty-four books of the Bible had to be learnt, besides knowledge of the religious laws concerning daily life, ritual practices and liturgy. General information about Judaea, Samaria, the Galilee and the surrounding countries was also required, and a good command of the Hebrew language. Although basic courses in Latin and Greek were offered, not all the pupils took them.

Every Sabbath day after prayers and the morning meal, Gorion sat down with Nikki in the living room to review one of the books of the Bible with him. This usually lasted for about two hours, with questions and answers following each other and occasionally a discussion on some interesting points. They both enjoyed these sessions very much, and Nikki was quick in answering every question. What he did not like was seeing Ruhama sitting close to Gorion and listening to everything that was said. He tried not to look at her but could feel her staring at him with her big brown eyes fixed on his face.

The girl was a nuisance, always underfoot. She pattered through the house with her doll clutched in her arms, looking into all the corners, following Rachela around as she supervised the household affairs. At least, she did not dare to come to the upper chamber where he studied every afternoon when he returned from school. His mother often reprimanded him for his cold and critical attitude towards the child, reminding him that she had lost her mother and was now dependent on her and his father for comfort and support. He should treat her like a little sister, talk to her, play with her occasionally.

"She doesn't like me," he protested. "In fact, I think she hates me after what happened in the upper chamber."

"I don't think so," said his mother. "She is just waiting for you to make the first move to become friends."

"Friends! With a girl like her, so unfriendly?"

"She is not unfriendly. You have made her so with you."

Nikki shrugged his shoulders and turned away. He could not be bothered with her now that he was so busy with his studies. The upper chamber was his refuge from her, and he stayed there most of the time while he was at home.

One day he entered the chamber and found some of the scrolls had been disturbed. His favourite scroll of Bel and the Dragon was missing. He rushed downstairs to find Ruhama and then grasped her by her shoulders and shook her.

"Where is the scroll you took? Who gave you permission to touch the scrolls?"

She was frightened at first and then angry. "I just borrowed it for a while to read. Why can't I read them? They aren't yours only."

Nikki was astounded. "You know how to read"

"I learnt how to read when I was three years old. My father taught me."

He knew that girls were not taught to read, only to recite some prayers and learn some of the blessings. There were no schools for girls, they were trained to sew, and cook, and take care of the younger children in the family. He wondered now if his father knew Ruhama could read and kept silent. He often found her in the evenings after supper sitting on his knees and talking softly to him. Was he teaching her as well?

"You can't take any scrolls out of the chamber upstairs. They have to be kept there always. Give me back the scroll you took, immediately."

She went to her room and brought him the scroll and thrust it at him.

"I finished reading it so you can have it back."

They stared at each other, neither ready at first to concede to the other. But Nikki was now beginning to see her as more than just a child, or some troublesome, ignorant girl.

"You can come and read in the upper chamber while I am at school," he said grudgingly. "But only as long as you are careful with the scrolls and other things in it."

Ruhama smiled, and Nikki noticed how her face was utterly transformed by her smile. She looked almost beautiful. He turned away quickly so that she would not see what he felt at that moment. Later on he would question his father and ask why he had not told him Ruhama could read, and whether he was also teaching her and asking her about what she read. He realised he was being jealous again, as he had been about his mother's warm affection for the girl.

From then onwards, he was more friendly, or perhaps just less hostile to her. He nodded whenever he met her on the stairs or in the house. And she in turn gazed back serenely at him instead of turning her back to him as she used to do. It was more of truce than friendship. He still could not accept her as part of the family.

Later on, when he spoke to his father about this, he understood that Ruhama had been taught very well by her father who was a scholar and a scribe in Babylonia. She knew all the blessings, prayers, and could read and speak Hebrew very well. She also knew how to sing many of the hymns that had been composed for the Sabbath and festivals and that were sung by Babylonian Jews in their synagogues or at home after their festive meals.

Nikki said he thought girls did not need to read or study since they were supposed to be learning how to look after household matters. What was the use of her studying when she would one day marry and have children to keep her fully occupied? Gorion said he agreed in general, but in some cases a girl may be gifted with a good mind and a desire to read and study. She should not be prevented from learning just because she was a girl. In his opinion, Ruhama was especially gifted and he wanted to encourage her to read and to talk to him about what she had read.

Nikki felt that perhaps, again, he was just afraid a girl being better than he was at his studies. He was one of the best pupils at school and always came at the top of his class. And he was sure he would be given first honours in the final examinations. And of course, after he went to Alexandria for his higher studies, he would far surpass any silly girl who thought she could ever be superior to him.

Comforted with this thought, he went upstairs to the chamber where he could be alone and undisturbed. He intended to show his father what an excellent student he would be.

****

Marcus was enjoying life in Rome. The trading office had gained many wealthy clients and won various contracts from the Roman government for the supply of goods. As a result, he and Gaius had gained a fortune from the commissions paid to them by his father's company, ten percent of every deal successfully negotiated.

He was having a good time with Gaius after the day's work, visiting the various places of entertainment in Rome. There was no lack of them. They had also become members of an exclusive club where young men gathered to drink and carouse, and then go to a brothel for a night of pleasure. Although he had gone there with them at times, he always returned with a sense of disgust. Gaius often laughed at him for his prudishness.

"It is the Jew in you still, Marcus. They gave you too good an upbringing in Jerusalem."

"It's not that I find Roman women unattractive. But I want to find a woman that I can respect and also love. Some woman whom I could marry perhaps, and raise a family."

"You are still young for that, only twenty-five! Plenty time for marriage. Have some fun first before you get entangled."

Marcus laughed, and then suddenly recalled Aurelia and his promise to take her out. She was barely seventeen now, some years younger than him. But he would like to know her better and would enjoy meeting her again. He decided to visit her at her uncle's house on the Esquiline hill and invite her to the theatre. There were always good comedies showing at the Theatre of Marcellus at the west end of the city near the Circus Flaminius. He had not told Gaius about his brief acquaintance with Aurelia and would not tell him of his plan to visit her. He would tease him unmercifully about her and might even make lewd remarks.

He went to see her the next afternoon, descending on foot down the Alta Semita, turning left towards the Argilentum and then up the Clivus Suburanus towards the Horti Maecenatis and the Auditorium within it built over a section of the old Servian wall. He found the villa after making some enquiries, and asked for admittance at the gate. Through the open gateway he saw Aurelia standing near the entrance to the atrium and called out to her. She came eagerly towards him, glad to see him again.

"So, you did not forget me, Marcus" she said archly. She looked lovely in her green robe and matching sandals, her golden hair tied up behind in a silk scarf.

"Well, it is only three weeks since I arrived in Rome from Caesarea and I was very busy with my work."

"Uncle is not yet at home, and my aunt is resting in her room. But come in anyway and wait in the peristylium for a while till my uncle returns. He will be here in a short while."

They walked through the atrium into the spacious garden and courtyard behind. It was pleasantly cool there and they strolled around and then sat down on one of the stone benches under the portico facing the central fountain. He admired the wall paintings that provided an attractive background to the flowers and shrubs planted along them.

"Actually, I also wanted to invite you to the theatre to see a play, perhaps a good comedy," said Marcus.

"Oh, I would like that very much," Aurelia said happily. "I have been begging my uncle and aunt to take me to the theatre but they do not enjoy watching plays. They think it is vulgar entertainment, mainly for the masses. They are a bit old-fashioned in their taste."

"I suppose they enjoy musical concerts and shows, or poetry competitions, and such things they give in the Odeon in the Pompey Theatre complex. I have never been there, have you?"

"No, not yet, but I hope to go soon, when my uncle decides to attend a performance there."

Just then her uncle arrived, walking hastily into the house and calling for her aunt. Aurelia hurried towards him and said that her aunt was still in her room, resting. But that a friend of her father whom she met in Jerusalem had come to visit her and was in the peristylium. He strode there immediately and greeted Marcus.

"I am Aulus, my young man."

"Marcus, sir. I am honoured to meet you."

Just then Aurelia's aunt entered a little bewildered at the scene.

"This is my wife, Aemelia, and this is Marcus, my dear, a friend of Aurelia from Jerusalem."

Marcus bowed in greeting to her. "I am now living in Rome," he said. "After nearly two months here, I feel quite at home already."

"Good, good," said Aulus. "Let us go into the atrium and have some refreshments. I want to hear from you about Jerusalem and my brother Rufus. When did you last see him?"

"It was about some weeks ago in Caesarea, when Aurelia was leaving. I left a week later to accompany my father from Caesarea to Rome."

"Why did your father come to Rome, for business or pleasure?"

"He came for a special mission to the imperial court."

"What special mission was this?"

"A petition to Augustus about the ruling powers in Judaea. The people are dissatisfied, to say the least, about the present ruler."

"You mean Archelaus, of course. We have heard very troublesome things about him. Rufus writes that he is both brutal and despotic."

"He is even worse than that. But the delegates from Jerusalem failed to convince Augustus to depose him, at least not for now. Perhaps he will do so in the future when Archelaus oversteps the boundary with his evil deeds."

"Augustus will certainly do so in time. He will not tolerate injustice and bad rule."

They went on to discuss other matters. Talking about his admiration of Rome and its wonderful buildings and gardens, Marcus mentioned how much he enjoyed the variety of entertainments, especially the theatres. He then asked whether he could invite them to see a play at the Theatre of Marcellus.

Aulus looked at his wife and she shook her head.

"We do not especially like the theatre, Marcus. But Aurelia does. I am sure she would like to see a play."

"I would be delighted to take her, then," he responded.

"Oh yes, please!" Aurelia said, turning to her aunt and uncle. "I would love to go."

When they assented, Marcus said he would come the next evening to escort her to the Theatre of Marcellus. They were now showing Mercator, a comedy by Plautus.

Aulus laughed when he heard this, and said he was sure they would enjoy the comedy, but personally after reading it he thought it rather silly. The play was based on typical, stock characters familiar to theatregoers. It was about a father as the *senex* and his son as the *adulescens amator*, both successful merchants in Athens, who fall in love with a slave girl as one the *meretrix* being sold at the harbour. They compete over buying her, using friends as their agents. When the father succeeds in acquiring her, his son is heartbroken and decides to leave Athens. But his friend confronts the father and tells him that his son is in love with the girl and she with him. He then proposes a law that old men should not be allowed to stand in the way of young lovers.

Aurelia found the play very amusing and Marcus was glad to be with such a lovely and lively young girl. He continued to visit her at her uncle's home and they visited some market places, public gardens, temples and other interesting sites and also the Pantheon built by Marcus Agrippa. He told Aurelia that his father had named him for Agrippa, the close friend and son-in-law of Augustus who had died about ten years ago. Joseph had known him personally when Herod invited Agrippa to visit Judaea to see all that he had built there—the new cities, the port at Caesarea, and the fortresses of Alexandrium and Herodium. He was royally entertained by Herod and presented with many gifts, and he was received at Jerusalem with acclamation for his benevolence and generosity towards the Jews in Cyrene and in Asia.

At the Pantheon, Marcus pointed out the capitals of the pillars that were made of Syracusan bronze, and decorations by Diogenes of Athens including the caryatides and statues that adorned the temple. It was said that one of Cleopatra's pearls was cut in half to serve as pedants for the ears of Venus. Besides building the Pantheon, Agrippa had turned Rome into a city of marble, renovated aqueducts, and provided a higher quality of public services, as well as bathhouses, porticoes and gardens.

Gradually, after a few weeks, as he and Aurelia began to grow closer to each other, Marcus approached Aurelia's uncle for permission to court her as a prospective husband. He thought he should also write to her father, Rufus, in Jerusalem as well as to his own father, about his wish to marry Aurelia. He could see that the girl was happy in his company and showing signs of affection as well. She was charming, intelligent and he loved her very much. He finally told Gaius about Aurelia and his serious intentions to marry her, and asked for his support in approaching her uncle and aunt. It would be necessary to have confirmation of his financial status and eligibility, and his support for obtaining Roman citizenship as well.

******

Joseph was in Ramatayim when he received the letter from Marcus about his proposed marriage. He planned to go to Jerusalem until the end of Succot, the Feast of Tabernacles, and would then travel on to Rome to see Marcus. By that time, he would know if his wish to marry Aurelia was accepted or not. He would of course visit Rufus in Jerusalem and see whether he agreed to the match. In his view, it would be a good alliance with one of the wealthy and well-established families in Rome. But he also felt glad of the chance to strengthen his friendship with a man of such noble nature and one he so highly admired and valued.

He arrived a few days before the Jewish new year at Gorion's house where he would be staying for the next three or four weeks. It was enough time for the marriage matter to be decided and he could also see what could be done to improve the situation in this City of David. It had already grown much bigger than the original city south of the Temple Mount, encompassed by a first wall surrounding the Temple and Mount Zion, and then by a second one that enclosed a large area to the north of the Temple. There were already some houses being built further north of this second wall by those who wanted a foothold in Jerusalem when they came three times a year on the pilgrimage festivals of Passover, Pentecost and Tabernacles.

Entering the Gorion house, he found the little girl Ruhama grown much taller and looking very much better than when he last saw her.

"I remember you," she said. "You are Joseph, the cousin of my father Hananel."

He was astonished at her memory. She had only seen him very briefly after she arrived the year before.

"And you are Ruhama," he said. "I also remember you. And you can call me Uncle Joseph if you like."

She smiled delightedly, and then taking his hand pulled him into the living room.

"Baba, here is Uncle Joseph. I will go and call Mama Rachela." And she sped off.

Joseph clasped Gorion's hand and then embraced him. They sat down facing each other and Joseph asked him how he was.

"I feel very tired with the work at court. Fortunately the courts will close over the coming few weeks for the holiday period and there will be time to rest."

66

"I see you have done wonders with the child," said Joseph. "The last time I saw her she looked so thin and miserable, crying ceaselessly."

"Yes, she has changed completely. We are so glad she will be staying with us permanently, as our adopted daughter."

"As your adopted daughter, Hananel? But what about her father in Babylonia?"

"He sent a letter saying he was getting married again and that his prospective bride did not want to raise the daughter of another woman."

Rachela came in, with Ruhama pulling at her hand, and followed by Nikki as well.

"Oh, Joseph! How good to see you? How is Marcus?"

He rose to embrace her, shook hands with Nikki, patting him on the shoulder. They all sat down on the couches to hear his news about Marcus and his doings over the past year.

He told them that Marcus was doing very well in Rome, earning handsome profits from his commissions in trade. Gaius was a good partner and they worked well together. He often went to visit Aurelia, Rufus' daughter, at the home of her uncle Aulus and he was now hoping to win her hand in marriage. Marcus wrote to her father and also approached her uncle about this and was waiting impatiently for their decision. In the meantime, Joseph intended to visit Rufus and hear what he thought of the proposal. It would take some time before anything was decided.

As for himself, besides the regular trading he had with Alexandria and Rome, his more recent business activities in the Galilee were beginning to show profit and was developing fast. He thought he could soon offer a joint partnership to one of his contacts there as it was becoming more than he could handle alone. In fact, he was getting restless and even bored, and was seriously thinking of leaving the entire business to his partners and to travel further afield in search of new opportunities.

****

Nikki was badly shaken when he heard that Marcus was intending to marry Aurelia. He had fallen in love with her and had dreamed of marrying her one day. But of course this was just a foolish fantasy, he told himself. He would of course write to Marcus and wish him well. He spent the rest of the holiday week moping around till his mother became worried to see him so miserable and out of spirits. She could not understand what was wrong with him.

He had just passed his examinations with high honours and had been looking forward to Alexandria and the prospect of seeing Maryam and Jeshua again. His eighteenth birthday was coming soon, within the next month. He was taller now, with wider shoulders, and his boyish face had taken on the look of a handsome young man. The grey-green eyes seemed darker and more intense, and the russet hair was browner with only a few reddish streaks.

He began taking out his resentments against Ruhama who always seemed to be there wherever he was, whether by chance or on purpose. She was the only one who noticed how upset he felt while Joseph was telling them about Marcus and Aurelia. His face had gone white for a moment and then regained its colour, and he saw her looking at him with her intense childlike gaze as if she knew what he was thinking. But she was only eight years old, so she could not have really understood why he had reacted in this way.

What angered him more was that she did not mind his resentment and kept silent when he spoke to her in a loud tone of voice. She merely turned away and quietly disappeared as if he had not said anything. He wanted anger to match his anger, not indifference. It made him feel as if what he said was no longer important to her. And he did not know why he cared about it. Why it made him even angrier with her.

Joseph went to see Rufus and came back encouraged. His brother in Rome had written to him that he found Marcus a good and steady person, highly responsible and financially sound, and recommended that Rufus agree to the marriage, especially since Aurelia had said she loved him and wanted to be his wife. Both Rufus and Fulvia would be returning to Rome very soon after his term of duty in Jerusalem ended and he would then decide finally on the matter. Joseph was also going to Rome after the holiday period in Jerusalem and winding up his business affairs in the north. He hoped that by then the marriage arrangements would be made and Marcus was happy and settled in his own home with Aurelia. He could then feel free to go on his travels abroad knowing that his son was well-established in Rome.

The festival period passed uneventfully. Gorion was glad that the situation in Jerusalem had stabilised and the people had become more or less resigned to the way they were ruled. He knew that the spirit of rebellion was just below the surface and could burst out at the least provocation. But they had learnt to bear their burdens and understood that further resistance would make things worse for them and for their families. Keeping the peace in spite of suffering was by far the lesser of two evils.

It would soon be time for Nikki to leave for Alexandria, and he would miss him very much. The boy was his youngest and his dearest, with his bright, inquiring mind and quiet ways. He was studious, intelligent, warm-hearted and above all, a devoted, loyal son. He would write to him often and was sure that Nikki would write back regularly. A whole new treasure house of learning would be opened to him in Alexandria, the famous hub of the intellectual world. And he would have Philo to guide him there, and Maryam and Jeshua to keep him happy and loved. To compensate for Nikki's absence, Gorion was glad now that he had the girl Ruhama to care for and teach as he had taught Nikki. She was the daughter he and Rachela had always wanted and could now have as their own.

****

Joseph returned to his home in Ramatayim to make a few necessary preparations before going to Rome. While he was still there, a special courier arrived with a letter from Scythopolis (Beth Shean), located at the junction of the Jezreel Valley and the Jordan River Valley. This was one of cities that belonged to the group of ten Greek city-states known as the Decapolis, each functioning autonomously but linked together with the other cities by their shared language and culture. The cities of the Decapolis were Scythopolis, Hippos, Gadara, Pella, Philadelphia, Gerasa, Dion, Canatha, Raphana, and Abila. Scythopolis was the leading city, the largest of them all and the wealthiest.

The letter was written by Agathon, one of the members of the *boule*, the Scythopolis city council. He addressed him as Joseph of Arimathea, the Greek spelling of Ramatayim, and invited him to come to Scythopolis at his convenience to discuss matters of trade and business. He requested that Joseph specify the date most suitable for him to visit the city and attend a meeting at the council house. He also mentioned that council members from Hippos and from Gadara on the eastern side of the Sea of Galilee were in Scythopolis and would also be attending this meeting.

Joseph had never been to any of these cities, but recalled that Herod had been given two of them, Hippos and Gadara, by Augustus. When Archelaus was in Rome to plead for his title to the kingdom ruled by Herod, a delegation from these two cities requested that they be included again once again within Provincia Syria. He also knew that the Greek population in these cities was highly educated and the citizens were rich enough to import expensive building materials to construct their monumental edifices, their temples and basilicas, their bathhouses and theatres, and to purchase luxurious goods.

Joseph sent a reply thanking Agathon for his invitation, but saying that he was on his way to Rome and would contact him as soon as he returned. He estimated that he would be back in about a month's time. He wondered what Agathon and the Greeks of the Decapolis wanted with him. They usually kept their distance from Jewish traders and businessmen, relying on the Nabataean trading network to supply them with their needs besides the agricultural produce and other provisions they obtained from the surrounding farmlands.

Another letter came just a day before he left. It was from Rufus, saying that he and his wife had agreed to the marriage of Marcus to their daughter Aurelia. With the permission of Augustus, he was going to leave Jerusalem before his term was ended and would be in Rome as soon as possible. He hoped to meet Joseph in Rome very soon and make all the necessary arrangements for the marriage.

****

The day soon came for Nikki to leave his home in Jerusalem. He woke up early that morning, and went to the upper chamber to look once more at the city in which he was born and loved so much. Some phrases from the books of the Bible resounded in his mind:

Awake, awake, Clothe yourself in your strength, O Zion; Clothe yourself in your beautiful garments, O Jerusalem, the holy city ...On your walls, O Jerusalem, I have appointed watchmen, all day and all night. ...Walk around Zion, circle it; count its towers, take note of its ramparts, go through its citadels, that you may recount it to a future age.

He saw the sun rising, its rays striking at the walls of the city and reflecting against the golden roof of the Temple. He would not see this again for the next few years. But he could keep the picture of it in his mind and in his heart.

He went downstairs to the kitchen and saw Martha already preparing the breakfast meal. She gave him a welcoming look and handed him the warm flatbread straight from the oven which she knew he liked. He rolled it around some cheese and dates and stood eating hungrily by the window looking out at the backyard. To his surprise, he saw Ruhama there, busily digging in the earth along the low wall enclosing the garden. A cat sat on the wall nearby stretching its paws.

"Yes, she is always there every morning. I always bring her some plant cuttings and flower seeds from my garden in Bethany," said Martha seeing his surprise. "She loves the garden and that cat follows her around because she feeds it with scraps of leftover food in the kitchen."

Then his mother came in and saw him standing there and eating. "Already having your breakfast before everyone else? Always so hungry and cannot wait for mealtimes," she scolded him.

"I like the bread just after it is baked in the oven. I am going to miss your baking and cooking Martha. What do they have for breakfast in Egypt, do you know?"

"Much the same I should think," she said. "At least among the Jews, I suppose."

Breakfast was served an hour later with all four of the family present. The carriage for the journey to the port of Joppa was already standing in the forecourt. Nikki was beginning to feel the coming parting and could not eat very much. The meal was eaten in silence until Gorion suddenly pushed back his chair, stood up, and left the dining room. Rachela then got up and followed him anxiously. Nikki sat still and looked at Ruhama who continued eating as if nothing unusual had happened.

Rachela found Gorion in his study, shoulders hunched, and hands against the arched window facing the garden outside.

"It is difficult, Hananel, I know," she said. "But you must not let Nikki see you upset at his leaving. He has to feel that you are confident about sending him away to study."

Gorion turned and she saw that he had already controlled his feelings and was ready to return to the breakfast table. He went to one of the shelves and took down a scroll encased in a silver sheath. Returning to the table, he placed this in front of Nikki and told him it was his parting gift.

"What is it, Father?"

"It is the scroll that my grandfather Hananiah wrote on the Book of Ezekiel. It is full of his commentaries and also esoteric speculations regarding time and future predictions he derived from the text. There are many mystical teachings, kabbalah, which I personally cannot clearly comprehend since I am not a scholar of such matters."

"What is kabbalah?" asked Nikki. "I don't understand."

"Kabbalah is the secret transmissions of sages who have tried to find hidden meanings in biblical texts that can reveal divine mysteries and predict future events. They use a system of numerological calculations of words in certain phrases used by the prophets. Perhaps one day you will be able to understand some of this."

Nikki rose to thank and embrace his father. He then turned to go upstairs and bring down his leather bag and shoulder satchel. His mother held him for a long while in her arms and kissed him goodbye. He turned to Ruhama and saw that she was waiting to hear what he would say.

"Goodbye, Ruhama. You can now stay as much as you like in the upper chamber. Look after the scrolls and other things there."

"Goodbye Nikki," she said softly.

He bent suddenly to kiss her on the cheek and quickly hurried out with his father following him. Gorion had decided to accompany him to Joppa and see him safely aboard the ship to Alexandria. There would still be time to talk, to advise, and to make his final farewells. They had to reach the port before the ship sailed in the late afternoon as the tide went out. He planned to stay overnight in Joppa at one of the many inns there for travellers and return to Jerusalem in the morning.

****

For Nikki, this was the first time he had travelled by ship. He was excited and happy after boarding it, even though the parting from his father had saddened him. He left his bag and satchel in his berth below and went up on deck to see the ship cast its moorings and sail out to sea. It was ebb tide and the ship moved slowly and smoothly over the water leaving a long wake behind. The sails caught the wind, and the ship began to sail more rapidly towards the southwest. It would take about three or four days to reach Alexandria if the winds were favourable.

They passed many other ships on their way sailing northwards carrying heavy loads of merchandise on their decks. This ship he was travelling on was for passengers only, not for cargo, although many of them had brought large amounts of baggage with them. He noticed some dark looking Egyptians among the travellers, and a few fair-haired Greeks. The captain was a Phoenician, and the sailors were mostly slaves from North Africa. Only a few elderly Jews were among the passengers and they remained below deck during the entire journey.

To occupy the time, he took out the scroll his father had given him and unrolled it to the first page. He saw a strange design of interconnected circles forming a tree-shaped pattern. On the top was a circle in which appeared the word *keter*, a crown. On either side below, it were two more circles, the one on the right contained the word *hochma*, wisdom and the one on the left had the word *binah*, understanding. Below the word *hochma* there were another two circles, the first with *hesed*, kindness, and the second with *netzah*, eternity, written in them. On the other side under the word *binah* there were also two circles, the first with *gvurah*, bravery and the second with *hod*, glory. In the centre, below the topmost word *keter*, there were four circles descending in a straight line like the trunk of a tree, the first containing the word *daat*, knowledge, the second *tiferet*, splendour, the third *yesod*, foundation, and the fourth *malchut*, royalty.

It said below that these were the *Sephirot*, the ten emanations or attributes of God. It was a strange idea to him, to think of God with emanations and attributes. He realised that he had never really conceived what the word God actually meant. It was some vague powerful being who caused things to happen in the world, who punished the wicked and rewarded the good, and who protected Israel as his chosen people. He was a very personal god, to whom one prayed every day and whom one blessed for all the good things in life.

Beyond that, he had never tried to conceive what God was in reality. No man had ever seen God, although the Bible said that God had spoken to Moses 'face to face'. But that contradicted another passage in the Bible in which Moses asks God to let him see his face, and God says that no man can see him and live. And then he lets Moses see his 'glory in passing' whatever that meant. Why had none of his teachers ever discussed this in school? Most probably because they themselves did not know what it meant.

He rolled up the scroll and put it away in his satchel. There would be a time for this later when he began his studies with Philo. He would begin with the

Greek philosophers of course, and then go on to study the various sciences and metaphysical systems concerning the creation of the world, astronomy and the movement of the spheres, as well as astrology. It would take four years of study to cover all that was laid out for him. What he would do afterwards, he did not know. He would like to travel and see the world before he settled on any course of life.

****

Ruhama went to the upper room after Nikki left. It felt strange to be there now in full possession of it. She touched her cheek where Nikki had kissed her so unexpectedly. Was it just cousinly duty or was he beginning to like her a little. She wanted to be regarded as his little sister, someone that he loved and protected. But all she had of him until now had been resentment and jealousy. He was so easily angry with her, though she had learnt to ignore it and control her temper.

The house was quiet. Father Hananel had gone away and would be back only the next day. Mother Rachela had retired to rest for a while and only Martha was there in the kitchen with no need to prepare a proper meal today. They would be eating some leftovers from the day before and some light dessert or fruit for lunch. Martha always prepared a hot soup and some fried chicken for supper before she left for her home. She wondered why Martha could not live downstairs in one of the rooms near the kitchen area instead of having to travel all the way from Bethany and back every day.

For the present, all she wanted was to sit and gaze out of the window and wonder what Nikki was doing now on the ship sailing to Alexandria. He must be enjoying the voyage and the fresh sea air. How she envied him! One day she would also travel to Alexandria and see all the beautiful sites there.

An hour or so later, Rachela called her down, and she hurried to answer her call. She found her in the living room, seated near the window and looking out at the approaching clouds that would soon bring rain and the winter season. Ruhama stood before her and Rachela put her arms around the girl.

"You know," she began, "now that you are our daughter and will be staying with us always, I want to speak to you as your mother would have spoken to you."

"You are my mother now," Ruhama told her.

"Well, I will try to be a good mother, Ruhama. I know you love reading and your father likes to teach you as he taught Nikki. But I also want you to learn things that every girl should know. You should learn to sew, to embroider, and to cook, among other things. You cannot begin now to spend all your time in the upper chamber or out in the garden. Martha will give you some lessons in cooking and I can teach you sewing and embroidery. One day, when you grow up and become the mistress of a house like this you will need to know these things."

"But Mama, I can always have a cook to make the meals and servant girls to do the sewing and embroidery. Why should I waste my time learning to do these things."

Rachela was surprised to hear such words from a child barely eight years old, and did not know how to answer them. She shook her head and pulled the girl closer.

"It is what you will be expected to know when you are older and will marry someone. Even if you are rich enough to have servants, you still have to learn the things that every woman should know."

"Then I don't want to get married, ever," she said decidedly. "Do I have to?"

Again Rachela was speechless for a while.

"No one will force you to marry. But one day you will want to live in your own house with someone you love and who loves you. And have children of your own."

Ruhama looked at her silently. "You mean like you did, Mama?"

"Yes, like I did, Ruhama."

"Then I will do what you say. I will learn to cook and sew. But I also want to read and study, and to know everything that Nikki knows."

Rachela hugged her and said she was very glad to hear this. Yet she wondered why Ruhama had this urge to study. How could it possibly be of use to her in life? For herself, it was sufficient that her husband and sons were educated and respected for their learning, while she was content to care for them and see they were well and happy.

****

Nikki arrived in Alexandria a few days after leaving Joppa. It was a pleasant voyage, the sea was calm, and the weather was fine all the way. As they approached the city he could see the marvellous Pharos lighthouse at the entrance to the Great Harbour. It had been built about three centuries ago during the reign of Ptolemy I Soter. During the day a large mirror reflected the sunlight to a great distance away, and at night a fire burned continually at the top of the tower to guide ships safely into the harbour.

There seemed to be hundreds of ships, boats and other sailing craft around them. And there was a lot of noise from people on them shouting to others on shore, the loud curses of sailors, the heavy thuds of wooden crates landing on the docks, and the shrill sounds of trumpets in the distance. As the ship neared the docks, a ramp was lowered from it to allow the passengers to disembark. Nikki waited with his bag and satchel on one side not wanting to be crushed by the crowd.

His father had told him that Philo's brother, Lysimachus, had one of his shipping agents at the port, and he would be notified as soon as this ship arrived. The agent was told meet Nikki on the dock and to bring him to Philo's house. As he came down the ramp, Nikki saw someone standing just below on the stone jetty and searching the faces of the passengers. This must be the man his father had mentioned. He went up to him and asked if he was sent by Lysimachus. The man instantly nodded, took his bag from him, and led him to a mule cart standing nearby.

They turned down the main colonnaded avenue till they reached its junction with the Canopic Road, the central street of the city that ran from east to west. From there, they turned right and drove westward, passing the mausoleum where Alexander the Great was buried, and reached the Musaeum. Nikki noticed that all the streets were at right angles to each other, laid out in a grid-like pattern. Philo's house was just beyond this, at the far end of a side street that turned northwards and almost reached the sea shore.

Philo was not at home when Nikki arrived. He was still at the Musaeum. But it was almost noon, and the servant who admitted him said that his master would be returning for his midday meal within the hour. The villa was spacious and luxurious. He was shown into a large room with a bed and a low table beside it, with some dried dates and nuts in a bowl and a jug of water. There was a cupboard for his clothes, and a long couch under a window facing the sea. The floor was covered with rush mats and silken curtains were draped over the walls. A door led into a tiled washroom with a toilet seat and a bathtub.

Nikki had enough time to wash and change his clothes before Philo arrived back home. He heard a knock on the door and the servant asked him to come into the dining hall to meet his master. As he entered it, Philo came forwards with outstretched hands to greet him, and warmly embraced him. Nikki was shy at first, but as they sat down and the food was being served, he found it easy to talk to him without reserve. Philo asked about his family, and then Nikki asked him about Maryam and Jeshua.

"Oh, they are very well and happy in their home in the Jewish quarter. I will take you there this afternoon to see them. They will be delighted to see you. They know you are coming and are very glad that you will be living here for a few years."

It was a light meal of fish in a delicious sauce and some cooked vegetables seasoned with herbs, followed by a cheese pancake and some fresh fruit. He was offered beer, which he tasted but did not like and preferred cold water. Philo drank buttermilk which he said was for his health but did not recommend it to Nikki. He told him that his brother Alexander would be coming in the evening for dinner which was the main meal of the day. He suggested that they both take a nap after their meal, and drive to the Jewish quarter in the late afternoon when it was cooler.

He must have slept very long and deeply because the sun was already low when he awoke. He dressed quickly and went out into the hallway. A servant saw him and said that Philo was in his study. Nikki felt embarrassed for having slept so long, but when he entered the study Philo smiled at him and said he was probably very tired from his journey and they could go to see Maryam and Jeshua the following day.

After a refreshing drink and some honey cakes, Nikki sat down with Philo in his study where he would be spending nearly every afternoon being tutored by him. It was a long and wide room, extending the length of the villa and opening out into the gardens beyond that faced towards the west. He was amazed at the numerous shelves that lined the walls crammed with scrolls of every shape and size. Some of the longer scrolls had their pages cut up to form books within leather bindings, which made for easier reading. There were also map drawings and paintings showing scenes from the Bible and from Greek and Roman history. A marble bust of Julius Caesar stood on a plinth in one corner near the window, tribute to the fact that Philo's father, besides having acquired Alexandrian citizenship which was not normally granted to Jews, had also received Roman citizenship from Caesar as a sign of special favour to him and his family.

"I usually sit near the entrance to this study," said Philo. "But I have placed a small reading table and chair for you at the far end just near the garden doorway. You will be undisturbed by anyone while you sit there and read or write down your notes."

He then explained that he had registered Nikki at the Musaeum for two lecture courses, one on Greek philosophy and the other on astronomy. The Musaeum had a roofed walkway, an arcade of seats, and a communal dining room where scholars routinely ate and shared their ideas. The building was filled with private study rooms, residential quarters, lecture halls, and theatres. More than a thousand scholars lived there, salaried by the institution, and paid no taxes. They had free room and board, and were even given servants.

Philo told him that Archimedes and Euclid had once been scholars living at the Musaeum. Its name was derived from the Nine Muses, whom Hesiod relates were the daughters of Zeus and Mnemosyne, the personifications of knowledge and the arts. Besides scientific research and the study of Greek works, many scholars were engaged in translating texts from Assyrian, Persian, Jewish, Indian and other sources. It was real treasure house of learning, and one could spend a lifetime there among its riches.

Nikki would go there with him every morning to attend the lectures and to use the library to follow them up with reading assignments. Philo would be spending most of that time either in the library or in one of the private study rooms with a few scholars in his field of research. At noon time, they would return home for the midday meal and a few hours of rest before meeting again in this study for his private tutoring.

"We will be working mainly on the interpretation of biblical texts, starting with the Book of Genesis. I call this kind of study 'Questiones' which means 'inquiries' or 'exegesis', an attempt to arrive at the real meaning of the texts and their allegorical implications. I hope to write and publish my work on this subject later on."

Nikki was not very sure he understood what Philo had said. He knew the Bible very well and did not think it needed to be interpreted or explained. The meaning of the biblical texts always seemed very clear to him. Philo saw his puzzled look and smiled.

"Yes, I know this is not what you have been studying at school in Jerusalem. There they teach you to read everything literally, and use the stories of the Bible as moral and religious instruction. That is their method of learning and teaching. I want to give you a different perspective of the Bible and other Jewish sources. And we will not be studying the Bible in its original Hebrew but only in its Greek version, the Septuagint."

"Why is it called the Septuagint?" asked Nikki.

"I thought your father would have told you the story of the Greek Bible. Or rather the legend attached to it!"

Philo told him the story of a Hellenic Jew who had apparently composed a fictitious letter about a century and a half earlier, presuming it to be from a man called Aristeas to his brother Philocrates, and relating how the Septuagint was created. The author, supposedly a courtier in the reign of Ptolemy II Philadelphus, said that the chief librarian of the library in Alexandria wished to have the books of the Hebrew Law translated into Greek for inclusion in the library collection. The high priest in Jerusalem sent seventy Jewish elders to Alexandria, and the king put them into separate chambers to translate the Hebrew Bible into Greek and every translation was found to be identical with all the others. The word Septuagint thus derives from the Latin words *versio septuaginta interpretum*, "translation of the seventy interpreters," and is usually referred to simply as the LXX.

Although the rabbis in Jerusalem rejected the Septuagint as a valid biblical text because they found many discrepancies between it and the approved canonical Hebrew version, known as the Masoretic text, Philo said that he considered it on equal standing with the Hebrew text. He also told Nikki that the Greek of the Septuagint was not the classical Greek that he had studied at school but the Koine Greek, the common dialect used by Alexandrian Greeks and by many Greek-speaking communities in the Hellenic East.

Nikki said that it was no wonder he had not heard about the Septuagint at school in Jerusalem. His father must have avoided telling him so as not to confuse him at that time while he was studying for his examinations. He hoped that he would very soon be able to converse with Philo in spoken Greek instead of Hebrew which Philo rarely used.

They went out into the garden for a brief stroll before dinner when Philo's brother was expected to join them. Nikki wanted to know about the Jewish community in Alexandria.

"Well, most of the Jews here are artisans engaged in various crafts and many have commercial enterprises. Some Jews are extremely wealthy merchants and moneylenders. We are an autonomous community with a council of elders headed by an ethnarch or what the Greeks called an archon, responsible for the general conduct of Jewish affairs in the city, especially in legal matters and drawing up of documents. We have our own Sanhedrin of seventy elders and a Jewish court, a *beth din*, as you have in Jerusalem. Our pride is in our large and splendid central synagogue on the Canopic Street with its famed double colonnade where the elders sit on thrones, and the congregants sit in sections according to their profession or occupation. You will see it on the Sabbath day when we go there for the morning services."

"My father told me of the rich contributions made by the Jews of Alexandria to the Temple" Nikki said. "There is a magnificent gate at the west end of the Women's Court made of Corinthian bronze that shines like gold, Nicanor's Gate, named for man who built it and donated it to the Temple, the most beautiful of all the nine gates there."

"There is a legend about those gates," said Philo. "They were so large and heavy that they had to be towed across the sea to Joppa. At one point they began to sink down and Nicanor threw himself over them saying 'Let me be cast down with them,' and by some miracle they floated again."

Nikki laughed. "I heard another version of this story. That a whale swallowed the doors and threw them up on the land."

They sat for a while watching the sun setting on the west, and the air filled with the flutter of birds coming to roost for the evening. Although he missed Jerusalem he thought he would be happy here at Philo's house and studying at the Musaeum. Also, there was Maryam and Jeshua here to visit as often as he wished. He was looking forward to seeing them the next day.

As the skies began to darken and the moon rose brightly in the sky, they went indoors to dinner. The house was lit with oil lamps and the table was laid with candlesticks in the centre. Nikki felt at peace now after the long day and in happy anticipation of the morrow.

****

Joseph arrived in Rome a few days after Rufus and his wife Fulvia had returned to their home. They reopened their house near that of Aulus and Aemilia and were happily reunited with their daughter Aurelia. She was, as they realised, very much in love with Marcus and happy that they had consented to their marriage. Marcus came with his father to visit her and her parents, and together they planned the wedding to be held in the early spring. Joseph would return to Rome to attend it before he went on to visit Britannia.

It was already late autumn, and Joseph wanted to see that everything was arranged before returning home to Judaea. He bought a house for Marcus and Aurelia in the prestigious Carinae area of Rome and saw to its furnishing and the provision of staff and servants for its proper maintenance. He also set about obtaining Roman citizenship for Marcus with the support of Aurelia's father and uncle and also of Gaius. Finally, he transferred the trading office in Rome into the full possession of Marcus and Gaius. It was now their own company and would give them all the financial support and stability that they required.

Two weeks later Joseph sailed back to Caesarea. Before returning to his home in Ramatayim, he decided to call on Agathon in Scythopolis. The Roman road to it ran almost in a straight line across the country from one city to the other, and it was an easy journey. The winter rains had not yet begun and the air was pleasantly cool. He could breathe here in this country after the stifling weather in Rome and the crowded atmosphere in that city. He did not like it there, although Marcus seemed to enjoy living in Rome and had no desire to leave it.

He knew that Scythopolis was the city built by the Ptolemies about 300 years ago at the foot of the mound on which the original town of Beth Shean had once stood. The town had been destroyed by the Assyrians when they conquered the northern kingdom of Israel more than 700 years ago. The new city below the mound was settled by veteran Scythian mercenaries, who named it the 'City of the Scythians'. A century later, after the Seleucids conquered the country, the name 'Nysa' was added to that of Scythopolis and it was given the rights of a polis. Nysa, Dionysus' nursemaid, was said to be buried at the city of Scythopolis which claimed Dionysus as its founder. When Pompey made Judaea part of the Roman Empire, he rebuilt Beth Shean on the mound which had been destroyed by the Hasmoneans, but the city centre remained in Scythopolis on the slopes below.

Joseph reached the city soon after daybreak, having ridden all night with a group of merchants and travellers bringing carriage loads of goods from Caesarea to Scythopolis. He refreshed himself at an inn, and had a quick breakfast before setting out to the city centre and the basilica where the city councillors and magistrates usually presided over the business dealings being conducted there. Scythopolis seemed to be a very prosperous place, with monumental buildings, a theatre, bathhouses, temples, shops and market places.

He finally found Agathon seated on the dais in the apse at the far end of the colonnaded basilica. As soon as the crowd in front of him had thinned out he approached and introduced himself.

"Oh, my dear sir, you are most welcome," said the councillor. "I have waited patiently for your visit and will be glad if you will come with me to my house as soon as I can arrange to leave."

There was a hurried and heated discussion with a few of the other councillors before Agathon led him out of the monumental gateway to the quieter residential area beyond the city walls. They walked along a broad avenue of palm trees in the direction of the amphitheatre and turned into one of the villas surrounded by an artificial lake. After Joseph was seated in the central room of the house and offered some wine and fruit, Agathon explained that his problem concerned the two cities, Hippos and Gadara. But the councillors of those cities had left Scythopolis two weeks ago and would not be able to come back for another week at least because of meetings with representatives from other cities of the Decapolis.

He outlined in general their problem and its possible solution. Hippos and Gadara came under the rule of Herod about thirty years ago, a gift from Augustus. Herod had an interest in them because they closely bordered his territory. After his death, a delegation to Augustus succeeded in releasing them from further Herodian rule and they reverted to the control of the Syrian governor. They had previously been supplied by merchant traders in the Galilee region, but Herod Antipas, tetrarch of the Galilee, was angered by the loss of the cities and refused to allow any further trading across the borderlines. On the other hand, the Nabataeans who supplied most of the cities of the Decapolis with their caravan trade were not prepared to go to the area east of the Sea of Galilee.

The only solution was to have supplies brought from the northern part of Samaria to Scythopolis and from there to the two cities on the eastern side of the Sea of Galilee. Greek traders had highly recommended the trading company of Joseph of Arimathea as the best and most reliable of suppliers with a wide range of goods. He hoped that they could come to some profitable arrangement on both sides. He was prepared to be the intermediary for these two cities, but the contracts would have to be signed by them individually.

"I would be quite happy to offer them my services," said Joseph. "In fact, I am interested in expanding my trading business northwards into the Galilee itself and perhaps even further. But I cannot wait here until the councillors from these two cities return to Scythopolis. May I suggest that we go to Hippos or Gadara and conclude this agreement without more delay?"

"That is a very good suggestion, my friend. We have a group of citizens who are traveling to Gadara tomorrow to enjoy the performance of two cynical satires by the poet-philosophers Menippus and Meleager. We could join them for this and then stay overnight to see the councillors in the morning. From there, we can travel to Hippos and conclude our business arrangements with both cities."

Joseph agreed to this proposal and returned to stay at the inn until the next day. He was a stranger to the life and culture of these Greek cities, but found it a pleasant experience to visit this richly built and well-ordered polis. He was told that Gadara was popularly called the City of the Philosophers and it would be interesting to visit it. As they travelled together with the lively young people eager for some cultural entertainment, Agathon told him something about these cynical poet-philosophers.

He said that Menippus was considered Gadara's first great son, although he later moved to Greece. He was said to have been a slave who had earned his freedom, made money as a ship-broker, and then hanged himself when he lost his business. His satires were actually pseudo-autobiographical works such as his Descent into Hades, and his type of philosophical satire had already become known as Menippean satire. Agathon quoted a famous line from one of them in which Menippus says:

> I have come from the hide-out of the dead, the very gates of darkness.
> I have left the home of Hades, set apart from other gods.

Meleager, a great admirer of Menippus, wrote many satires in imitation of him, and also liked to write epigrams for various occasions. He even composed a mock epigram for his own tomb:

Tread softly, Stranger, over the sacred dead
Here lies in well-earned sleep the aged
Meleager, Son of Eucrates ...

A school of rhetoric was also founded in Gadara. But in his view, the greatest of Gadara's sons was Philodemus, the Epicurean philosopher and poet who was born in Gadara and later moved first to Rome and then to Herculaneum. He had studied under Zeno of Sidon in Athens and after going to Rome he became involved in the violent attack in the Senate by Cicero against his friend Lucius Calpurnius Piso, the father of Caesar's wife Calpurnia.

Joseph had read some works of Greek literature but had never heard of these authors or realised that philosophers and poets had been living in the Decapolis region. He was not much interested in philosophy or literature and thought Greek writers were clever and intellectually gifted, but did not have the depth of thought and emotion that the Bible contained, and the high visionary images of the biblical prophets. It was all surface glitter with the Greeks, their love of external beauty, symmetry and perfection of form. They lacked something more profound, more serious and meaningful.

Still, he enjoyed the visit to Gadara, if only to see its impressive buildings and streets. It was built on a mountain ridge which gave it the shape of a long and narrow rectangle. There were two theatres on the northern and western slopes of a hill rising at the eastern end of the ridge. The city itself spread along the ridge towards the west with its main building complexes on either side of the main street, the colonnaded *decumanus maximus*, traversing the city from east to west. Various edifices could also be seen on the north and south sides of this street, including the forum, the covered market, a large bathhouse and other decorative structures such as a nymphaeum.

He attended the theatrical performances that evening although he would have preferred to go to bed after the long ride from Scythopolis. He hoped they could wind up the business dealings in a day or two and he could return home. He did not wish to linger too long in this region. The next morning, he and Agathon successfully wound up the business arrangements for supplying the city with the goods it required and by noon they were on their way to Hippos to confirm and authorise the contract drawn up in Gadara.

They travelled by carriage along the eastern shore of the inland lake, the Sea of Galilee, till they came almost as far as halfway up its length. And then, on the right, Joseph saw the mountain that rose suddenly above the shore, with its symmetrical southern and northern slopes descending into deep valleys, and a winding, snake-like path leading up to its flat-topped crest surrounded by the walls of the city. He was amazed at the sight, a city on the top of a high hill, and seemingly impregnable from attack.

"How will we get up there, Agathon? The ascent is very steep along that winding snake path for the horses. It must also be hard for mules to climb up with their carts."

"That way is not the one we will take. There is an easier road on the other side of the mountain where a saddle ridge extends across the valley. We will circle around towards it to the city gate on the eastern side."

Entering with Agathon through the arched gateway, Joseph saw a massive round tower to his left, and then they crossed over a beautifully paved oval plaza. They soon found themselves walking along the decumanus maximus colonnaded on both sides to provide protective shade. The fronts of shops could be seen behind the colonnades and on the left the impressive edifice of a bathhouse was visible. Within a few minutes, they could glimpse the attractive gateway marking the approach to the forum, its paved surface bathed in sunlight. Granite columns of colonnades bordered the forum on the north and east sides, supporting single-sloped roofs that created shady aisles. Three large doorways led from the forum and the decumanus maximus to the basilica.

As they went up the steps to the interior of this building, Joseph was surprised by its size. It was pleasant to stand in its cool dimness after leaving the sunlit street and forum. At the far northern end, he could see the tribunal and the statues of the city notables mounted between the columns that supported the ceiling and roof of the basilica. Councillors were seated on the tribunal platform and someone was standing in front of it speaking to them in excited tones, so they held back for a while.

"These Nabataeans are boycotting us and supporting Herod Antipas and his spiteful border blockade because his wife, Phasaelis, is the daughter of their King Aretas. Now that we are under Roman rule again we should complain to the Governor of Syria to force these people to supply us with the provisions we require."

"Demetrios, you are dreaming" one of the councillors said. "The Romans will do nothing for us. Not after Aretas assisted Varus in his attack against the

Jews after Herod's death. They are now allies, even though they are constantly suspicious of each other."

"Well, we shall have to depend on the Jews of Judaea and Samaria then" another councillor remarked. "I am waiting for Agathon of Scythopolis to arrive with a Jewish trading agent very soon."

Agathon walked towards the tribunal and Demetrios turned around to see him and Joseph approaching.

"Talk of the devil!" he said smiling. "How timely is your arrival."

"Yes, and I have brought Joseph of Arimathea as your prospective trading agent. We have already been to Gadara and received their consent and approval."

Joseph came forward to greet Demetrios, the archon, and bowed in the direction of the other councillors on the platform.

"I am glad to see you, Joseph" the archon said. "We can sit down immediately and discuss the terms you have agreed upon with Gadara. I am sure they will be acceptable to us as well."

It did not take long for the terms of the contract to be laid out and approved, and the councillor in charge of signing such agreements put his seal upon it. Joseph was glad that there was enough time for him and Agathon to reach Scythopolis by the late evening instead of having to stay overnight in Hippos. Demetrios accompanied them both back to the east gate where their carriage was waiting and parted from them with many thanks and good wishes.

****

Winter was approaching in Alexandria, but unlike Jerusalem, the climate in this city during the winter months was pleasantly mild, cool at night, with occasional rainy days. Nikki quickly became used to life in the city, going every morning with Philo to the Musaeum, listening to the lectures and reading in the library. He wrote every week to his father and always received a warm letter in return, but not in his father's handwriting. Nikki guessed that it was Ruhama who penned the letter dictated by him in small delicate script.

He was very busy with his studies and often did not return with Philo for the midday meal but remained in the library to read or went to visit Maryam, Josiah and Jeshua at their home in the Jewish quarter. He always brought something for them when he came, a toy for Jeshua, or some delicacies from the market for Maryam and Josiah. He also spent time playing with the four-year old boy, now grown taller, but with his fair curly hair still long over his shoulders. He knew that his mother had vowed him to be a Nazirite, and she frequently tied his hair back with a braided tassel to keep it off his face.

Jeshua was a good and quiet child, but Maryam told Nikki that he dreamed in his class at school, hardly paying attention to what the teacher was saying, although strangely enough he knew all the answers to any question put to him. At times, instead of coming home after school, he wandered off somewhere, usually towards the sea shore where the fishermen went out in their boats to cast their nets. She would find him sitting there watching them and gazing into the distance, his blue eyes reflecting the colour of the sea.

Josiah was becoming restless at their prolonged exile in Alexandria. He was fairly content with living here with Maryam and Jeshua, and was a kind and loving husband and father. But he longed to be back in his home in Nazareth and to see his sons again. They had done well with the family carpentry business and were fairly well to do. He received letters from them regularly and wrote to them as well. He felt that Maryam was now well established in the Jewish community here. The boy was well cared for and his mother had decided that he would be tutored at home by a private teacher rather than be sent to school, which meant that Josiah no longer had to worry about his education.

Maryam wrote a letter to Joseph suggesting that Josiah should be released from his agreement with him and be able to return home. Nikki sent the letter to his father to be forwarded to Joseph who was often traveling and may not be in Ramatayim at present. A month later a reply came making arrangements for Josiah to leave Alexandria by one of the trading ships going to Joppa. He was both sad and happy to leave, and hoped that Maryam and Jeshua would be able to come to Nazareth when the danger that threatened them had passed.

****

That winter in Jerusalem was a bitterly cold one. Snow fell on the city, turning it into a wintry wonderland. Ruhama loved playing in the snow and building castles with it in the garden. Gorion had a bad cold and did not go to work for more than a week. Rachela was busy in the kitchen with Martha making hot soups and other nourishing food to keep all of them warm and well fed. Ruhama spent many hours at Gorion's bedside, chattering about everything that interested her, reading to him from letters that arrived, and writing letters for him in reply.

Hannukah, the Festival of Lights, came and went. Candles were lighted for eight days in memory of the restoration of the Temple after the Maccabean victory over the Syrian Greeks two hundred years earlier. January came with thunderstorms and torrents of rain, and then February with strong winds and a sudden sweep of hail stones striking the roofs of houses. By March, the winds were softer and then came the latter rain, that final downpour that washed the earth in preparation for springtime and a burst of red poppies over the surrounding hillsides.

Purim, the Feast of Esther, was celebrated with colourful processions in the streets and merry festivities with masks depicting the characters in the Book of Esther—Mordechai, Haman, Ahasuerus, and Queen Esther. Ruhama enjoyed it all, watching the processions from the rooftop, dancing around the garden now with its first flowers, playing with her cat, feeding the birds. The house was always full of guests, many staying for dinner and late into the night.

Gorion retired from the magistrates court and was elected to the position of adviser to the Sanhedrin over civil and political matters. Its members often came to visit him at his home for consultations and discussions on various topics. He was also busy making a record of the legal cases he had tried over the long period of his position as magistrate, intending this to provide younger magistrates with precedents for future legal cases.

Joseph came for a short visit before leaving for Rome and the wedding of Marcus and Aurelia. He brought some gifts for them, a few scrolls of Greek literature and philosophy for Gorion which he had acquired during his brief stay in Scythopolis, some perfume from Arabia for Rachela, and a golden pendant for Ruhama. He noticed she had grown quite tall, become prettier, and looked much happier than she had been before. She was delighted with his gift and shyly kissed her Uncle Joseph in gratitude.

"How long will you be gone, Joseph," Rachela asked him.

"I will be in Rome for about a week or so for the wedding and for other business matters. But I will leave afterwards for the journey I planned to Britannia."

"It will be a long journey and I assume you plan to remain there for several weeks" said Gorion.

"For several months I think, Hananel. I will remain there until the late autumn. They have an abundance of mineral deposits of tin, lead, iron, gold and silver that can be mined and that are in high demand in the Roman Empire. Besides I have a keen curiosity in seeing new places and exploring foreign lands, I hope to establish a foothold there, a trading post for a regular exchange of goods between the southern coastal towns of Britannia and the Mediterranean countries."

"I heard it was a wild country, the people are like savages with a fierce and warlike appearance. Julius Caesar describes them as barbarians who wear animal skins, dye their faces with blue paint, and charge naked into battle."

"That was more than fifty years ago, Hananel. It may be true of the warring tribes in the north of the island which is heavily forested and swampy. There are a lot of farming settlements now along the southern coast, sheep grazing and cattle herds. The people there are more peaceful. Intrepid Phoenician traders used to sail to Cornwall in the southwest to buy tin as an alloy with copper to produce bronze. But since the destruction of Carthage, the trade with them has almost completely ceased. I wish to renew trading in tin and in other metals."

"Well, I wish you luck in your new venture and enterprise. For my part, I am content with remaining in Jerusalem for the rest of my life, and so is Rachela. I am not sure about Ruhama of course. She has an adventurous spirit, much like yours, and is eager for travel. She constantly wants me to take her to visit other parts of the country."

"Perhaps I can take her with me to Alexandria when I go there next spring. She could stay for a while with Maryam."

"Yes, that would please her very much, Joseph."

Joseph left the next day for Caesarea and then Rome. The marriage would be held after the Passover festival, and Marcus was planning to take Aurelia for a wedding trip to Capri before settling down in their new home. Joseph would then go north across the Alps and Gaul to the shores of Brittany and sail over the channel to Britannia. It would take him about a month, travelling slowly and enjoying the new scenes and stopping at the Roman settlements and outposts along the way. Britannia would be reached in the late spring when the weather was usually warm and sunny but sometimes interrupted with clouds and rain.

On the advice of a trader in Rome, he would go to Tintagel on the northern coast of Cornwall. A Phoenician trading post had once been established there. He intended to build a small villa overlooking the sea and order some ships to be built by local shipbuilders. It would be his annual summer retreat far from the turmoil of Jerusalem, Rome or Alexandria.

⁂⁂⁂⁂

Philo was pleased with Nikki's progress in his studies. They had made a beginning in the interpretation of the first chapter in Genesis on the creation of the world. He had a bright, inquiring mind and was open to new views and perspectives. Now that he was hearing lectures on Greek philosophy and astronomy, he could bring in the cosmological concepts in Plato's *Timeus*, Aristotle's *On the Heavens*, and Ptolemy's *Almagest* for contrast.

Plato believed that the world was created by a benevolent demiurge who tried to fashion it according to a perfect and ideal model but failed to do so completely. Aristotle believed that that the universe was eternal, timeless, that it was not created but had always existed. Philo's personal belief was similar to this, in that the world was made of primordial matter and not a creation *ex nihilo* but he still believed, as it says in the Book of Genesis, that God gave it form, creating heaven and earth by shaping what had previously been formless and void.

He wanted to give the boy a critical mind, to be able to think in abstract, metaphysical terms. Later on he would also introduce him to that wonderful work of the Epicurean poet Lucretius, *De Rerum Natura*—on the nature of the universe. Lucretius believed that the world operated according to physical principles, by chance rather than by divine intervention. He was doubtful about the theory of Pythagoras in which the earth, the planets, and the sun, all revolved around a 'Central Fire'. This was in complete contradiction to the view of Ptolemy showing the spherical form of the heavens revolving around the earth at the centre of the universe.

Philo noticed that his brother Alexander had also taken an interest in Nikki. He often came to dinner and there was a special rapport between them. Alexander was more practical and had a realistic and common sense attitude to the world as a place where men had to find a way to live together in harmony for the greater good of all. Philo was more sceptical of this possibility, and preferred to distance himself from public affairs, although this was not always possible. There was also considerable tension in the Alexandrine Jewish community between the more orthodox members who remained loyal to the national and religious beliefs of Judaism and those like himself who stressed the universal aspects of Jewish

90

law and the views of the prophets, avoiding stress on national aspects of the Jewish religion and emphasising its rational aspects.

At dinner one evening, Nikki asked Alexander how long it was since Jews were living in Egypt. Alexander raised his eyebrows and looked at him in amusement.

"I thought you were the great Bible scholar, Nikki. Our nation was born in Egypt. Don't you remember that about a thousand and five hundred years ago Jacob and his family of seventy members came down to Egypt? And their descendants stayed here for four hundred years and turned into a nation of six hundred thousand."

"Yes, those were the Hebrews, the Israelites, before they became Jews. I mean the Jews, those of later generations, of the time when they were established as an independent people in their own land."

Alexander said that there were no Jews in Egypt for a long while until a small force was sent there by Menashe king of Judah to assist the Egyptian Pharaoh Psammeticus in his Nubian campaign. Later, when Cyrus king of Persia conquered Babylon and allowed Jews to return to their land, he also conquered Egypt, and to protect it against the Nubians in the south, he stationed a large force of Jewish mercenaries in a fortress near the Nubian border on the island in Nile called Yeb, now known as Elephantine.

"What happened to them?" asked Nikki.

"They remained there for nearly a hundred years. And because they were so far away from Judaea and the Second Temple built there by Jews who returned to Jerusalem, they built their own temple on the island dedicated to Yahweh and even offered sacrifices to him on the altar. There is a copy of a letter in our archives from the Jews of Elephantine to Bagoas, the Persian governor in Judaea, asking for his help in rebuilding the temple that other soldiers stationed on the island had destroyed in hatred of them."

He told Nikki that the garrison was withdrawn when Alexander the Great conquered Egypt and founded the city of Alexandria. Many Jews came to settle in it and under the Ptolemies the Jewish community grew larger and developed a unique social and cultural life of its own. Most of them became completely Hellenised, although they retained their loyalty to the Temple in Jerusalem. He was also going tell Nikki about another temple that Jews had built in Egypt, the one in Leontopolis, but thought it best to leave it till another time.

****

Before he left for Britannia, Joseph wrote to tell Gorion about the wedding in Rome and Gorion read it aloud to Rachela and Ruhama in the evening as they sat together in the living room.

Dear Hananel,

Greetings from Rome! The wedding was conducted with great festivity in the palatial residence of Rufus and Fulvia. It was held according to both Jewish and Roman custom. The young couple was feted by nearly five hundred guests. I cannot tell you the names of those who were there since I only recognised a few of them, but Rufus tells me these were the most prominent persons in the government and at court. The bride was beautifully dressed and Marcus looked very handsome as well. I have never seen him happier than on that day.

The good news is that Marcus has received his Roman citizenship. It was granted personally by the emperor a few days before the wedding. And I was invited with Marcus to a special audience before him. He was most gracious, and was pleased to hear that Marcus had been named for his former son-in-law, friend, and adviser, Marcus Agrippa, whose death he still mourned. I took the opportunity to speak about the situation in Jerusalem and Judaea, recommending the replacement of Archelaus by some other ruler from among Herod's grandchildren in Rome. He listened very carefully, nodded his agreement, but said nothing.

Marcus and Aurelia have gone on to Capri for two weeks. Their home is ready for them when they return, and I am sure they will be busy entertaining their friends and business acquaintances for weeks to come. Marcus will soon resume working with Gaius, and Aurelia, besides maintaining her household, plans to open a literary salon for women. This will be an innovation for Roman women who usually meet only at formal social events and spend most of their time in idle gossip. She wants to invite writers and historians to give a talk on some interesting subject, answer questions on it, or hold a general discussion on the topic.

I told Rufus of my plan to travel to Britannia next week for several months and gave him a copy of my will in which I named him and you as my trustees. I enclose the original with this letter and ask you to have it legally recorded and approved. In it, I leave all my personal property and effects to my son Marcus,

92

except for a few bequests to charity. I do this in case I encounter some misadventure during my travel to Britannia and my stay there. I will write again to you as soon as I arrive there, although I do not know how long the letter will take to reach Jerusalem.

In the meantime, my love and good wishes to you and Rachela, and love to Ruhama as well. I hope to find you well on my return in the autumn.

With warmest regards,

Joseph

Gorion looked at the will, folded it up with the letter, and placed it in his leather folder where he kept his official documents. He would go to the Council House the next day and have the will registered. Rachela said she hoped Joseph would return safely home and that there would be no need for the will to be executed.

Ruhama asked what a 'will' was, and told her that a will is a written document in which a person says what he wants to be done with his property after he dies. Usually it was to give the property to his children with a few gifts to other people or to charity. Sometimes a will was bad or unfair, like Herod's will, and a judge could change a will if people complained or protested against it. He said he was sure that very soon Herod's will would be changed. But he was not sure who would be chosen instead of Archelaus. The Romans might want to rule the country directly by a governor as they do in Syria.

He got up to go at once to the Council House, but a visitor was suddenly announced. It was Johanan ben Zakkai again from the Sanhedrin. He took him into the study and closed the door. Ben Zakkai told Gorion that there was a religious but also a legal and civil matter under discussion by the elders. It concerned Glaphyra, the widow of Alexander, the daughter of the king of Cappadocia. When her husband was executed, Herod took custody of her children and sent them to Rome but forced her to remain in Jerusalem. After Herod died she returned to Cappadocia and brought her children back from Rome. She reverted to her pagan religion and told her children to renounce Judaism.

"Well, good riddance to her, then," said Gorion.

"But recently, during a tour of the eastern Mediterranean countries by Gaius Caesar, a grandson of Augustus, together with Juba, the king of Mauretania, they visited Cappadocia and Juba fell in love with Glaphyra. They will soon be married."

"It is all perfectly legal" said Gorion. "She is a widow now and can remarry."

"Yes, but her children are opposed to the marriage, and wish to return to Judaism and to Jerusalem, and be accepted once again as Jews by the Sanhedrin court. Shammai is of course against this and wishes to deny their request. But Hillel is in favour of accepting them, saying that they were what is called in Hebrew *tinok shenishba*, an abducted baby, those unwittingly or unwillingly kept away from or left ignorant of their Jewish heritage."

"This matter will have to be voted on in the Sanhedrin. It is a religious, not a civil matter," said Gorion.

"There is another complication, a civil one," said Johanan. "Archelaus is against accepting them as Jews for the obvious reason that they are Hasmonean and could challenge his rule one day. He wishes to prevent them from becoming citizens of this country and deny them the right to do so. The question is whether he can do this legally."

"In my opinion, he cannot," said Gorion.

"But who is going to prevent him from using his lawyers from bringing some false charges of heresy against the children," Johanan insisted. "Or prevent him from corrupting the magistrates at the civil court?"

Gorion was silent for a few minutes. He understood immediately what Johanan was going to request from him on behalf of Hillel the Elder. He wanted Gorion to act as the children's defence lawyer if the case came to court. He believed Gorion's experience and prestige among the magistrates would win the day.

"Johanan, you must realise that if the Sanhedrin votes in favour of the children and Archelaus brings charges against them, that my defence of the children will antagonise him. He would find some means to harm me personally and endanger me and my family."

"I realise this and so does my old master Hillel. But he said to tell you that if good men did not stand up and be counted in times of evil, and try to avoid confronting it, they would inevitably suffer the consequences of that evil."

"Your master is wise above all men, Johanan. Tell him I shall think seriously about this matter and will wait first to hear what the Sanhedrin decides before I give him my answer. Perhaps Archelaus will not do what we assume he will do."

"You can trust him to do everything he can to hurt the Hasmoneans. Look at the way he treats his Hasmonean wife, Mariamne, the daughter of Aristobulus. He might even try to have her eliminated as Herod eliminated her grandmother Mariamne."

Gorion grimaced with disgust. The man was more than just cruel and depraved. He was a threat to all civil justice in the country. It was time that Augustus deposed him before worse things were done. He accompanied Johanan outside and said he would go with him as far as the Council House. He had just been about to go there when Johanan arrived. They walked together and continued discussing problems with the Sanhedrin so deeply divided between the two schools of thought. As long as Hillel was alive the more rational and liberal members could still hold the upper hand. But in the end, extremism would win because the people could no longer bear the oppression of its rulers.

****

After four years in Alexandria, Nikki completed his prescribed course academic studies with honours. He was now thoroughly familiar with Greek philosophy from its earliest beginnings to Aristotle and beyond him to his followers, the Peripatetic school at the Lyceum of Athens. He had also taken a great interest in astronomy and in the various cosmological theories about the universe. Personally he tended to disagree with the accepted Ptolemaic system of a fixed geocentric earth with the sun, moon, stars and planets circling it.

He had read Philolaus, a disciple of Pythagoras, who supported his theory of a spherical earth that, together with the sun, moon, stars and planets, circled a Central Fire in the universe. This sounded more plausible but could not yet be scientifically proven. At least, it was better that the Babylonian conception of the earth as a flat disk. But he found the idea of Philolaus of a Counter-Earth circling on the other side of the Central Fire as too speculative and mysterious.

He also greatly enjoyed his studies with Philo on the Bible and was intensely interested in the new perspectives that it opened for him. They had studied Genesis for almost a year, and they spent the next year on Exodus. He understood the need for Philo to avoid the literal reading of the biblical text, but he was not convinced that an allegorical interpretation was the right one. It seemed to him as though Philo was writing for the benefit of Gentiles and making the Bible palatable to their tastes. It was an adaptation of the Mosaic legislation for a better acceptance and appreciation of it by non-Jews with constant references and comparisons with Greek lore and legislation. Nikki thought that a historical approach was better and would explain things that no longer seemed credible in the biblical account of the world and of past events. He tried to make this clear to Philo.

"The story of the creation of the world in the Bible is the way the people of the Bible saw it. For them, the world could not have created itself. It had to have a Creator, an all-powerful and omniscient God. They understood that creation had be something gradual, moving gradually from the more elementary creations, the earth, the heavens, plant growth, animal growth, to the creation of man and then woman. Six days were enough for a God who could make time run as fast as he wished or slow down as long as he wanted."

"Yes, that may be. But what can we say about their conception of God? Was it not a very primitive one if taken literally?"

"That is how they thought of him in those days. A god was always some supernatural being who was powerful and protected his people as long as they worshipped him and made sacrifices to him. It was like the relationship of a king and his subjects. He ruled them and defended them against their enemies and they paid him taxes, built him a grand palace, and honoured him with much pomp and ceremony. It was far from the abstract and spiritual conception of a supreme deity, or from Aristotle's unmoved mover."

Philo said that he did not like the God of the Bible with his arbitrary moods, his vengeful treatment of sinners, the plagues, the destruction of people and cities, his threats against his own people, and the need for someone to placate his anger, like Abraham or Moses. Nikki laughed in agreement and said the biblical God was very much the Greek Zeus with his thunderbolts and his arbitrary, changing moods, from extreme anger to benevolent mercy. Just like any human father towards a troublesome child.

"And the problem of the Exodus from Egypt and all the miracles that God performs for his people," Philo added. "I do not like the favouritism, the idea of a chosen people superior to all others."

"I do not think chosen people means superior people, just those with a special mission, with a special relationship to God, one that is closer and more meaningful. God is still thought of in the Bible as the God of all human beings, and those who followed the moral precepts of the Bible, the seven Noahide commandments, were considered as righteous gentiles."

"There are a lot of contradictions in the Bible" Philo explained. "That is why I feel the need to interpret it in a way that will be accepted to rational minds, to use allegorical explanations for the difficult passages."

Philo believed that the Torah was of divine origin and that the Bible was both a source of religious revelation and philosophic truth. He claimed that some Greek philosophers had borrowed from the Bible. One of his main ideas was the identification of the Hebrew phrase *Malach Adonai*, the Angel of the Lord, with the Greek concept of the Logos. He had derived this idea from the post-biblical work, 'The Wisdom of Solomon' which was included in the Septuagint. Philo's Logos was an intermediary divine being, like Plato's demiurge, which could bridge the gap between God and the material world. Philo called it 'the first-born son of God', the bond that linked the divine and the human in a great chain of being.

Nikki was a little doubtful about all this metaphysical speculation and was more interested in what Alexander had told him about the ancient Jewish colony in Egypt. After dinner one evening, he questioned him again about the history of Jews in Egypt. Alexander was only too pleased to tell him more about it.

"Thousands of Jews came to Egypt from Judaea over the past three centuries to escape from life under the Seleucid rulers. Many of them became military colonists serving in the army of the Ptolemies. They were allowed to settle in the Nile delta region. History repeated itself, because this was the very same Land of Goshen where Jacob and his family had originally settled."

"Did they go on pilgrimage to Jerusalem for the three festivals?"

"Perhaps at first they did. But you remember that the Temple was eventually desecrated by Antiochus Epiphanes, the mad ruler of Antioch, by erecting a statue of Zeus in it. He deposed the legitimate Zadokite High Priest, Onias III, and appointed a Hellenised priest, Alcimus, instead. Onias was executed in Antioch but his son Onias IV fled to Egypt with his family while other Zadokite priests went to found a small colony on the shores of the Dead Sea a little north of the Essenes in Ein Gedi. Ptolemy gave Onias the city of Leontopolis where he built his own temple on the ruins of Bubastis, an old Egyptian temple. The whole area of the delta around it was called the Land of Onias."

"Was it like the Temple in Jerusalem," asked Nikki.

"It was a much smaller replica of it, but the Jews even offered sacrifices on the altar. Onias also built a fortress around it for better protection. Ptolemy endowed it with large revenues and supplied it with wood and animals for the sacrifices."

"So they forgot about the Temple in Jerusalem. Even after the Maccabees restored it and rededicated it?"

"No, they continued to make pilgrimages to Jerusalem and the Temple, to send the annual tax and make many other contributions to it. In time, the Jews ceased going to the temple in Leontopolis after the great synagogue was built in Alexandria. I can take you to see this temple one day. It is still standing."

Nikki decided that he wanted to be a historian, to write a history of the Jewish people from its earliest beginnings to present times, as Livy had done for Rome. The Bible ended with the Book of Chronicles which summarised its history up to the reign of Cyrus the Great and the return to Zion more than five hundred years ago. Since then there had been a few post-biblical works such as the books on the Maccabees, but nothing that gave a continuous account of events since then.

He would go to Rome now that he had completed his studies at Alexandria. He was nearly twenty-one and he thought he could find a position in Rome as a tutor to the son of some noble family and begin working on his projected history. It was an ambitious project but he hoped to find some scholars among the Jews of Rome who would assist him in it. They were one of the oldest Jewish communities and were as well established and organised as the Jews of Alexandria. Marcus was there with Aurelia. They already had two children, a boy and girl, and were living very happily in their lovely home on the Carinae. It would be good to see them again. He did not want to return to Jerusalem as long as Archelaus was still in power. His father had also encouraged him to go to Rome and not to come home.

****

The rule of Archelaus was a disaster in progress. It had begun badly and grew worse in time. He was greedy, a predator, only looking for his own pleasure and profit. He did not govern but merely sat in his palace and left matters to his hirelings. They, of course, took advantage of this to treat people with contempt and did not give attention to miscarriages of justice.

Then there was the affair with Glaphyra, Alexander's widow who had married Juba II and became the Queen of Mauretania. Archelaus had always been attracted to her and when he met her again on a visit to Rome they became lovers. He then divorced his wife and she divorced Juba to marry him. There was a public outcry in Jerusalem against this marriage because it was considered incestuous. She had been the wife of his half-brother Alexander, and according to the law, a man was forbidden to marry the wife of his brother unless his brother died without a child to bear his name.

Anger against Archelaus was also because Alexander had been the handsome young prince adored by all the people and whom they had hoped would be Herod's heir. To them it was like a double usurpation by his hated half-brother. It was said that divine punishment would fall upon her, and sure enough, soon after her marriage, she fell ill and died. A story circulated among the people that Alexander had appeared to her in a dream two days before her death to castigate her. Her two children were then sent back to Cappadocia as the grandchildren of the king of that country and withdrew their request to be recognised as Jews.

By the end of the eighth year of his rule, those who had supported Archelaus in the past realised that he was a barbarous and tyrannical despot. Strong accusations against him were sent to Rome and he was brought before Augustus to answer for his crimes. Augustus banished him to Vienne, a Roman colony in Gaul. The interpretation of his dream by Menahem the Essene of the nine ears of corn was finally fulfilled.

****

Ruhama had grown up. It was ten years since she had come to stay with the Gorions and she was now sixteen. Rachela had kept her close at home, and was over-protective of her, while the girl longed to go out and see the world. Joseph had not kept his promise to take her with him to Alexandria. He was so busy with his own business affairs with traveling around the world that he hardly came to Jerusalem any more. The only time she had been allowed to leave Jerusalem was when Martha took her to her home in Bethany for a week. This was when Mother Rachela was feeling tired and unwell and Father Hananel took her down to the Essene colony at Ein Gedi on the shores of the Dead Sea for a curative treatment.

Bethany was only about a mile from Jerusalem but it always took Martha more than an hour to reach the Gorion home. She wondered why Martha was not married. She was now nearly thirty years old but she seemed much younger. Martha told her that her parents had died when she was only ten years old and left two young children, Elazar and Mary, only a few years old. She had cared for them ever since and they were now grown up and could take care of themselves. But they remained together in their family home in Bethany and were happy together.

Ruhama enjoyed her visit to Bethany and the mountain scenery around it, but was afraid to go near the leper colony on the Jericho Road. Mary told her that she often went there to tend to the sick, and like the Essene doctors, she wore long white robes and a veil to protect her from contamination. Elazar was a student at the local religious seminary, the *Beth Midrash*, preparing to become a teacher. The people living in Bethany were poor but hospitable and open to all people, whether Jews, Samaritans, Essenes, or travellers from abroad who passed through their town on the way to Jerusalem, taking very little payment for those wishing to stay in a guest room for the night.

Ruhama said she would like to study medicine at the Essene clinic on Mount Zion near her home. Martha had taught her many things about the plants and herbs she always brought her over the years for the garden, and told her about their medicinal properties. She now had planted many beds of flowers and herbs there, rosemary, basil, chamomile, feverfew, lavender, lemon balm and others. She often had tried to persuade Mother Rachela to drink the teas that Martha made from these plants, but she refused to do so.

When she returned home, she found Rachela no better after the treatment at Ein Gedi. She was afraid that something more serious was wrong with her health than mere fatigue, and offered to take over some of the household affairs to relieve her from over-exertion. The servants had to be supervised while they cleaned and dusted the rooms, the clothes washed, beds aired and remade, the windows polished and the floors rugs beaten outdoors. Then there was the market shopping which she and Martha did together, and she helped with the cooking and preparations for the midday meal. This took up most of the morning. Her parents usually rested for two hours after the meal, but she always went to the upper chamber to read and write till the late afternoon. In the meantime, Martha baked fresh bread and cakes, and prepared the evening meal before she left for her home. She had to leave at least an hour before sunset in order to reach Bethany while it was still light.

In the evenings, Ruhama sat and talked with Father Hananel, wrote some letters for him and also the weekly letter to Nikki who was now living in Rome. He always wrote regularly to them, about once a month, giving them news about his studies and also about Maryam and Jeshua. In his last letter, he told them that they were planning to return to Judaea now that Archelaus was deposed, and would live in Nazareth with Josiah and his family. Jeshua was now nearly twelve years old and Maryam felt he needed a father to teach and guide him as he grew to be a man.

Nikki had visited Marcus and his family soon after his arrival in Rome and sent warm regards from them. Through Marcus, he found a family who wanted a tutor for their young son and he lived quite comfortably in the guest wing of the house. He hoped to visit Jerusalem in the summer when the family went down their seaside villa near Naples. Gorion told Ruhama he did not want to worry him with any mention Rachela's illness in the letter, and just to say that they were looking forward to his visit. She was now almost an invalid and kept to her room for most of the day.

****

Gorion was at the Sanhedrin court more often since the banishment of Archelaus. Instead of a new ruler from among the Hasmonean or Herodian family, Augustus had decided to rule more directly through a prefect or a procurator. The first of them, Coponius, of equestrian rank, arrived together with Quirinus, the Governor of Syria, who would be responsible for the political and military control over the province. Judaea was now a Roman province and the customary census for new provinces had to be taken.

There was an immediate uprising against the census considered a religious violation by the Zealots, a new party formed under Judas the Galilean. He incited the people to rebellion and attacked Sepphoris which was then the administrative centre of the Galilee, sacked its treasury and took the weapons in its armoury for an armed revolt against Rome and Herodian rule in the Galilee under Antipas. He and his followers were suppressed by Roman forces and much of the city was burnt down during the battle with the rebels. A fanatical wing of this party also emerged, the Sicarii, extreme religious nationalists who held hidden daggers under their robes to assassinate those they considered pro-Roman collaborators.

Fortunately, the High Priest was able to pacify the people before it led to open revolt and the census was taken. Coponius proved to be a capable man who maintained good relations with the Jews. He was very considerate about the sanctity of the Temple and increased its protection after Samaritans penetrated into the inner court and desecrated it by scattering human bones on the floor. He repaired one of the gateways to the Temple Mount and it was named the 'Gate of Coponius' in his honour.

But at the Sanhedrin, violent debates were held about direct Roman rule. Not because of national pride but for religious reasons. The presence of Roman soldiers in the Tower of Antonia overlooking the Temple was a violation of its sanctity since they did not show a respectful attitude towards it. Coponius also had some coins struck with his name and of Augustus Caesar that bore his image. These could not be used in money dealings in the Temple. He also held the power of life and death, and could order executions without consulting the Sanhedrin.

Gorion was asked to head a new delegation to Augustus asking for the restoration of Jewish rule. He advised the Sanhedrin that this would be a useless attempt and might even lead to harsher measures imposed on the people. Augustus realised that unlike other nations under Roman rule, the Jews were exceptionally troublesome and unruly with so many warring factions among them. The idea of a delegation was dropped, although a special committee was formed to deal with the problem of the coinage and with the Roman soldiers. They had to lay down some red lines before more trouble broke out.

Coponius was replaced after three years by Marcus Ambivulus. The Jews of Judaea gradually became used to this ruling system and made no further protests, while the Samaritans of Samaria were glad to be free of the Herodians. There was still a lot of tension in Jerusalem, and Gorion found himself in constant demand for liaison between the Sanhedrin and the Roman government authorities stationed in the Antonia Tower. The Roman soldiers were told to refrain from standing on the roof of the tower and looking over at the Temple compound, and the new coinage was excluded from use in Jerusalem and confined to commercial exchanges between Judaea and the surrounding countries. Compromise was better than conflict, and this was the policy that all had agreed to for the present. Gorion found enough reasonable men on both sides to keep the peace.

When Maryam and Jeshua returned from Alexandria to Joppa, Gorion went to meet them. Philo had sent him the name of the ship and the day of its expected arrival at the port. He wrote that they were both glad to go back to Judaea. The boy had been taught by private tutors and had a good knowledge of Hebrew and of the Bible. He could speak the local Greek language but was not taught to read

Greek or Latin. He and Maryam conversed in Aramaic which was also used by the Jews among themselves in their neighbourhood.

Jeshua would not be a scholar like Nikki, but he was highly intelligent and had a warm heart. He liked to wander in the fields and accompany his mother in gathering healing herbs and plants. They were close to each other and she was very tender and protective of him. Philo said he saw them only once a week on the Sabbath at the synagogue and they sometimes came back with him to his house for a brief visit. He would miss them and hoped they would be happy when they returned to Nazareth.

****

Gorion brought Maryam and Jeshua to stay at his house in Jerusalem for a while before traveling to Nazareth. Rachela met Maryam for the first time and they liked each other. But Ruhama found her a little strange in the way she dressed and spoke, although she was very interested when she heard of her work in herb healing and her other medical skills. Perhaps Maryam could find a cure for Mother Rachela or at least relieve her of pain.

She thought Jeshua was a beautiful child, with his large blue eyes and long curly hair tied back with a band. He spoke to her very gently in Aramaic although he understood Hebrew very well. She liked his soft voice and manner, and could see his love for his mother as he sat close to her and looked up into her face. Maryam was delighted to be in Jerusalem again after more than ten years in Alexandria. Although she was happy to stay for a while with the Gorions, she knew she would soon have to rejoin her husband in Nazareth.

"Next year Jeshua will be thirteen years old and we will bring him to the Temple to stand before the priests and rabbis and be examined for his knowledge."

"We will be glad to have you stay with us again when you come back to Jerusalem. It will be good to see Josiah again."

"Yes, so will I," said Maryam. "He wrote to say that he was retired now and could not work any longer because of the pain in his back. He has even stopped coming to Jerusalem for the pilgrimage festivals, though his sons always come."

"I think taking some ginger in hot water would be good for back pain," said Ruhama.

"Yes it is, and I also have some herbal preparations for it which I intend to use for him."

"You must be tired, Maryam," Rachela told her. "Ruhama will show you and Jeshua to your room to rest until the evening. Then come down at sunset and join us for dinner."

They went upstairs. Rachela retired to her room and Gorion went into his study. During his absence a letter had arrived from Joseph who was on his way back from his annual stay in Britannia.

Dear Hananel,

Sorry I have not written to you for some time. I returned a few days ago from Britannia to spend the winter months in Rome. I bought a house on the Aventine overlooking the Tiber on one side and the Circus Maximus on the other. I shall not be returning to my home in Ramatayim for the present. My partner who is handling all the internal trade in Judaea and Samaria lives there now.

Marcus and Gaius handle all the trade coming into Ostia from Egypt and other ports of the Mediterranean, while I deal with the importation of tin and other metals from Britannia which comes down overland through Gaul to Massalia and is shipped to Genoa. From there, it is distributed to various cities in Italia and also to Rome according to specific orders.

This allows me to visit Marcus and Aurelia and my grandchildren at least once a week. I have also seen Nikki who visits them occasionally. He seems to be doing very well here, teaching, studying and writing. He has grown into a serious young man, and very handsome looking as well. You should be proud of him.

While I am in Rome, I frequently meet with Rufus who has become a partner with me in the Britannia trade. He has a good head for business and will take full charge of it while I am away in Cornwall during the spring and summer months. In the autumn, I usually go to Alexandria for a few weeks. But I am happiest when I am in Britannia and at the house I built on an island that rises up opposite one end of the bay on the southern coastline. The main port is located at the other end of the bay. This part of Cornwall is the area furthest to the west and juts out into the sea like a long finger.

What brought me there in the first place was what I read in the Bibliotheca Historica written by the Greek historian Diodorus Siculus. He calls Cornwall by its Greek name Belerion and this is what he says about it:

They that inhabit the British promontory of Belerion by reason of their converse with strangers are more civilised and courteous to strangers than the rest are. These are the people that prepare the tin, which with a great deal of care and labour, they dig out of the ground, and that being done the metal is mixed with some veins of earth out of which they melt the metal and refine it. Then they cast it into regular blocks and carry it to a certain island near at hand called Ictis for at low tide, all being dry between there and the island, tin in large quantities is brought over in carts.

This is the island where I built my house. At low tide, it is easy to cross to the mainland on horseback or on a mule cart. The mines are some distance northwest of it and I own the largest one in Cornwall which has twenty-two lodes of tin in them. The people here call it the Ding Dong mine because I installed a bell in it to be rung at the end of the last shift of the miners. Besides mining, there is large fishing industry here, and a large amount of trade between the tribes of Britannia and those on the coast of Gaul. Interestingly enough, there is an identical and larger conical shaped island on that coast just opposite this one.

I feel very much at peace here, and live like a king. The people are friendly and consider me as a good employer who cares for their welfare. Some were curious about the country which I came from, and have never heard of Judaea before, or of Jews for that matter. Their religion is one of gods and goddesses representing various forces of nature. But further north, the people are ruled by the Druids, a powerful priestly caste with their barbarous cult of human sacrifices and who practice divination. Their horrifying practices are mentioned by Caesar in his account of the Gallic Wars and also by Diodorus. I have yet to encounter them, since fortunately, they are not found in this area.

Write to me care of Marcus and let me know how you and your family are doing. I understood from Philo that Maryam and Jeshua are now on their way back home to Nazareth with Josiah and are well and happy to return after such a long exile.

Give my love to your dear wife and daughter.

With my warmest regards,

Joseph

****

Maryam left for Nazareth a few days later with many presents of food and other provisions. She was also given some of Nikki's clothes that he had outgrown for Jeshua, including the clothes he had worn for his presentation at the temple when he was thirteen years old. Josiah was glad to see her and the boy, and his sons were also delighted to have a younger half-brother they could play with and pamper, taking him for rides on horseback across the green fields around Nazareth and through the lovely Valley of Jezreel with its many dotted farms and settlements. Jeshua was happy in their company, and was also ready to learn the carpentry trade in the workshops. He had a natural instinct for working with wood, especially with carving the shapes of flowers and animals on cabinets and wooden screens for wealthy clients.

Josiah began to prepare him for the Temple presentation and found that the boy knew the Bible almost by heart and also had a good knowledge of the laws and customs of Judaism. On the other hand, he found him indifferent about it and showed no interest in further study. When the time came to travel to Jerusalem, the whole family set out together, his older brothers riding on horseback and he and his parents in a closed wagon.

Gorion had been advised by letter of their coming and was at the Temple on the day they had fixed for the presentation. The priests and rabbis were seated in the eastern part of the Royal Stoa used as a court for elders. Jeshua stood before them, his hands clasped behind him and his family ranged themselves behind him. Gorion watched the proceedings from one side and saw that the rabbis and priests were looking at Jeshua and talking excitedly among themselves. He approached nearer to listen to what they were saying.

"He is the image of the prince, I tell you Hanina."

"No, it cannot be, Nehunia, the boy cannot be his."

"What do you say, Gamaliel? Can it be so?"

They looked at each other and then shook their heads.

One of the priests posed the first question:

"What can you say about the Song of the Sea? When Pharaoh and all the Egyptians drowned?"

Jeshua thought for a while and then said: "They should not have been singing when the Egyptians drowned. It says in the Book of Proverbs that you should not be happy when your enemy falls."

106

There was a long silence, and then Gamaliel said, "You are right, Jeshua. There is a midrash on this sentence by one of the men of the Great Synagogue in the time of Ezra which says that God told the angels in heaven not to sing because these people were also created by him."

They questioned him about other passages in the Bible, and he gave them surprising interpretations of them. But they could not find any fault in his answers and gave him full acceptance as a *bar mitzvah*, one who accepted the Torah and its commandments. Gorion invited them all to his home for a special celebration before they set out for the north. Jeshua received many gifts from everyone and his face shone with happiness and gratitude.

****

It was already late in autumn as Josiah and his family travelled northwards to the Galilee. They followed the line of wagon transports going along the Valley of Ayalon towards the city of Lydda, where they stopped overnight. The next day they went on to Aphek, now called Antipatris after it had been rebuilt by Herod and named for his father Antipater. They then turned towards the northeast and the road leading to Shechem in Samaria and would go beyond it to find the main highway that ran from Sychor to the Galilee.

Unfortunately, just outside Shechem, the axle of a wagon wheel broke down and had to be mended. James, the oldest of Josiah's sons, went into the city to look for help and came back with a Samaritan blacksmith to tow the wagon to his forge. While they waited for the wheel and axle to be replaced, the smith invited them to rest at his house nearby. They were hesitant at first, as it was not usual for Samaritans to be friendly towards Jews. But the wife welcomed them graciously and offered them food and drink.

They sat near the hearth where an elderly man in long white robes was already seated. He greeted them with the words *Shalom Aleichem*, may peace be upon you, and Josiah replied with *Aleichem Shalom*. He realised that this was a Samaritan priest, yet the Samaritan temple was still in ruins, destroyed over a hundred years earlier by the Hasmonean king John Hyrcanus. Enmity between them and the Jews was bitter and often led to bloodshed.

Jeshua was sitting nearest to the old priest and gazed at him with wondering eyes. The priest bent towards him and asked him for his name.

"Oh, Jeshua, which is the same as Joshua. Do you know who Joshua was?"

"He was the servant of Moses and became the leader of the Israelites after Moses died. And then he led the people across the Jordan River and conquered Canaan."

"Joshua was of the tribe of Ephraim," said the old priest. "Of all the tribes of Israel, the tribe of Joseph received a double share for his two sons, Ephraim and Menashe. Just look at the size of their inheritance when the country was divided among the tribes. Ephraim is in the centre with a large area, and Menashe is to the north with an even larger share. And this was only half of Menashe's territory. The tribe had a huge area across the Jordan together with the tribes of Reuben and Gad."

Josiah said that this was because Joshua had shown preference for the tribes of Joseph.

"But Joseph was considered by Jacob to be his first born son, and was entitled to a double share," the Samaritan priest protested.

"Jacob's preference only made his brothers jealous," said Josiah. "And they sold him to the Ishmaelites going to Egypt."

"Joseph forgave them in the end. He had a higher intelligence, a greater soul that all his brothers. He could see the future in his dreams. The kingdom of Israel was meant to be his and his sons."

"Then why did God give the kingdom to David of the tribe of Judah?"

"Well, he first gave it to Saul, of the tribe of Benjamin, the younger brother of Joseph. Saul was brave and fought the Philistines, but he was not a wise king, so God gave the kingdom to his son-in-law David. And David then made Jerusalem his capital and his son Solomon built the first temple there. But the temple was originally meant to be built here in Shechem, the city that Jacob gave to Joseph."

"Yes, I remember now," said Jeshua. "Joshua was told to build an altar of unhewn stones to God on Mount Ebal and to make sacrifices on it. Six tribes would then stand on Mount Gerizim and six on Mount Ebal facing each other across the city of Shechem to recite the blessings and the curses."

"The stones of this altar are still there on Mount Ebal. And do you remember, Jeshua, the passage which says that when Joshua was old and dying, he gathered the people together at Shechem, gave a farewell speech and then, as it says in the Bible:

He wrote these words in the book of the Torah of God, and took a great stone, and set it under the doorpost which is in the sanctuary of the Lord."

Josiah interrupted their discussion by reminding the priest that Joshua had placed the Tabernacle with the Ark and the holy vessels in Shiloh north of Bethel and not in Shechem. Shiloh remained the centre of worship for centuries until the time of Samuel. The Philistines captured the Ark but later returned it when it caused a plague among their people. Finally, David brought it to Jerusalem which then became the capital city and centre of worship. The Temple was built there by Solomon, but after his death ten tribes broke away to form another kingdom in the north and made Shechem its capital. This kingdom was eventually destroyed by the Assyrians and most of the people were exiled.

The old priest was silent and then answered Josiah. He admitted that this was true, but a small remnant of the Israelites in the north remained in Shechem and slowly returned to their faith and to the Torah. They were still there when the Babylonians exiled the Jews of Judaea and were there when they returned seventy years later. They had offered to help rebuild the temple in Jerusalem but were rejected.

Josiah said it was because they were no longer considered as Jews. Most of them had intermarried with other people the Assyrians had settled in the area. When Nehemiah arrived to rebuild the walls of Jerusalem, they allied themselves with the local forces of Sanballat the Horonite, Tobiah the Ammonite, and Geshem the Arabian to try and interrupt the work on the walls but they eventually failed.

Again the priest was silent. He no longer had any answer to this. But he placed his hand on Jeshua's head and said that perhaps the time had come for both the Jews and the Samaritans to make peace between them. They parted from him with mutual blessings and then entered the repaired wagon and continued their journey to Nazareth. As they drove out of Shechem, Jeshua looked at his father and said that at least there were some good Samaritans, and the old priest was one of them.

******

Winter came round in full force a month later. It did not snow this year, but there were heavy rains that flooded the country in many places and a cold wind blew relentlessly through the city. Rachela was becoming weaker by the day and did not have the strength to rise from her bed. Ruhama remained constantly by her bedside and slept on the couch near her to keep watch all night. Martha came in the morning to relieve Ruhama for a few hours. They took turns to keep her warm and dry, and to take some light nourishment as she found it difficult to swallow. Ruhama feared she would not last the winter.

"I think I must write to Nikki now," she told Gorion. "I know she does not want me to do so but he should come home now."

"He said he will be here in the summer," he answered. "She seems calm and confident that this illness will pass when the winter is over, and she insists that he not be told anything for the present unless she becomes worse."

Ruhama did not want to tell him what she thought. She could see that he was in a state of denial, not able to face the idea of losing her. Without telling him, she consulted one of the Essene doctors who had been teaching her privately about medicines and curative treatment. He came one day when Gorion was away to see Rachela and then told Ruhama that the illness had progressed beyond the hope of any cure. In his opinion, she had only two or three weeks left to live.

After consulting Martha and finding that she also thought Rachela could not hold on to life much longer, she wrote to Nikki. She told him that his mother was seriously ill and that he should come home as soon as possible. It would take a week for the letter to arrive and another week or more for him to return, and she hoped he would be back in time.

Nearly three weeks later Nikki finally reached Jerusalem. It was a difficult journey in wintry weather, and he was thoroughly exhausted by it. Gorion was shocked to see him appear so suddenly, pale and drawn. He quickly realised that someone must have told him about Rachela. They embraced and Nikki asked him about her.

"She is still holding out," he said. "But I am beginning to lose hope."

"You should have written to me earlier. I had a letter from Ruhama, although she said mother did not want her to tell me."

"Ruhama was right to do this," Gorion admitted sorrowfully. "You had better go up first and change out of your wet clothes before you see your mother."

He went upstairs, and in the lighted landing above him saw the figure of a tall girl in flowing robes, her long tresses plaited like a crown around her head, and her large brown eyes gazing down at him. She had heard his voice and came out from his mother's room to meet him. He was stunned by her beauty and stood looking up at her for a long moment.

"Nikki," she said softly. "You have come at last and just in time."

"Ruhama, is that you? I hadn't realised you were …" and his voice broke off.

"That I was what, all grown up?"

He felt embarrassed and was too confused to reply.

"How is mother? I was just going up to change first."

"She is a little better today, and sitting up. She will be so glad to see you."

A few minutes later they were both at her bedside. Rachela was moved to tears to see him after so many years of absence. He had grown taller and broader, but his face was the same she had remembered, the russet hair, the grey eyes, the high forehead, the firm mouth. He gazed at her with anxious looks, holding her hands against him, bending to kiss her wasted cheeks. He could not speak, but there was no need for it. He sat down on one side of the bed and Ruhama sat on the other. Rachela gave a hand to each of them.

"So you wrote to him, you naughty girl," she whispered.

"She was right, mother," Nikki said. "I should have been called home long before this."

After a while, Rachela lay back against the cushions and closed her eyes. Ruhama signalled to Nikki that they should let her rest now and come back later. They tiptoed out and left her asleep. They went downstairs and into the kitchen where Martha greeted him with loud cries of joy, and hugged him in her strong arms.

"Come and sit down. You must be hungry and I have just baked some fresh bread. And there is a plate of chicken and vegetables from the midday meal still warm."

While he ate, she peppered him with questions about his life in Alexandria and Rome. Ruhama left him there and went up again to Rachela.

She now spent nearly all day in that room, leaving only when Martha came in the afternoon for a few hours. Nikki came in several times during the day but did not stay long, and spent most of his time in the upper chamber. Gorion came every morning and every evening but could not bear to stay more than a few minutes. He knew she was dying and there was nothing he could do to save her.

A week later, Martha came in and found Ruhama fast asleep on the couch. She approached the bed and saw Rachela lying motionless and not breathing. Touching her face, she found it cold as ice. When she shook Ruhama awake and signed to her wordlessly that Rachela had died, the girl looked at her uncomprehending and then rose to see for herself that Rachela was gone. Slowly Martha lifted the sheet to cover the face, and Ruhama sat gazing blankly at Martha who tried vainly to comfort her.

"Martha, go down and tell Father Hananel" Ruhama finally said. "I will go up and tell Nikki."

Martha nodded and went out. Ruhama mounted the stairs very slowly to the upper chamber. She found him sitting and leaning over a partly open scroll with his forehead on his hands. He lifted his head when he heard her step in the doorway and saw her standing with tears welling in her eyes.

"It is mother," he whispered standing up and approaching her.

"Yes, Nikki. She's gone."

She came nearer and he lifted a hand to wipe the tears from her cheek.

"I have shed all the tears I have and can cry no more," he said.

He lifted his other hand and cupped her face, drawing her closer to him. He bent his head slowly to kiss her gently on the lips by way of comfort, but then pulled her even closer and began to kiss her passionately on her eyes and forehead. Her arms went around him, and they clung to each other, locked in a tight embrace for a long while.

Ruhama was the first to draw away with a sigh, and looked up at him.

"We must go down to see Father, Nikki," she said tearfully. "Martha has gone to tell him and he will need us there."

Wordless, he put his arm around her and led her out and down the stairs.

****

The funeral for Rachela was held the following day. The house was filled with people from all over Jerusalem and some from outside it. There were Sanhedrin elders, priests, magistrates, councillors, Temple officials, Roman officers and a representative of the Prefect of Judaea. Gorion was known and respected by so many during his long career in the courts, and he received them all with restrained sorrow and dignity, with his son Nicodemus by his side to see he was not crushed by the crowds.

A long procession of mourners followed the litter carrying the body down the hillside and along the Valley of Hinnom leading into the Kidron Valley, and up the Mount of Olives. The Gorion family tomb lay inside the large orchard of olive and fruit trees they had owned for many generations. After the burial, Gorion recited the mourner's prayer, the Kaddish, which was composed in Aramaic.

> *May His great name be exalted and sanctified in the world which He created according to His will. May He establish His kingdom, may His salvation blossom and His anointed come near, during your lifetime and during your days, and during the lifetimes of all the House of Israel, speedily and soon. And let us say Amen!*

It was not really a prayer of grief and sorrow, but a reaffirmation of belief in the God of creation whose will must done on earth, an acceptance of pain and anguish, an expression of hope for ultimate salvation. This was the strength of Judaism, this looking forward to a future time of happiness and glory in the midst of sorrow and suffering.

Nikki wondered why all the most beautiful prayers like the *Kaddish* were in Aramaic such as the *Kol Nidre*, recited on the Day of Atonement. At the beginning of the Passover Seder, they chanted the song *Heh Lahma Anya*—this is the bread of affliction, while holding up the matza—the unleavened bread that the Jews baked hastily before they departed from Egypt. Perhaps it was because Aramaic was the language of the people, a language that could express greater intimacy and affection. It was the *lingua franca* of the region, the one in which different nations and peoples could communicate.

They returned to the house and began the seven days of mourning seated upon the ground for most of the day while visitors came to pay their condolences. Nikki could see how his father was agonised with grief, how much he had depended on Rachela for comfort and support. He also realised that Ruhama would never leave him, would try to keep up his spirits and help him in time to overcome his loss. If he hoped to marry her, he had to stay at home with her and his father.

He decided to remain in Jerusalem and resign his position as tutor in Rome. He would now devote himself entirely to composing the history of the Jewish people which would extend from the time of Ezra and the return to Zion up to the present day. There were the archives in the building near the Council House where he could find much of the material he needed, and there were many scholars among the Sanhedrin members he could consult.

At the end of the week, he sat with his father in his study and told him of his plans. He did not mention Ruhama at first, and only said that he had enough of Rome and wished from now onwards to make his home in Jerusalem. He offered to help him in dealing with the Sanhedrin, the Temple authorities, the Roman administration, and any legal matters that required arbitration or pacification.

Gorion was very glad to hear this, and Nikki could see that his father was heartened to have him by his side. He then told him about Ruhama, and said that they were in love with each other and wished to be married later, perhaps in the summer. Gorion looked at him with delight but also with astonishment.

"I always thought you did not like her, Nikki. You used to be so aggravated and angry with her when you were younger."

Nikki laughed ashamedly. "That was a long time ago, Father, when I was a callow young fool. I love her very much for herself and also for her loving care of mother during her long illness."

"You have made me doubly happy now. I will have my son and also my daughter with me. Your mother would also have been very happy."

When Ruhama came in later, Gorion opened his arms wide to hug her. His eyes shone with tears of joy and also of sorrow that Rachela was not there to see them now. They sat down, with Nikki and his father on either side of Ruhama, and made plans for the future. They would have the wedding in the summer and then go on a brief honeymoon trip to Alexandria and to Rome. Martha would stay at the house while they were away. In the meantime, Ruhama wanted to continue her medical studies at the Essene clinic nearby and Nicodemus would work with Gorion in the mornings and study at the archives in the afternoons for his historical project.

The situation in Jerusalem was slowly improving. There was less conflict among the different parties and with the Roman administration. Most of the unrest was in the Galilee under the rule of Herod Antipas who was regarded as being, like his father, too pro-Roman and in favour of Hellenism. His wife, the daughter of the Nabataean king Aretas, was a sore point as well among the Jews. But so long as Augustus was alive he would not dare do anything to aggravate the Galileans and end up like his brother Archelaus in exile.

****

114

A year later, when Hillel the Elder died, the whole city mourned his death. The old man had lived till he was 120 years old, the age of Moses when he died, the oldest age in popular belief that a person could reach. And like Moses, when he died, *his eye was not dim nor was his strength diminished*. His son, Simon, succeeded him as President of the Sanhedrin, but he was already nearly ninety, and was mostly unable to conduct the sessions, so Shammai, who was the Av Beth Din, the Chief Court Judge, became Acting President until Gamaliel, Simon's son, took over the leadership of the Sanhedrin.

Gamaliel, so highly honoured and respected that he was later called Rabban Gamaliel, held the reputation of being an unquestioned authority on religious law and ritual, and his advice was constantly sought on many other matters. Over the head of Shammai, with the majority of Hillelites in the Sanhedrin, he authored some legal ordinances on community welfare and the rights of women, arguing that women should be protected in divorce, and that if they wanted to remarry after the death of their husband, a single witness was sufficient to testify that her husband had died. He sent out three epistles on new religious rulings, one to the Jews in Galilee, the second to those in southern Judaea, and the third to the Jews of the Diaspora. He also instituted the intercalary month, the Second Adar, once every four years, in order to adjust the lunar calendar to the solar one.

In spite of his strict orthodoxy, he was tolerant of other religions and cultures. Gorion found it easy to discuss with him various matters arising out of religious conflicts and tensions in Jerusalem. He also consulted him about tensions between the Temple officials and the Roman administration that involved questions of Jewish law and ritual. A very delicate balance had to be maintained and Gamaliel proved to be an excellent partner in this endeavour.

Nicodemus also found it a great pleasure to talk to Rabban Gamaliel. He was a mine of information about Jewish history, and Nicodemus was especially interested in his knowledge about the *Knesset Hagedola*, the Men of the Great Assembly or Synagogue, that had preceded the Sanhedrin as the foremost religious authority. This was a synod of 120 scribes, sages and prophets whom Ezra the priest had gathered together to guide the people who returned to Jerusalem from their exile in Babylon. In fact, this assembly was often called 'Ezra and his Court of Law'.

This would be the first period of his history. The second period was from Simon the Just, the last of these men, to the time of the Hasmonean revolt against the Greeks. The third period was from that time to the present, a time when religious authority was passed down to succeeding pairs of master scholars, the Zugot, beginning with Antigonus of Socho. This was the chain of transmission of the Oral Law which in his own day continued with the pairing of Hillel and Shammai.

It would take him several years to complete the history, but he felt a need to do this. Some well-researched historical record of post-biblical times was necessary for the sake of posterity. He would begin with Ezra the Scribe who was regarded by some rabbis as a 'second' Moses. During the long period of the Babylonian captivity, many of the people had become assimilated into the culture of the country, even worshipping its gods. The small group of the Israelite nobility, the priesthood and members of its intellectual elite remained loyal to the faith of their forefathers and preserved the sacred scriptures that were meticulously copied by scribes and studied. Ezra was both priest and scribe and had a comprehensive knowledge of all the scriptures and of the laws of Moses.

When Cyrus the king of the Medes and Persians conquered Babylon, he encouraged the people of Judah to return to their land and rebuild the Temple.

The last two sentences in the Bible, at the end of the Second Book of Chronicles, records the declaration of Cyrus:

> *Thus says Cyrus King of Persia: All the kingdoms of the earth has the Lord God of heaven given me; and he has charged me to build him a house in Jerusalem which is in Judah. Who is there among you of all his people? The Lord his God be with him and let him go up.*

Cyrus gave them all the treasures of the Temple that the Babylonians had taken, and more that forty thousand people returned to Zion. The Temple was rebuilt but the people had little knowledge of the laws and rituals. So much had been forgotten. Ezra then decided to go to Jerusalem and instruct the people. He assembled them and made them swear once again to be faithful to the covenant with God.

****

Summer came round at last, and preparations for the wedding began. Gorion told Nikki that he could no longer mount the stairs with his stiff knees and wanted to refurnish the room next to his study on the ground floor as his bedroom. The entire second floor would be for Nikki and Ruhama. He arranged for a complete renovation of it to form a central living room facing east, a bedroom and bath on the south side, and a small study on the north side. A wide balcony would extend along the entire eastern side overlooking the Temple Mount.

By the time they returned from their honeymoon in Alexandria and Rome, the renovations were completed. The upper chamber remained untouched and was only for reading and discussions with some of the scholars he would invite for consultation. The study was where Nikki could to do his writing and where he could keep the copies he made from the archive documents. Ruhama said she wanted to build a small clinic at the end of the garden where she could prepare the herbal medicines and cures for distribution among the poorer families in the Lower City.

Gorion was happy when the twins, Jonathan and Joanna, were born a year later. It was a joy to see them grow and fill the house with their laughter and their boisterous play. The years now passed peacefully without much tension or revolt among the people. The procurator Marcus Ambivulus was soon replaced by Tineus Rufus. Augustus had apparently decided to send these men for only three or four years. From his experience, too long in a position of power would lead to corruption and exploitation.

Joseph came for a visit when the twins were four years old. His own grandchildren, Arius and Arianna, were a few years older and he wanted Marcus and Aurelia to bring them on a visit to Jerusalem to meet their young cousins. At the next festival of Succot, they finally came with Joseph to stay for two weeks at a house he had rented nearby. The children enjoyed eating in the large succah Gorion built in the garden, and they all went to the Temple to see the wonderful ceremony of the drawing of the water.

This was when the Levites go down to the Shiloah pool below the southern wall of the Temple, bring up jugs of water to be poured over the altar, and recite the prayer for abundant rainfall in the autumn and winter. They were always accompanied by joyous throngs of people singing and dancing all the way down and up again to the Temple. When they arrive at the altar, the trumpets are blown, and the people shout in response to the blessings of the priests. At night, fires are lit in the Temple courtyards, and people hold flaming torches while they danced and sang.

Gorion stood with Joseph and watched it all with delight. "There is a saying that he who has not seen the water-drawing ceremony has never seen joy in his life."

"And there is another saying," countered Joseph, "that he who has not seen Jerusalem and its splendour and the Temple in its glory, has never seen beauty in his life."

He hoped this period of peace and harmony would last for a long while. But he was beginning to have fears about what would happen after Augustus died. Everyone had assumed that his heir would be Marcus Agrippa who married Julia, the daughter of Augustus. When Marcus Agrippa died, Augustus adopted Gaius and Lucius, the two sons of Agrippa and Julia, as his heirs. But later on, during their military service abroad, Lucius died of an illness in Massilia, and two years later Gaius suffered the same fate in Lycia. The rumour was that Livia, the wife of Augustus, had had them poisoned to ensure the succession of her son, Tiberius, from her previous marriage to Tiberius Claudius Nero.

Tiberius has started out brilliantly, marching east with Marcus Agrippa to Armenia which was then under Parthian influence and returning with the standards of the legions that had been lost to them. He married Vipsania, Agrippa's daughter, whom he loved very dearly. He was then sent with his brother Drusus on campaigns in the west and achieved many victories and celebrated his triumph for his campaigns in Germania. Although he continued with his successful military campaigns and was elected consul twice, he decided suddenly, at the age of thirty-six, to withdraw from politics and to retire to Rhodes, perhaps angry at the adoption of Gaius and Lucius as the heirs of Augustus.

After the death of his beloved grandsons, Augustus confirmed Tiberius as his heir, but forced him to divorce his beloved wife Vipsania, Agrippa's daughter, and marry Agrippa's widow Julia, the only daughter of Augustus. It was not a happy marriage. Tiberius was also deeply saddened when his brother Drusus died after falling from his horse during a campaign in Germany. Drusus had married Antonia Minor, the younger daughter of Mark Antony and of Octavia, sister of Augustus. The sons of Drusus, Germanicus and Claudius, were adopted by Tiberius after the death of his brother and were brought up with his own son Drusus.

A year later, while Joseph was in Britannia, he heard that Augustus had died and Tiberius was the new emperor in Rome. He feared that anti-Jewish sentiments in Rome were bound to rise very soon because of the many conversions to Judaism among the wealthy matrons of the city. After forty years of peace and stability under this great emperor, nothing would be the same again. He was doubtful whether Tiberius would rule as well as his stepfather. Tiberius was now in his fifties, of a gloomy disposition and given to long periods depression and fits of anger. He was well known for his aversion to Jewish religious practices and had more than once arbitrarily expelled some Jewish merchants who had been trying to gain a foothold in the city.

Joseph realised that he would have to warn his son Marcus in good time before new measures were adopted against the Jews of Rome. Perhaps Marcus should transfer all the business to his partner Gaius and remove his name from the company register. Marcus and his family could return to live in Ramatayim, their ancestral home and bring up his children in the traditional Jewish manner. He felt now that it was time for him to retire from his many business ventures and live from now onwards on his family estate in his own country.

The Senate confirmed the position of Tiberius as Princeps as it had done for Augustus. Tiberius assumed the administrative and political powers of Princeps but refused at first to bear the titles of Pater Patriae, Imperator and Augustus, and declined to wear the civic crown and laurels. He allowed the Senate to act without his orders, and whenever he gave them they were usually only vague suggestions.

Coins were struck to mark his accession to imperial rule and the Senate rejected his half-hearted proposal to restore the Republic. When the Senate wished to name a month after him as they had done for Julius Caesar and for Augustus, he drily asked what they would do when there were thirteen Caesars. He supported a return of Roman society to the traditional public morals, the *mos maiorum*, and deplored the vulgar degeneration of the aristocracy. He checked extravagance and told provincial governors who were always trying to collect more revenue that "a good shepherd sheared his sheep but did not fleece it." His mother, Livia, took advantage of his reluctance to rule more strongly by taking charge over many of the important decisions that had to be made.

****

Chapter 2 (14–26 CE)

It was late August, sometime after the death of Augustus, when Gorion first heard of pending trouble. The High Priest Ananus ben Seth asked him to come to an urgent meeting at the Temple. He went out with Nicodemus who was on his way to the archives building near the Xystus, and told him about his fears for the future.

"The old order is changing, my son, and not for the better."

They walked slowly along the road leading through the Upper City towards the Hasmonean Palace. It was early in the morning and the air was still cool before the midday heat.

"History shows that change is inevitable" Nikki said, "but we must try not to repeat the mistakes of the past."

"Still, history often repeats itself, Nikki, as you may well have noticed in your studies."

Gorion was now nearly eighty and feeling his years. He no longer attended sessions of the Great Sanhedrin which now met very rarely. Although it continued to act as a supreme court for capital crimes, most civil and legal matters were now debated and decided by the smaller Sanhedrin court in the Council House building near the southern entrance to the Temple. The High Priest also presided over a court for sacred and ritual matters at his residence in the Upper City. But Gorion did not choose to be involved in these courts and had long since resigned from the magistrates court in the Council House.

Once past the Hasmonean Palace Nikki entered the archives building while Gorion continued along the royal bridge spanning the valley from the Upper City to the Temple Mount. Descending a sloping corridor that led towards the suite of the High Priest, he found a large group of priests and elders gathered near the doorway.

Ananus was standing on a dais within the reception room, but when he saw Gorion entering he hurried forward to meet him.

"I have been waiting to see you, my friend. Thank you for coming at my urgent request."

"What is the matter Ananus? Why do you have this large gathering here?"

Ananus drew him inside and mounted the dais again. He extended his arms for silence as all those in the doorway entered and filled the room.

"Let me welcome you to this meeting, Temple priests, elders, honoured guests. I have served as High Priest for over seven years since the banishment of Archelaus and the evil house of Boethus with him. Gone is the corruption of the Herodian court and of the pagan influences introduced into our traditional way of life. We had the support and approval of the late emperor Augustus in restoring the rightful line of the priesthood. But now that he is gone, a new prefect, Valerius Gratus, has been sent to Jerusalem. There is a new policy in Rome. Prefects in Judaea will now serve for a longer, ten year period, and the prefect is the one who controls the high priesthood and selects the person of his choice. I was informed by him that Ishmael ben Phiabi, will replace me as High Priest."

Cries of anger and disapproval came from all around him. Gorion was shocked but stood silent in front of Ananus. When the room became silent again, Ananus beckoned to him to come up to the dais.

"You all know Hananel Gorion, the esteemed and long-serving magistrate of Jerusalem. I have invited him here today to consult with us as to the best way to counter this decision. This upstart, Ishmael ben Phiabi, or Fabus as he now calls himself, was chosen by Gratus because he is a willing puppet of the Roman authorities. He is young, handsome and enjoys a life of pleasure and luxury. The high priesthood is only a means to his greater influence and wealth. This is scandalous. He should not be allowed to wear the sacred robes of a High Priest."

He then appealed to Gorion, as Chief Councillor, to bring this matter to the Governor of Syria and explain the need to countermand the decision of the prefect. Gorion looked down at the faces raised to him. He knew so many of them, and had worked for years on their behalf. But he could not think of any way he could help them.

"Ananus, and you my dear friends and colleagues! There are times when we must bow before unfortunate events and wait for divine deliverance from them. Any appeal against the new prefect and his choice for the high priesthood will only lead to a worse fate. From my experience, it will be better to show compliance at first, and to work against Ishmael and expose him for what he is to the government in Rome. He will not last long in this high position, I can assure you."

There were murmurs of dissent and some spoke of public protests and demonstrations. But after a prolonged debate, wiser heads finally agreed with Gorion. When all those present began to depart, he remained with Ananus for another hour to advise him on what should be done. First, a complete inventory of the Temple funds and treasures should be made, a list of all the priests and laymen working in the Temple and their various functions had to be drawn up. And then a full account of the annual expenditure for the Temple sacrifices, rites and ceremonies.

"I already have everything on record here," said Ananus. "My son Eleazar has been keeping my accounts and I trained him well to follow me in my position as High Priest when I eventually retire. There is also my son-in-law Joseph Bar Caiaphas who has helped me with the Temple administration."

Ananus brought out the scrolls and documents with copies he had made for submission to the authorities.

"Good, excellent. Give me a copy and I will see that they are transmitted to Rome through my cousin Joseph of Arimathea who has connections with the emperor's court. They will be impressed by your good management for the past eight years and realise that your replacement was unjustified. In a year or two, you and your family will be back here again. Rome always appreciates good government and administration."

As Gorion left the Temple to return home, he was surprised to find Johanan ben Zakkai waiting outside.

"I wanted to talk to you about the Sanhedrin, Gorion. We are also having some trouble there."

"I thought Gamaliel, Hillel's grandson, is now actively in control of the Hillelite faction in the Sanhedrin. The School of Hillel his grandfather has prevailed over the Shammaites in nearly every matter, and it is still the dominant faction, even though Shammai is now the acting head of the Sanhedrin."

"It is not the Shammaites I am worried about. There is a new group demanding representation in the Sanhedrin, the Zealots. Some of them have received ordination as rabbis by followers of Shammai and are causing great dissension among the elders."

"But Judas the Galilean was suppressed or exiled. We have not heard of him or the Zealots for the past few years."

"It is his sons, Jacob and Simon who are now active in the Galilee and have a large following there. Most of them are brigands, a boorish lot, with little learning but a fierce spirit of national zeal and hatred of the Romans. Some of them have educated themselves at the small Torah centres in the Galilee and serve as rabbis in the local synagogues. Now they want to become members of the Sanhedrin."

"Legally, I would say they have the right. But the Sanhedrin can bar them on certain grounds, such as not complying with the halachic ruling of *dina malchuta dina*, the obligatory acceptance of the law of the land, and to keeping the peace."

"The Shammai faction is mostly supportive of them and its members sympathise with their aims. If we overrule them, they will become antagonistic and disruptive in our sessions."

"I don't know what to tell you, Johanan. You will find more and more of such people in the coming days with extremist views. The times are worsening."

"The times of my old master Hillel are over, I know. But I hope Rabban Gamaliel will prevail in the end. I will leave you now since we are nearing your home."

He turned away and retraced his steps while Gorion went on towards his home. It was nearly noon and he felt hot and tired. Ruhama would be waiting there with the children to have their midday meal together. Afterwards he would take a nap and then write to Joseph in Rome, enclosing the scrolls and documents from the Temple with his letter in a protective satchel. He decided to have Johanan deliver it to him personally. That young and learned scholar would benefit from a visit to Rome.

****

Nazareth was a small town perched on a mountain ridge, surrounded by the verdant hills and valleys of the Lower Galilee dotted with villages and farmland. The houses on the terraced slopes were built of stone and were surrounded by trees and orchards. Below, in the valleys, there were rich fields of wheat and barley, and sheep grazed on the hillsides around the town.

Josiah had built his home and his large carpentry workshop in the valley near the ancient well. It was also near the road that led northward to Sepphoris and from there eastward to the Sea of Galilee. He and his four sons, James, Jose, Jude and Simon, were known for their good carpentry work commissioned by the rich residents of Sepphoris. During his absence in Egypt, his sons expanded their woodwork enterprise to the towns around the Sea of Galilee, to Capernaum, Magdala, Bethsaida and many others. James, the eldest, remained in Nazareth, while his brothers travelled back and forth to these towns. They had even set up a workshop at Capernaum to build boats for the fishermen.

When Maryam and Jeshua returned to Nazareth, Josiah had already retired from work. He spent much of his time teaching Jeshua, while James began training him in carpentry work. There was a close rapport between him and the boy, and he encouraged him in his clever decorative furniture carvings. But he could see that Jeshua was restless, often straying from the workshop to the hillsides around it.

Maryam was also worried about Jeshua. He was now almost eighteen. Although he was willing and obedient to the wishes of his father and brother, his mind seemed to be elsewhere. He was often silent during his work and at meals, and could sit for hours in the evenings lying on the grass and dreaming. She knew these were his teenage years, the time when the boy was growing into a man, and wondered what he would choose to become.

His brothers often teased him for his shyness, for his fair looks and long hair which remained uncut since childhood. He smiled at them affectionately and was not offended. He knew they loved him and also his mother who took such good care of them and their father. But sometimes they were angry at him for wandering off from the workshop without a word.

"Where do you go, Jeshua?" Jude asked him one day. "You just disappear in the middle of your work and are gone for hours."

"He always comes back and finishes the job very well," said James in his defence.

"Still, he can at least tell us where he was going so we need not have to worry about him."

Jeshua hesitated, and then said: "I usually go to see an old man I met on the other side of the hill. We go for a long walk towards the village of Cana where he lives and then I come back."

"Who is this old man?" asked Josiah.

"I don't know, Father. He talks in Greek like the Egyptians in Alexandria and he lives in Cana. But he goes out every morning for long walks in the hills around. He invited me to his home but I did not go."

"You must not go there, my son. And you should stop meeting him."

"He is very well-mannered and learned. He told me many interesting things about Egypt and the Pharaohs before the time of Moses. Did you know there was a Pharaoh who did not worship idols but believed in only one God?"

Josiah stared at him in disbelief. But Jeshua was animated, and his eyes were bright with certainty and conviction. He told them that this Pharaoh, called Akhenaton, had closed all the temples in Thebes and dismissed the priests. He then built a new city further south in Amarna to worship a god he called Aten who appears as the sun in the heavens. He wrote some hymns to this god which were inscribed in the temple he built. Jeshua then recited the lines:

How manifold it is, what thou hast made!
They are hidden from the face (of man).
O sole god, like whom there is no other!
Thou didst create the world according to thy desire,
Whilst thou wert alone: All men, cattle, and wild beasts,
Whatever is on earth, going upon (its) feet
And what is on high, flying with its wings ...

"Isn't this like our Psalms, Father? Such beautiful lines ...Perhaps Moses knew them when he was at Pharaoh's court. But the old man said that by that time the Egyptians had gone back to worshipping idols."

Josiah was angry. "I don't want you to fill your head with Egyptian beliefs. It is good you left Egypt while you were still young. I forbid you to see this old man anymore."

Jeshua was silent and went outside. He could not understand what he had done wrong. What harm was there in meeting other people and hearing about their beliefs and the stories they could tell.

He decided to walk eastward towards Mount Tabor. It was a steep mountain but he would try to climb it. From the top, he would be able to see the whole of the Galilee. A week later, against his father's wishes, he set out early morning on the long walk of about twelve miles to reach the mountain before nightfall. He would climb it the next day and rest in the lodge other climbers had built on the mountain top.

Mount Tabor was where the Israelites had won the battle against the Canaanite King of Hazor, Jabin and his general Sisera. It was Deborah the Prophetess who organised the battle under Barak and the tribes of Naphtali and

Zevulun. What a great judge and leader of the people she must have been! And her song of victory was inspiring:

> In the days of Shamgar son of Anath,
> in the days of Jael, the highways were abandoned;
> travellers took to winding paths.
> Villagers in Israel would not fight;
> they held back until I, Deborah, arose,
> until I arose, a mother in Israel.

From there, he went towards the Sea of Galilee and wanted to stay for a while with his brothers at Capernaum. He could work with them on the fishing boats they were building and go sailing on the beautiful lake. They called it the Kinneret, because it was shaped like a harp, a *kinor*. His brothers would welcome him and would be glad to have him work with them. He would meet new people there, and visit the towns around the lake. And perhaps even cross over to the other side of it to see that city built on a mountain top that shone in the early morning light.

****

Valerius Gratus was infuriated. He had spent the past few years struggling with the difficult task of governing Judaea and Jerusalem and was frustrated at every turn. First there was the resentment at his appointment of Ishmael ben Fabus as High Priest. The man was young and handsome, an ideal figure to preside over the Temple and its holy rites. He was urbane, educated, well-mannered and gracious towards all, especially towards the Roman authorities. Yet the people resented him, the priests did not cooperate with him, and he had decided to resign the office after serving for only two years.

There seemed no other way but to reappoint Ananus, but he decided instead to appoint his son Eleazar who was younger and perhaps more malleable. It was disappointing to find that this young man was even more difficult to manage than his father. So he deposed him after two years, and appointed Simon, the son of Camithus. Again the people began complaining about this choice, so he went back to the family of Ananus and chose Joseph Bar Caiaphas, the son-in-law of Ananus ben Seth. It was maddening that he could not seem to please anyone by

126

his choice. In fact, he felt the people were becoming hostile. He was constantly being accused of corruption and of harsh government. The other day, as he was driving past a house where repairs were being made to the roof, a tile fell down on his head and nearly killed him. He was sure it was not an accident, but could not prove it.

The news from Rome was that Tiberius was also having trouble with the Jews. Too many women of patrician families were being attracted to Judaism and some had even converted openly. There was an edict against Jews who engaged in conversion and some of them had been expelled from Rome. No new grants of citizenship were made for Jewish merchants and traders wanting to reside in the city. They were an enterprising people, going out to many of the Roman provinces throughout the Empire, especially in the west, in Gaul and in Spain.

There were Jews in nearly every port of the Mediterranean, and of course the large Jewish community in Alexandria. That was another problem for him, as there was also a sizable community of Alexandrian Jews in Jerusalem with great influence among the people and highly honoured for their contributions to the Temple. He had to show deference to them and to the wealthy families in the Upper City because he needed them as buffers between him and the people. Whenever there was a sign of trouble they could always find some way to calm the situation.

The main problem for Gratus was the pilgrimage festivals when the city was filled with people from all over the country, most of them from the Galilee. These were the worst of the lot, rowdy, demanding, fiercely resentful of the soldiers he sent to keep them in order. He had to line the streets with his men and keep them posted at the city gates, on walls and on rooftops. A reserve force was always on guard in the Antonia Fortress overlooking the Temple in case of riots. So far he had not had any serious trouble with them.

He found that the magistrate Gorion was a useful adviser on matters concerning the Sanhedrin and the Temple. His son, Nicodemus, was also an intelligent and friendly person, easy to talk to and helpful with administrative problems. He had also met with Joseph, Gorion's cousin, when he came on occasional visits to Jerusalem and heard that he was planning to buy one of the luxurious houses in the Upper City as a second home. More people like them should be encouraged to settle in Jerusalem.

Rome had informed him of the death of Archelaus in Vienne, but it did not seem of any interest to the Judaeans after all this time. Antipas, the tetrarch in Galilee, was also unmoved at the news, since there was no love lost between the brothers. Both had been the sons of Herod from his Samaritan fourth wife Malthace. Antipas would continue to maintain the extensive Herodian estate in Vienne, in the Rhone valley, a gift to Herod from Augustus. Founded as a Roman colony during the time of Julius Caesar, Vienne had turned into a major urban centre and trading axis. Many Jewish merchants had settled in it as well and had made a fortune from the business opportunities there. After his term of duty in Judaea in about six or seven years, he hoped he would be given a house and land in Vienne as former prefects had received for their services.

****

Joseph made up his mind to retire from all his business enterprises in the west. He would go back to Ramatayim but would spend most of his time in his new home in Jerusalem and resume his charitable activities there for the improvement of the city and its population. Rufus agreed to take over the Cornwall mining enterprise and trade with Britannia. He told Rufus of his fears about Tiberius and his antagonism towards the Jewish population in Rome and that this might affect Marcus as well.

The first sign of danger was a scandalous report about a gang of Jewish embezzlers who solicited large gifts of money, presumably for the Temple, from a prominent matron in Roman society who had converted to Judaism. Tiberius was so enraged that he brought this matter and other such scandals before the Senate. It was only a matter of time before the Jews of Rome would be put under severe restrictions or even expelled. There was no time to be lost.

Joseph persuaded Marcus to leave everything to Gaius and dissolve their partnership immediately. He and Aurelia could return to Ramatayim with their two children, and make it their home. He knew that Aurelia would not be happy to leave Rome, and the children would also find it hard to adapt to a different kind of life in Judaea. Arius was now nearly fourteen and Arianna twelve. But they would enjoy all the comforts and luxuries they were used to in Rome and also learn a little about their Jewish heritage.

Once they began their preparations to leave, Joseph sailed to Judaea to make the house in Ramatayim ready for them and then travelled to Jerusalem to see about his new home there. His unexpected arrival at Gorion's house surprised and delighted the family and he was warmly welcomed.

"I was expecting you only after your new home was renovated," Gorion said.

"You have not heard the latest news from Rome yet, about the threat of expulsion for the Jews of Rome?"

"What expulsion? How did this happen?"

Gorion was aghast when Joseph told him all he knew so far. Nikki said that he had heard some rumours about it but thought they were false. A few days later a full report of the decision of the Senate was sent from Caesarea to Gratus. Joseph obtained a copy of this and brought it to show Gorion and Nikki.

"It says that there is a large number of Alexandrian Jews residing in Rome who will be sent back to their country. Most of the Jews in Rome are redeemed prisoners who had eventually gained Roman citizenship. Tiberius will conscript 4000 young men of military age to be sent to Sardinia to guard against the bandits harassing the Roman population. Temporary Jewish residents in Rome, the *peregrini*, will be sent away, and the rest will be allowed to stay only if they renounce their Judaism. Since only a handful will accept this condition, there will be a general exodus, many of them going to various Mediterranean ports and a few back to Judaea."

"The man is mad," said Gorion. "It will only harm the economy in Rome. The Jews can survive anywhere and will always land on their feet. Mark my words, Rome will beg them to return one day."

"That may be," Joseph agreed. "But if they do, they will have to avoid further attempts to convert people to Judaism. This is not the first time Jews were expelled from Rome. According to a historical account written by Valerius Maximus, Jews and also star-gazing Chaldeans were banished from Rome and from the entire country about a hundred and fifty years ago for their corrupt values and false beliefs."

"Romans are seeking a more meaningful faith than the worship of their gods," Gorion remarked. "The time has passed for such pagan beliefs."

"You know what Habakkuk prophesied," Nikki reminded his father. "*For the earth shall be filled with the knowledge of the glory of God, as the waters cover the sea.*"

"That will only be at the end of time," Gorion told him. "It will certainly not happen in our days!"

Joseph nodded and then began to tell them of what he was planning to do in Jerusalem now that he had been forced to leave Rome. All the large funds he had accumulated from his various business enterprises in the west would be invested in building up the northern part of Jerusalem, in the broad new area of Bezetha beyond the second wall. There were a few buildings there occupied by commercial and transport agencies and hardly any residences. He wanted to build stone houses with central courtyards to serve as inns and hostels for those coming on pilgrimage to Jerusalem or for traders from the east. They would pay a nominal sum for their stay to cover the maintenance and upkeep of the buildings. This would relieve the situation in the Lower City during the festivals when the crowds overflowed into the streets and the congestion led not only to quarrels and even violence, but was also unhealthy.

"That is a tremendous enterprise, Joseph, and a very costly one," Gorion protested.

"But it is a very necessary one. I believe I am the only one who can afford to do it."

"Ruhama has been telling me about how crowded the Lower City is even during normal periods. She has been working there among the poorer people to give them medical care and remedies for illness."

"I think I will also install a bathhouse, a medical centre, and of course a good sanitation system in the new area."

"You will need a lot of people to manage these buildings properly."

"Yes, I have thought of that. I will offer managers free housing and let them open a food and shopping centre for the residents which will give them a steady income."

He unrolled a sketch of his building plans, and Nikki found it very interesting. He asked Joseph about the water supply to the area and to Jerusalem in general.

"About three miles southwest of Bethlehem there are three large reservoirs called Solomon's Pools hewn into the bedrock and fed by two aqueducts from several springs and by rainwater flowing down from the hills. The area south of Jerusalem is higher than the city and two aqueducts convey the water to it, the high level one goes to the Upper City here, and the low level one to the Temple Mount. A third aqueduct was also built to convey water to Herodium."

"Yes, I noticed the one to the Temple Mount goes across the valley over the royal bridge," said Nikki. "But Jerusalem will soon need much more water than it has now. All we have here is the Gihon spring."

"Well, more water from other collection pools further south could be brought to Solomon's Pools by building a longer aqueduct conveying water to them. But it would be a very expensive project. In Rome, several aqueducts have been built at various times to supply the city and there is always need for more of them."

Gorion asked Joseph about his trading enterprises in Judaea and Samaria, and whether he would resume control over them.

"No, I left them to a local partner who gives me a percentage of his profits. But Marcus and I have plans to begin trading with eastern countries, with Babylonia, Persia, even India. So far the trade ties have been monopolised by the Nabataeans and the Arabs, but I think we can exploit more possibilities than they have done up to now."

They went into the dining room for the midday meal with Ruhama and the twins, Jonathan and Joanna. Joseph had brought some presents for them as well as for their parents and randfather. The children were now ten years old, a few years younger than his grandchildren. He hoped they would be seeing more of each other at festival times when Marcus and Aurelia would be in Jerusalem. It was good they were all going to be home again.

****

James went to Capernaum to bring his brothers home to Nazareth. Josiah was ill and Maryam said that there was little chance of his recovery. He found them at the sea shore frying fish over a makeshift fire and laughing at a story Jeshua was telling them. He stood in the shadows for a moment to listen to what he was saying.

"And so I made a bet with that fisherman that I could walk on the water, and he challenged me. He took me out on his boat and told me to walk back to the shore. I took two long pieces of flat wood lying on the bottom of the boat, those the fishermen keep in case the boat leaks, and bound them tightly to my feet. I held a rope tied to a fishing boat and then just skimmed and skated along the surface of the waves behind the boat till I reached the shore."

"It's a miracle you did not drown," said James coming into the circle of light.

131

There was a general shout and outcry of welcome and a lot of back slapping. And then a flood of questions were asked till they noticed that James was struggling with his tears.

"It is Father," he finally whispered. "You have to come home with me at once. There is not much time left for him."

It took nearly the whole night and the following morning before they were back in Nazareth. Josiah was lying in bed and Maryam sat by his side. He smiled at them and lifted a weak hand in greeting, but could hardly speak. They knelt at his bedside for a long while, talking to him about their journey, about Capernaum, about their work and the people there. Then Maryam said Josiah should rest and called them to have their evening meal.

Later, before she came to put out the light and let him sleep, Josiah took her hand and asked her to stay for a moment. He had one last favour to ask now that he knew his end was coming. He had never asked her before who was Jeshua's father, and she need not answer if she did not want to tell him. But he would like to know who he was.

"Josiah, you are Jeshua's real father, the one who always loved and cared for him."

"I love the boy and his good and gentle heart, so much like yours. But I still want to know …," he said, and then his voice failed him.

Maryam quietly told him about Alexander and how it all had happened so many years ago.

"A Hasmonean prince, a royal prince, and growing up in my house, as my son," Josiah said, his eyes alight with wonder and delight. And then it clouded over with fear, and he said she must never reveal this to Jeshua or anyone else. There was still that evil Herodian, Antipas, who might want to kill him if he knew. She told him that only Joseph and Gorion knew the truth about Jeshua, and also her cousin Elizabeth and Zacharias. So the secret was safe.

She remained with him until he fell asleep and then retired to her bed. Three days went by, with each of his sons staying by the bedside in turn while Josiah lay with his eyes half-closed in semi-consciousness, until he quietly passed away. They sat in mourning for a week and at the end Joseph arrived in answer to the message Maryam had sent him.

She cried then after not being able to cry for over a week. She knew she could no longer stay in Nazareth. The boys were grown men by now and would soon find wives for themselves. She wanted to return to Jerusalem, to stay once more with Elizabeth and Zacharias who were now old and would be glad to have her with them. But she was not sure whether Jeshua would want to go with her or stay with his brothers.

"He should come back to Jerusalem and stay with you for a while. And then he can stay with me in my new house in Jerusalem. I will take care of him like a son and give him every opportunity to do whatever he wishes to do. He can live like the prince that he really is."

"You know, when Josiah was dying and asked about Jeshua, I told him the truth about his birth. But he said I should not tell Jeshua or anyone else."

"He was right of course," he told her. "But one day he might ask you about it. He certainly knows that Josiah is not his real father, however much he loves him."

After Joseph left, Maryam made preparations to leave and spoke to James about her plans. He told her that the house in Nazareth would be sold and the carpentry workshop closed. His brothers decided to move the entire woodcraft business to Capernaum and he himself wanted to go to Emmaus where his mother's family lived. It was on the road from Joppa to Jerusalem and they had an inn there for travellers. He would help to manage the inn since his uncle was getting too old to run it well.

Maryam, Jeshua and James travelled together to Jerusalem and then James went on to Emmaus. After selling their home and closing the workshop, Jose, Jude and Simon took all the furniture and the carpentry tools with them to Capernaum. It was a painful goodbye for them all but they hoped to meet again in Jerusalem during festival visits.

****

Herod Antipas was in his element. He was glad at the news that his hated brother, Archelaus, had died at last. He had been cheated out of his inheritance by him and left with only the Galilee and Peraea, but it proved to have been for the best. Judaea was almost impossible to rule with the Temple priests and the Sanhedrin interfering with political decisions and measures. There was also the constant friction with the Samaritans in the north and with the Greek population around them. Here in the Galilee he had the people under full control in spite of their tendency to revolt at the least provocation. It was like riding a restive horse, challenging but with the satisfaction of curbing it completely.

Now that Tiberius was emperor, all he had to do was to get into his good graces. He would do what his father had done with Augustus. Build a city in his honour and name it for him. He would build it on the western shore of the Sea of Galilee, and model it after the other Greek cities and fill his palace with Greek statues. To populate the city, he would compel Galileans to settle there, building them good houses at his own expense and giving them land in the surrounding area. Religious Jews were reluctant to reside there because the city was built over a large burial site which made it impure for residence. To fill out the numbers, he invited wealthy Greeks and other non-Jews to build luxurious villas and mansions along the main street that led from his grand palace on the hill down to the lakeshore.

Tiberias, built in honour of Tiberius, was completed in the sixth year of the emperor's reign. People came from afar to admire the gleaming white city with its broad paved avenues sloping down the mountain side towards the sea, the luxurious villas, the palace overlooking it from above, the thermal baths near the hot springs south of it, and the sports stadium near the shore.

The dedication of the city was a grand occasion, attended by Drusus, the son and heir of Tiberius, accompanied by Herod Agrippa the son of Aristobulus, who was raised in Rome at the imperial court with his brothers and sisters. Also attending the dedication were his half-brother, Philip the Tetrarch, who had built a city in honour of Augustus near Paneas, at the foot of Mount Hermon and called it Caesarea Philippi. The brothers were not very friendly with each other, but kept up a formal, polite relationship.

The only shadow over the dedication was the death a year earlier of Germanicus, the son of Tiberius' brother Drusus. Much loved by the people, and praised for his successful campaigns in Germany, he became famous for having avenged the defeat of the Roman legions under Varus at the Battle of the Teutoburg Forest six years earlier and for retrieving two of the three legionary eagles that were lost to the enemy. As he lay dying, Germanicus accused his legate Piso, the Governor of Syria, of having poisoned him in Antioch. Piso was an arrogant man with a violent temper, and after a bitter quarrel over his disobedience, Germanicus had ordered his recall to Rome.

After the death of Germanicus, Piso made an armed attempt to regain his control over Syria. Popular outrage against him forced Tiberius to bring him to trial, but to avoid his conviction Piso committed suicide. There were rumours that Tiberius had been behind Piso's actions for fear that his nephew Germanicus would become emperor instead of his own son Drusus. He could discount his other nephew, Claudius, who was a scholar and a social misfit because of his stuttering.

Antipas was eager to curry favour with the emperor by serving as an intermediary between Rome and the rulers of eastern states under Roman domination or patronage, inviting many of them to visit him at his palace in Tiberias. He saw himself as following the path of Herod his father in allying himself more closely with the emperor and the imperial court. He was often in Rome, entertaining and being entertained by the members of the court. But the people of the Galilee hated him for his harsh cruelty and exploitation of them and for his licentious, pagan style of living.

Most of the Galileans were farmers or workers in house building, road construction, quarrying, among many other occupations. Many were employed by the rich estate owners in the fertile Jezreel Valley. Others gradually improved their living conditions by becoming stewards of these estates and tax farmers for the government. The people were heavily taxed and were kept under tight control by the authorities and by the Roman auxiliary units in the area.

The sons of Josiah in Capernaum were becoming prosperous, with many commissions for woodwork from Tiberias and other cities in the Galilee. They were highly praised for their excellent craftsmanship and for the decorative furniture they produced for the palace and the villas of rich estate owners. There were also more orders for large boats to carry supplies to the city from the towns and farms around the sea. The three brothers built a synagogue of basalt stone in Capernaum in memory of their father and inscribed his name over the doorway. They were now married and well established in the town and had built fine houses for themselves.

****

Maryam and Jeshua arrived in Ein Karem accompanied by Joseph, much to the delight of Elizabeth and Zacharias who had both grown old but were still fairly active. Their son Johanan was no longer with them. Against his father's wishes, he left to join the small exiled community of Zadokite priests living on the shores of the Dead Sea north of Ein Gedi.

Zacharias was happy to see Jeshua, only a few months younger than Johanan, and to see how he had grown. He was tall, sturdy, blue-eyed, and with long fair hair curled over his shoulders. Zacharias liked his gentle, gracious manner, the melodious Aramaic that he preferred to speak, although he knew Hebrew well enough. He looked so much like his father now that he was nearly the same age as Alexander had been at the time of his execution twenty-seven years ago.

Joseph said that he would leave Jeshua for a few weeks in Ein Karem, but would return to bring him back to Jerusalem where he would care for him like a son. He would have all the advantages that wealth and connections could give him. He also thought that it was time to tell him who he was, a Hasmonean prince. Zacharias disagreed, thinking that the danger had not yet passed so long as the Herodians still had some power, especially Antipas in the Galilee who was now trying to match his father Herod in his ambitious building projects and close relations with the imperial family in Rome.

"One day the Hasmoneans will rule again, Joseph," Zacharias told him. "Look at Herod Agrippa in Rome with his close ties to Tiberius and his son Drusus. Perhaps he will succeed Antipas his uncle in the Galilee."

"That young man has no such ambition. He prefers his high and extravagant life in Rome as a favourite in the imperial court. Why should he trouble himself with ruling over a land with so many contentious people to control?"

"Well, you know best I suppose with your experience of Roman life. The Hasmoneans may have had their day. My son Johanan has no love for them or for the Herodians since they have exiled the true priesthood of Zadok to Egypt, and left only a small remnant in the desert of Judaea. He has now joined them and is living the hard life of a hermit."

Joseph took his leave in the evening to get to Jerusalem before nightfall. Maryam thanked him for all he had done for her and for what he promised to do for Jeshua. She hesitated about letting her son know who his real father was, but said that when Joseph thought the time was right he could do so. She still wore Alexander's signet ring on a chain around her neck and kept his royal blue cloak wrapped in a silken bag in her clothes chest. She had worn it only once, during the journey to Bethlehem after Herod's death.

Joseph had left one of the carriage horses for Jeshua so that he could go for rides around the countryside. He spent several hours a day on horseback, going further afield every day to explore the surrounding villages. One day he decided to ride as far as Emmaus to visit James and return the next day. He took some gifts of fruit and a woollen coat Maryam had knitted for him but which he wanted to give James instead. He would soon have to wear the more elegant clothes that Joseph intended to buy for him when he went to Jerusalem.

Emmaus was now a thriving town and an important crossroads, with houses owned by wealthy landowners in the area. It was also the historic site of the famous battle that Judah the Maccabee had fought against the Seleucids about a century and a half ago. Twenty-five years earlier, soon after Herod's death, pro-Hasmonean rebels fortified themselves in the town and tried to prevent Varus from reaching Jerusalem to quell the rebellion against the succession of Archelaus as Herod's heir. Although the town was totally burnt and destroyed, it was quickly rebuilt and soon became an administrative centre under Roman rule.

James was living in the house of his elderly uncle and aunt and had taken over management of the large inn on the road from Joppa to Jerusalem. He was glad to see Jeshua again and to hear that he would soon be living in Jerusalem with Joseph in the Upper City. He wanted to know what the connection was between Joseph and Maryam.

"She told me that when she was very young, her uncle Zacharias had arranged for her betrothal to Joseph's son Marcus."

"So, what happened to prevent this betrothal?"

"Zacharias told me that he had sent my mother to serve as one of the Temple virgins. But that some priests who did not like him for his Zadokite origins began to accuse her of immoral behaviour. As the daughter of a Cohen, a priest, this could bring a charge of capital punishment by stoning, although they no longer have the power to carry out such measures."

"Did Joseph cancel the betrothal because of this?"

"He only wanted to postpone it until my mother was cleared of any suspicion," Jeshua said. "But Uncle Zacharias decided to have her married to your father, Josiah, and send her away to Egypt. He knew these hostile priests would soon demand to put her on trial."

James looked at him for a while, and then said very quietly.

"My father cannot have been your real father, Jeshua. You do not look like any of us in the family. You have your mother's fair looks and blue eyes, but you also have something else that makes you very different from us."

"Are you saying I am a bastard?" Jeshua shouted at him. "That my mother was a whore?"

"I never meant to say such a thing, Jeshua. Your mother is a good and pious woman and was a faithful wife for my father. All I am saying is that she must have been married to someone else before, someone who had died or been killed."

"Why did she not tell me? Why was it kept a secret?"

"It may have been for political reasons. I don't know, Jeshua. You must ask your mother or Joseph."

"Then we are not really brothers?" His eyes filled with tears and his voice broke.

"We will always be brothers, Jeshua. I love you more than any brother could, and all my brothers love you as well."

Jeshua spent the night in Emmaus tossing and turning, unable to sleep. Early next day, after embracing James and saying goodbye to the old uncle and aunt, he rode back to Ein Karem. His mother was not at home but had gone to a nearby village where a child was ill and in need of medical care. Zacharias saw that he was unhappy but did not ask any questions. But Elizabeth tried to draw him out and find what was troubling him.

"I was in Emmaus with James yesterday, as you know. He told me something about myself that I did not know before."

"I think you mean about your father, of course. That Josiah was not your real father."

"Then who was he? Why couldn't I have been told?"

"Your mother thought it best to let you grow up without feeling a stranger in Josiah's family. It was to give you a father's care and a sense of belonging. Your brothers love you very much, and except for James who now knows the truth, they believe that you are their father's son."

"I love them also. But I want to know who my father was and I am sure you can tell me."

"He was of a noble family who loved your mother and married her. But he had enemies and they accused him of treason towards Herod and his family. In the end, they caught him and killed him. Your mother came to stay with us until you were born. But two years later after Herod died, we were afraid that Archelaus and his spies would find out where she was living and she had to escape to Egypt. Josiah agreed to marry her and to take her there until the danger had passed."

Jeshua sat with his head in his hands. He found it hard to accept all this. What was this danger that made it necessary to stay in Egypt for over ten years? He wanted to know the name of his father, but Elizabeth said she could not tell him. He must ask his mother first. An hour later he decided he could not wait for her. He packed up his clothes and told Elizabeth that he was going to Jerusalem to see Joseph. It was time for him to be there and begin a new life. Joseph would surely tell him about his father and his family. He kissed Elizabeth, mounted his horse and set off eastwards towards Jerusalem, promising to be back on the Sabbath.

****

Herod Agrippa was only five when his father, Aristobulus, was executed by Herod. He was then sent with his two brothers and two sisters to Rome together with their mother Berenice, the daughter of Herod's sister Salome. He was named Agrippa for Herod's friend and the son-in-law of Augustus, Marcus Agrippa. Exceptionally handsome and intelligent, he won the affection of Tiberius who had him educated with his own son Drusus and with his nephew Claudius. Thirty years were spent enjoying all the extravagant pleasures and luxury that life in Rome afforded. He and Drusus were as close as brothers. With Claudius, who was more reserved and stuttered, he was friendly though he found little interest in his scholarly and literary pursuits. A few years earlier a marriage was arranged for Agrippa with Cypros, granddaughter of Phasael, Herod's eldest brother.

Feeling sure of his favoured position at the imperial court, he had recklessly borrowed money and allowed his debts to mount. Drusus, who was expected to succeed his father one day as emperor, was sent to command legions in Illyricum while his cousin Germanicus was restoring order in Germania. When there was an uprising among the legionnaires in Pannonia, he was sent to quell the rebellion together with Sejanus, Prefect of the Praetorian Guard. Drusus realised that Sejanus was trying to expand his power in Rome, and there was constant animosity between them about the growing control of Sejanus over the civil and political administration of the empire. After the death of Germanicus, Drusus began to serve as co-emperor with his father, but he knew that the real power was held by Sejanus whom his father seemed to trust more than ever before. On one occasion, Drusus lost his temper and struck Sejanus with his fist and their enmity became known openly. But by that time, the man was too powerful to depose.

Agrippa had accompanied Drusus to the dedication of Tiberias and met his uncle Antipas whom he did not like very much, although he appreciated his wealth and power. His sister, Herodias, estranged from her husband, was living there with Antipas as her lover. He admired the city on the beautiful lake, the Sea of Galilee, and they had spent some enjoyable trips around it.

Unfortunately, not long after their return to Rome, Drusus became ill, suffering from fever and indigestion. His wife, Livilla, tended him without success, and he gradually became weaker. He was sent away to Capri in the south to gain back his health, but it was useless. Within a year, his illness became fatal, and Agrippa suspected Sejanus of having seduced Livilla to poison her husband.

When Drusus died, Agrippa lost all hope of maintaining his position in Rome. Deeply distressed, hopelessly in debt to the imperial treasury and many of his former friends, he fled Rome in fear of his creditors and found refuge in the fortress of Malatha in Idumea which he had inherited from his grandfather. He was depressed, and in his enforced seclusion contemplated suicide. It was Cypros, his wife, who stood by him and tried to reverse his fortune. Even when their young son, Drusus, died in infancy, she had remained strong and refused to despair. She appealed to Agrippa's sister Herodias, for help, and Herodias then persuaded her lover, Herod Antipas, to appoint Agrippa as his *aedile* in Tiberias with a yearly income.

He resented the fact of being indebted to Antipas. Adding to his bitterness was the fact that Sejanus had now taken full power in Rome. Tiberius was a broken man after the loss of his beloved son and soon retired to his villa in Capri leaving everything to the one he called his *socius laborum*—the partner of his labours. Sejanus began a series of purge trials for senators and equestrians who opposed him, and sent Agrippina, the widow of Germanicus, and her two sons into exile. Darkness was falling over Rome and it would take seven long years before it ended.

****

Arriving on horseback and almost breathless at the main entrance to Jerusalem, Jeshua asked for directions to the house of Joseph of Ramatayim. Apparently the man was well known, because the Roman guards outside gave him clear instructions. He walked the horse through the streets and found a large mansion with a walled garden and a stable on one side. A hostler at the gate took his horse and the gatekeeper sent him with one of the gardeners to the house. Jeshua realised that Joseph must have left instructions with them in case he arrived unexpectedly.

As he entered the large airy living room, he saw Joseph standing on the balcony at the far end overlooking the Lower City with the mountains of Judaea in the background. The floor was covered with a richly designed mosaic. He stood in great amazement while Joseph hurried across to greet him.

"Jeshua, you are welcome!" Joseph said, with hands outstretched to clasp his. "I am very glad to see you."

He tried to answer, but the words would not come. Joseph saw his troubled face and asked if all was well with the family in Ein Karem. Jeshua nodded and allowed himself to be drawn to one of the couches on the side. Taking a deep breath he said he was sorry to have come without notice.

"This is your home, Jeshua, or a second home from the one in Ein Karem. There is no need to apologise."

Joseph ordered some fruit juice and other refreshments and after Jeshua felt more relaxed he began to explain why he had come so suddenly. Joseph listened with close attention and saw that the time had come to tell the young man the truth. He told him all that had happened more than twenty-six years ago when Herod ordered that his two sons from his second wife Mariamne should be executed for plotting against him, how Alexander had found temporary refuge in the Temple with Maryam, and how they had fallen in love and were secretly married.

"You are a Hasmonean prince, Jeshua, the son of Prince Alexander and one of the heirs to the kingdom of Judaea. It no longer exists, but perhaps one day it will be restored to its rightful rulers."

Jeshua was stunned into silence. All this did not seem real to him and he could not be sure it was true, although he knew that Joseph would not lie to him about his birth. How could he ever assume the role of a prince?

Joseph saw the fear and confusion in Jeshua's face and tried to calm him. He need not worry now since no one knew about this except for the few people involved at the time. Besides Zacharias and Elizabeth, there was only Gorion, his wife Rachela, and his son Nicodemus. Even Josiah had not been told at the time, although Maryam had told him about it just before he died. The priest at the Temple who married his parents and the witnesses would have long forgotten their involvement. They had been well paid for their silence.

"You must rest now," Joseph told him. "I will show you to your room. Later on we will talk about the plans I have for you and see what you think of them."

After Joseph left him, Jeshua stood still in the centre of his room gazing with wonder at the luxury and comfort around him. He felt he had entered into another world so different from his own plain and simple one, a world in which he would have to play a part he had not been prepared for. He could enjoy the luxuries and comforts but they were not really essential for him. In fact, he would feel more comfortable to live with ordinary people out in the countryside than with the rich and powerful people in this city.

But Joseph had spoken of his royal heritage and his future prospects as a prince who might one day rule over his people and give them back the independence they had lost. Something deep inside him responded to this call, to this challenge to do what he could for them, to improve their lot, to restore their hopes for a better life. He had seen how the people in the Galilee were suffering under the rule of Herod Antipas and perhaps one day he could help in getting rid of this tyrant.

****

Nikki sat with Gorion in his study looking over the plans received from Joseph for improvements to the city. Jerusalem was in need of expansion and the new quarter in the north was an ideal solution. But there was also need for more water to be brought into it and to provide for a better water supply system. Storehouses would have to be built to ensure a constant supply of basic goods and materials, food, firewood, oil and sheep for the Temple sacrifices.

Gorion had spent several years as adviser to the City Council on legal and administrative matters, but was now getting weary of this task. He wanted Nikki, who had been assisting him in this for the past two years, to take over his duties from him entirely. He had a good head for administration and could undertake the work besides his scholarly studies and interests.

"These are very good plans, Father," said Nikki admiringly. "They cover all the essential things that a city should have. But I think Joseph should not have to do all this alone. We should try and get some of the wealthy people in Jerusalem to share in the endeavour and in the expense. There is that extremely rich man

Kalba Sabua who owns a huge sheep farm north of the city and supplies the Temple with his animals. Also Ben Zizit Hakeset who owns large fields of wheat and barley and oil presses. Both of them have commercial ties with the Roman authorities and deal in the import of various goods and merchandise."

Gorion agreed, and said that in return for their help he would have them nominated as city councillors. Joseph had good relations with the Roman authorities in Jerusalem and they would not object to the improvements in the city to relieve the crowded population in the Lower City, especially during pilgrimage festivals. Rome would of course object to the construction of a third wall to enclose the northern area of the city as marked in the plans or of any kind of fortification of the city that might be used in case of some future revolt.

"I doubt the people have any inclination to revolt," said Nikki. "They already had a bad taste of it ten years ago. The might and power of Rome cannot be matched by any stretch of the imagination."

"Yes, you may be right, Nikki," Gorion replied. "But we are a hot-headed, proud, and stubborn people, and it will take little to ignite a rebellion, however futile."

They walked out into the garden where the children were playing. Jonathan had climbed an apple tree and was pelting Joanna with the green unripe ones. He stopped as soon as he saw his father coming out and slid down immediately.

"Time you both went in to wash up before dinner. Uncle Joseph will be coming with someone you will like to meet."

"Who is he?" the twins said at the same time. They often spoke in chorus with each other, in identical words.

"Never mind, now, you will soon find out! Off with you to your mother."

Gorion smiled as they scampered away. He could see Ruhama at the doorway grabbing an arm of each and leading them inside. What a wonderful wife and mother she was. She and Nikki were as much in love as they had been when they married, and they were perfectly suited to each other.

At dinner that evening Joseph introduced Jeshua as the son of a dear friend in Ein Karem who had come to live at his home in Jerusalem and assist him in his work in the city. Ruhama was delighted to see that angelic child she had seen so many years ago when Maryam came back with him from Egypt. Jeshua did not recall her or Nikki, but he remembered Gorion who had come to meet them in Joppa, and how kind he had been to him and his mother after the long sea voyage from Alexandria.

Joseph sat at the opposite end of the table from Gorion, with Jeshua on one side of him and Nikki on the other. Ruhama then came in with Mary, Martha's sister, who had taken her place in the household, helping with the cooking and cleaning. After serving everyone, they both sat down to enjoy the meal together. Mary was sitting next to Jeshua and could not help taking quick looks at this fair, handsome young man, dressed in such elegant robes.

"I hope your mother will also come to visit us occasionally for a Sabbath eve dinner and a day of rest in our house," said Gorion.

"I am sure she will be glad to see you again, sir," Jeshua said in response.

"We will bring her here one day very soon," Joseph promised. "She mentioned the common interest in herbs and plants that she had with Ruhama many years ago."

"I recall what she told me then," Ruhama said. "She knew much more than I did at the time, when I was learning about them from the Essenes living nearby."

"I would very much like to meet some Essenes," said Jeshua. "I am curious about their customs and beliefs."

"Jeshua, you are welcome to join our weekly study group on the Sabbath in the upper chamber of this house," Nikki told him. "We have Essenes and other people from different Jewish and non-Jewish sects meeting to discuss various religious issues and sometimes even political ones."

"Is this in connection with your historical research, Nikki?" asked Joseph.

"Yes, and no," he answered. "It is also to resolve differences and tensions. It is good for people to know each other better and to lessen ignorance and fear among them."

"Do you have any Samaritans in this group?" asked Jeshua. "I remember meeting some of them on our way from Jerusalem to Nazareth when I was a boy."

"Not yet," said Nikki. "But I would be glad if they could be persuaded to come."

When they ended their meal, Gorion invited them to go outside to the garden for an after-dinner stroll. The children gathered around Jeshua asking him a lot of questions about Alexandria where he grew up and what he had seen there. They kept begging their father and mother to take them to Egypt to visit the pyramids and to ride through the desert on camels. Jeshua sat on a bench with them and held them spellbound with his boyhood memories.

Gorion and Joseph walked around the garden talking about their building plans and the costs they would entail, while Nikki went to speak to Ruhama who was busy clearing away the table together with Mary. He drew her aside and led her into Gorion's study. From the darkness of the room, they looked out of the open doorway to see Jeshua sitting with the two children. With his arm around her, he told Ruhama of his idea to have Jeshua come and tutor the children. They would enjoy being with him and he would be a good influence on them.

"I know that with my research and administrative work I have not been giving them enough attention. They need a guiding hand besides your own motherly care. And I can see that Jeshua loves children and has the patience to listen to them and talk to them."

"Yes, Nikki," Ruhama told him. "I think it is a very good idea. It will make him feel part of our family. But Jeshua also needs some guidance from you. He needs to know more about our history, our political situation, the people in this country, and many other things that he has not had any knowledge of before."

"Well, Joseph will also see to it that he is instructed in many of those things, but I will do my best as well to give him all the instruction he needs."

He kissed her and went outside to wait until Jeshua and the children finished their talk. He then sat down near him and suggested that he should come during the late afternoons to spend an hour or two with the twins. Jeshua said he would be glad to do so. They were bright and curious children, and interested in whatever he could tell them. He could teach them Aramaic, the language their mother had once spoken, and tell them some of the parables he had heard from itinerant wise men and teachers in the north.

Just before Joseph and Jeshua left, Gorion and Nikki invited Jeshua to join them and the children on a tour of the city and the Temple on one of the Sabbath days. Jeshua hardly knew Jerusalem and had only been to the Temple once as a boy. Nikki would tell them all he knew about the different sites and their history. The early autumn weather was perfect for it. They would take a picnic basket and spend the afternoon at the King's Garden in the Kidron Valley before climbing back uphill to Mount Zion.

****

When Elizabeth told Maryam about Jeshua's discovery that Josiah was not his real father, she realised that Joseph would tell him the truth about his royal birth and also explain the reasons why this was kept so secret from him. Joseph could give him all the care and assistance to live the life he should have more rightfully led as a prince of Israel. Still, she felt that she had lost him in some way, and that he now belonged more to his people than to her. Elizabeth had felt the same way when her son Johanan decided to leave the family home to find some greater purpose in life by joining the small community of exiled priests near the Dead Sea.

They rarely heard from him, but some news of him reached them through Nikki who received information from the Essenes about this community and of Johanan as well. He had become a wandering preacher of their doctrines, calling the people to repent of their sins before they were destroyed in the coming apocalypse. Nikki told Zacharias that Johanan had been seen in the Judaean desert and in the Jordan valley, living the kind of ascetic life that Elijah had led during his years of exile. He was as the prophet said, like a voice crying in the desert for the return to God and his revelation on Mount Sinai.

Maryam was reminded of that dramatic story about Elijah on Mount Carmel where the prophet proved to the people the falsity of their belief in the Canaanite god Baal. But after killing the priests of Baal and being threatened with death by the queen, Jezebel, he fled to the desert. It had taken him forty days and nights to reach Mount Sinai where God had first revealed himself and where the covenant was made between him and his chosen people.

"You know the story of course," said Elizabeth. "When God asks him 'What are you doing here, Elijah?' he answers: 'I was jealous for you because the children of Israel have forsaken your covenant.' Nikki says Johanan is trying to re-enact the story of Elijah. But I am afraid for him. They will try to kill him as they tried to kill Elijah."

She was in tears by then and Maryam put her arms around her. Johanan had been only six months old when Jeshua was born and they had played together in their early childhood. She promised that she would send him to look for Johanan. The Essenes near the Dead Sea might be able to help in the search. This kind of fierce religious zeal was dangerous and could only lead to destruction and death.

Maryam decided to go to Emmaus and see James. He should be told about Jeshua and his true identity. She wanted to ask him to accompany Jeshua in his search for Johanan. She knew he loved and was completely devoted to his young brother. There were always carts and wagons going up and down from Jerusalem to Emmaus so she could easily find a ride in one of them.

146

The inn was crowded when she arrived there. People were going in and out, travellers, wagon drivers, horse riders, and Roman cavalry officers and men passing through. She walked around to the back where she found one of the serving girls fetching water and asked her to tell the innkeeper that his mother, Maryam, was waiting outside. A few minutes later James came out to look for her, embraced her lovingly, and led her into his private quarters on one side of the inn.

"You must be very busy, James," she told him. "I can rest here and wait till there are less people to serve."

"I will take you to the house of my uncle and aunt where you can spend the day and perhaps stay overnight. But first tell me why you have come. Is Jeshua well?"

In a few words, she told him about Jeshua and his Hasmonean father. James was at first astounded but then said he had always felt there was something special about him. He had an innate grace and charm which made him liked and even loved by all who met him. Maryam told him that Joseph was now taking care of him and giving him all the privileges of his royal birth. But she was not sure he would care much for living in idle luxury and would try to do something worthwhile with his life.

She was warmly received at the home of James' uncle and aunt, and after sharing their midday meal retired to the room they gave her. Later that evening, when James returned from the inn, she told him about Elizabeth and her anxiety for Johanan, and of her intention to ask Jeshua to go to the Zadokite settlement in the Judaean desert and search for him.

"It is better if he does not go alone. Perhaps you could leave your work at the inn for a week or two and travel with him. Elizabeth told me he promised to be in Ein Karem for the Sabbath and you could come and meet him there."

"I will come, of course, Maryam," James assured her. "I have two good assistants at the inn to keep it running well in my absence."

She left early the next morning thanking the elderly uncle and aunt for their hospitality. James had arranged with one of the drivers to take her back to Jerusalem. He behaved so much like his father, Josiah, with the same kindness and consideration, and she hoped to keep him and Jeshua closer together.

****

147

Antipas had been ruling the Galilee and Peraea for the past twenty years. He was confident that his rule would be as long as that of his father's thirty-three years as king. Although he was only a tetrarch, he already had all the influence of a king. He occasionally spent festival periods in the Hasmonean palace in Jerusalem and gave generous gifts to the Temple. Besides this, he followed his father's example as a builder. Sepphoris was rebuilt after its destruction by Varus and fortified, and he added a wall to Betharamphtha in Peraea, the biblical city of Beth Haran, which he renamed Livias in honour of Augustus' wife Livia, the mother of the emperor Tiberius. He was ambitious, and tried to persuade Rome to extend his tetrarchy, to take over Judaea and Samaria, but was refused.

He made every effort to retain favour with his Jewish subjects by not letting his coins carry any human images, and he built a sanctuary for prayer in Tiberias. He knew that at first pious Jews did not like to live in the city because it was found to have been built on the top of a graveyard and was therefore subject to ritual impurity, but this applied mainly to priests who were forbidden to enter a cemetery. In time, many Jews came to live there.

He spent most of his time either in Sepphoris or in Tiberias at the royal palace he had built on the hilltop overlooking it. At other times, usually in the winter season, he stayed in the fortress of Machaerus in Peraea near the border with Nabataea so that his wife, the daughter of its king, could visit her family. It was a useful alliance since Nabataea agreed to stop supplying the two wealthy and prominent cities, Hippos and Gadara, located on the eastern bank of the Sea of Galilee which rivalled him in their trade with the surrounding regions.

Another problem was his nephew Agrippa, whom he had appointed as his *aedile*, the chief administrator, in Tiberias. The man was taking too much advantage of his position and becoming extravagant in his style of living. They often quarrelled over the money he expended. He was behaving in the same way he had in Rome where he mounted up such huge debts. And he was also trying to ingratiate himself with the Jewish population in the Galilee, favouring them over the Greeks and other non-Jewish inhabitants. He often took long walks on the seashore as far north as Bethsaida across the Jordan from Capernaum, hobnobbing with the fishermen and sailing in their boats back to Tiberias. They liked him for his courtesy and charming ways. He probably saw himself as heir to the tetrarchy and was overfriendly with the Roman governor of Syria.

In spite of all he did for the people he ruled, Antipas remained unpopular. In reaction to their open dislike, he became cruel and repressive, and a vicious circle of hatred was created. He was also not much liked by the Roman soldiers stationed in various military camps around the Galilee and did not gain their respect as an able ruler.

****

Marcus was in great distress when Aurelia told him that her father, Rufus, was dying. Fulvia had written to beg her daughter to come to Rome as soon as possible and to bring the children with her. Aurelia had not agreed to live in Ramatayim and had rented a house in Caesarea where she felt more at home among the Roman population there. Marcus spent every weekend with her and the children, but during the week he was at his father's home to manage the now prosperous trading company he had organised with his partners in eastern countries.

Aurelia wanted him to come with her to Rome, even though the restrictions against Jews were still in force and Sejanus, the Praetorian Prefect, was conducting what could only be called a reign of terror in the city. Marcus was reluctant to go back there. He felt a certain resentment and distaste for the place where he had once enjoyed living. Two weeks later, he received a letter from Aurelia to say that her father had died. It also said that she decided to remain in Rome with the children.

"We will be staying here with mother for a while," she wrote. "She is deeply grieved and has also become very ill after caring for Father for so long. Father's will says that he leaves the house and all its contents to her and sufficient funds for all her needs. But the bulk of the estate and his business enterprises abroad are left to the children. I think they can now take full advantage of their fortune and their place in Roman society. I would like to buy back our previous home in the Carinae area, and I hope you will soon be able to join us."

It was inevitable, he realised. Aurelia had not been happy to come here to Judaea and did not fit in well with the social circles in Caesarea. Even though they still loved each other, they had grown apart over the years and perhaps for her sake they should separate or even divorce. He wrote back to her with his condolences to her and her mother, and said he agreed with her plans for herself and the children. Arius was now sixteen and Arianna fourteen, both old enough to look forward to making their own way in life. He supposed that Arius would soon be taking an interest in his grandfather's business enterprises and Arianna would eventually be married to some rich nobleman's son.

He decided to take the long-postponed visit to Damascus and to the cities of the Decapolis for which he was now the main supplier. He had won them over from using the expensive Nabataean trade routes, those which ran from Damascus down through Bostra to Petra and from there southwards into Arabia and eastward to Babylon, Persia and also along the silk trade route to China. Damascus had become the hub of all the commercial activities in the region, a major trade centre between East and West, from which he could expand his contacts.

He wrote to his agent, Alcimus, in Damascus, the most enterprising of all his trading partners. The man was half Greek and half Syrian, and as devious as they come. He had originally worked with the Nabataeans but quarrelled with them over his commissions and Marcus offered him a partnership in his trading company. He wanted to move the headquarters of his trading company from Judaea to Syria and told Alcimus to buy a house suitable for business as well as for comfortable lodging.

When Marcus arrived in the city, he had to admit the man was efficient with an eye for architectural beauty. The two-storied building was on the Via Recta west of the theatre, not far from the city gate facing the road to Sidon and Tyre on the Mediterranean coast.

"Excellent!" said Marcus, clapping Alcimus on his shoulder. "It is a perfect choice. We shall do good business here and I shall also enjoy living in such elegant quarters."

"It is spacious and airy," Alcimus said. "As you see, the entrance is on the north side facing the street, but there is a large paved courtyard on the south side and a walled garden beyond it."

Alcimus then took him to see some of the city sites—the bazaar, the citadel, the government house and the magnificent east gate with its three arches, a central one for chariots and two side ones for those entering on foot.

"We will now go and see the marvellous new Roman temple of Jupiter being built. They are building it over the Canaanite temple of Baal-Hadad, the god of thunderstorms and rain, who is now identified with Jupiter and his thunderbolts. It will take decades till it is completed, but the Romans intend it to rival your grand temple in Jerusalem."

"I doubt any sanctuary in the entire east will ever be as large and grand as our Temple in Jerusalem. Have you seen it?"

"No, not yet, but perhaps you will invite me to visit your famous city and temple one day," Alcimus suggested. "I have heard much of its splendour."

On the way back they passed, a walled enclosure with the design of a candelabrum on the iron-barred gate. Marcus stopped and looked through the bars to the building inside. It looked like one of the typical synagogues in Judaea. Alcimus told him this was the place where some exiled priests from Jerusalem had found refuge more than two centuries ago. They were now a large community living in single-storied houses behind the enclosure. Marcus was curious to know more about them, and was about to knock at the gate with the iron clapper, but Alcimus stopped him and advised him to leave them alone.

"They are different from other Jews in Damascus, the merchants and shopkeepers merchants living near the bazaar area. These are pious people who call themselves the Bene Zedek, the righteous ones. They dress in long, white robes, bathe frequently in the purification pools beneath their houses, rarely go out into the streets of the city, and hire servants to supply them with food and other necessities."

"What do they do all day, then?" asked Marcus.

"I heard they sit and study old scrolls and documents, and make copies for all their members. They do not eat meat, only vegetables and plants, make their own bread, weave their own clothes, and some keep beehives for honey on the flat rooftops of their houses."

They returned to the house and spent the next few days furnishing it and setting up their business centre in the courtyard at the back. Alcimus would bring him clients and provide for everything he needed. Marcus would still travel to see his father in Jerusalem at least once a year, but this would be his home from now onwards.

****

James arrived in Ein Karem the following week on the eve of the Sabbath and found that Joseph and Jeshua were already there. It was an emotional meeting for them all, and the first time he met Elizabeth and Zacharias. They both saw how much he was like his father Josiah in his manner and character, and spoke of him warmly.

After the lighting of candles, the blessing over wine and bread, and the Sabbath evening meal, they sat together to plan the proposed search for Johanan. First of all James wanted to know who the Zadokites were and what the name Zadok meant. Zacharias told him that they belonged to the family of priests descended from Zadok the first High Priest to serve in Solomon's temple. He himself was in the legitimate priestly line from Aaron's son, Eleazar and grandson Phineas. Ezra the scribe was a tenth generation descendant of Phineas.

"You remember Phineas, the one who was so zealous for God when many of the people were tempted by Moabite and Midianite women to adultery and the worship of Baal-Peor. A plague broke out among the people as divine punishment, but it stopped as soon as he killed the tribal prince Zimri and his Midianite woman for openly defying Moses."

"Yes, of course," said James. "I remember the verse in the Book of Numbers." He recited it out aloud:

> *Phineas the son of Eleazar the son of Aaron the priest: Behold I give to him my covenant of peace, and will be his, and his progeny after him, a covenant of everlasting priesthood in turn of his zealousness for his God, and he atoned for the sons of Israel.*

Zacharias applauded him for his good memory and continued by saying that the prophet Ezekiel praised the sons of Zadok as staunch opponents of pagan worship during the period before the Babylonian exile. Ezekiel also prophesied their return as priests in the future temple to be rebuilt. In fact, this was what happened after the Return to Zion. The high-priesthood remained in their hands until the time of Simon the Just and of Onias I and II. But the High Priest Onias III was usurped by his younger brother Jason, who was a Hellenist and who introduced idolatrous practices in the Temple. Onias fled to Antioch and was brutally assassinated there by order of Menelaus, the envoy of Jason to the king of Syria, Antiochus IV.

Zacharias said that his son, Onias IV, fled to Egypt where he gained the protection of Ptolemy VI Philometor and received permission to build a temple in Leontopolis, modelled on the one in Jerusalem but comparatively smaller. The reason why Onias did not return to Jerusalem after the restoration of the Temple was because the Hasmoneans wanted to take over the high priesthood instead of the legitimate Zadokite dynasty.

"Some of the Zadokite priests did not go down to Egypt," Zacharias added. "Instead they set up their small exiled community on the shores of the Dead Sea near Jericho. For them, Onias III had been their beloved Moreh Zedek, the teacher of righteousness, who had been slain by the Wicked Priest Menelaus, who had bribed Antiochus to take over the high priesthood from Jason. The Zadokite priests called themselves the community of the Yahad, the watchers or keepers of the covenant. They are still waiting for the future restoration of their priesthood to the Temple, keeping themselves pure in body and soul, and predicting that one day there would be a war between the sons of light against the sons of darkness."

"Dreamers," said Joseph. "After two centuries of Hasmonean rule they can never regain their former position. By now, I have discovered that some of the members of the Dead Sea community have gone to other places, such as Damascus. Marcus wrote to me about the strange community he found there which seem to have an identical way of life as those in this community."

James then asked Zacharias how it was that his family, who were of Zadokite descent, had remained as priests serving in the Temple.

"Many members of our clan felt they had to remain if only to preserve some representation of the true priesthood in the Temple. Unlike the Zadokites in the settlement near Ein Gedi, we accepted the situation and remained as priests in Jerusalem. Some of the Hellenised priestly clans who were then ascendant in Jerusalem also claimed to be descendants of Zadok and called themselves Sadducees, the Hellenised form of the name."

Joseph reminded Zacharias that in time the Hasmonean rulers allied themselves with the Sadducees against the rising power of the Pharisees who began to oppose them for their Hellenistic leanings. It was ironic that the heroic Hasmonean family which had fought so bravely against assimilation with Greek culture began promoting it. Herod had also favoured the appointment of high priests from among the Sadducees after having rid himself of the last Hasmonean high priest, Aristobulus, the young brother of Mariamne. He had him 'accidentally' drowned while swimming with his 'friends' in the pool at the palace in Jericho. He was only sixteen at the time, but was much loved and adored by the people, and therefore a threat to Herod.

"Although the high priesthood is still being held by the Sadducees, their popularity among the people has been in decline since the Pharisees are now more dominant," said Zacharias. "The Pharisees are now the moving force among the people, teaching and preaching their doctrines and their elaborate interpretations of the Bible, going far beyond the literal sense of the text, often distorting its meaning completely. The Sadducees refuse to accept these new doctrines, and hold strictly to the biblical laws in their original, literal sense."

Joseph agreed with him. There were too many new religious restrictions being applied by the Sanhedrin. But fortunately, the stricter Shammaite faction was not in the majority with their 'holier than thou' attitude towards the more liberal Hillelites. He thought that Rabban Gamaliel, Hillel's grandson, was doing well in restraining some of their excesses.

It was getting late, so they all decided to retire. They had all of the next day to relax, to walk around the countryside, to continue their talks, and to plan the journey that Jeshua and James were going to take to look for Johanan.

****

The desert was fiercely hot and his leather sandals sank into the burning sands. Johanan followed the road along the shores of the Dead Sea to Jericho, and after bathing in the river he sat in the shade of a palm tree to eat some of its sweet, ripe dates with the bread he had brought from the settlement. He had spent more than two years with the priests in the small community centre before he was finally accepted as a member of the Yahad, those committed to obey the rules of the community laid down in the Manual of Discipline.

Because of his fervent devotion and his strong, charismatic personality, the community leaders had assigned him the task of spreading the true word of God among the people living in the Judaean desert and in the settlements along the Jordan valley, to warn them of the approaching 'end of days' when only the children of the spirit of truth would receive their reward and survive. His good looks, dark, flashing eyes and black hair matched a commanding presence that comes with deep conviction.

The time he spent in the Judaean desert brought little success and only a few converts. So he had decided to go further north to Gilgal where there was a circle of twelve standing stones formed by the Israelites who had collected them from the river bed as they were crossing the Jordan into Canaan. They still stood there as a memorial to this historical event, and ceremonies were often held there in commemoration of it. This was where Samuel the prophet had crowned Saul as king, and this was also the place where Elijah stayed during his final years after returning from his journey to Mount Sinai together with Elisha, who was to succeed him as the leading prophet in Israel.

He stood for a while in the centre of the stone circle trying to infuse himself with the faith of those times, the fervent love of God the prophets of the Bible had felt which was now lost. For all their piety and their deep study of the scriptural texts, the Zadokites could not reach that level of prophetic inspiration. Their strict discipline and rigid adherence to rituals and bodily purification lacked the elements of emotion and passion which was necessary if they wanted to convince others of their beliefs.

The story about the prophet Elisha and Naaman the Aramean came to mind. Naaman was the commander of the armies of Ben-Hadad, King of Aram-Damascus. When he became infected with leprosy, he was told that there was a prophet and miracle worker in Gilgal who could cure him.

So Naaman came with his horses and his chariot, and stood at the door of the house of Elisha. And Elisha sent a messenger to him, saying: Go, wash in the Jordan seven times, and your flesh will be restored and you will be clean. But Naaman was angry, and went away saying: I thought he would come out and stand and call on the name of the Lord his God, and strike his hand over the place and recover the leper. Are not Abana and Pharpar, the rivers of Damascus, better than all the waters of Israel? May I not wash in them and be clean? So he turned away in a rage.

His servants finally persuaded him to obey the prophet, so he went to the Jordan and dipped into the water seven times. His skin was cleared of the disease and he returned to thank Elisha saying that he now believed in the God of Israel.

The story gave Johanan an inspiration. He would go to the Jordan River, to Bethabara, the river ford between Judaea and Peraea. This was where the Israelites had crossed the Jordan when they entered Canaan to conquer it with Joshua at their head. Here was the place where Elijah had crossed over the river to be taken up in chariot of fire and ascended in a whirlwind to heaven. He could still hear the voice of Elisha crying: "My father, my father, the chariot of Israel and the horsemen …" when he lost sight of him. This would be the place where people could come and purify themselves in the waters of the Jordan. He would tell them that all their sins would be washed away and they would feel reborn.

******

As soon as they returned to Jerusalem, Joseph sent a message to Nikki, asking him to find some of the Essenes in the community living near the Mount Zion gate not far from the Gorion house. Ruhama was also a frequent visitor there. He wanted one of them to take Jeshua and James to the Zadokite settlement north of Ein Gedi. The Essenes were friendly with the Zadokites, although they were not allowed to enter their compound. There were also some Essenes living with their families outside the compound who worked in the pottery kilns, brought supplies to the settlement from Jericho and sent letters or documents to the community in Damascus.

"It is not very safe on the road to Jericho," Nikki told Joseph when he heard of the planned search for Johanan. "I advise James and Jeshua to dress like ordinary travellers or pilgrims and ride down on donkeys or in mule carts. They should leave early in the morning before it gets too hot, and take a lot of water with them."

"You are right, Nikki," Joseph agreed and added that James and Jeshua had just gone to the Temple with a message from Zacharias to one of the senior priests he knows there.

"What was the message about?" asked Nikki, already guessing what it might be.

"He wants to find the priest who married Alexander and Maryam and receive the written legal document from him for their marriage. There must have been some official document of it in the Temple records. This was what James wanted, so that no one could say Jeshua was born out of wedlock."

"It is nearly thirty years ago, Joseph. The man must be quite old by now."

"Zacharias recalls it was a young priest of the prominent Jehoiarib clan and feels sure he can be found. Besides, Jeshua looks so much like Alexander that this priest will surely see the resemblance."

Nikki waited with Joseph until the brothers returned, and was glad to see that they had indeed obtained a copy of the document. The old priest who had married Alexander and Maryam could not forget that day and the tragic parting between them. They also met his son, Matthias, who would soon take his father's place in the Temple. Jeshua was now confident of his true birth.

He and James began preparing for their journey. Nikki went off in search of his Essene friends to find one of them to accompany the brothers to Jericho and from there to the Zadokite settlement. By the time their preparations were made, Nikki had returned with a young Essene who had agreed to go with them and show them the way. As they all sat down to have a meal together, James told Joseph that he and Jeshua would not be returning to Jerusalem after their journey but wanted to go up to the Galilee to visit their brothers in Capernaum. Perhaps they would also stay there for a while to be together again.

****

After James and Jeshua left with their Essene guide, Nikki remained with Joseph to hear of his plans for the young man's future. Jeshua had so far led a fairly simple life among the working classes and was totally unfit for his royal status.

"I will groom him carefully, and teach him how to wear fine clothes, to enjoy good food and some of the luxuries of the elite in Jerusalem. I will also introduce him into upper class society and to some of the Roman authorities as a person of noble lineage without disclosing his true identity."

"I think you are wrong, Joseph. You are trying to make him into the Hasmonean prince with ambitions for regaining the kingdom of Judaea. That is both a highly unlikely dream and a real danger to his life."

"I want to give him a chance to regain his rightful place as a Hasmonean heir and a future ruler. He has by nature all the beauty, character and fine qualities of a prince. All it needs is a little nurturing and polishing. He will be loved by the people as his father was, and many of them will recognise Alexander's face in Jeshua."

"You are dreaming of the restoration of the Hasmonean monarchy. History shows that most of them were tyrants, cruel despots and greedy for more power and conquests rather than for the good of the people. They massacred some, exiled others, and forcibly converted the Idumeans. Thanks to this conversion we received a Herod who outdid them in ferocity. A true Edomite who came to rule over Jacob and regain his lost birthright as the Bible predicted."

"Nikki, I know what you have in mind. The blessing that Isaac gave to Esau after Jacob had stolen the one given to the firstborn son. *By the sword you shall live and you will serve your brother, but if you gain dominion you will break his yoke over you.* But Herod is now dead and Rome rules."

"The people identify Rome with Edom because Herod identified himself with Rome and Roman interests against his own people. Even if a Hasmonean regains the throne it will be the same as it was with him, as a client kingdom at the mercy of Rome. What is the value of that? Why should we have the same kind of situation in the Galilee with a ruler buttressed by Roman legions?"

"Antipas rules like a Herod. Jeshua could be a benign Hasmonean ruler who softens the edges of Roman rule and slowly acquires greater autonomy and independence. He will have the good of the people as his primary interest."

"Joseph, you are being naïve. With all his good nature and moral standards, power will corrupt him. He will not be able to withstand the persuasion of his advisers and the influences of the wealthy elite. They will turn him into the ruler they want."

Joseph shook his head and said he did not agree with this prediction. Jeshua had a pure soul, and he would be incorruptible. He would see to it that he was protected with good advisers and against the sharks among the powerful families in Jerusalem, especially the corrupt priestly ones that Herod had favoured.

"Rome's dominion will not last forever. They too will pass one day and Israel will gain its independence once more. It is only a matter of time."

"How much time do you think it will take?" Nikki said, almost angrily. "A thousand years, perhaps two thousand years? I am a historian, and I believe that even if we gain a measure of independence one day, it will always be conditioned on the political situation around us. We will always be at the mercy of greater powers, of foreign influences."

"What you do not realise, Nikki, is that we already have a strong influence over the world through our economic power. There is a wide network of Jewish traders like myself and Marcus that stretches across the entire Mediterranean from Alexandria in the south to Tarsus in the north, and from Antioch in the east to Spain and beyond in the west."

"But independence requires political power, military might, and also territorial conquest. Even if Rome falls one day, another such power will rise and take its place. We cannot compete among nations with our sliver of a country and complete lack of any military force. Those who try to oppose these forces will only destroy themselves."

He felt exhausted by this argument and so was Joseph. They would just have to agree to disagree, and part as friends. They were both deeply concerned for Jeshua and wished to remain united in their efforts on his behalf.

****

James and Jeshua arrived in Jericho just before noon. It was always a busy place for travellers and for traders between east and west, and also those coming down from the north along the Jordan River. They found lodgings in an inn, while their driver and Essene guide went southwards to the Zadokite settlement to ask about Johanan and where he could be found.

It was late autumn so the weather was not too hot to explore the city. Jericho was a garden city covered with date palms. Cleopatra had once owned it as a gift from Mark Antony and leased it to Herod, but later on it was transferred to him by Augustus. He built his winter palace there over the ruins of the former Hasmonean palace destroyed by an earthquake, and built two more which were skilfully constructed with a combined network of aqueducts and pools and extended over a large area along the edge of the valley to the west of the city.

It was a long walk, but the two brothers enjoyed it, going as far as the old Hasmonean fort. There was a tacit understanding between them that no reference would be made to the family connection with these sites. Jeshua already knew some of their history and how it had tragically ended. The last Hasmonean king, Antigonus Mattathias, the younger son of Aristobulus II, was exiled with his father and brother to Rome. With the aid of the Parthians, he managed to usurp the throne from his uncle Hyrcanus and to reign as king in Jerusalem for three years. Herod, with Rome's blessing, ousted him and sent him to Antioch where he was executed by order of the Governor of Syria. Some reports said he was beheaded but it was more likely that he was crucified. His body was taken down and hidden by a faithful priest who managed to bring his remains to Jerusalem and to bury him secretly.

By the time they returned to the inn, the Essene guide and cart driver had already come back from the Zadokite settlement. He said the community overseer told him that Johanan had been there a week earlier after wandering for a month in the Judaean desert and then went north to Jericho and beyond. James thanked the guide and said he could return to Jerusalem with the cart driver and Joseph would pay them both for their services.

The next morning the two brothers set out on foot along the Jordan Valley road looking carefully at all the people traveling back and forth to see if Johanan was amongst them. They went as far as Elisha's spring where they rested for a while and filled their water-skins from it. Among many miracles performed by this prophet was turning the bitter water of the spring into fresh, sweet water by throwing salt into it.

"Reminds me of the miracle Moses performed by throwing a log into the waters of Marah, the bitter spring," said James. "It was three days after they crossed the *Yam Suf*—the Reed Sea, and entered the desert of Sinai, when they had no more water to drink."

"Why do people always need miracles in order to have faith and believe in God," said Jeshua. "All they need to do is to look at the wonders of nature, at its beauty."

"Not everyone has your eyes, Jeshua. Nature is only something they see and cultivate as useful for their benefit and profit."

They walked on towards Gilgal, intending to spend the night there before going on to Bethabara where Johanan was last seen. If he was not there, they would go further north up the Jordan Valley.

****

Herod Antipas was in his element. His beautiful new city Tiberias had begun to attract many of the wealthier Greeks and Jews in the Galilee and even many from across the border in the tetrarchy of his half-brother, the tetrarch Philip. He had a grand palace on the hill above the city, where he could entertain royal guests and friends. But he left the administration of Tiberias to his nephew Herod Agrippa, who proved very efficient although he was becoming a spendthrift with his love of luxuries. He had lived a pampered life in Rome and still thought himself entitled to the privileges of a Hasmonean prince. But Antipas overlooked this for the sake of Agrippa's sister Herodias.

Herodias was alienated from her husband, Herod Philip, who had once been called Herod II and the designated heir of his father. He and his mother, Mariamne, daughter of a former high priest Simeon Boethus, were banished from Jerusalem for suspected involvement in a plot against Herod. Mariamne was given a palatial home in Ashkelon where she lived for most of the time, but often went back to her native city, Alexandria for the winter season.

Herodias had always despised her husband for being more interested in books and learning instead of more manly pursuits, and also for his lack of interest in asserting his position as one of Herod's sons. Although it had now become common knowledge that she and Antipas were lovers, her husband remained indifferent to the gossip and was still refusing to divorce her.

Sepphoris, after its rebuilding, was becoming a rich, cosmopolitan city, deeply influenced by Greek culture but also inhabited by the many nouveaux-riche Jews owning large estates in the region. The city was popularly known as the 'Ornament of the Galilee'. This was the capital city for Antipas for more than twenty years ever since Augustus had elected him as tetrarch, and it was in his honour that Antipas renamed it Autocratoris, although the name was rarely used.

Antipas had never given up his desire to expand his boundaries beyond the Galilee and Peraea. He continued to act as the loyal client ruler of the Roman emperor, making himself indispensable to Tiberius in maintaining the balance of power between Rome and Parthia. In fact, he was bent on bringing the two sides into some kind of mutual accommodation to avoid further conflict and tension.

A year earlier, when Antipas went to Peraea as usual to spend the winter months at Machaerus with his Nabataean wife, Phasaelis, she realised that he was planning to divorce her and marry Herodias. When she confronted him and found that this was his intent, she left him and returned to her father in Nabataea. Aretas was furious and vowed revenge for this shameful treatment of his daughter. But he bided his time, waiting until Antipas should fall out of favour with Rome. He was sure that in time he would soon become entangled with his double dealings between the various Roman provinces in the East and with Parthia. That man had delusions of grandeur, thinking he could match the great Herod with his wiles, and he would regret breaking his alliance with Nabataea, which bordered Peraea on the east. Invasion and conquest would be easy.

Antipas was not unduly worried about this danger. Tiberius would never allow Aretas to conquer his territory. The Governor of Syria had enough legions to protect him against attack. In the meantime, he would sever all his trade connections with Nabataea and make use of the new trade route being set up from Damascus to the east by an enterprising Jew and his Greek partner. He heard that they were extremely efficient and less expensive. Marcus, that was the name he was given. His father was a prominent figure in Jerusalem. It would be a very good connection in every respect.

****

James and Jeshua found the road from Gilgal to Bethabara filled with people going towards the river. There were men, women and children, many of them family groups riding in wagons and carts, but most of them were walking on foot, striding forward with the early morning sun on their faces. They followed them, merging with the crowds. It was not very far to go, just a few miles from Gilgal, but it took a long while because of the slow-moving vehicles and people. It was already after the noon hour when they arrived near the river bank, and were glad to find tents set up under the trees that could be hired for an overnight stay.

They could see Johanan in the distance standing waist deep in the water. It was near the end of summer when the river was at its lowest level. More than a hundred people surrounded the tall, dark figure, bearded with unkempt hair straggling over his shoulders. His hands were stretched out to each one in turn, pushing them down into the water.

"What is he doing to them?" asked Jeshua.

"He is showing them how to immerse themselves in the water," said James. "This is the purification ritual for priests before serving in the Temple. It must be done in flowing water or in the fresh water of a spring."

They could hear his thundering voice calling out to the people: "Repent, purify yourselves of your sins before the coming Day of Judgment!"

James said that this was what the Zadokites were preaching. They foretold that a war was going to happen within the next forty years between the sons of light and the sons of darkness, and that the Temple would be destroyed. Only those that repented of their sins would be saved. Johanan was their emissary, a prophet like Elijah come to warn the people against pagan practices and the influence of Rome.

It was impossible to approach Johanan now, so they decided to wait until the evening, but by the time they had eaten some of the food they had brought with them they felt too tired to stay up, and postponed their meeting with him till the morning. Sitting outside their tent after sunset, they saw the full moon rise above the tree tops and then, as darkness fell, the stars began to appear. Jeshua gazed up at them with wonder and asked James whether he thought the stars predicted the future.

"I doubt they have anything to do with such things. Stargazing is a lot of foolishness."

"Perhaps you are right, James. But when I was a boy in Alexandria I used to wander around the city. One day I met three old stargazers near the Serapeum who were looking at me strangely. One of them approached and said: 'This is the child the stars have foretold.' Then the second one asked me: 'What is your name?' When I told him, the third one said: 'We predicted your coming.' What do you think they meant?"

James was silent, and then said: "Mother Maryam once told me that on her way to Egypt she met some stargazers in Bethlehem the night she spent there with you and our father. They gave her a small gift for you, a silver orb with a cross above it. Does she still have it?"

"Yes, she showed it to me once. It is just some childish toy. I opened it and found some incense inside."

"They must have simply guessed you were the same fair-haired child they saw then."

"Do you believe in destiny, James? I mean that your life is determined from the very beginning? Or do we have free will to choose what we want to be?"

"It's a difficult question, brother!" James said with hesitation. "My father always said that everything is already known by God before it happens. This means that our fate is determined in advance whatever we decide to do."

"That is not what it means," Jeshua protested. "Even if God knows what will happen in the future it does not mean we cannot choose what we want to do freely. He just knows in advance what we will choose, but he does not determine it."

"Look, I am not a philosopher and do not know the answer to your question. I only want to follow what the prophet Micah says: *I shall tell you, man, what is good, and what the Lord requires of you: only to do justly, and to love mercy, and to walk humbly with your God.*"

Jeshua sighed wearily as he rose and entered the tent. James remained outside thinking about Jeshua's future. It was difficult to see him as a royal heir, a Hasmonean prince, even though he had all the looks and grace of inherent nobility. He had a simple and loving nature, without any ambition for social position or wealth. But he was now faced with all the temptations of his rank, all that Joseph wanted to provide for him, riches, social esteem, political power, even kingship. The people were hungry for leadership, for some divine sign of redemption, of release from Roman rule and oppression. If they knew who Jeshua was they would force him into the role of redeemer, of a saviour, and he would be destroyed in the process, driven like a lamb to the slaughter. The secret of his identity must be kept.

᛭ ᛭ ᛭ ᛭ ᛭ ᛭ ᛭ ᛭

As dusk fell over the Jordan valley, Johanan crossed over to Peraea on the east bank of the river. He made his way towards the nearby town of Betharamptha, now called Livias by Antipas. How he hated and despised this Herodian ruler in his hilltop fortress, Machaerus. One day he will confront him, as Elijah confronted Ahab, and call down the curses of God against him.

He did not enter the town, but took shelter in a cave he had discovered outside it where there was a small stream and some date palms. At the back of the cave, he had found a burial niche with a large stone tablet covering the opening. A local shepherd told him this cave was where the rebel slave Simon of Peraea, was buried, the one who had burned the royal palace in Jericho soon after Herod's death and declared himself king and messiah. The Romans pursued him when he fled to his home in Peraea and beheaded him. There was a strange inscription on the stone tablet which seemed to say that the archangel Gabriel predicted he would die and rise again after three days.

Simon and his followers must have been influenced by pagan beliefs like those about the Egyptian god Osiris or the Babylonians god Tammuz, dying and returning from the dead. He remembered what the prophet Ezekiel had said in one of his visions, the abomination of the Temple where women sat at the gates weeping for Tammuz. How ironic it was that the names of Babylonian gods were adopted by the Jewish calendar. How many people realised that the names Esther and Mordechai were those of the Babylonian gods Ishtar and Marduk? The Zadokites were right to omit the Book of Esther from the biblical texts. It was some fairy tale written by exiled Jews in Persia, priding themselves with the belief that the Persian king was of Jewish ancestry.

The overseer at the Zadokite settlement had made his mission clear to him. The people had to turn back to their origins, to the revelation at Sinai, to the pure faith of the biblical teachings, and to eliminate all those pagan accumulations. It was his mission to bring the message of repentance and return to God, but the method he used was the voice of fear, a warning against divine anger that would destroy all the unfaithful.

164

So many false messiahs had risen after Herod's death, and the people still longed for another. What they wanted was a heroic figure like Judah the Maccabee to lead them to victory and independence. But what they really needed was a spiritual guide to warn them like the biblical prophets had done, to rebuke them, to threaten them with dire punishments if they disobeyed the commandments. His was the fearsome voice of Isaiah in his earlier prophecies. *Ah sinful nation, a people laden with iniquities ...they have forsaken the Lord ...they are gone away backward. ...Wash you, make you clean, put away the evil of your doings ...*

****

Jeshua woke with the sound of birds twittering in the trees above. It was still very early in the morning, with the dawn just breaking. James was fast asleep, so he rose quietly and went outside. No one around them was stirring as he made his way down to the river bank and gazed at the water streaming down towards the south. He waited there for a long while, and then noticed someone approaching from the other side of the river. He soon recognised the tall figure of Johanan as he reached the water's edge, flinging off his camel-hair robe and entering the river only in his loincloth. He saw him dip himself seven times in the water, and then swimming with strong strokes towards the western bank.

The sun was just rising as he came nearer. Jeshua stood there waiting to greet him, a smile of welcome on his face. Johanan stood up, knee deep in the water as a ray of sunshine struck Jeshua's forehead, turning his fair hair into gold. He gazed at the young man in amazement, the bright face, the blue eyes and golden hair. He thought he was seeing an apparition, an angel come to bring good tidings.

As Jeshua came towards him, walking into the shallow edge of the river, he stood in silent wonder, and then opened his arms wide with joy. Was this the answer to his prayer, the one sent by God to fulfil the prophecies of divine redemption?

"Johanan, I am your cousin Jeshua!"

He was speechless. He was barely three at the time, but he still remembered the boy he had played with back in Ein Karem. They embraced and then Jeshua said he wanted to be immersed in the river as well, to be cleansed of his sins.

"What sins, Jeshua? You surely cannot a sinner!"

"Well, perhaps not sins of commission, but certainly those of omission. I should have searched for you long ago, and not waited for your parents to send me."

"My parents, how are they? This is *my* great sin of omission, to show respect and love for them."

"They are well but anxious to know how you are. You have been away so long."

"It is nearly ten years since I left them. But I cannot leave my mission now. I have sworn an oath to be the messenger of the Zadokites to the people of Israel."

Jeshua immersed himself, coming up refreshed and filled with a sense of peace. Johanan was struck again at the purity and beauty of the face, the almost ethereal look in the blue eyes lifted to the skies. He returned to the eastern bank to retrieve his robe, holding it aloft as they both moved back to the other side.

Jeshua saw James coming down towards river and waved at him.

"That is my brother, James," he told Johanan. "He accompanied me on our journey to find you."

The two men greeted each other warmly, and they all went up to the tent together. James laid out the food they had brought with them from Jericho—bread, cheese, olives, and some dried dates and figs. Johanan said that there was still enough time to sit together and talk, since no one would go down to the river before the sun had warmed the area.

"How did you know where to find me?" he asked.

"We had an Essene guide who went to your settlement to ask about you. We were not sure we would be welcome there."

"Strangers are often suspected by us of being spies or agents of the government. The Romans see us as potentially subversive and inciting to rebellion because of our teachings. We regard Essenes as friendly neighbours though we differ from them in our views."

"How are they different from you?" James asked hesitantly. "They also live as a community, share their goods with each other, eat together ..."

"Yes, but they accepted Herod and his government. They have no quarrel with Roman dominance in this country while we do not accept it and never will."

"I admire the Essenes," said Jeshua. "They are peace-loving, welcome all people and care for the poor and sick."

"We care more for the purity of their souls, for their adherence to the teachings of our fathers. We accept only the rule of God and await his kingdom on earth which will surely come one day."

"You want Israel to be once again 'a kingdom of priests and a holy nation' as God told Moses on Mount Sinai"

"Yes, you have said it exactly! And we, the Zadokites, the sons of Zadok the high priest who served in the Temple of Solomon, are the true priests of Israel, not those hypocrites and sycophants in the Temple in Jerusalem."

Johanan then said that the prophet Ezekiel, one of the Zadokite priests of the First Temple exiled to Babylon, had a vision of a future Temple in which the sons of Zadok will minister to God. His detailed description of it shows how completely different it would be from the Temple of Herod. This was how they believed it would be built one day.

"Your father, Zacharias, is a Zadokite," said James. "Yet he served in the Temple nearly all his life, before and after Herod rebuilt it."

"That was my quarrel with him," said Johanan. "He wanted me to serve there as well but I refused. He is a Sadducee, a Zadokite who accepts the rule of priests of a lesser rank, who compromises for the sake of keeping his position. I regard the Sadducees as disloyal priests and hypocrites."

"He is old now, Johanan," Jeshua said gently. "He wishes to see you before he dies. Can you not go and visit him just for one day?"

"I cannot leave my mission here, Jeshua. But I will send a letter to him and my mother when I return to the settlement where I always spend the Sabbath."

He stood up and said he would have to go now to attend to the people who had come to the riverside. James said they were going up the Jordan valley towards the Galilee to visit their brothers in Capernaum.

"Come here again on your way back and I will take you to visit our settlement."

They parted with warm embraces and Johanan strode away with his camel hair robe fastened with a leather girdle clearly marking him as a desert preacher or prophet. The sun was already higher up in the sky, reflecting its golden light on the waters of the Jordan. James and Jeshua waited for a while till they saw Johanan enter the river, and then turned northwards towards Galilee. They had been strongly impressed with him, and Jeshua said that he would like one day to visit him at the Zadokite settlement.

James was not in favour of such a visit. He pointed out that although Johanan did not know Jeshua was a Hasmonean prince, some of the Zadokites might identify him merely by his looks. He was also a grandson of Herod, which would make him doubly hated.

"A man should be judged for himself, not for his parentage," Jeshua protested.

"Not in this country or even in Rome itself. Parentage is all you are judged by and rated. Johanan thinks your father was some nationalist rebel killed by Herod and that you and your mother had to flee to Egypt to avoid being arrested. Your mother is also his cousin, his father's niece, and therefore of a Zadokite heritage. So he considers you as someone who could join his Zadokite sect in the desert."

Jeshua looked at him in anguish. He did not want his cousin to know of his Hasmonean origins.

"Will he hate me if he finds out? We liked each other instantly as soon as we met on the river. I cannot forget his wonderful smile of welcome."

"Then you must hide your identity. Only a few people know of it. Do not even tell my brothers when you see them. Who else knows besides Johanan's parents, Joseph, Gorion, Nikki, Ruhama? My father, Josiah, knew just before he died."

"I think Philo in Alexandria must have guessed the truth," said Jeshua. "Or my mother may have told him when he asked her to confirm his suspicions."

"The truth is safe with him, I think," James assured him.

They set out northwards along the river bank on the long road to the Galilee. For Jeshua, it was like going home again to the green hills and valleys that he had always loved.

****

Joseph came to visit Gorion at his home when he heard that he was feeling ill and was laid up in bed. Ruhama had been giving him some medicine and nourishing food to strengthen him.

"What news of your projects, Joseph?" he asked as soon as he saw him.

"Going very well I think, Hananel. The buildings in Bezetha are being occupied by young families as well as by a few rich merchants. It has become the main entry for goods from the north and there are many storage depots for grain, oil, wool, and wood to provide for the needs of the city for several years. All we need is a third wall to enclose the area for better protection from bandits and marauders."

"And what is going on about the Temple? How are they progressing with all the additional buildings and interior decorations?"

"It is a slow business. The priests are reluctant to spend more money than they have already. It is already forty years since Herod began building it and it will probably take another forty years to complete everything he had planned for it."

"Nikki says the city needs more water, and that an additional aqueduct will have to be built. He made a complete survey of the water supply system and submitted the plans to the Roman authorities. The plan is to have water from sources further south conveyed by aqueduct to Solomon's Pools, the three large reservoirs near the Ein Eitam spring southwest of Bethlehem, so that more water can reach the Temple."

"It is a very expensive project, Gorion. They will demand money from the Temple treasury. And you know how the priests and the people will react."

"But what is all the money, the half-shekel they received from every Jew in the country and in the world every year, intended for if only to build and improve the Temple."

"There is a lot of corruption among the priests. You remember that after Valerius Gratus replaced the High Priest Ananus with that upstart Ishmael ben Fabus, he backed down a year later and appointed Eleazar ben Ananus. But now, as you know, Caiaphas, the son-in-law of Ananus, has taken over the high priesthood and is now firmly in charge."

"I told Ananus at the time not to accept him into his family. That man is power hungry. I understood from Nikki that he is in close collusion with the Roman authorities and with Gratus as well."

Gorion asked Joseph if he had any news from Zacharias about his son Johanan, and heard that he received a letter from him but that he still refuses to abandon his mission.

"Zacharias must be approaching his hundredth year," Joseph told him. "And Elizabeth is already in her seventies. She had Johanan when she was over forty I believe. He is their only child after waiting so long for him. It must be hard for them without him near them. I am glad that Maryam decided to stay with them, although she is always welcome to come and live in my house to be near Jeshua."

Ruhama came in, bringing a tray for Gorion's midday meal. She invited Joseph to join her and Nikki in the dining room where they and the children were having their meal. Later on, while Gorion was taking a nap, Joseph and Nikki went to the upper chamber to discuss various matters. They were both anxiously waiting for Jeshua to return to Jerusalem and to find out about his meeting with Johanan.

It was quiet and cool in the upper chamber as Joseph and Nicodemus sat down at the round table. A few scrolls lay scattered over it. One of them was opened almost at full length in which there was a sketch of the entire city. Another had the design of the Temple and all its various sections. Joseph looked at them admiringly and praised Nicodemus for his architectural skills.

"I see you have already sketched in the line for the proposed aqueduct."

"Yes, and I have also estimated its enormous cost," Nicodemus told him. "Some of the richer people in this city have agreed to join me in setting up a consortium to finance this project. Gratus will ask the Roman governor in Syria for his assistance in obtaining funds. What remains to be done is to persuade Caiaphas and the Temple priests to pay their share."

"He will do so only under duress," Joseph warned him. "He can always threaten to incite the people against Rome for touching the Temple treasury which is only meant for its upkeep. It does not take much to arouse a rabble in Jerusalem."

Nicodemus rolled up the scrolls and cleared the table, putting them all in their niche on the shelves. Joseph stood up and went to one of the arched openings overlooking the Temple. He gazed into the distance where a glimpse of the Dead Sea could be seen.

"I am beginning to worry about Jeshua meeting Johanan," he said. "I hope he has not told him of his true parentage. I tried to warn him before but he did not seem to understand the reason. He has to wait until he is ready to rule."

"You have to give him time," Nicodemus advised. "You are teaching him how to dress more elegantly, to mix socially with people, with the Jerusalem upper class, the priesthood, the Romans as your adopted son and protégée without telling anyone of his true rank. And I will try to round out his education in Jewish studies, history, theology, and the political situation today."

"I think the time will come for his public appearance as the Hasmonean heir when Herod Antipas either dies or is deposed. Rome will see the need for a princely or even kingly figure to satisfy the desires of the people for a return to

Hasmonean rule. Many of them will still remember Alexander and recognise Jeshua as his son."

"He will need a few years to become accustomed to his new position. James is a good and steady influence on him and I suggest that you bring him to Jerusalem to give him the brotherly support he will need."

"That is a very good idea, Nikki! He can be his constant and loyal companion or adviser," Joseph said in glad agreement. "He can still remain as general manager of his inn at the Emmaus crossroad now that he has a few good partners in the enterprise. He can always go down there once in a while to see to things, to visit his aunt and uncle. I am sure he will agree to be with Jeshua now that he knows of his Hasmonean parentage and that his father Josiah would have wanted him to do so."

Nicodemus added that he would also invite James to join Jeshua at the regular meetings held in the upper chamber with a few people such as Johanan Ben Zakkai, Matthias, a priest of the Jehoiarib clan, and some of his Essene friends.

It was getting late in the afternoon and the room grew darker. They went down again to be with Gorion for a while. The children soon came in, and they all sat talking together until supper time. Joseph enjoyed being part of this warm family gathering, promising to come again with Jeshua when he returned.

****

Life in Rome was no longer what it had been in earlier days. Tiberius had practically abdicated his authority as Caesar to Sejanus, Commander of the Praetorian Guard. Sejanus kept trying to marry into the Julio-Claudian family, and after divorcing his wife, he wanted to marry Drusus' widow Livilla. But Tiberius denied his request, so he began to isolate the emperor from Rome, persuading him to retire to the countryside and finally to Capri. Since he was in charge of the Praetorian Guard he could control any information between Tiberius and Rome.

The only barrier to his plans for complete control was Tiberius' mother, Livia, and he would have to delay his plans to extend his power until her death. He also had many opponents among the senators and wealthy equestrians in Rome. He formed a network of spies with the intention to bring false accusations of treason amongst them. He took advantage of the distrust between Tiberius and

Agrippina the Elder, widow of Germanicus for trying to place her sons as his heirs instead of his young grandson Tiberius Gemellus, the son of Drusus and Livilla.

Aurella tried to keep her children away from all these intrigues and to avoid any attention from Sejanus. But Arius was becoming more and more angered by his behaviour and sided with the senators in opposition. After consultation with Marcus and Joseph, it was decided to keep him out of trouble and send him to the now large colony of Roman tradesmen in Britannia. Their company had an important trading post in Tintagel on the west coast of Cornwall and he would gain good experience there in trading.

Arius was at first very reluctant to go, but Joseph said that he would soon arrange to travel there with him and see him well settled in this new country. As a Roman, he would be welcomed in the small colony of tradesmen, a colonial outpost of the Empire, and among the Cornish natives who were friendly and cooperative. The plan was to go the following spring when the weather was favourable.

Joseph was sure Arius would like living there once he adapted to his new life. At his age, he was young and impressionable enough to do so. It would be good to visit Britannia again after so long. He had been happy and at peace there for a while, far away from the turmoil of Jerusalem or Rome.

****

It was now early winter in the Galilee, and although it rained sporadically the days were still fine. James and Jeshua arrived in Capernaum after their long journey, partly on foot and partly hiring rides on wagons driving northwards. Jose, Jude and Simon, were overjoyed to see them and they were also glad to meet them again and their families. The brothers were now living in well-furnished houses and had a large workshop with several men employed to handle all the demands from Tiberias and other cities in the Galilee.

Jeshua felt happy to enter the workshop with the fresh scent of wood shavings and the soft dust under the tables. Some of the finest timber from the forests of Lebanon had recently been floated down by way of the various tributaries that fed into the Jordan River which emerged into the Sea of Galilee at Bethsaida, not far from Capernaum.

"We have already used some of it to build a new ark in the synagogue named after our father," said Jose. "You must come to see it this Sabbath day when we hold our services there."

"And we will take you in our new boat on the lake to visit some of the cities around it—Bethsaida, Magdala and of course Tiberias," Jude added.

"You will like Tiberias. It is a really beautiful city now with all the new houses on the hillside and the wide shoreline."

"Are there still many fishermen working along the shores?" Jeshua asked. "I would like to go out fishing with them again."

They laid many plans for their visit, and then retired to rest. James said that they should not stay longer than a week or ten days because Joseph would become anxious. Each day, one of their brothers would take a day off work to take them around the area. They sailed first to Bethsaida with Jose in the large boat recently built to transport some materials and goods from there. The city was located within the territory belonging to the tetrarch, Herod Philip, and lay on the eastern bank of Jordan River near the juncture between it and the Sea of Galilee.

"Philip the Tetrarch, intends to develop this place, and perhaps even turn it into a polis," said Jose. "He is a much better ruler than Antipas, and cares for his people. Many have come over the border to benefit from the good commercial opportunities he offers."

"His nephew, Agrippa, is in Tiberias working under his uncle Antipas," Jude told them. "He is a very likeable and charming, and the people adore him, which of course aggravates Antipas. They quarrel very often over the city management."

James smiled. "Joseph told me he was a popular figure at the court of Tiberias in Rome, having a good time with the emperor's son and heir Drusus."

"He certainly enjoys the good life," Jose laughed. "He has to have the finest furniture we can provide for his house near the river. His extravagance will be his downfall one day when Antipas gets fed up with him."

They set out to sea again on the way back to Capernaum. After the Sabbath, Jude would take them to Magdala further south along the coast. He said it was a lively town, mainly filled with tradesmen and artisans. And the day before their departure, they would all go together to Tiberias where they had to make a large delivery to the palace of Antipas.

****

Winter came early that year to Jerusalem and the city lay under a deep layer of snow. Fires were lit in the hearth in all the rooms of the Gorion house. It was now too cold in the upper chamber so Nikki spent most of his mornings in his small study on the second floor, and then kept his father company in his ground floor room. They held long discussions on various matters and Gorion, who was in better health and felt stronger, tried to give his son some of his views based on his long experience.

"The Romans, with their practical and logical minds, cannot understand Jews. It makes no sense to them to worship some invisible, unknowable god. They ask how can one feel close to such a deity, and also worship him to the exclusion of all other gods. For political expediency, they will respect the religion of the people under their rule, allow them to follow their customs and rituals, and only demand submission to their civil administration. Yet many Jews refuse to accept their rule willingly and they will destroy themselves in their refusal."

"It is not just national pride, Father," Nicodemus said. "We are not like the British tribes or the Germanic tribes, or many of the people in the Roman provinces who try to rebel against Roman domination to gain independence. Revolt for us is for religious reasons as well. No one should rule us but God and his representatives on earth. Our very nationhood is defined by religion and is inseparable from it."

"This will lead to our self-destruction, Nikki. What the people must be told is that Roman rule is what God has ordained. They must wait for deliverance through divine intervention and not by human rebellion."

"But, Father, that is just why they have been so easily led by so many messianic figures over the past two or three decades, ever since Herod died. They believe that the time has come for redemption and will follow anyone who claims he was sent by God to deliver them."

"At least, Johanan does not claim to be a messiah," Gorion said. "He only says he is heralding his coming."

"And the approaching Day of Judgment," Nicodemus added.

"There is a rising tide of rebellion in the country. You should warn the Roman authorities to hold off, to intervene less with religious matters. You know, they have the authority to decide who should be the High Priest and his

174

Temple garments are stored in the Antonia Fortress not in the Temple. It is demeaning also to have Roman soldiers up there, overlooking the Temple area."

"I have already advised Gratus against allowing Roman soldiers to enter Jerusalem with their standards—the eagles that symbolise imperial power and domination." Nicodemus told him. "I reminded him of the tragic events after Herod mounted a golden eagle over a Temple gate, the terrible massacre that followed its removal by the zealous rabbis and their disciples. Every violation of this kind gives Zealots and religious fanatics more influence over the people. The Romans do not seem to understand that such things are the direct cause of all these messianic revolts and their response is to be even harsher and more repressive—it's a vicious circle."

He promised to speak to Joseph about this when he returned from Rome. Joseph had gone there for Arianna's wedding to a Roman senator, and afterwards to accompany Arius to Britannia. He hoped he would be back in Jerusalem in time for the Passover festival, the most problematic time in the city.

****

Marcus arrived in Rome a week before his daughter's wedding, bringing her a wedding gift of rich silks from the East, besides other luxury items. She would also have a large dowry and her new home would not be far from her mother's mansion. Aurelia had organised a grand reception and festive dinner after the marriage ceremony which would be conducted with Roman rites and an exchange of vows.

He found his father, Joseph, residing at his old lodgings near the Tiber River. He was reluctant to attend the marriage ceremony, but would come to the following reception and dinner.

"It is still not easy for me to see how completely Aurelia and the children have abandoned their ties to Judaism. You, Marcus, at least retain your national loyalties even if you no longer observe Jewish laws and customs."

"Now that I am living in Damascus, even my national feelings have weakened and frayed. But I still become angered when I see Jews wronged and abused, especially those in the Galilee under Antipas. He has some important trading contracts with our company so I am familiar with what goes on there."

"Yes, I heard he no longer trades with the Nabataeans since divorcing his wife, the daughter of King Aretas," Joseph remarked.

"He was a fool to do so, even though we have profited from it," said Marcus. "He will regret it one day. The Arab is a vengeful foe when he is wronged, when his honour and pride are hurt."

"And a faithful friend once you gain his love and loyalty," said Joseph. "I found true and tried partners in them during the years they drove my caravans across the desert."

"The Arabs are descendants of Ishmael, the eldest son of Abraham" Marcus remarked. "They still resent his expulsion into the desert and being deprived of his heritage by the younger son Isaac."

"But the Bible says the children of Abraham will inherit the land from the Nile to the Euphrates, which means both Ishmael and Isaac. The children of Isaac will receive only the Land of Canaan, while all the rest will be the heritage of Ishmael and his children, which means that Ishmael will have the bigger portion."

Joseph then quoted the passage in Genesis in which God tells Abraham that his wife Sarah would give birth to a son and heir. "When Abraham pleads for the future of Ishmael, God tells him: *Behold, I have blessed him and will make him fruitful, and will multiply him exceedingly. Twelve princes shall he beget, and I will make him a great nation.*"

"Well, let us hope that will satisfy him and his descendants" Marcus said sceptically.

They talked of the old days in Judaea, their old homestead in Ramatayim now in the hands of caretakers. Joseph said that one day he would retire and spend the rest of his life in the mountains of Ephraim away from everything. There was now only the need to see Arius settled in Britannia and to ensure the future of young Jeshua.

****

Maryam wrote to Ruhama to say that Zacharias was feeling weak and failing fast. He wanted to see Gorion before he died because he had a special message to give him. She begged her to bring him to Ein Karem as soon as possible. A few days later, Nikki and Ruhama brought Gorion in their carriage to the home of Zacharias and Elizabeth. The roads were still covered with frost and badly rutted in places, but the day was bright and sunny for December.

They found Zacharias sitting near the hearth, and his face lit up when he saw them.

"Gorion, it is so good of you to come!"

"I am glad to see you, old friend. It has been too long since we last met together."

Maryam and Elizabeth had prepared a good meal for them, and they sat around the table to enjoy the food and family talk. Elizabeth wanted to know all about the grandchildren, and Zacharias asked about Joseph, Marcus and his children in Rome.

"I had a letter from Joseph," Gorion told him. "There is a change of plan. He will be returning to Jerusalem soon after Arianna's wedding, and take Arius to Britannia only next spring after he has graduated from school."

"He also wrote to me about Jeshua," Nicodemus told Maryam. "He asked me to keep an eye on him when he returns from the Galilee."

"He could come here and stay with his mother till then," Elizabeth suggested.

Nicodemus said he would urge him to do so, and to let James go back for a while to his home in Emmaus. He was told that a younger brother of James's uncle, Cleopas, had come to live in Emmaus, and may be willing to take charge of the inn so that James could remain permanently in Jerusalem with Jeshua.

"I would be glad to have James with him constantly," said Maryam. "He has always taken special care of him ever since we came to Nazareth. It was such a confusing time for him then."

"It is now another confusing time for him, I think," Nicodemus said. "He needs guidance and support after discovering who he is."

"Joseph will give him the support and you must give him the guidance, Nikki," said Zacharias. "Between you both he will be protected from any future harm."

They retired to the couches around the hearth. Gorion looked expectantly at Zacharias, and the old man noted his questioning look.

"Yes, my friend. I wanted to tell you and Nikki something very important before it is too late for me to do so. I intended to tell this to my son, Johanan, but he will not be coming to visit me as I had hoped."

He told them a secret that had been handed down in his family for three generations and entrusted to him. When the Zadokite priests were deposed from the high priesthood and many of them fled either to Egypt with Onias or to the settlement near Ein Gedi, they hid large quantities of Temple treasures in various places on the outskirts of Jerusalem and in the Judaean desert. A list of the treasures and their locations was inscribed on a copper scroll for better preservation. The Zadokites hoped one day to return to their former high position in the Temple and recover the buried treasures.

"Where is this scroll now," Nikki asked.

"It is in a small box in an underground vault in the Temple which I marked on this map of the Temple interior. I am entrusting the key of the vault to you Gorion and to Nikki until Johanan returns and takes charge of it. Please keep it safe for him."

Gorion was amazed to hear this, and also afraid to be responsible for such a task. But Nicodemus seemed eager and excited by this revelation. He did not like Caiaphas and the corrupt priests in the Temple administration and hoped that they would be replaced at some future time. This treasure would give the Zadokites the power to regain control if they had a strong leader like Johanan.

Zacharias was glad to see that his request was accepted. He handed over the key to Nicodemus and recited the priestly blessing for him and his father. They remained with him for another hour until he retired to rest, and then drove back to their home in Jerusalem.

****

Jeshua was glad to be back in Galilee near the beautiful lake and in the company of his brothers. They spent a few evenings around a camp fire near the shore, watching the fishermen going out in their boats to cast their nets. Some of them remembered him and invited him join them on one of their fishing trips far out into the lake. They were good men, charitable, regularly attending synagogue services, hospitable to strangers passing through their town. He liked their simple piety, their faith in God, and the good comradeship amongst them. Every fisherman was ready to help his fellow in trouble if his net was caught in a rock underwater or his boat sprang a sudden leak.

He went with his brothers to the small synagogue they had built to attend the Sabbath morning prayers and the reading of the weekly portion in the Bible. After every sentence that was read, someone translated the Hebrew into Aramaic for those who did not understand the holy language. Then a rabbi stood up and gave a sermon on the selected portion, explaining the meaning more clearly and deriving certain moral principles from it.

Afterwards, a few hymns were sung before everyone went home to enjoy the main Sabbath meal. The entire family was gathered together that morning, and as James was the eldest brother, he was asked to make the blessings on the wine and the bread. Jeshua was reminded of the way Father Josiah had always conducted the Sabbath meal with such warmth and good spirits.

They spent the afternoon walking about the town, meeting a few friends and watching the children playing in the fields around it. If it was not for the discovery of his true identity, this is where he would gladly like to live. James must have noticed this, because he smiled at him sadly and said they could always come back here later on for longer visits. He could enjoy the benefits of both worlds as long as no one knew who he was.

The next day Jude took them in his wagon to Magdala where he had to buy some food supplies and wine. After making his purchases, they went to the central inn to have their midday meal, leaving the wagon and mules in the stables behind. It was very noisy and crowded, and the serving girls hurried back and forth from the kitchen to the tables. After they finished eating and paid the fare, Jeshua saw some rough fellows seated in the corner laughing and making lewd remarks at a young serving girl, no more than twelve of thirteen, with a lovely face and long red hair. One of them thrust out an arm to bar her way and encircled her waist, making her cry out in fear.

Jeshua immediately went to her rescue. His blue eyes blazed as he tried to pull the girl away. The fellow lifted his other arm to strike at Jeshua, but James and Jude were already at his side and held the fellow's arm back with all their strength. The girl managed to slip away and ran back to the kitchen. The brothers stood firm against the loud roar of fury and attack, until the innkeeper came quickly with his assistants to evict the man and his friends. He did not want a fight that would cause damage to his customers and to himself.

Jeshua was still trembling with anger as they went outside. James put an arm around his shoulders to calm him down.

"This sort of thing is quite common in public inns, especially in Magdala," Jude told him. "Some of the worst people come here to engage in thievery, smuggling, and other criminal activities. Young unprotected girls are often kidnapped and forced into prostitution."

"It should not be tolerated," said Jeshua. "I cannot stand by when I see such things."

"You have lived a protected life so far, Jeshua," James told him. "The world has travelled far from Adam's Garden of Eden. There are more Cains than Abels."

They travelled southwards towards Tiberias where Jose and Simon were to arrive by boat the following day from Capernaum. It was late afternoon by the time they arrived, and as arranged, were given lodgings at the service and delivery centre behind the palace. From the top of the hill, Jeshua looked down at the city with its wide avenues and white limestone buildings leading down to the lake glimmering in the last rays of the sun. He felt calmer then, and more purposeful. He wanted to do as much as he could to bring into being the kingdom of heaven Johanan was preaching about although he still did not know how he could do this.

****

It was the day following the Sabbath, and the young priest, Matthias ben Joseph, was in charge of assigning duties for the members of his clan for the coming week. His family was a prominent member of the Jehoiarib priestly clan, the first one among the twenty-four courses serving in the Temple in weekly rotation. There was an earlier Matthias several generations ago, who had married the daughter of Jonathan the Maccabee, which meant that his family was of Hasmonean descent through the maternal line.

He completed his assignments as quickly as he could because he had an appointment that morning with Nicodemus ben Gorion at the Council House on the south side of the Temple. This was where the one of the minor Sanhedrin courts in Jerusalem was located, the one that dealt with criminal offences and civil disputes concerning property and financial claims. Another minor court was located near the western gate adjoining the Xystus which dealt mainly with religious matters and laws concerning the Temple.

He rushed across the Court of the Gentiles and out through the Triple Gate into the plaza beyond. He saw Nicodemus standing near the entrance of the Council House talking to the prominent Sanhedrin rabbi, Johanan ben Zakkai, whom he knew very well from their regular meetings in the upper chamber of the Gorion House. They seemed troubled and also angry.

"Matthias, good morning," said Nicodemus. "Thank you for coming to meet us."

Rabbi Johanan also greeted him with a warm handshake. They moved inside to one of the side benches in the Council House to avoid the flow of people going in and out and also to prevent being overheard.

"It's about the high priest Caiaphas," Johanan explained. "The Sanhedrin has heard complaints about the administration in the Temple and the handling of funds."

"We have a board of fifteen Temple officers, *memunim*, to administer the various functions of the Temple," said Matthias. "And there are seven trustees, *amarkelim*, to oversee the treasury, besides three cashiers, *gizbarim*, to empty the contribution boxes. They are all pious and reliable priests, in my opinion."

"Yet it seems there is never enough money to do the necessary repairs after the three festivals," said Nicodemus. "Nor can the building plans and necessary improvements be financed."

Johanan said that Rabban Gamaliel, the head of the Hillel faction in the Sanhedrin, has requested that Caiaphas submit a financial report on Temple income and expenditure, but he refused to do so, claiming that the Temple is outside the jurisdiction of the Sanhedrin. But there was a strong suspicion that he was embezzling the treasury through false receipts for supplies such as oil, wood, incense and other requirements. Matthias promised to look into this matter personally and also to consult with one of the treasury trustees on how to prevent such embezzlement.

"There is also another matter," said Nicodemus. "Some serious complaints have been made about the vendors and money changers in the Court of the Gentiles during the festivals who charge high prices and rates of exchange."

"Yes, I have heard of this, but we have no control over them," said Matthias. "There are Temple guards at the gates only to keep order among those entering."

"I doubt Caiaphas cares much about such matters," Johanan remarked. "He does not take an interest in the people, never enters the Temple through this area but only across the bridge from the Xystus."

"Don't forget he was appointed by Gratus and the Roman authorities and not by the people," Nicodemus reminded him. "It was most probably through bribery and cooperation with their administration."

"He is not liked by the priests here," said Matthias. "Herod favoured these Sadducean families over the Hasmonean ones like my own family. They are now well entrenched in power and wealth."

He had to return to his duties, but he promised to report back to them about the treasury as soon as possible. Nicodemus and Johanan saw him to the Temple gates and then turned back to walk down towards the Pool of Siloam. This was the main source of water supply in Jerusalem, especially convenient for people coming to Jerusalem for the three pilgrimage festivals.

The water came from the Gihon spring outside the eastern wall of the Temple, and flowed down through the tunnel that King Hezekiah had built more than seven centuries earlier. There was also the Pool of Bethesda on the north side of the Temple near the Sheep's Gate, as well as the Mamilla Pool outside the western wall of the city. Herod had built aqueducts leading from that pool into three reservoirs within the city. But all this was no longer sufficient.

"Nearly every house in Jerusalem has a cistern to collect rainwater during the winter season," Nicodemus said. "And Roman soldiers have dug deep wells in the valleys around the city for their own use. But water is still a problem in Jerusalem."

Watching the crowds around the Siloam pool, he felt frustrated at the slow process of creating the consortium for building the aqueduct from Solomon's Pools near Bethlehem. That was the only possible solution for an adequate water supply to the city and to the Temple.

"Perhaps the Sanhedrin should intervene in this matter," Johanan suggested. "Rabban Gamaliel says that the public good is a basic principle in Judaism."

Nicodemus said he was doubtful Gamaliel could use this principle against Caiaphas to finance the aqueduct or even to share in the cost. The only way was to go to Gratus and lay out their case. But he thought they should wait until Joseph returned to Jerusalem, since he would have more influence on him and on the Roman administration.

****

Agrippa was now thirty-five and dissatisfied with his life so far. All those wonderful years in Rome had come to nothing. He had hoped that when his dear friend Drusus came to power after his father's death, that he would regain the Hasmonean crown over the entire country and even beyond it as in the days of Alexander Janneus and his queen Salome Alexandra. Instead, he was here in Tiberias, forced to endure the whims of his uncle Antipas and the incestuous relations he had with Agrippa's sister Herodias.

His hope was that Antipas would one day fall foul of the Roman authorities and be deposed as his brother Archelaus had been nearly twenty years earlier. Then there was a good chance he could take over the tetrarchy. He had already gained the friendship of the Governor of Syria and took every opportunity to curry favour with him. The city was well run under his administration, and he was well liked by the citizens. And wherever he travelled through the Galilee, he found the people glad to welcome him as a Hasmonean prince.

This morning he decided to leave the palace and go down with his assistant to the waterfront where the supply boat from Capernaum was to arrive, bringing the new doors and some furniture for his villa by the lake. Those Galilean carpenters were excellent craftsmen, and he was ready to pay them the price for their work.

Although winter was not yet over, the weather here was warm and pleasant. Standing on the docks, he watched the fishing boats on the lake, most of them returning with their haul from a long night on the water.

As he gazed out to the left, waiting for the boat to arrive, he saw three men talking and laughing together, and also looking northwards expectantly. One of them, younger than the other two, was fair-haired and handsome, not at all like his Galilean companions. He then recognised the oldest of them as the man he had spoken to about the doors he ordered from Capernaum.

"You there, my good man," he called. "Aren't you Jude the carpenter, the one I spoke to before about the doors for my villa?"

Jude turned around and then bowed in greeting.

"Yes, my lord Agrippa, I am. As promised, my brothers are bringing the doors by boat this morning and will arrive very soon."

"Excellent! I have a wagon ready nearby to take them to my new villa a little further down the coast near the hot springs."

"These are also my brothers, James and Jeshua," said Jude. "They live in Judaea and came here for a short visit to see us."

"They are very welcome, I am sure," Agrippa said, smiling at them. But he seemed puzzled to hear that the younger man was Jude's brother.

James noticed his puzzled look, and told Agrippa that Jeshua was their half-brother from a different mother.

"Oh, I see," said Agrippa. He turned to Jeshua and looked at him more closely.

"You seem very familiar to me. Have we met before, in Rome perhaps?"

"Not that I can remember," said Jeshua. "I have never been in Rome."

James looked at Agrippa with wary eyes, noting the family resemblance between him and Jeshua, although Agrippa was of a darker complexion. Luckily, they were all distracted by a loud hail from one of the boats approaching the docks. As it came alongside, Jose and Simon leapt out to greet their brothers, while the boat rowers lifted out the two doors as well as other items of furniture.

Agrippa sent his assistant to bring the wagon down to the docks. After receiving the payment for their work, the brothers thanked him and began walking up the road towards the palace where they would stay overnight. Agrippa watched them go, a band of brothers, happy to be reunited. How he envied them for their warmth and spontaneous love for each other, so unlike the way his family treated each other.

Although his sister, Herodias, had gained him this position, she was cold and distant with him, taking the side of Antipas whenever they had an argument. His brothers in Rome had been jealous of his popularity at court, especially Aristobulus, the youngest in the family, who was named after his father. He promised himself that he would one day return to Rome and regain his position there.

****

Joseph returned from Rome to find that James and Jeshua had arrived back in Jerusalem a few days before him. He was glad to find them both looking well and happy to indulge themselves again in the comforts of warm baths, soft, padded robes and fur-lined slippers, good food and kindly servants. Gathered around the hearth in the evening, Joseph heard all about their experiences over the past three weeks and told them about his own visit to Rome.

"In about two or three months from now, when spring arrives, I intend to go with my grandson Arius to Britannia to get him established at his trading centre there."

Jeshua looked up with an eager face and asked if he could go as well. Joseph thought it was a good idea. He could enjoy a brief visit to Rome and then a pleasant sea voyage to Britannia, stopping at various ports on the way. It would be a kind of grand tour to supplement his education.

"On condition that you begin studying Latin with the tutor I have arranged for you," Joseph told him, "and also with the studies that Nicodemus has planned for you, mainly on Jewish history. We arranged that you will be here in the mornings and at the Gorion house in the evenings."

He saw that James was looking anxious and smiled reassuringly at him.

"I would like you to continue staying here with us James," he said. "While Jeshua is studying, I would like you to assist me in the mornings with my various projects in the city. I need someone to manage the charity institutions, to talk to the people and gain their trust. You will be with Jeshua in the afternoons and if you wish you can also go with him to the Gorion house in the evenings."

James felt relieved and said he would be glad to help Joseph. He wanted to know more about these institutions, and he was more than willing to undertake their management. Joseph gave him a general summary of them and then told him that he intended to leave him in charge of them while he and Jeshua were away in Britannia.

"You will be working closely with Nicodemus and also with his wife, Ruhama. They have both taken an interest in promoting the welfare of the poorer people in the city. Ruhama has set up medical centres in the Lower City mainly with the help of Essene doctors and healers. Nicodemus is more concerned with the city administration, food and water supply, and financial matters."

They had a late supper and retired to their rooms. Before going to bed, Joseph went out onto the balcony overlooking the eastern part of Jerusalem, the Temple Mount to the north and the Lower City descending southwards to the Kidron Valley. It all seemed so peaceful under the stars and the new moon near the horizon. He thought back to the time when this was simply a hill fort held by the Jebusites in the time of David, and then even earlier to the time of Abraham, when it was called Salem, one of the small city states in Canaan ruled by its priestly king Melchizedek, the king of righteousness, who served El Elyon, the High God.

Could the idea of one god have already preceded Abraham? He would have to discuss this with Nicodemus one day, or with Philo in Alexandria. On their way back from Britannia, he and Jeshua could stop over in Egypt and visit him. Jeshua would enjoy seeing the city where he had lived as a child. He might even leave him there with Philo for a few months after their return from Britannia to be taught Greek and philosophy to round out his education as a prince.

****

185

A special session of the Sanhedrin was called by Shammai, now almost eighty years old. For many years, he had served as the Av Beth Din, the head of the Sanhedrin law courts. After the death of Hillel and of his son, Simon, who died shortly after him, he was elected as Nasi, the President of the Sanhedrin. Hillel's grandson, Gamaliel, was now the head of the Hillelite faction which still comprised the majority of its members, and the laws were nearly always passed according to their ruling.

For Shammai, this was his final attempt to push through his eighteen ordinances to sever contact between Jews and Gentiles. The Hillelites had consistently opposed such ultra-orthodox decrees as provocative and unrealistic. It would aggravate relations among the various inhabitants of the country and cause even more enmity than was already felt between them. However, times were changing, and there was now more support for the Shammai school of thought among the members of the Sanhedrin. At the entrance to the Hewn Chamber, Shammai caught hold of Johanan Ben Zakkai and pulled him aside.

"I know about the meetings you are attending with sectarian groups at the Gorion home, and even with some Alexandrian Jews and Greek scholars."

"These are purely for academic discussions on comparative religion, philosophy, and ethics to find out points of agreement or difference."

"But from what I hear, Gamaliel intends eventually to establish a college for young rabbis where such matters will be taught. And eventually, these rabbis will be teaching the pupils in our schools. It will contaminate their Judaism with pagan culture and ideas."

"Judaism will only be strengthened when it stands up as intellectually equal to other beliefs and philosophies."

"You are a fool, Ben Zakkai!" Shammai shouted at him. "This is the kind of thinking by Jews during the period before the Hasmonean revolt. They became entranced with Greek culture and were ready to assimilate with it."

The bell rang for the beginning of the session, and they joined those entering the large chamber. Shammai strode up to the dais and opened the session with the usual blessings and convocations. He then rose and addressed the assembly. He still had a commanding presence in spite of his years, and many of the Hillelites respected his vast learning and deep convictions even when they voted against his proposals.

"We are gathered here to discuss the eighteen ordinances proposed by me and my disciples," Shammai began. "These are very strict decrees about ritual purity and contact with Gentiles who will be regarded from now on as causing impurity in wine or oil simply by touching, handling or transporting the vessels that contain them."

Gamaliel rose to protest that such ordinances would cause bitter hatred between Jew and Gentile and may lead to even greater strife and violence among the people living in this country. But Shammai ignored his protest and went on to speak about his proposed legislation.

"We have forgotten that we are the chosen people of God. And as Balaam predicted, we shall always dwell alone, and not be counted among the nations. Our numbers are small in this tiny stretch of land and many of our people are no longer living here with us. Thousands are living in Babylonia, in Alexandria, in Rome and elsewhere, and although they are still loyal to us, they have slowly adapted themselves to living within foreign cultures. We here are the last bastion of our nation in the Promised Land and we must preserve our faith and heritage from assimilation with other people and their cultures. The only way to do this is to separate ourselves from contact with the foreign elements in this country."

He then laid out the eighteen ordinances that he wished to legislate as binding upon all the people. As he read them out, there were murmurs in the assembly that grew louder and louder as he went on listing them. Cries of astonishment were heard from the rear where the younger members were sitting. When Shammai finished, pandemonium broke out. Some stood up and came forward to the lectern set up for response and criticism by members of the assembly. Quotations were brought from the Bible about 'loving the stranger in your midst', that God loved all his creatures, both Jew and Gentile. Others spoke about the political implications, the tensions that this would create with the Roman administration.

Shammai was undeterred. He spoke again on a different subject that he felt was equally serious—the daily sacrifice in the Temple that was made in the name of the emperor. This was hypocrisy, since the emperor considered himself to be a god. Was he perhaps sacrificing to himself? It was a ridiculous farce and should be stopped.

Gamaliel replied that this arrangement was made in the time of Augustus when the Romans wanted to set up an open air temple in Jerusalem for the imperial cult, with the statue of Augustus Caesar as a god to be worshipped. Fortunately, after protests by the Temple priests, it was decided to replace this tribute to Caesar by a daily sacrifice in his name.

Shammai then asked everyone to be seated so that a vote could be taken for the eighteen ordinances. Two urns were passed around from hand to hand, one that was marked with the word *ken* (yes) and the other with the word *lo* (no). Each member was given a token to drop into the relevant urn. At the end of this process, the tokens were removed and counted.

The tally was twenty-five in favour of the ordinances and forty-five against them. Everyone turned to look at Shammai, but strangely enough, he was not angry or disturbed. He drew himself up and spoke in a voice strong in passion:

"You will regret this rejection, my respected colleagues. The day will come many years after I am gone, and it will be filled with blood and tears."

The entire chamber was still and silent as Shammai walked slowly down the aisle and out of the building followed by a few of his disciples. A curtain seemed to have come down between the opposing groups. They would no longer be able to differ from each other with genial banter but with bitter diatribe and denunciation. Johanan sensed how deeply they were split, not merely over religious matters but also over national and political issues. A house divided against itself was sure to fall.

****

Sitting in his study, with its window overlooking the garden and a view of the sea beyond, Philo felt content. In retrospect, already past the age of fifty, he had spent more than half of his life in these quiet surroundings, reading, writing, and conversing with scholars at the Musaeum. He was fortunate in having all the privileges of wealth and high social standing.

His family had been one of the very few to be granted Roman citizenship. But he had always insisted on his identity as a Jew. The Jews were known as the *Ioudaioi* (literally Judaeans) and he called himself Philo Judaeus. As an Alexandrian Jew, Judaea and Jerusalem was his motherland and Alexandria and Egypt his fatherland, and he was the loyal son of both. He loved the Bible, but he knew it only in its Greek version, the Septuagint, and had little knowledge of the Hebrew language aside from certain basic terms and concepts.

His younger brother Alexander, now the alabarch, held a commanding position in the Jewish community. As the official director of customs and taxes appointed by the imperial government, he was in constant touch with the Roman authorities in the city and influential in preserving good relations with them and with his counterparts in the Macedonian Greek community. His two sons, Marcus Julius Alexander, generally called Mark, and Tiberius Julius Alexander, were brought up more like Romans than Jews, frequenting the Gymnasium to engage in sports and athletic exercises, the hippodrome or the theatre, rather than the synagogue.

Philo occasionally tried to engage his nephew Tiberius in philosophical dialogues and discussions. The young man argued well against him in negating the idea of divine providence and affirming the rationality of animals. But Tiberius was soon tired of such speculations and was more interested in his own social promotion and success in business affairs like his father.

Well, at least he could use his dialogues with Tiberius on providence and animal rationality as written treatises. One would be *De Providentia* and the other *De Animalibus*. In his view, God governs the world in accordance with justice and by the unchangeable laws of nature. He has the authority of a leader or a parent who cares even for ill-behaved children, and is compassionate and anxious for their welfare. As for animals, he believed that they do not possess reason and are therefore not rational beings with the free will to make ethical evaluations and choices.

He was glad at least that he had kept up his correspondence with Gorion's son Nicodemus in Jerusalem and to hear of his historical and theological pursuits in relation to Judaism. They differed in their approaches but always found some common ground of assent in the sphere of ethics and human nature. His main work, which he had begun when Nicodemus was his pupil, was in harmonising the Bible with Greek philosophy through the use of allegory. This was similar in some ways to the exegetical method used by the Pharisee rabbis in their interpretations of the Bible and in relating it to the world of today. But his approach was more universalistic, with greater stress on the moral aspects of the commandments rather than on the ritualistic aspects of religious practice.

Nicodemus must be in his mid-forties by now and the children, the twins, grown up already. He had often invited them all to come to Alexandria but they could not leave Gorion who was old and often unwell. He always sent copies of his writings to his former pupil and always received his comments or criticisms in return.

He hardly saw his brother Alexander except for his weekly visits on the Sabbath because he was usually busy with his many duties and other activities in connection with the imperial family in Rome. He had warm ties especially with Antonia Minor, the younger daughter of Mark Antony and Octavia, the sister of Augustus. She and her elder sister, Antonia Major, still owned property in Alexandria inherited from their father, Mark Antony, and Alexander was in charge of their interests.

As the widow of Drusus, the brother of Tiberius, Antonia Minor was held in high regard in Roman society and famed for her beauty and virtue. Years ago, she had taken an interest in the two young sons of Herod, Aristobulus and Alexander, during their stay in Rome, and even after their death, she continued to give care and attention to their wives and children exiled in Rome.

Sadly, her eldest son Germanicus, died several years before of poisoning at the hand of his legate Piso. After his death, his wife, Agrippina, daughter of Marcus Agrippa and Julia, quarrelled with Tiberius and was banished from Rome with her six children to forestall any claims for them as rival heirs to the children of Drusus, his son.

During the past decade since the death of Augustus, the situation in Rome had become critical. Tiberius, in mourning for the death of his son Drusus, had retired to Capri, leaving the city to be governed by Sejanus. Emboldened with his new powers, Sejanus had managed to seduce Drusus' widow Livilla, Antonia's daughter, hoping through her to gain entry into the imperial family.

Antonia's younger son, Claudius, was scholarly and retiring, without any interest in political matters. Although tall and well built, he limped, was slightly deaf, and suffered since childhood from a severe stutter. He was therefore not considered as a prospective heir as his elder brother Germanicus had been.

Philo felt glad that Joseph and his son Marcus would no longer be living in Rome. In the continued absence of Tiberius, Rome was a dangerous place to be. He doubted that even the wife of Marcus, Aurelia, and her daughter Arianna were safe from the wiles of Sejanus.

****

Spring had come round again, and Joseph was eager to leave for Rome and then Britannia. The ban against the Jews in Rome was gradually being lifted and restrictions were no longer made on travelling back and forth between Judaea and Rome. Joseph was eager to see Aurelia and his grandchildren again.

During the past two months Jeshua had gained a good knowledge of Latin, and had regularly attended the daily sessions on Jewish studies with Nicodemus.

He still retained his basic knowledge of Koine Greek from his early days in Alexandria, and could converse easily in it.

Well outfitted for the journey with warm clothing and with two young servants to see to their needs, they sailed from Caesarea in one of the swift, luxury ships. When they arrived at the busy harbour and port of Ostia at the mouth of the Tiber, a boat was chartered to take them upriver to the city of Rome. All had been prepared for their arrival at Joseph's house on the Aventine.

Standing on the balcony of the house, Jeshua was amazed at the view of the city within its walls spread out beneath him, with the gleaming marble buildings and temples in the Forum surrounded by the famed Seven Hills of Rome. The Aventine was the southernmost hill of the city, located very near the Tiber River, and overlooking the Circus Maximus to the north. To his left he could see the bridge that crossed over an island in the river and on to the western bank. Joseph, standing behind him, pointed out another hill beyond the river, the Janiculum, with a red flag flying at the top. This was the signal that Rome was safe, and it was lowered only when the city was threatened by an attack.

"Arius will take you on a tour to visit the Forum and to see many other famous sites. We have about a week before we sail to Britannia."

"I would like to visit the Jewish quarter as well, Joseph. Where is it located?"

"It is just below us, along the western bank of the river, opposite the Theatre of Marcellus on the eastern side. Sadly, most of the Jews in Rome were expelled some years ago. Only those with Roman citizenship, like Aurelia's family, have remained in their homes."

Arius arrived in the evening to take them to his home on the Carinae, one of the many grand residences in that area. He was a strong and well-built young man, friendly and good-natured. Jeshua liked him instantly. They conversed in Latin, and although Jeshua was still hesitant in his speech, Joseph was sure that during their long voyage together his Latin would become much more fluent.

Aurelia was in the atrium to greet them in a flowing elegant robe, and introduced Jeshua to her daughter Arianna and her husband Laurentius. She had thoughtfully ordered food from a Jewish caterer for the sake of her father-in-law and his young companion. It was just an intimate family meal, and Jeshua felt very much at ease with everyone. Conversation was lively, and all the latest gossip of Roman society was aired.

"You both must come here tomorrow evening for my literary soirée. Antonia will be here with her son Claudius who always enjoys listening to the readings, especially from the works of his late mentor Livy. And we will also have some musical pieces on lyres and lutes."

Joseph gladly assented. It would give Jeshua some acquaintance with Roman high society. He knew Antonia well and had met her frequently during the years he lived in Rome. But he had never met Claudius and wondered what this almost forgotten member of the imperial family was like. He must be close to forty by now, still living with his mother and generally a recluse from society except for select occasions in the company of writers and artists.

The next morning, Arius took Jeshua on the promised tour of Rome, leaving him greatly impressed by its grandeur and wealth, its temples, theatres, stadiums, and beautiful gardens. They had only a few hours to rest in the afternoon before setting out again to join the guests at Aurelia's house. Jeshua stayed well behind as they entered the large reception room and then found a seat on a corner couch as Joseph and Arius mingled with the crowd. It was not long before he saw Joseph approaching his corner, bringing an elderly matron with him. He immediately stood up to greet her.

"Antonia, this is my young protégé Jeshua who is traveling with me and Arius to visit Britannia."

"I am very glad to meet you, Jeshua," she said in a soft, low voice. But he could see that she was looking at him with extreme surprise and wonder. She turned towards Joseph with an enquiring gaze.

"He is so like Prince Alexander and exactly the same age when I last saw him."

Joseph was stunned into silence. He had forgotten that Antonia knew the Herodian family very well and especially the two sons of Herod who had been raised in Rome. Jeshua was also startled and afraid to meet someone who knew his father. Antonia sat down on the couch and drew him to sit next to her.

"You must be Alexander's son, I am sure of it," she told him.

Looking up at Joseph, she saw him nod in assent and then she smiled at both of them. Joseph sat down at the other end of the couch and told her the story while Jeshua listened once again to it. Antonia was completely overcome by what she heard. Joseph then asked her to keep the story a secret as it was not yet time to reveal Jeshua's true identity.

"Yes, you are right Joseph, especially not now with Tiberius away and Sejanus in power. One day his machinations will be exposed and I will see to it that he is either executed or banished."

She rose then to join Claudius and the circle of people to hear a reading by one of the well-known actors of the day. It was from the opening lines of Virgil's *Aeneid*:

Arms and the man I sing, who first made way,
predestined exile, from the Trojan shore
to Italia, the blest Lavinian strand.
Smitten of storms he was on land and sea
by violence of Heaven, to satisfy
stern Juno's sleepless wrath; and much in war
he suffered, seeking at the last to found
the city, and bring o'er his fathers' gods
to safe abode in Latium whence arose
the Latin race, old Alba's reverend lords,
and from her hills wide-walled, imperial Rome!

Jeshua could barely follow the lines in Latin but was impressed by the dramatic voice reciting them. This had been the language and culture in which his father had been brought up far from the land of Judaea where he was born. He wanted to know more about it, to find out what gave them such greatness and power in the world. Perhaps Caesar should be given his due and his rule accepted by Judaea, as long as it was granted religious liberty. What did it matter who ruled the country, since every ruler taxed his people, made them submit to his will, and repressed any sign of revolt. He could not imagine himself as a ruler. He would not have the strength to impose his will on others. But people must have some form of government and a system of laws or there would be anarchy.

As the evening drew to a close, he went with Joseph to say goodnight to Aurelia and Arius. They arranged to meet the next day to see the horse racing at the Circus Maximus, spend the noon hours at one of the many bathhouses in the city, and see a play at the theatre in the evening, a typical day for leisured Romans like themselves.

****

The last light of day was fading in the west as Nicodemus made his way home from Council House near the Xystus. It was a balmy evening. He always loved this time of day when the rays of the dying sun turned the stones of the houses to gold. Passing along the streets one could feel the warmth of the walls when they were touched.

He had been meeting with the priest Matthias and the Temple administrators regarding the supplies of wood and oil for the Temple. He had also shown them the plans for the aqueduct which would lead directly into the Temple complex running under the bridge from the Xystus to the Gate of the Priests and down into an underground reservoir. This was becoming a dire necessity with the growing population in the city and the ever increasing numbers of people arriving for the three festival pilgrimages every year. Passover was approaching, the Lower City would be crowded with pilgrims, and the cisterns and wells filled with the winter rains, would soon be depleted.

The High Priest, Caiaphas, had apparently vetoed expenditure for this project, saying it should be paid for entirely by the Roman authorities in Jerusalem. The consortium Nicodemus had built up to finance the project was faced with an impasse even though Gratus seemed ready to cover half the expense. He had to wait until Joseph returned and used his influence to solve the dilemma.

Entering his home, Nicodemus saw through the door to the dining room that the table for supper was laid out and Ruhama and Mary were bringing in the hot tureen of meat and vegetable stew from the kitchen. Jonathan rushed down noisily from the floor above and Joanna entered from the garden with some flowers for the table. No one had noticed him entering the vestibule and he turned into the side washroom to bathe his face and hands.

As he came into the dining room he saw his father shuffling into it from his study at the other end. When he saw Nicodemus, his face lit up and Ruhama smiled up at him as they embraced.

"We were nearly going to begin without you," she said, as they all sat down to enjoy the evening meal. It was always then that they could come together as a family. For Nicodemus, after long hours at the archives and in the Council House, it was the best time of his day. Gorion inquired if he had received any news from Joseph since he left for Rome.

"Yes, he wrote that they had arrived safely and were making preparations for the voyage to Britannia. In the meantime, Arius has been introducing Jeshua to the pleasures of life in Rome and they have become firm friends."

Jonathan looked up suddenly to ask when Jeshua would return. He had lately become sullen, almost resentful, and was not doing very well as school. Now almost sixteen, he was at that difficult age between boy and man.

"I don't know, Jon," his father said very gently. "It will probably take at least three months or more, if my calculation is right. It's a long journey."

He knew how much his son had become attached to Jeshua during the past few years. Whenever he came to join the study sessions held in the upper room, Jeshua always spent some time with Jonathan before the sessions began, and there was a strong bond of affection between them. He looked across the table at Joanna, so much like her twin brother in looks, but so unlike him in character. Quiet, modest, and content with life at home, she helped her mother and Mary with all the household duties and also took special care of the gardens around the house.

"Joseph wrote to James that he expected to be back in Rome towards the end of the summer," Ruhama told him, "and that he would be in Jerusalem soon afterwards."

"Yes, I know," Nicodemus answered. "I will be going to Rome to meet and consult with him. The Temple authorities have appointed me as their official delegate to visit the Roman Jews still living in the city to see about the transfer problems of the Temple tax to Jerusalem, and many other matters."

"Judaism has been recognised as a *religio licita* and therefore Jews have the right to transfer these funds by law," Gorion said angrily. "Julius Caesar granted them the freedom to practice their laws, to observe the Sabbath, to send contributions to the Temple, and even to be exempt from military service. Augustus confirmed these privileges, and even sent costly gifts to Temple. He agreed to have daily sacrifices offered in his name instead of installing his deified image there."

"All these privileges have been suspended by Sejanus. He is also actively encouraging anti-Jewish sentiment among the people. Luckily the Jews of Rome have some support at the imperial court. Tiberius' mother Livia still holds the reins of power and Antonia, his sister-in-law, is highly influential. We can appeal against him to the Senate."

"I wonder, Nikki, if you know the story about the Valerius Flaccus, the proconsul of Asia Province. It was just a few years before the First Triumvirate was formed in Rome with Caesar, Pompey and Crassus. He issued a decree cancelling the right of the Jews to send their Temple tax to Jerusalem and confiscated the funds. When he was brought to trial two years later, he managed to get acquitted through the eloquent defence by Cicero. He claimed that he had merely curtailed a privilege that was outdated, and that he had paid all the money into the Roman treasury."

"I remember reading about it among the records in the Temple archives. Cicero apparently swayed the court by calling the Jews a clannish people who have too much influence over politics and public affairs. That has always been the argument against the Jews and always will be."

"How long will you be in Rome," Ruhama asked him.

"No more than a week I think," he replied. "I will be staying at Joseph's house on the Aventine. Although he will already have left for Britannia, the house is maintained in constant readiness for occupation by him and those he invites to use it."

He turned to Jonathan, seeing the pleading look in his eyes and smiled.

"You can come with me, Jon," he told him, to his delight. "We will go to Rome and then perhaps to Alexandria on the way back."

The meal was soon over, and after the table was cleared, Gorion remained seated with his son and grandson. It was the family tradition to spend an hour every evening studying the weekly portion of the Bible together. Each read out a few verses and then they discussed them. This time it was the story in the Book of Numbers about Balaam who was offered rich gifts by the King of Moab to curse the Israelites encamped in the desert nearby. Instead, the words that came out of his mouth were blessings.

> *How shall I curse, whom God has not cursed? How shall I defy whom the Lord has not defied? From the top of the rocks I see him, and from the hills I behold him. Lo, they are a people who shall dwell alone, and not be reckoned among the nations.*

Nicodemus wondered whether this could really be called a blessing and not a curse. Always having to 'dwell alone', never to be accepted among the nations. Do we not share in everything that makes us all human? The same desire to live in peace and freedom, to enjoy all the good things on earth, to hope for a better world? What was it that kept this people perpetually apart from the rest of the world, so different from its neighbours, so peculiar in character?

He would pose these questions at the next session of the study group in the upper chamber. It was now a much larger one, this time with the attendance of two Greek philosophers from Gadara who were visiting Jerusalem, mainly to meet Greek Jews at the synagogue of the Alexandrians and to learn something of Jewish philosophy.

******

Joseph was becoming impatient with the slow preparations for their voyage. He had to make sure that the merchant ship was seaworthy and fitted out with all the necessary supplies for at least three weeks if not more. Arius was spending his last two weeks in Rome enjoying all the pleasures of the city with Jeshua before going into 'exile in Britannia' as he saw it.

They had been out and about everywhere, returning late in the evenings completely exhausted. It was all so new and amazing to Jeshua, but he seemed to regard it all from a distance and not with the same enthusiasm as Arius, more like an interested observer than a willing participant. Although Arius liked Jeshua very much, he could not understand him. Even when he was always ready to do whatever was suggested, he regarded everything dispassionately, as though he was not really enjoying it. Still, they got on well together, both of them generous in affection and friendly cooperation. Joseph was sure that by the time they reached Britannia, they would be firm friends. Arius could influence Jeshua with some of his vigorous Roman exuberance and Jeshua could temper it with his softer and gentler spirit.

Yet he recalled what James had told him about his young brother, and how on rare occasions his fierce anger could be aroused when he saw injustice and cruelty towards the weak and defenceless, how his blue eyes would blaze like an avenging angel. He had seen this only once, when the chief steward of the house had struck a young Nubian slave for dropping a heavy tray of food in the dining hall. Jeshua caught up the fleeing boy in his arms and shouted at the steward with such enraged fury that the man was terrified and quickly retreated to the kitchen.

It was this strong trait of character that revealed the nobility of his nature. All he needed to regain his birthright as a Hasmonean prince and rightful heir to Herod's kingdom was to give him the power and the will to rule for the good of the people. It would take another ten years at least to transform the young man into the future Prince of Israel, to give him some knowledge of the Roman world,

197

of the principles of good government and economic stability. This tour to Britannia would be an important part of his education.

The day of departure soon came around. Aurelia had already said her farewells before going to stay with her daughter Arianne and her husband in their country villa in the Roman Campagna. These days, with Sejanus in power, many senators preferred to spend more time outside Rome than in it, often neglecting attendance at the Senate sessions in the Curia Julia.

A covered carriage was hired to take the travellers to Ostia where they would board one of the merchant ships of Joseph's trading company. They would travel along the northern coast of the Mediterranean, stopping at various ports for unloading merchandise and taking on kegs of water, fresh vegetables and fruits. Most of these ports also served as trading posts for the business that he and Rufus had built up over the years and that his grandson would now have to manage.

They set out at noon, eager to be on their way at last.

"We are traveling on the Via Ostiensis," Joseph told his two young companions.

"How far is it to Ostia?" Arius asked him.

"About thirteen miles I think. It will take us about half a day to reach it. We travelled faster by river boat up the Tiber when we came from Judaea. We will stay at Ostia tonight and board ship early tomorrow morning."

They found the harbour noisy and crowded with ships and the docks piled with bales of wheat, rolls of papyrus, and many other goods. Porters were rushing up and down between the docks and the storerooms, while sailors strolled by on their way to the bars that lined the street fronting the shore.

The carriage stopped at a large inn owned and managed by a Jewish family. As they entered, they were greeted by the innkeeper who came forward, grasped Joseph's arms in a strong grip, and gave a hearty laugh.

"Never thought I would see you here again, my friend," he said.

"Nor did I, Zedekiah," Joseph replied with a smile. "This is my last voyage, I think, before I turn seventy next year."

"You seem fit and strong, Joseph, and your looks belie your years!"

Arius and Jeshua were introduced to him and he invited them all to rest in their rooms and then to dine. During the meal, Joseph talked about his earlier days as a frequent traveller through this seaport. Ostia was the main entry from the outside world into Rome and its lifeline. Years ago pirates had sacked it, set fire to the port, and cut of the supply of grain to the capital. It took more than a year until Pompey raised an army and defeated them. The city and a new harbour were built, with a canal linking it to Tarracina. There was a large Jewish merchant community in Ostia, and a few years ago he had contributed to the building of a synagogue at the far end of the city.

Just as they finished eating, the door to the street opened and a large burly man strode towards them. Joseph realised that it was the captain of the merchant ship, and rose to greet him. The man saluted in the Roman manner and introduced himself.

"Captain Aegidius at your service, sir," he said. "I heard that you had arrived and came to tell you that we sail at sunrise tomorrow."

"Thank you, Captain. We will be ready to board your ship in good time."

"I will send two sailors early in the morning to bring your baggage and lead you to the Aurora. I have prepared the itinerary for you and left it in your cabin. It is a three to four week voyage, as you know of course, barring bad weather."

Joseph invited the captain to join them at table and to have a cup of wine. They spoke generally about maritime navigation and the sea trade. The Aurora was a well-built, sturdy ship with three masts, large square sails and steering oars off the stern. It could carry nearly 3000 amphorae of wine, oil, and grain, and usually plied the major trading routes in the Mediterranean, the *mare internum*.

Roman warships protected these routes against pirates and sometimes came to the assistance of merchant ships in dangerous weather conditions. They did not travel during the winter months, from November to March when the sea was declared as a *mare clausum*. They also discussed the written sailing directions, the Greek *periploi* for coastal voyages.

"As you know, although we follow the coastal route, we cannot come too near the coast because of our low V-shaped hull and the ship must sail deep in the water. But you can use the rowing boats that transfer our merchandise in order to visit ports of interest to you."

They talked together for a while and answered many questions that Arius had about the various coastal cities along their route. Both he and Jeshua were eager to hear about them and Joseph promised to be their guide during the voyage.

****

James was feeling more and more frustrated with the task that Joseph had imposed upon him. He was in charge of improving the conditions of life in the

199

Lower City, supervising repairs to the paving of the narrow, winding streets and the walls of houses in danger of collapse. With the help of Nicodemus, he had organised a crew of inspectors to report to him about problems in the supply of food and water, and to make sure the public areas were kept clear of refuse, and to see that the drainage channels and gutters were cleaned regularly. He also opened an infirmary where Ruhama and Joanna came twice a week to provide medical care for the poor.

Many of the houses were two or three stories high and had cisterns on the roofs to collect rain water during the winter months. There were several inns to accommodate travellers and many taverns and wine shops around the market areas frequented by noisy, drunken revellers. Fortunately, the city was patrolled by night watchmen who handled any outbreak of violence or drunken brawls.

It was a pity that, unlike the Upper City where the streets were laid parallel and perpendicular to each other, the Lower City had just grown and expanded in a rambling fashion, with winding streets and flights of stairs going up or down. The stark contrast between the upper and lower parts of the city was all too evident to James, as he came down every morning from Joseph's house to the administrative centre he had set up at the south-eastern edge of the city overlooking the Siloam Pool, located near the South Gate and the stepped street that ran up along the valley towards the Temple walls.

It was the first day of Nissan, and the Passover festival was just two weeks away. This morning, when he arrived at the centre he found that a messenger had brought a summons from the High Priest Caiaphas to appear at his official quarters in the Temple. The day was hot, one of those that usually occurred at the change of the seasons, and by the time he had climbed up the stepped street and entered the Temple, he was tired and irritated. What could Caiaphas possibly want from him? He never liked the man, and thought he was unworthy of his high position, unlike what his father-in-law Ananus ben Seth had been.

As he entered the hall leading to the High Priest's suite he heard angry voices raised and saw Caiaphas dressed in his official robes striding out into the hallway and shouting at the priests who were following him. As soon as he saw James he came to an abrupt stop and glared at him.

"So, you have come, James son of Theudas!" he sneered.

James stood still, a stunned look on his face. How did Caiaphas know about his true parentage? No one besides his father Josiah had known that he was the son of a Greek convert who had died before he was born, and had been adopted by Josiah and his wife as their own. Even Maryam had not been told.

"I am about to hold the ceremony and sacrifice for the new moon. You will have to wait in the Court of the Gentiles till I send for you."

As the High Priest swept by, James gazed furiously at the retreating figure with rage in his eyes. He had a sudden desire to just leave the Temple and return to the Lower City. But he realised that antagonising the High Priest might cause harm to Joseph and his many charitable enterprises in Jerusalem. He knew about the tyrannical methods that were used to keep the high priesthood as the dominant power in the city. And that Caiaphas regarded Joseph as his main rival in his influence over the city and its wealthy families.

It took more than an hour before James was called back to the suite. He found Caiaphas disrobed and sprawling in an armchair drinking wine. He invited James to sit on a couch near him, fixed him with a glaring look and began to berate him.

"I was informed that you are advising the people in the Lower City to avoid making frequent sacrifices at the Temple as they used to do, and that prayers and good deeds will please God more than sacrifices. Far fewer of them attend the new moon and other ceremonies as I noticed today. How have you dared undermine the traditional authority and prestige of the Temple and its priests?"

James was silent at first and then took courage. His answer was that the poorer people could not afford the exorbitant amounts charged for sacrifices. Even the simplest sacrifice of two doves that once used to cost a few *prutot* was now a dinar each. He quoted Isaiah's famous words:

> *To what purpose is the multitude of your sacrifices to me? ...Your new moons and appointed feasts my soul hates ...Wash yourselves, make yourselves clean ...learn to do well, seek judgment, relieve the oppressed, judge the fatherless, plead for the widow ...*

Caiaphas was furious. He heaved himself up from his seat and began striding up and down the room until he finally stood squarely in front of James.

"The Temple is the heart of the nation, and I am the heart of the Temple. Without the ceremonies and sacrifices the people have nothing to unite them and keep them loyal to our faith. Prayer and good deeds is for the individual, but sacrifices are for the nation as a whole. You do not understand the spiritual power and symbolic force of the sacrificial act, the sense of release and redemption from sin that it gives the one who offers it, the feeling of grace and gratitude which fills him."

"It is a false kind of absolution and redemption," James responded with fervour. "So, according to you, anyone can sin and do as much evil as he likes and then absolve himself by making a sacrifice in the Temple? Can he bribe God to exempt him from punishment? Sacrificing in the Temple is like buying pardons from God through his priests."

"Your words will one day be your downfall, James son of Theudas," Caiaphas warned him. "You may go now. I shall speak to Joseph about this when he returns and make him understand how dangerous and subversive your views and actions are among the people."

Outside, under the hot noon sun James thought of going back to his rooms in Joseph's house where it was cool and comfortable. He crossed the bridge from the Gate of the Priests into the Upper City and made his way towards the house. His mind was so troubled that at first he did not hear his name being called. And then someone appeared alongside him and he saw it was Nicodemus.

"What are you doing here, James? Were you at the Temple?"

James nodded but found he was unable to speak, and turned his face away. Nicodemus immediately realised that something was wrong.

"Come with me, James," he suggested. "I was just going home for the midday meal and you can join me."

He accepted gratefully and they walked together in silence until they reached the house. Ruhama and Joanna were still at the infirmary, and Gorion was resting after his early meal. Mary set out the table for the two men saying that she had already eaten. As they sat down to enjoy the food and the coolness of the room, James began to tell him of what had occurred between him and Caiaphas.

"He is a proud and dangerous man," Nicodemus said quietly. "There is no point in arousing his anger. We will need his agreement on the water problem and I am sure Joseph will pacify him after his quarrel with you."

James agreed that it would be best to avoid antagonising Caiaphas, and he would therefore refrain from saying anything more about the Temple sacrifices. They talked about city affairs and then about Joseph and Jeshua who were on their way to Britannia.

"I did not really like the idea of Jeshua going on this long voyage and seeing the world outside Judaea," James admitted. "I know that Joseph wants it for his good and for his princely prospects, but Jeshua is not suited to the role of a Hasmonean ruler."

"I said the same thing to Joseph before he left," Nicodemus told him. "But he would not listen. He believes that the young man is pliable and can be moulded into the right shape and form."

"He will destroy his real nature if he does so," James insisted. "I know him better than anyone else. He will suffer for it."

Nicodemus invited him to stay for supper, but James wanted to go home and rest. They parted with a promise to meet the next day to begin making preparations for the festival which was fast approaching.

****

Joseph stood on the deck near the prow of the Aurora in the early morning sunshine and threw out his arms to the wind and the waves. How he loved the smell and taste of the salty spray on his face. Travelling was his chief joy, and it was only when he was sailing on the sea that he felt young and full of life.

The words of a Psalm came into his mind: *They that go down to the sea in ships, who do their trade in great waters* ...How often had he taken a ship just for the pleasure of sailing anywhere! He wanted Arius and Jeshua to share the same pleasure, and to enjoy seeing cities and countries unknown to them.

The first port of call was Genoa where they arrived after a two days' journey. The ship would dock for only one day in the fine harbour where many trading vessels were moored. They went ashore to explore the city and climb up to the old Celtic *oppidum* at the top of a hill. The city was once the capital of Liguria which had been inhabited by Celtic tribes, but was later settled by Phoenicians and Etruscans. Joseph told them how the Carthaginians had burned down the city during the Punic wars because it had allied itself to Rome, and was rebuilt by Romans after their final victory. It was now a major trading centre although he had not thought it worth establishing a trading post there.

"What is the meaning of the name, Genoa," Arius asked.

"Most probably it comes from the word 'genu', meaning 'knee' in the local dialect, because it lies inside the knee of the Italian peninsula."

They spent the day in the warm sunshine and mild breezes, ate the food brought from the ship in baskets, and lay on grassy slopes overlooking the blue sea sparkling in the distance. By next morning, they were on their way again, sailing towards Massalia. It would take another two days to go along the coastal route, and the weather was fine and breezy. Most of the time they stayed on deck, looking towards the coastline as the ship passed by, and looking out to sea to see if any dolphins or whales might appear. The Greek sailors told them stories about dolphins saving the lives of drowning people and bearing them to shore on their backs.

Many hours were also spent with Joseph telling them about the wars that the Romans had fought to gain dominance over all the countries bordering the Mediterranean and which they now called the *Mare Nostrum*, our sea. Arius was especially interested in Caesar's Gallic Wars and his attempt to conquer Britannia that eventually failed.

"Why didn't he succeed as he always did in his wars?" Arius wanted to know.

"Well, he nearly did so, but he had bad luck," Joseph explained. "At first, it was just an expedition to prevent Belgian tribes which had settled there from assisting the Gallic Belgae against him. He found some allies among British chiefs who hoped to use the Romans against rival tribes. His first invasion failed because although his two legions managed to land on the southern coast, the ships with his cavalry were blown off course by heavy gales and most of the Roman fleet was wrecked on the beachhead. He defeated the British in a pitched battle but he could not follow up the victory without cavalry."

"And what happened the second time, a year later?"

"This time he was a little more successful. He came with five legions and two thousand cavalry, but again the weather was against him. Forty of his ships lying at anchor along the beach were wrecked when a storm dashed them against each other, and many days had to be spent repairing them. Yet he managed to advance northwards and several tribes surrendered to him. He took some hostages and an annual tribute to Rome was negotiated. Caesar then decided to return to Gaul before the winter season began."

All this about Caesar was new to Jeshua, but he knew about Pompey who, a century ago, had marched into Judaea to end the civil war between the Hasmonean brothers, Hyrcanus and Aristobulus, the sons of King Alexander Jannai, both contending for the throne. He entered Jerusalem and thousands were slaughtered trying to defend the Temple against him. When he finally breached the walls with battering rams, he forced his way into the Temple and defiled it by entering the Holy of Holies. Could his defeat by Caesar nearly fifteen years later have been divine punishment for this desecration?

He was roused from his reflections by shouts from the sailors, and everyone crowded into the foremost part of the ship to see that it was now approaching the harbour of Massalia. The sunlight shimmered on the waves and they could already see the dockyards, and behind them the walls of the city and the gate with its broad ramparts. As the ship neared the port, boats set out towards it from the shore to carry back the merchandise from Rome. Among them was a larger vessel with a tall figure standing at the helm. Joseph instantly recognised him.

"Manilius!" Joseph shouted and waved his arms. His voice did not carry over the waves, but the other man waved in return.

"Who is it?" asked Arius.

"He's the company director of the Massalia trading post. His name is Manilius and he is the younger son of Gaius, your father's former partner."

After their strong hand clasps and warm embrace, Joseph introduced Manilius to Arius as the son of Marcus, his father's close friend and one time partner, and as the young man who would soon take over his grandfather's large trading company.

"You can be my trading partner young Arius," Manilius said with a broad smile. "You will find the trading post here in Massalia is the largest and most profitable one outside Rome."

"We will be glad to visit it and to know all about its work and commercial enterprises," Joseph told him. "Since we have three days in this port, we also hope to see something of this famous city, the oldest to be founded in Gaul."

"Yes, of course. You must come and stay at my home while you are in Massalia. I have a villa up in the hilly outskirts with a view over the city. You should rest there today, and I will take you around tomorrow."

They sat on the terrace of the villa in the late afternoon after having enjoyed a good meal and a brief nap. Spread out below was the city and the sea coast that stretched from east to west. The wide harbour was filled with ships lying at anchor, and boats plied back and forth between them and the shore. There were also many pleasure craft sailing in the distance, while seagulls soared and dipped over them. In answer to the many questions, Arius had about the city and its origins, Manilius began telling them the story as he knew it.

"According to Thucydides, Massalia was founded about six hundred years ago by Greek colonists from Phocaea, the most northern of the Ionian cities on the coast of Asia Minor. Herodotus says that the Phocaeans were the first Greeks to make distant voyages and were familiar with the Adriatic, Tyrrhenian and Iberian seas. In fact, they were the first Greeks to go beyond the Pillars of Hercules and reach Tartessos, at the mouth of a great river stretching far inland from the southern coast of Iberia."

"I have read many fabulous accounts of that region," Joseph said. "It was so rich in silver, gold, and ivory, that the Phoenicians, who first came as traders, finally settled there and colonised it. Like us, they imported tin from Britannia and copper from Hibernia to make bronze which brought high prices in the markets of Rome."

The sun was already setting by the time they went indoors to have their supper, and they all retired early to their rooms. The villa was large and airy, with cool breezes from the sea wafting into it. Joseph lay on a low bed, feeling tired but content with the journey so far. Arius would soon be forming his first contact with the company trading posts and Jeshua would become more familiar with the Roman world and be more able to relate to it with poise and confidence. He had an innate nobility of character and all he needed was the education and polish that he should have acquired as a prince. Nicodemus was mistaken in thinking Jeshua was not suited to the role of a Hasmonean ruler, and he was determined to prove him wrong.

Thanks to Manilius, they thoroughly enjoyed their stay at Massalia. The visit to the trading post was an impressive experience even for Joseph. The commercial ties, the variety of merchandise, and the enormous profits that accrued were more extensive than he had thought possible. They welcomed his suggestion to take them out for a visit to the four islands near the coast, especially the small rocky one that had once been the lair of pirates and now had a fortress built on it for a small Roman contingent guarding the harbour. Roman warships patrolling the Mediterranean often stopped there on their prescribed routes from east to west.

During their circuit of the islands, Manilius had many stories to tell about Massalia where he had been living for many years. He told them that a few centuries ago, Massalia was a rich city-state ruled by an oligarchic government with a network of cities under its influence and patronage, and had gained dominance over the sea trade in spite of constant harassment by Etruscans and Carthaginians. Massalia even assisted Rome during the Second Punic War by sending provisions by ship for the Roman army.

Returning from their sailing trip around the islands, Manilius took them to a small eatery near the port where they were treated to an excellent fare of cooked or roasted fish with fresh vegetables and fruit. The sea air had given them a good appetite and they lingered near the busy port afterwards to watch the stevedores loading and unloading the ships on the docks while gulls screeched overhead.

It was already after the noon hour and the weather was becoming quite hot, so he took them back to his villa in a horse-drawn carriage to rest for a while. Later that afternoon they visited the city centre and the marketplace, and then took a long drive along the esplanade fronting the sea. It was clearly more a Greek city than a Roman one and nearly all the signs on the road were in Greek rather than in Latin. People in the streets were dressed in the Greek style, in plain linen chitons pinned at the shoulders for coolness and comfort and the language they spoke was more often Greek than anything else.

Back at the villa and at a well laid table for supper, the talk centred around their continuing journey to Britannia along the Atlantic coast. Joseph speculated about the early travellers, the adventurous Phoenicians who had first gone there more than a thousand years ago, braving the winds and the weather. Manilius then told him about the journey that the famous mathematician, astronomer and navigator, Pytheas, a citizen of Massalia, had taken to the northern lands about three hundred years ago. He made instruments that allowed him to establish the latitude of Massalia, and was the first to connect the sea tides to the phases of the moon. He organised an expedition by ship to circumnavigate Britannia, and then went on as far as Iceland and Norway. Like the Phoenicians, he wanted to establish a sea trading route for tin from Cornwall but was unsuccessful.

"Now, as you know, our company ships ply that route during the summer season to avoid bad weather. But we still have to endure the occasional gale that blows a ship off course until the gale passes. You will most likely have a fairly good passage at this time of year."

For their last day in Massalia, he suggested taking them in his private vessel to Arelate to visit the city with its theatre, amphitheatre and hippodrome, and also to the huge aqueduct and water mill complex a few miles to the north of it. The city lay near the mouth of the Rhodanus, and he could sail the vessel up the canal which had been built about a century earlier to link it to the sea. It was a very enjoyable trip for them and when they returned it was time to board the Aurora which would be sailing at dawn.

Agrippa was enjoying his life in Tiberias in spite of the distaste and constant irritation he felt working for his uncle Antipas. The lovely villa which he had recently built on the shores of the inland Sea of Galilee, the fact that his wife Cypros had finally joined him there, and that she was now carrying his first child, made him happy. He was now thirty-five years old, living in high style and comfort, and felt that all his former troubles could be forgotten, the death of his dear friend Drusus, heir to Tiberius, his flight from Rome because of his debts, his brief seclusion in the fortress of Malatha in Idumea where he had even contemplated suicide.

Cypros had saved him by appealing to Herodias his sister who persuaded her lover Antipas to give him a position in the administration of the city. He had almost full authority there since his uncle preferred to live in Sepphoris most of the year. He was very successful in keeping this beautiful city well cared for and organised, and the people living in it were pleased with his efficient management and friendly attitude towards everyone.

Although his duties were administrative with the legal authority of a magistrate, he began venturing into the world of political power. Without letting Antipas know, he made surreptitious contacts with the Roman authorities in Syria and allowed them to assume that he would most probably succeed his uncle as the Tetrarch of Galilee and Peraea, since Antipas had divorced his Nabataean wife and was childless. Besides this, everyone knew that his sister was his uncle's lover and supposed that she would influence him to declare her brother his heir, although Agrippa knew this was not what Antipas would ever do.

A visit to Tiberias was expected soon by Herodias and her young daughter Salome, a pretty child, graceful and light footed, who was now about ten years old. Antipas seemed to be kind and affectionate towards her, and treated her as his own daughter. Herodias had not yet received her divorce from her husband who was still living in his mother's palatial house in Ashkelon. She had been Herod's third wife, also named Mariamne, and the daughter of Simon Boethus whom Herod appointed as high priest until he fell out of favour. Her son was once considered as Herod's heir and named Herod II, but was cut out of his will because Mariamne was suspected of disloyalty and even perhaps of treachery. People now called him Herod Boethus, or Herod Philip, instead of Herod II. It was confusing since his half-brother Philip the Tetrarch, was also known as Herod Philip.

One morning, at his offices in the palace complex on the hilltop above the city, Agrippa found a man of about fifty, dressed in fine robes, standing in the centre of the reception room. He had a tall, striking figure and his fine-featured face was bronzed. As he approached him, the man held out a hand in greeting which he met with his own.

"I am Marcus, the manager of the trading company in Damascus which handles nearly all the trade between Galilee and the surrounding areas. I have just come from visiting your uncle in Sepphoris, and was requested by him to see you here in Tiberias."

Agrippa gestured towards the couch and invited him to be seated. He had heard of this man who owned a large trading network covering almost the entire region and with links as far as Babylonia in the east. He ordered some wine and fruit to be brought in and settled himself in an armchair opposite the couch to hear what Marcus had to say.

"Your uncle is interested in renewing trading ties between Galilee and two cities of the Decapolis, Hippos and Gadara, on the eastern side of the lake. As you know, these were once given to your grandfather, Herod, but are now part of Provincia Syria like their sister cities. For the past few years my father, Joseph of Arimathea, had been supplying them with goods and merchandise and I have continued to fulfil the agreement he made with them."

Agrippa assented that renewed trade with these cities would be most desirable. Merchants in Tiberias often complained that they could double their profits if there was cooperation and trade with those cities so close by. Instead, there was enmity and rivalry between them and Tiberias. He listened as Marcus proposed setting up a trading post in Tarichaea, located south of Tiberias and near the south-eastern corner of the lake, almost opposite Hippos on the other side. The trading post would be privately owned by his company and would be an intermediary agent between the Galilee and the two Decapolis cities.

"Your uncle wants you to assist me in allocating the land for this and to supervise the construction of the trading post."

"Gladly," Agrippa told him, thinking how he could profit from this. "I will travel with you to Tarichaea tomorrow and see that all is arranged to your satisfaction."

"There is something else I would like to ask you personally, Agrippa," Marcus said hesitatingly. "Your uncle Philip is tetrarch of the lands to the northeast of the lake, Batanaea, Trachonitis and Gaulanitis, what we Jews call the Golan and Bashan."

"Yes, he is," said Agrippa, surprised to hear that Marcus was Jewish. He had thought him to be Roman or at least a Syrian with Roman citizenship. "I hardly know him though he was always courteous and kind whenever we meet. He keeps to himself and rarely visits his half-brother here."

"I was hoping during my stay in Tiberias, to pay him a visit and try to interest him in my services as a trading agent. It would complete the network I have been building up for the past ten years. I would be grateful for an introduction to him through you as his nephew, and even perhaps being accompanied by you."

"Why not go through my uncle Antipas?" Agrippa asked.

"I sensed a certain coldness and reserve from him when I indirectly introduced this idea," Marcus replied. "I thought that your uncle Philip would find it more amenable to it if it was proposed by you."

"Well, I would like an excuse to visit Caesarea Philippi up near Mount Hermon. I am told the city is beautifully built in the Roman style, and I have always wanted to see the spring and waterfall at Paneas where a temple is erected to the Greek god Pan. The river from there must be full at this time of year, just after the winter rains."

They decided to travel there together after the visit to Tarichaea. Although Antipas had assigned a suite of rooms in the palace for Marcus and his attendants, Agrippa invited him to return with him to his villa on the seashore at noon after he completed his duties at the administration offices. He liked the man and thought he would be a useful friend in his contacts with the Roman authorities in Syria.

****

Nicodemus was feeling a little more relaxed. He was glad that the Passover festival had passed without more trouble than had been expected. He had gone to see Gratus, the Roman prefect, and had insisted that Roman soldiers keep to their quarters in the Upper City and that no soldiers in the Antonia fortress be stationed near the walls. He organised a small force of local guards to line the streets leading to the Temple and to man the entrances so that the crowds entering the Temple grounds moved in an orderly manner. Water barrels were placed at intervals along each route and a few tents were set up below the Hulda gates where anyone who needed urgent medical care could be treated.

After a ten-year assignment, beginning from the year after the death of Augustus, this was the last year that Valerius Gratus would serve as the fourth Prefect of Judaea. A new man was due to replace him during the summer months. Joseph promised to be back in Jerusalem when that occurred in order to establish good relations with the new prefect from the very beginning.

Nicodemus was on his way that morning to the Mariamne Tower near the Joppa gate where Gratus always resided whenever he came to Jerusalem. He had come up before the festival from Caesarea Maritima, his permanent place of residence, and was due to return there on the morrow. This would in all probability be their last meeting before he left the country, and perhaps it was intended merely as a matter of courtesy rather than for administrative problems.

He found the prefect in the large reception room on the ground floor which opened on to a central court with benches and flower pots lining the sides. Gratus invited him to go out there and they strolled together in silence for a while before seating themselves on a bench at the far end.

"I wanted to tell you how much I appreciated the good arrangements you made for the festival. Every time I come to these festivals in Jerusalem I always anticipate having to deal with disorderly crowds and riots which can easily be stirred up into rebellion and revolt by fanatical extremists among the people."

"The people are usually peaceful if they are not provoked," Nicodemus said quietly. "They want to feel that at least in the Temple they can have a sense of freedom from Roman rule, even if they accept it as a political necessity."

Gratus looked at him haughtily and with a little distaste. This talk of freedom was not to his liking.

"I cannot understand your people, Nicodemus," he said angrily. "I have been here for ten years and still find it the strangest country I have ever seen. All the benefits of Roman rule are totally unappreciated, passions rule more often rather than reason, and I found this province almost ungovernable."

"We are what our own Bible calls a 'stiff-necked people'," Nicodemus said without rancour. "Nothing you say is worse than what our prophets have always told us. Just read what it says about the troubles Moses had with the Israelites in the desert. They even caused him to lose his temper and be denied entry into the Promised Land."

"There is another thing I do not understand," Gratus told him. "You are first called Hebrews, then Israelites, and now Jews. Your people are disunited, scattered all over the Roman Empire—in Rome, Alexandria, and throughout the provinces, as well as Babylonia in the Parthian Empire."

"For all our diversity and dispersion, we are united by three things—our faith in God, our Bible and our love for our country. Jews all over the world send contributions to the Temple as the centre of our faith, they pray in the direction of the Temple in Jerusalem, and they teach the Bible and the tenets of our faith to their children."

Gratus was silent, considering what he could say to this. He always felt confounded by this faith in some invisible god who seemed to have such power over the minds of this people, so unlike the Roman gods who were far more natural and humanised. He shook out these thoughts and turned to other matters.

"I also wanted to tell you that I received a letter from Rome telling me about the new prefect who will be appointed to replace me. His name is Pontius Pilate, and he is an equestrian of the Pontii family which originates from the Samnium region in Italia. He was chosen for this position by Sejanus who has always promoted his career, and he is more of a military man than I am. Sejanus believes that Judaea needs a stronger hand to govern the people."

"A softer and more generous hand would be more effective. Compliance and submission can come through greater leniency and consideration in the attitude of rulers," Nicodemus suggested. "What the people need is to have their own ruler, even if he is merely a figurehead. In fact, I would advise the emperor to appoint one of the Hasmonean grandsons of Herod as a client king and rule through him."

Gratus shook his head. "We have tried that before and it won't work now. You will have him and Antipas in Galilee at each other's throats. There is a long history of interfamily quarrels, assassinations and executions over the past century to deter any emperor of Rome to consider such a step. Besides, you have your figurehead in the person of the High Priest, Caiaphas, a strong man whom I appointed instead of his weaker in-laws."

"Caiaphas is strong, but not loved. He is harsh and inconsiderate of other people and their needs. I have failed to persuade him about providing the funds to improve the conditions in the Lower City, to build the aqueduct, to repave the streets leading to the Temple."

"Well, that is his privilege, of course. Rome will make some contribution for the aqueduct when the time comes, but the funds for it must come from the Temple treasury which I know is rich enough."

"He claims otherwise and refuses to allow us to inspect the financial records of the Temple. Administration of the Temple is regarded as separate from the administration of the city, like an autonomous state within a state."

"Rome has always respected the religious practices and privileges of the people she governs. We cannot interfere with the Temple priests and their financial administration. As you know, since the time of Augustus, a daily sacrifice is paid for by us in the name of the emperor."

He rose, and Nicodemus followed him back to the reception room where they found Caiaphas and his retinue. He had also come for a final meeting with the Roman prefect before his departure. Bowing briefly to him, Nicodemus hastily said his farewells to Gratus and went out into the forecourt. He was surprised to find James outside waiting for him. It was bad news, if he read his face rightly. They walked out into the street and then huddled in a small recess to talk privately away from the sight of passers-by.

"Ruhama has just received message sent by Maryam from Ein Karem. It said that Johanan, Zacharias' son, was arrested by Antipas for incitement against him and for the threat of insurrection. Zacharias had a stroke after hearing about this and is not expected to live for long."

"I will go there immediately," Nicodemus said. "I will pack some clothes and take the carriage out to Ein Karem."

James left him at his house and went down into the Lower City. He thought about Johanan who was most likely imprisoned in the fortress of Machaerus in Peraea without any chance of contact by his followers. Some way might be found to send one of the Arab nomads in the desert to bribe the guards and get a message through to him. If his father died, he would have to be told.

****

Nicodemus arrived within the hour at the home of Elizabeth and Zacharias. He left his horse in the open field nearby to graze and knocked softly at the door. Maryam opened it quickly and warmly embraced him. He saw how her golden hair was becoming streaked with white and how tired she looked with the lines on her face and the shadows under her eyes.

213

"We have not slept all night," she said. "Zacharias is still conscious but he cannot move his body or speak. He can only communicate with his eyes, closing once for yes and twice for no."

"Can I see him now, or is he sleeping?" he asked.

"He is awake and Elizabeth is with him. You can go to his room whenever you wish."

"I would like to ask you a few things first, Maryam. Has he left anything in writing, perhaps a will or some document to be opened in case of death? Also, has any message come from the Zadokite settlement about Johanan? Or have you tried to contact them about him?"

"The answer is no to all three questions, Nikki. I think James will try to contact the priests at the settlement and find a way to communicate with Johanan."

She brought Nicodemus some cool fruit juice to refresh him after his ride from Jerusalem. He sat down tiredly as Maryam went to tell Elizabeth that he had arrived. A few minutes later, he followed her into the room and saw Zacharias propped up on his bed with pillows. Elizabeth was sitting next to it and holding her husband's hand. The old man's bleary eyes turned towards him as he approached the bed and they seemed to smile. He bent over him, placing his lips on the wrinkled forehead, and then sat on the other side of the bed. After a while, when Elizabeth left the room with Maryam, he leaned forward until their eyes met.

"I am going to ask you a few questions, Zacharias," he said.

The old man closed his eyes once.

"Do you want me to take the box with the copper scroll out of the Temple?"

The eyes closed again in assent.

"Should I send it to the Zadokite settlement?"

The eyes blinked twice in the negative.

"So you want it to be kept with me for the present?"

Once again, the eyes closed in assent.

"All right, Zacharias. I will use the map you gave me to find the vault and take out the box. It will stay with me until I know what happens to Johanan. If they release him, I will give it to him. If not, I will keep it until the right time comes to hand it over to priests in the settlement."

Zacharias closed his eyes once and then turned his head to the pillow to rest. Soon Nicodemus noticed that he had fallen asleep and he quietly rose and left the room. He found that Elizabeth and Maryam had laid the table for the midday meal and sat down to eat with them. They talked for a while and then Elizabeth went back to her seat in the bedroom to watch over her husband, while Maryam cleared the table.

"I will return now to Jerusalem," he told her. "There is something that Zacharias wants me to do for him."

Maryam did not question him but accompanied him outside to see him mounting his horse and riding away. Tears came into her eyes then, as she watched his figure fading in the distance. How time had flown since they were all younger and closer together! She missed Jeshua, her son, who was now far away in a distant land and living in a different world from hers. Joseph was turning him into what his father Alexander had been, a young and handsome Hasmonean prince with all the wealth and manners of a Roman nobleman, and the prospect of a royal appointment at some future time. It was what he rightfully should have, but in her heart, she wished he had remained ignorant of his heritage and without the dangers that it might bring.

****

Nicodemus arrived home to find that Ruhama and Joanna had returned from the infirmary. He told them he had seen Zacharias and that the old man was still conscious. He could not move his body, but his mind was alert and he could hear and respond by eye movement. It was now late afternoon, and he wanted to get to the Temple before the doors closed after the evening service.

"I will tell you later about this, Ruhama," he said, taking her aside. "I won't be long, and will be back in time for supper."

He hurried through the streets, and instead of going across the Bridge of the Priests to the Temple Mount, he took a more southern route that descended to the street that ran down the valley, and made his way towards the Valley Gate in the southern part of the western wall. Entering through it, he hurriedly passed through a long corridor that sloped downwards to the vaults. The one marked on Zacharias' map was the furthest one from the entrance, and he used the key to open it. There were several things in it, high priest vestments, robes, golden cups and other vessels. On the lowest shelf, he found the small wooden box or rather casket, in which the copper scroll was resting. It was not too large to hide under

215

his cloak, and after closing the vault, he made his way back to the valley and ascended the road leading to the Upper City.

No one had noticed him coming or going, as most of the priests were busy with the evening sacrifice and prayers. Caiaphas never stayed in the Temple beyond the time for the afternoon sacrifice before sunset. Nicodemus returned home in good time before the family gathered for their evening meal. He had a secret niche in the western wall of the upper chamber where he kept a few important documents and some precious stones, and he went up there to hide the casket with the copper scroll in it. As he came down from the chamber, he saw James entering the hallway and looking about hesitantly. He called to him and invited him into the dining room to have supper with them.

"I am glad you have come, James," he said. "I have seen Zacharias and after supper I will tell you what I have done since then."

James sat down with the family around the table, as he often did before returning to his rooms in Joseph's house nearby. Sometimes he stayed later when there was a meeting of the study group in the upper chamber or whenever he and Nicodemus had to discuss various matters about the Lower City and its administration. They were both of the same age and understood each other very well, finding that they agreed about most things and worked well together. He was almost like one of the family by now, and felt very much at home in the Gorion household.

****

Darkness was approaching over the Judaean Desert. The sun was setting in the west, and the priests stood outside their settlement facing towards it and chanting the evening prayers. Dressed in their long white robes, they stood ranged in lines with the youngest ones in front, and remained there until the sun dipped under the horizon. As the shadows gathered over desert landscape, they turned towards the buildings of the settlement and entered the large dining area.

Seated on benches on either side of a long table in the centre, each one had a plate of food and a cup of water placed in front of him. Elimelech, the head of their order, pronounced the blessing over the food and they ate and drank in total silence. At the end of the meal, after the tables were cleared, each one in turn recited some verses from the thanksgiving psalms they had all learnt and memorised. Finally, one of the older priests rose to give the lecture of the day based on a verse of the Bible and its interpretation.

This is the oracle that the prophet Habakkuk saw: How long have I cried out, and you do not hear? I cry out 'Injustice!' and you do not liberate us.

This refers to the entreaty of the generation and the events to come upon them.

Why do you let me see such wickedness, why do you behold such turmoil.

This refers to those who rejected the Law of God with tyranny and treason.

The wicked man hems in the righteous man, therefore judgment comes out perverted.

This refers to the Wicked Priest, and the Teacher of Righteousness.

Behold you among the nations, regard and wonder marvellously, for I will perform something in your time which you will not believe if it were told to you.

This refers to the traitors and the Man of Lies because they have not obeyed the words of the Teacher of Righteousness from the mouth of God. These are the traitors of the New Covenant because they did not believe in the covenant of God and desecrated his holy name.

The old priest read on from the scroll of Habakkuk the prophet who pronounced five oracles against the Chaldeans, the old name for the Babylonians. In his interpretation, however, the old priest referred these to present day events and castigated the 'Kittim', by which he meant the Romans whose dominion will end in the near future.

When he ended his lecture, all the other priests stood up and filed out to the rooms set aside for sleeping. Night had fallen over the desert by then, and the only light came from the moon, still in its early phase. Amram, the overseer, was the only one who did not go in to sleep but went outside to make a tour of the walled settlement and then to check that the Levite guards were at their posts.

The small Levite community, which had followed the priests into the desert, lived to the north of the settlement, and served as a link between them and the outside world. The women did the cooking and washing, and the men did all the handy work needed for general maintenance, and for the delivery of supplies from Jericho.

The reason for his extra concern for safety was that in the morning, a follower of Johanan brought the news of his arrest by the soldiers of Antipas in Peraea. Someone had betrayed his hiding place in the cave. Amram sent a Levite to Jericho to find out where Johanan was imprisoned, but the man had not yet returned.

The next day three finely robed men rode down to the settlement from Jerusalem and asked to speak to him. They introduced themselves as Nicodemus, James and Matthias, friends of Johanan's father, Zacharias who had suffered a stroke when he heard about his son's arrest. They wanted to know if there was any news at the settlement of his whereabouts, and assumed he was in the fortress of Machaerus.

"I have already sent someone to Jericho to find out what he can," Amram said. "I suggest you go to the inn there and wait until I send you further news of him."

They thanked him, rode on northwards along the seashore to the city, and stopped at the inn. James remembered that he and Jeshua had stayed there when they came looking for Johanan. They took rooms at the inn and decided to stay in the city for a few days. James would go north to Betharaba to enquire among the followers of Johanan if anyone of them had seen the arrest or knew where they had taken Johanan. Nicodemus wanted to explore the city and the surrounding area where Herod had built his famous palaces. Matthias said he would go to the date plantations outside the city where many Nabataean Arabs worked. He thought he could hire some of them to go to Machaerus and find out from the guards whether Johanan was there.

On the third day, it became clear that this was indeed the case. Machaerus was originally a hilltop palace built by Alexander Jannai about a century earlier and destroyed by Pompey's general Aulus Gabinius. Herod later rebuilt it as a fortress with a palace in its centre. It had a large courtyard, an elaborate bathhouse, and floor mosaics. An aqueduct brought water from the east to fill the cisterns. Antipas now used it as his winter palace, and furnished it with all the luxury enjoyed by an eastern potentate. Johanan's followers had told James that deep ravines surrounded the fortress on all sides, so it would be difficult to gain easy access to it.

The three men returned sadly to Jerusalem. When he arrived home, Nicodemus heard that Maryam had come to tell them that Zacharias had passed away the night after his visit. Temple guards came to take his body for burial in the section for priests in the tombs north of the city. Elizabeth and Maryam were staying at Joseph's house for the seven-day mourning period, and he went immediately to see them. It was distressing to give them the bad news about Johanan's imprisonment at Machaerus with little hope they would ever see him again.

****

Herod Antipas was jubilant because, at long last, he had caught this madman, Johanan the Baptizer, who was constantly castigating him for his sinful relations with his brother's wife. He had been gathering a large following, preaching against sin and transgression of the sacred laws, and calling for repentance and cleansing of the soul through baptism. The situation was dangerous and might lead to disturbances and even actual revolt, so he had paid spies to join the crowds and follow him to wherever he was hiding during the night.

He had Johanan safely incarcerated at Machaerus with no possible means of escape. When he went there for the winter season, he intended to question him thoroughly and to find out whether he or his accomplices had hatched a plot to overthrow him. The very fact that he was announcing the imminent coming of the Kingdom of God implied the advent of apocalypse and messianic times. There had been a rash of self-declared messiahs ever since his father Herod died, and they had all proved false, but the credulous people were always ready to follow anyone who had the power and passion of voice to lead them.

Another source of satisfaction was that his wealth and influence was expanding. Although he no longer enjoyed trade relations with Nabataea because he had divorced the daughter of King Aretas, he managed to restore relations with two cities of the Decapolis, Hippos and Gadara, on the other side of the Sea of Galilee, and with the regions to the northeast under the rule of his brother Philip.

One day he would also take over Judaea, which he felt was rightfully his after Augustus had banished his brother Archelaus, and exiled him to Vienne in Gaul nearly twenty years ago. Archelaus died there childless and alone. His sister Olympias, now living in Rome, had wisely married off her daughter, Mariamne, to Herod, the elder brother of Herodias and Agrippa. Their son, named Aristobulus, was already nearly fifteen, a handsome lad when he saw him a year ago, and perhaps a potential heir to the Hasmonean dynasty. His own Hasmonean connections would strengthen even more when he could finally marry Herodias.

What annoyed him was this upstart Agrippa, so urbane and debonair, so charming and friendly, that everyone instantly took to him. He did not like the way he sauntered into his presence, not even condescending to bow in greeting, and talking to him with such familiarity. Telling him what he should do and not do with that careless insouciance so typical of a young Roman noble. He probably thought himself the heir to his uncle Antipas. It would never be!

Here he was again, after riding on horseback from Tiberias to Sepphoris, as usual in less than an hour and without any effort.

"What are you doing here in Sepphoris again, Agrippa?" he shouted, as the young man strode in. "You were here not two days ago."

"I heard the news, uncle," Agrippa answered with his face full of consternation. "You arrested Johanan the preacher of Betharaba."

"Good news, I think you mean Agrippa," he said with a smirk. "How can it be otherwise?"

"It will be bad news in the long run, as you will see later on. Instead of eliminating his influence it will only arouse his followers to greater condemnation and opposition to you."

"His preaching was turning to incitement, and his followers have become so numerous that they pose a real danger to public order."

"How could you arrest him when he was preaching in Judaean territory under Roman jurisdiction?"

"The foolish fellow liked to go over the Jordan every night to sleep in a cave in Peraea. The spies I hired to lead my soldiers to his hiding place said that he needed the peace and solitude of the desert after spending the day with the crowds near the river, so we caught him there."

"I advise you to release him after you have questioned and cautioned him against insurrection, or you could complain to the Roman authorities in Judaea to have him exiled to some remote region."

"I think that if he remains in prison long enough, the people will eventually forget him. You do not understand politics, Agrippa. The best way is to cut off any sign of criticism or protest immediately before it becomes opposition."

"Have it your way, uncle," Agrippa told him. "Don't say I did not warn you."

He left abruptly without a farewell, and mounted his horse outside to return to Tiberias. He felt frustrated that he could never find any meeting of minds with his uncle Antipas, so set in the same mould as his father Herod. In fact, he was becoming even more repressive of late, afraid of the threatened attack by Aretas of Nabataea for divorcing his daughter, and anxious to ensure the support of Rome against him.

Thinking of Rome made him wish he could have remained there where he felt most at home. What a gay life he had had in his younger days! His youngest brother, Aristobulus, named for his father, had taken his place there and was now a familiar figure at the imperial court as he had once been. He was a spiteful fellow and had always been jealous of him because he had been so intimate with the emperor's family, and especially with Drusus. There was no love lost between them.

One day, when he had settled his debts in Rome, he would return there and regain his position at court. He might even persuade Tiberius to make him Ethnarch of Judaea. Or he might receive the Galilee and Peraea after Antipas died. Like Philip the Tetrarch, Antipas was childless and he would be the natural heir.

****

Agrippa's visit with Marcus to Caesarea Philippi was a great success. His uncle Philip was in his late forties, unmarried, but quite happy and content with his tetrarchy and with his peaceful life away from contentious Judaea and any need to conform to Jewish laws and customs. Most of the people under his rule were a mixture of Greeks, Nabataean Arabs, and a host of other small ethnic groups living in harmony with each other. Expansion of trade and commercial ventures were always welcome, and he received Agrippa and Marcus with pleasure and warm hospitality. They had a good interview with him, and he was very forthcoming in response to what Marcus requested.

"You know my dear Agrippa that Bethsaida, our major fishing port, lies just at the junction of our two territories. I intend soon to raise it to the rank of a polis and rename it Julias. This will be our main trading centre, Marcus, and you can set up a trading post in it besides the one you will have in Tarichaea."

"I would be very grateful for this privilege, your honour," Marcus said, putting his hand on his heart and bowing in the Arab way. He had often travelled through Nabataean lands and adopted many of their courteous manners. Although they were trade rivals, there was a large measure of cooperation between his company and their merchants.

"I am, of course, also interested in trade contacts with the cities of the Decapolis and with the northern capital of Nabataea, Bosra. I have learned since I began to rule here that economic profit can override political borders and ethnic differences."

"That is what I have always believed," Marcus said in agreement. "I speak nearly all the main languages of this region and am familiar with all their customs and religious beliefs, so that I can treat everyone in the manner in which he is accustomed."

"Spoken like the true diplomat!" said Philip, smiling.

They enjoyed his hospitality in the city for a few days, and then went the surrounding uplands, and had a dip in the ice-cold and refreshing waters of the Paneas at the foot of Mount Hermon. From there, they travelled down to the Lake of Galilee and along the eastern bank to make a complete circuit of it, rounding the southern end where the lake ran down into the Jordan, and coming up on the western side to Tarichaea and then to Tiberias.

At the villa, after a good supper, with Cypros joining in the cheerful conversation, they went out to the seashore for an evening walk before retiring. Marcus told him a little about his own life, about his father, Joseph, and their family estate in Arimathea, and also about his Roman wife and two children, and the many years he had lived in Rome as a merchant trader.

Fishermen were now going in their boats to their usual fishing spots on the lake where the best catches could be made. Long shadows lay across it, but a bright moon was slowly appearing in the western skies to cast its glow on the water.

"I have to set out for Damascus early tomorrow," Marcus said. "It has been a wonderful visit to this part of the country, a veritable paradise! But my partners must be getting restless by now."

"I am sorry you are leaving, but I hope you will be back again to check on the trading posts being built"

"Agrippa, you are welcome to visit me in Damascus, which is not too far away from here. I see you can easily leave administrative matters here for a week or two with your good assistants in the city. Like me, you know how to delegate authority and make management much easier."

They parted regretfully the next morning, and Marcus took the road northwards along the lakeshore and then headed up towards Damascus with some travelling companions. The pleasure he had felt with the friendship now firmly cemented between them promised to last for a long while afterwards.

Agrippa went up to his offices in the palace. He found that all was in order, and his chief assistant was glad to tell him the good news about their plans for building a theatre on the lakeshore. He had postponed them for lack of funds, but he now received the money that Tiberius had allocated for it when he named the city in his honour. He suspected that the Roman authorities in Syria had held on to these sums for years, and that only now had forward them under pressure from Rome.

This city would at last have some culture and enjoyable entertainment as every city in the Roman should have. He would bring over theatre productions and perhaps some literary and musical programs from Hippos and Gadara now that relations were about to be restored. In a year's time, when the theatre in Tiberias was ready, he would visit those cities to see what was offered in their theatres and odeions.

Returning home for his midday meal, he had a short nap, and then went out with Cypros for their daily stroll along the shore. He showed her the area a little to the south where he had planned to build the theatre, and the promenade that he would construct along the waterfront to make it easily accessible. As they turned back northward towards the port, they saw a large fishing boat approaching the docks. Descending from it were the three carpenter brothers who had worked for him a year or so earlier when he was building his villa.

He hailed them, and they turned towards him and his wife. Their faces seemed drawn and anxious.

"What are you doing in Tiberias?" Agrippa asked with interest. "Do you have some new building project here?"

"No, we do not," Jose said. "We came to see you, Agrippa, and are glad to have found you so quickly."

"Well, let us not stand here then. Come back with us to our home and let us talk there."

They hesitated and then accepted his invitation, grateful for a place to rest after the long boat trip from Capernaum. Offered refreshment, they accepted only some fruit and a drink of cold water. Agrippa waited patiently until they were more relaxed and ready to talk. The brothers looked at each other, neither of them wanting to be the first to speak. Jude finally turned to him and explained why they had come.

"A few days ago some people from Judaea came to our synagogue in Capernaum to tell us about the arrest of Johanan, the preacher at Betharaba, by your uncle Antipas."

"Yes, I know about it and am very angry that he did so," Agrippa assured them.

"There is a special reason why we are more angry and concerned than anyone else. Johanan is the cousin of our youngest brother, Jeshua, who is actually our half-brother. His mother, Maryam, who was our father's second wife, is the cousin of Elizabeth, the mother of Johanan, now living in Ein Karem near Jerusalem."

"I remember that young man when we last met. I did think he was very unlike you in appearance and was surprised to hear he was your brother."

"We have come to you to ask for your help in persuading your uncle to release Johanan. He is the son of a priest and a holy man, and means no harm to anyone. He preaches against sin, but not against sinners. He will never preach violence or act violently. Like all the prophets of Israel, he feels impelled to denounce those that disobey the words of God."

"I have already tried to speak to my uncle," Agrippa said earnestly. "I urged him very strongly to release Johanan. There is no reason to imprison him. He has done nothing to show he intends revolt or insurrection. But I could not persuade him."

Simon then said they knew that thousands of people were still encamped along the Jordan River hoping to see Johanan released. If not, they planned to march to Machaerus and surround it in protest. This might lead to the very revolt that Antipas feared by the followers of Johanan.

Agrippa tried to think what he could do to prevent this. He had to find some other means to influence Antipas.

"What I could do is to write to the Roman prefect in Caesarea and claim that Johanan is a Judaean and therefore under Roman jurisdiction and not subject to arrest by Antipas, the tetrarch of Galilee and Peraea. The Sanhedrin must also demand the transfer of Johanan to Jerusalem to stand trial there for any suspicion of inciting revolt. You will then have to find as many witnesses as possible to defend him against such charges. I am sure many will come forward including his family in Jerusalem."

Jose looked up with a spark of hope in his eyes. "Could you write such a letter for us, Agrippa, in Latin, and signed by you. It would have much greater effect if you did. Perhaps you could even deliver it personally."

He thought about it for a moment and looked at Cypros questioningly. She nodded her agreement, as he knew she would.

"I will do it," he promised. "Stay overnight at the workmen's quarters in the palace, and we can travel together to Caesarea tomorrow and then go to Jerusalem."

Jude mentioned that their eldest brother, James, was living in Jerusalem and was working for a wealthy patron of his, Joseph of Arimathea. He had contact with the Roman authorities and could support Agrippa in his efforts to release Johanan. They had not seen their elder brother for more than a year and it would be good to visit him and find out what Joseph could do for Johanan.

As he accompanied them out, Agrippa tried to think why the name Joseph of Arimathea seemed so familiar. He was sure he had heard it recently. Then he remembered. Arimathea was the family estate of Marcus and his father. How strange the way so many lives crossed each other without anyone realising the intricate links they formed. Was it all just random or was their some predetermined pattern that controlled it all. He did not believe in fate, as many did. He had always grasped life as it came, and seized opportunities before they vanished. That was his way and would always be.

****

Chapter 3 (26–31 CE)

Summertime had arrived, and Gratus was waiting impatiently in Caesarea for the arrival of his replacement as Prefect of Provincia Judaea. All he knew was that the man called Pontius Pilate outranked him in status. He also heard through his deputies that the selection of Pilate was by a special appointment of Sejanus because of his strong temperament and ruthless repression of anyone who dared oppose him. In a way, it indicated a subtle criticism of his own inability to cope more efficiently with the unruly and exasperating inhabitants of the province.

This evening, after a tiring day sorting out the records of his ten-year tour of duty, he felt he needed some air. Leaving his aides behind to finish the work, he stepped out of what had once been Herod's palace in the southern part of the city and walked to the far end of the terrace. Built on a rock promontory that jutted out into the sea, the cool westerly winds made it a pleasant place for the governors of Judaea to live in as their official place of residence.

He could see to the south the large semi-circular structure of the theatre with thousands of seats resting on vaults and an orchestra paved with imitation marble. To the north lay the hippodrome where thousands of spectators could sit to view the chariot races and the athletic contests. Just beyond it was the temple of the city that Herod had dedicated to Rome and Augustus, with the statues of Dea Roma and Caesar Augustus placed on either side of the entrance. It stood on a high podium facing the harbour of Sebastos, with steps leading down to the pier. His gaze then went further north to the aqueduct that Herod had built, along which water flowed down from the springs of Shuni on the southern slopes of Mount Carmel. To the east of it, a new amphitheatre was in the early stages of construction to provide additional entertainment for the growing city, although he feared there would be some delay because of opposition among the local population.

What a marvellous engineering feat Herod had accomplished in building this harbour, besides the many other impressive buildings, sanctuaries and temples around the country! What a great ally he was for Rome! Yet how his ungrateful people hated and despised him and rejoiced at his death thirty years ago. He had built that magnificent temple in Jerusalem unequalled in splendour and beauty, but he could not gain their hearts.

Gratus was glad to rid himself of them now. He intended to return to Rome on the same ship that brought Pilate. The port authorities said they expected it to arrive at sunrise the next morning and that it would sail back to Brundisium within a week. It would take just a few days to hand over his authority to the new prefect and provide all the necessary information he needed. He could hardly wait to be on his way back home from Brundisium along the Via Appia to Rome.

The sun was setting as Gratus went into the palace. The suite for Pilate and his wife had already been prepared for them. The woman was reputed to be a clairvoyant and expressed a strange reluctance to come to Judaea after having nightmares about it, but her husband was adamant and insisted that she accompany him. She might prove to be right, he thought, reflecting on his own years in Judaea as some bad dream he would try to forget.

He was up early the next morning expecting at any time to receive notice of Pilate's arrival. When it came soon after he had breakfasted, he mustered his aides and the small company of soldiers to accompany him to the docks. They were just in time to see Pilate and his wife in their full finery descending the ramp, with his retinue close behind. As he approached, he could see that the man was taller and stouter than he was, and bore himself with a certain degree of arrogance.

"Ave, Valerius Gratus!" Pilate called out in a loud voice.

"Welcome, Pontius Pilate," Gratus answered. "And my respects to your honoured wife."

He bowed to her in greeting, and after exchanging a few words with them, he led the way back towards the palace. Pilate looked around with interest and seemed pleased to find everything built in the Roman style. He strode into the palace with an imperial air and gazed around the spacious hallway leading into the grand reception room with approval. They seated themselves on the silken covered couches while servants placed some wine and a variety of fruits on the low table in front of them.

"You will find all the comforts and luxuries of Rome here," Gratus assured him. "Your suite has been prepared with the best furniture available and anything you may require will be obtained as soon as possible."

Pilate nodded in brief acknowledgment and bit greedily into a succulent date. Gratus noticed his florid face and heavy-lidded eyes that betrayed his sensuality and self-indulgence. His timid wife was just the opposite, sipping her wine slowly and hesitantly. A strange pair, he thought to himself, but then it was not so strange for strong and self-conceited men to choose women of a weaker nature.

They conversed casually for a while on general matters, and arranged to meet later in the afternoon for a longer talk, and even take a walk along the shore to the south past the theatre. After conducting them to their suite, Gratus went to his own apartments. He was due to hold a final meeting later that morning with members of the city council and community leaders and arrange for an introductory session with the new prefect the following morning.

These meetings were always contentious and frustrating for him. The Greeks and the Jews were constantly aggravating each other and it was impossible to resolve their disputes. The Jewish quarter was at the northern end of the city, but many of the wealthier Jews were now living closer to the centre of it and were planning to erect a synagogue almost adjoining a Greek temple. He had begged the city council to deny them the right to do so or at least to persuade the Jews to relocate it. He felt sure it would lead to trouble. Pilate may be better equipped to handle such matters, but he should be aware of what to expect before he met with the council members and community leaders in Caesarea. Delegations from the High Priest and the Sanhedrin were also due to arrive from Jerusalem the following day to present themselves before Pilate and to submit their reports and petitions.

Some days later, after these meetings and presentations had concluded, the time came for Gratus to leave. He and Pilate went out for an evening stroll, walking together through the porticoes surrounding the palace. They had dined well and felt more relaxed in each other's company now that they were to part very soon.

"I understand you will be sailing with the tide tomorrow evening, Gratus," Pilate said in his suave and urbane manner. "I wish you fair weather and a happy return home."

Gratus thanked him politely, trying to match the long strides of his companion.

"And I wish you fair weather during your tour of duty, Pilate," Gratus said in return. "I doubt you will find it easy to govern this province."

He had done his best to explain the problems of governing Judaea and dealing with the complex realities of the country, the bitter quarrels and protests that occurred so frequently, but Pilate had seemed unfazed by his words of warning.

"I intend to be stern and uncompromising with any disturbances of the peace," Pilate declared. "From what I have seen and heard so far, it will be necessary to be harsh with the people here."

Gratus could hardly suppress a bitter smile. From his experience, the harsher he treated them for their unruly insubordination the more obstinate they became.

"My advice to you is to avoid direct conflict with them. Play one sector against the other and let them vent their anger at each other and not at Rome. Divide and rule!"

"Is that how you managed for the past ten years, Gratus?" Pilate said in contempt. "Change and change about, favouring one and then the other to keep trouble at bay? That is not my way!"

They walked on silently for a while. Gratus felt this as a criticism of his governing policy, but held his peace. Pilate would soon come to realise that a head-to-head confrontation with the people of Judaea would never succeed. To change the subject he spoke about the few friends he had made in Jerusalem whom he could consult whenever difficulties arose.

"When you go to Jerusalem for the festival period, you will find some very capable and influential people who could be helpful in case of need. One of them is Joseph of Arimathea, a wealthy philanthropist who has contributed much towards building the city and its maintenance. The other is Nicodemus ben Gorion, the chief of the three city councillors who provide for its good administration."

"I think Rome must have more direct control over that city and its administrative system. It is not a polis with an autonomous system of local government. Besides my authority in financial and military matters, I have been invested with the *ius gladii*, which gives me criminal jurisdiction. This means that I have the sole right and power to judge and execute anyone who threatens Roman rule over this province."

"Do you mean the Sanhedrin no longer has the authority to carry out capital punishment?" Gratus asked in astonishment.

"They will still retain the power to condemn a person to death for transgressing their religious laws. From now on, execution can only be carried out by permission of the prefect and by Roman soldiers."

"What about the authority of the High Priest?"

"He has jurisdiction only over the Temple and its administration. He can recommend punishment for offenders or violators of his authority and send them to the Sanhedrin or to us for trial and punishment, depending on whether the offence is religious or political. Sometimes it is both."

Gratus believed Sejanus must have granted this new judicial privilege to Pilate in order to enhance his position and power. There was a full legion, Legio X Fretensis, stationed here in Caesarea with an auxiliary cohort of it garrisoned in Jerusalem at the Antonia Fortress. In case of serious disturbances or revolts, the governor of Syria would come with his legions to Judaea to suppress them.

They had now come around again to the palace entrance and went in. Gratus felt tired and hoped the day would pass quickly. Preparations were in process for the ceremony on the following morning for the official transference of the prefecture from Valerius Gratus to Pontius Pilate. A colourful march past by soldiers and officers of the tenth legion bearing their standards and eagle was to be held, followed by the presentation of an award to Gratus for his services.

After this, they would all attend a chariot race in the hippodrome and then return to the palace for a celebratory banquet in honour of the new prefect, and in the afternoon, to attend a performance of acrobats and dancers at the theatre. A delegation from the government authorities in Syria was arriving to participate in all these events. Pilate was of course looking forward to all the pomp and circumstance of his new position. Gratus did not begrudge him the pleasure and satisfaction. Let him enjoy his first two or three months in Caesarea Maritima before he went to Jerusalem to face the situation there.

It was a relief for him when all this was over and he finally boarded the ship in the early evening. He stood on deck as it slowly left the harbour, going past the lighthouse at the far end of the breakwater. Gazing for the last time at the shores of country and roofs of the city beyond, he turned towards the open sea ahead, leaving all thoughts of the past decade behind him.

Pilate was also relieved that Gratus had gone. The man was a weakling, worn down by the constant friction with the people here, and losing his Roman pride and sense of imperial power. One of the changes Pilate decided he was going to make was to introduce the imperial cult into Judaea and especially into

Jerusalem. Every other nation in the Roman world had accepted emperor worship and recognised the Roman gods, except this little backward country.

The first thing he did was to order the construction of a small edifice next to the theatre, which would be *res sacra*, a sacred site, devoted to the worship of the emperor Tiberius. His next attempt was to send a troop of auxiliary soldiers to relieve those stationed in Jerusalem. By his order, they entered the city at night carrying standards with the imperial image of Tiberius engraved upon them. The people might protest at first, but at the end, they will accept this as a *fait accompli.*

He was astounded a few days later to find a large delegation of Jews headed by some priests and religious leaders assembled in the hippodrome with vociferous demands for the removal of these standards. For five days, he simply ignored their presence, thinking they would eventually disperse and return to their city. Some of them did leave, but many more came to replace them. Then a small group of notables asked for an audience with him at the palace. He received them politely, but listened with growing impatience to their words.

"I cannot understand your request. These standards are the official and accepted symbols of honour carried by Roman soldiers whenever they march to their stations. Why should Jerusalem be the exception?"

"We have no objection to their carrying the standard of their legion, the *vexillum* on their marches and in their own stations. It is the *imago*, the human image on them, which violates Jewish religious laws against the presences of deified images and statues in our holy city."

"I thought only your Temple was a sacred place, not the entire city of Jerusalem," Pilate said angrily. "We will continue to respect the sanctity of the Temple, but no more than that."

He left them, walked out towards the hippodrome, and entered the royal box overlooking the arena. He stood there, staring at the massed crowds gazing upwards at him expectantly, hoping to hear that he had relented. Instead, he commanded the troops standing guard near the hippodrome to enter it and surround the crowds. At a signal from him, they drew their swords.

"I have refused your request to withdraw the military standards," he shouted. "If you do not accept my decision and leave at once, you will be considered as rebels against the government of Rome and be executed."

Struck dumb by his refusal and cruel threats, the people flung themselves on the ground, ready to die rather than to yield. Pilate looked at them in amazement.

He could not understand this madness, this fanatic zeal for their laws and their willingness to die in defence of them. He had only meant to frighten them into submission. The last thing he wanted was to begin his period as prefect with a massacre. These Jews would make a strong protest directly to the emperor, and Tiberius would immediately recall him.

After ordering the troops to sheathe their swords and return to their former position outside the hippodrome, Pilate went back to the palace to face the group of notables still waiting there. They saw what had happened at the hippodrome from the palace portico and were relieved to see the troops withdrawing.

"You people are madmen," he told them with angry frustration. "This kind of crazy obstinacy will lead to your destruction one day. Mark my words!"

"It is this obstinacy that has always kept them from being totally destroyed," responded one of the men quietly.

Pilate looked at him for a while, noticing his tall figure and his calm, regal appearance. It was clear that this man was a leader.

"And who are you, then?" he asked. "I was not told your name or the names of those in your delegation."

"I am Nicodemus son of Gorion, one of the councillors of Jerusalem, and these are my fellow councillors and other notables."

"I heard about you from Valerius Gratus. He thinks very highly of you."

He invited them into the reception room and sat down opposite Nicodemus to question him further. In answer to his request to explain the behaviour of the people in the hippodrome, Nicodemus tried to inform him of their history.

"What is not generally understood, sir, is that our people did not create their religion but their religion created them as a people. According to our history, about two thousand years ago our forefather—Abraham—heard the voice of God speaking to him and telling him to leave his home in the land of the Chaldeans and to go to the land that God promised to give to him and his descendants. This was the land of Canaan, which now belongs to the people of Israel."

"So you people are usurpers, occupying a land that did not originally belong to you?" Pilate said with a sneer. "You conquered it by a belief in your manifest destiny, as the people chosen by your god to inherit it?"

"This was called the Land of Canaan because the Canaanites were the main people living here at the time," Nicodemus explained. "They were not a united nation with a sense of national identity, but lived in different fortified city states each with its own king and constantly fought against each other. These city states were mainly located in the north, in the hilly regions, while several other peoples occupied the rest of the country such as the Amorites in the southwest, Hivites in the centre around Shechem, Jebusites in the Judaean hills and Jerusalem, as well as Hittites, Kenites, Girgashites, and Gibeonites, some of whom still live amongst us."

"Well, all that is past history. You have won your place among the nations. But it is time your nation wins its place in the Roman Empire and adapted itself to imperial policy and civil principles of conduct."

Nicodemus thought it was useless to continue this conversation and rose slowly to take his leave.

"I hope you will reconsider the matter of the standards, sir," he said anxiously. "We all wish to live in peace and harmony, and I assure you the people will remain submissive to Rome and its representatives once their traditional laws are respected."

"I see I have no choice in this matter since I also wish to maintain the peace in this province," Pilate answered with some bitterness. "I will order the standards returned from Jerusalem to Caesarea."

He rose as well and left the delegates to find their own way out of the palace. He had given way this time but he would have other opportunities to enforce his will. Although he liked that fellow, Nicodemus, and his dignified manner, they could never see eye to eye. Promised land, forsooth! Chosen people, indeed! They had to realise that Rome was now in power in this country.

A great shout went up outside when the people heard the good news given to them by the Jerusalem councillors. They streamed out of the hippodrome with jubilant cries to climb into their carts and wagons for the journey back to their city. Nicodemus and his companions waited until the last of them had left before they mounted their horses. The long line moved slowly southward along the Roman road to Antipatris. From there, it would go further south to Lod and Emmaus before turning east towards Jerusalem The distance was about sixty Roman miles, and would take them about three days at the pace they were going.

Night had long fallen before they stopped to camp on the outskirts of Antipatris. Here were the abundant springs of water that fed a river leading down to the coast. As he lay down to rest, Nicodemus remembered that this was the site of ancient Aphek, where the Israelites fought one of their main battles against the Philistines. After the defeat of the Israelites, they brought the Holy Ark from Shiloh in the belief that it would lead them to victory in a second round, but the

Philistines captured the Ark and thousands of Israelites died on the battlefield. He tried to imagine what the people must have felt then, that God had deserted them in their hour of need. It was long ago, but the same situation kept repeating itself throughout their long history.

The next day, instead of following the line of carts and wagons, he left it and his other companions to ride along another Roman road towards the east in the direction of Arimathea. From there, he could later on continue on that same road to Gophna and then southwards to Jerusalem. It was also the quicker way, although more mountainous than the other. The reason for his decision was that before leaving for Rome, Joseph was worried about his estate now that Marcus was no longer living in it. If all was well there, he could assure Joseph about it when he met him in Rome.

The steward of the estate welcomed him and took him into the rooms always kept ready for visits from Joseph or Marcus. After a brief rest and something to drink, he rode out with the steward across the fields and vineyards, and into the orchards surrounding them. All seemed to be well cared for, as well as the farm behind the main buildings on the estate where the steward and his family lived. There was also an outhouse where the estate workers lived during the autumn planting season and the summer harvest. It was so pleasant and peaceful here that he decided to stay on for a few days before going back to Jerusalem. He needed the solitude and a chance to think about the new prefect that had arrived from Rome. Pilate was sure to be troublesome, and in comparison, Gratus was much easier to handle.

Besides the standards sent to Jerusalem, Pilate had already sent the moulds for casting the first coins to be minted with his name on them. Fortunately they did not bear a human image, but one of them had the design of a *simplum*, a ladle used for libations during the sacrifices made by priests to the Roman gods. Another coin had a *lituus*, a curved staff ending in a curlicue held by an augur. Most of the people in Judaea were probably ignorant about these objects and their function, but some of them would notice and realise what they were.

Finally, the worst thing that could happen with this new prefect was in connection with the aqueduct they had to build to prevent the water shortage becoming critical. During the last meeting he had with Gratus, he was warned that Pilate was sure to demand that Temple funds should cover the entire cost. Although Pilate had previously agreed to pay half the expenses, Sejanus vetoed his decision, and instructed him to demand full payment for it from the High

Priest. With both men so headstrong, it would be impossible to find some compromise.

Thinking of Caiaphas, he could easily see his venality and love of luxury. The Romans liked him because he was strong and determined to have his way in everything. His treatment of those under him and of the people in general was harsh and even cruel.

He recalled what ben Zakkai had told him at one of their meetings. During a discussion about the behaviour of Simon Boethus, a former Sadducean High Priest, an elderly member of the Sanhedrin stood up and cried out in anguish:

Woe is me because of the house of Boethus,
Woe is me because of their staves.
Woe is me because of the house of Hanan,
Woe is me because of their whisperings.
Woe is me because of the house of Kathros,
Woe is me because of their pens.
Woe is me because of the house of Ishmael ben Phabi,
Woe is me because of their fists.
For they are high priests, and their sons are treasurers, and their sons-in-laws
are temple overseers, and their servants beat the people with clubs.

****

Agrippa and the brothers of Jeshua decided to go to Jerusalem first before Caesarea after spending some time at Bethabara and talking to some of the followers of Johanan. Many of them were still encamped outside the fortress of Machaerus where Antipas had incarcerated him. They hoped that an appeal to the Roman authorities in Jerusalem would help to release him, but Agrippa, knowing his uncle's vengeful spirit, was not very optimistic.

They found James at home in Joseph's house in the Upper City, and he arranged for their accommodation in the guest wing where he also had his rooms. Agrippa received a suite meant for visiting dignitaries from abroad. Although he was glad to see his brothers, James told them that Gratus was no longer in Caesarea and that the new prefect, Pilate, was not expected to come to Jerusalem until the end of the summer season.

Besides this, there had been trouble in Caesarea about the military standards Pilate sent to Jerusalem and the city councillors had gone there to resolve the issue. They could do nothing about Johanan until Pilate was in Jerusalem and the Sanhedrin elders and city councillors could make their petition and submit the letter Agrippa had written to him. From what he heard of the new prefect, he doubted that he would be inclined to help them in this matter. In fact, he might even applaud Antipas for arresting Johanan and saving him from having to deal with potential rebels and revolutionaries.

"But you are welcome to stay here for a while before you return northwards again," James told Agrippa, after his brothers decided to leave the next day. "You might be interested in touring the city and seeing the new buildings going up in the Bezetha quarter."

Agrippa accepted his offer gladly. He had not been in Jerusalem since he was a young boy of five when Herod had his father executed for supposed treason. He hardly remembered anything of the city, only the palace near the wall and gate of the city at the western end. This might have been his home if his uncle Alexander or his father, Aristobulus, had lived to inherit Herod's kingdom, as was their due. James took him around the following morning, first to Herod's palace where he had once lived as a child, then to the Hasmonean palace in the east from where he could overlook the Temple and its courts. Finally, they walked northwards, past the city wall to the new Bezetha quarter.

"All these new buildings are so well designed and very impressive," Agrippa said. "I like the way they are all built around large central courtyards with water fountains and plots of garden plants and flowers surrounding them."

"As you see, this area is on a more elevated level than the rest of the city and will be expanding further to the north in time," James told him.

"It will eventually be necessary to have a wall around it to link it up to the city walls below," said Agrippa. "It is too exposed as it is now and unprotected."

"Yes, I see what you mean," James answered. "I will suggest it to Joseph when he returns."

As they walked back to the Upper City, Agrippa asked him about Joseph.

"Joseph went to Rome about two months ago and took my brother Jeshua with him. They are now in Cornwall with Marcus' son Arius who has inherited the large trading company from his grandfather Rufus. Arius will be stationed there permanently to manage it."

"When will Joseph return to Jerusalem," Agrippa asked. "I would very much like to meet him."

"Not till the end of the summer," James told him. "He might even be going on to Alexandria before returning here."

"Alexandria," Agrippa said with memories of this beautiful city coming back to mind. "That is where one should live these days. Rome cannot equal it in beauty and culture."

Reluctantly, he left Jerusalem a few days later, thanking James for his kind hospitality and promising to visit again during the autumn festival season. His uncle usually spent that period at the Hasmonean palace, and this time he would join him. Perhaps they could then resolve the problem of Johanan's imprisonment with the help of Joseph and the Jerusalem councillors.

He made a leisurely journey back to Tiberias, going first to Joppa and then along the coastal highway to Caesarea. He thought he might pay his respects to the new prefect of Judaea and try to assess the man, to see if he was what James had thought—arrogant, overriding in asserting his power, insensitive to Jewish prohibitions against deified images, although his final rescinding of his orders about the military standards was common sense prevailing over pride.

He found comfortable lodgings in the city and decided to look up some of his former acquaintances whom he had known in his earlier days in Rome. Most of them were merchants and traders dealing with commercial matters between the two cities. They would certainly be able to gain him entry into one of the official receptions at the prefect's palace. Meanwhile, he would enjoy some of the entertainments offered in Caesarea, the theatre, the sporting events, the luxurious baths, and other things.

The opportunity to meet Pilate came the next day when he received an invitation to attend the dedication of the newly built Tiberieum. It stood adjacent to the theatre, so that the rites of the emperor cult could precede every performance. The dedication was a grand affair, the first major event of his prefecture to inaugurate a new period of government for Provincia Judaea in its capital city, Caesarea. Agrippa joined the crowds of elegantly dressed men and women and saw Pilate standing on a podium at the entrance to the edifice with his right hand resting on the stone inscribed with his dedication.

DIS AUGUSTIS TIBERIÉUM
PONTIUS PILATUS
PRAEFECTUS IUDAEA
FECIT DEDICAVIT

"Hail Tiberius Caesar, son of the divine Augustus, to whom this edifice is dedicated," he announced in his stentorian voice.

A priest offered the sacrificial rites at the small altar, poured a libation of wine over it, and recited a brief prayer the health of the emperor and his family. Then the crowds streamed into the theatre for the grand performance in celebration of the occasion. Agrippa was included among the leading citizens of Caesarea invited into the palace nearby for refreshments and for introductions to the prefect. When it came to his turn, he introduced himself as Herod Agrippa, a grandson of Herod. Pilate looked pleased to meet him and led him aside to converse more privately.

"I believe you are one of the young Hasmonean princes living in Rome, Agrippa. I recall seeing you some years ago at the imperial court. What are you doing in Judaea?"

After hearing about his present situation and employment by his uncle in the Galilee, Pilate said that he would be glad to meet Antipas whenever it was convenient to arrange this.

"My uncle will probably be in Jerusalem for the autumn festival when I assume you will also be visiting the city," Agrippa told him. "I am sure he will be glad to meet you then."

"Good," said Pilate. "Give him my regards and say that I look forward to seeing him."

Agrippa thought Pilate appeared to be friendly and gracious, far different from what he had expected. Perhaps he was a little pompous and patronising, but that was part of his public demeanour. Still, this was not the right time to broach the problem of Johanan with him and it would have to wait until he was in Jerusalem. He must make sure to present the petition officially with all the influence that could be brought to bear.

He stayed on for another two days in the city, feeling very much at home in this Roman environment. As much as he hated his grandfather Herod for the death of his father, he had to admire his genius for building this grand port city and harbour. He was truly a master builder! Whatever Antipas had done with

Sepphoris and Tiberias, he could never match what Herod had done, nor could he equal the rich splendour of the Decapolis cities.

He decided to return to Tiberias by taking the road directly across the country from Caesarea to Scythopolis, the only Decapolis city on the western side of the Jordan, and then ride northwards along the river road and up to Tiberias on the shores of the lake. After his overnight stopover in Scythopolis, he set off early in the morning and arrived home in the evening tired but happy after the long day's journey.

Cypros was glad to see him back after nearly two weeks absence. She had been feeling anxious because Antipas was in his palace here and fuming to find that Agrippa had gone away for such a long time. She knew they had quarrelled about Johanan's imprisonment and Antipas was now threatening to dismiss him from his position.

"Do not let this trouble you, my dearest," he reassured her with a smile. "My uncle can never manage without me in Tiberias."

A bath and a good meal refreshed him and he retired early to bed. As they lay together, he told Cypros what he had been doing during his absence and what he was now planning to do. They had been through good and bad times in the past, but whatever happened in the future, he was confident he would always land on his feet. Their first child was due to be born during the coming winter, and she must not let anything worry or upset her.

He slept late, and it was nearly noon before he made his way up to the palace. He found his uncle seated at a table in the large dining hall, haranguing the servants for the delay in serving his midday meal. He scowled at Agrippa when he saw him enter, but did not say anything to him.

"May I join you, uncle?" he asked sweetly, and seated himself without waiting for an invitation.

Antipas reddened in sudden fury and banged a fist on the table.

"Where the devil have you been you lazy scoundrel?"

"Just a brief visit down south," Agrippa answered calmly. "I had some matters to attend to."

"What matters?" Antipas demanded. "What could possibly take you away from your duties for so long?"

"I had to see some people in Jerusalem, and then I went to Caesarea to visit the new prefect, Pontius Pilate. By the way, he sends his greetings to you and hopes to meet you in Jerusalem during the autumn festivals."

The lines of anger on the face of Antipas softened, and Agrippa saw the beginnings of a smile on the thin lips, but all he did was nod before beginning his meal. Agrippa poured out some wine for both of them.

"And where is my dear sister and her lovely daughter Salome?" he asked.

"She's gone to Rome for a holiday with her girl to spend some time with your mother, Berenice. Your grandmother, my aunt Salome, passed away last week, and your family is in mourning."

"I barely remember her, always moving like a shadow behind everyone in the house," Agrippa said, and then added solemnly "May she rest in peace!"

"Herodias was the only one of all you children that she loved," Antipas told him. "It was she who got her married to that fool, Herod, son of Mariamne Boethus, my father's third wife. Salome thought this boy would be my father's heir and wanted Herodias to be his wife and queen."

Agrippa had heard enough about the intricate relationships of his Herodian relatives, and he was no longer interested in hearing anything more about them. He knew his sister's husband and did not find him a fool, as his uncle thought. He was like all the members of the Boethus priestly family, proud, highly educated, and a serious scholar, which, of course, had made him extremely unsuitable as a husband for his volatile and capricious sister. Pride made him deny her a divorce, but now that her incestuous relations with his uncle came under such violent condemnation by that troublesome preacher, Johanan, he might finally do so.

Inevitably, the subject of Johanan came up as soon as the meal was over. Antipas said he had received disturbing reports of the large crowds encamped around Machaerus and of nightly attempts to scale the walls in spite of the heavy guards posted on them. He would have to send some troops there to disperse the people and prevent them from even crossing the Jordan into Peraea.

"You can't do this," Agrippa said in agitation. "As soon as the people see soldiers coming at them they will riot and then there will be a massacre. Do you want this to happen?"

"What choice do I have, Agrippa," Antipas countered. "Tell me what you think should be done, barring the release of the man."

They stared at each other with undisguised hostility. Finally, Agrippa raised his arms in surrender and told Antipas it was his decision and he had said all he could say about it. He got up from the table and began walking out, but then turned back.

"What would you say if I went there first and tried to persuade the people to leave? I might even get Johanan to speak to them if he wants to save them from being beaten or killed."

Antipas was amazed at his suggestion. Would he place himself in harm's way just to protect a crazy mob? They would most likely tear him to pieces.

"I believe I can do it," Agrippa said with conviction. "I know how to go about it. I will not need your troops. In fact, they will only make it more difficult for me if you send them."

Antipas shrugged his shoulders and thought this was a foolhardy mission, but if this high-minded nephew of his was so determined, he had no objection.

"You may go, Agrippa," Antipas agreed. "But do not go alone. Take a few soldiers or at least some bodyguards with you."

"I will take a few people with me, but none of them will carry arms. All I need is a letter with a seal from you to the guards at the fortress to give me access to Johanan."

The next day Agrippa sent a messenger to Capernaum to bring the three brothers back to Tiberias. He also sent a messenger with a letter to James in Jerusalem asking him to meet him in Jericho. They might help him to convince Johanan to speak to the people and send them away from Machaerus. Antipas had told him that supply wagons arrived once a month from Jericho at the fortress with a change of guards.

Agrippa met with James and his brothers several days later at the inn in Jericho. They heard from the guards that more than five thousand people were in Peraea, most of them waiting passively, but some of the younger men tried to scale the walls and when beaten back by the guards they were now inciting the crowds to make a massed attack and break into the fortress. It was already nearly three weeks since the arrest and the early summer heat was beginning to wear away their patience.

When they arrived at the gates of the fortress, the guards allowed the five men into the huge pillared courtyard with a tessellated pavement. Several rooms opened from it and there was a bathhouse at the far end. Steps led down on one side to the lower level where the guards had their quarters with prisoner cells in the centre. Two of the guards went down to bring Johanan up into the courtyard.

What a sight he was to the horrified eyes of Agrippa and his companions. His black hair was matted, his beard was thick and untrimmed, and he was clad only in a loincloth. He gazed at them questioningly with his large black eyes until he recognised James.

"You came once to see me in Bethabara," he said. "You came with your half-brother, my cousin Jeshua. Where is he?"

"He has gone away to visit Britannia with his patron and protector, Joseph of Arimathea," James told him. "I and my brothers have come in his place to see you."

Johanan then turned towards Agrippa and fixed him with a piercing look.

"Have you come to release me, Agrippa?" he asked. "I have done nothing to deserve this imprisonment. You can tell your uncle Herod Antipas that I am preaching against sin and not against sinners. All I want is for sinners to repent and to be able to enter the Kingdom of God."

Taken aback at first that Johanan knew who he was, Agrippa told him that he had argued with Antipas about this but his uncle refused to listen.

"Then why have you come here at all?"

Agrippa explained that more than five thousand men, women and children were outside the fortress and had come to demonstrate against his arrest. They had been there for nearly three weeks, and Antipas was afraid that some of them would become violent and attempt to break into the fortress. He was planning to send soldiers to expel all these people from Peraea, which would almost certainly lead to a general massacre if they refused to go.

"We came here to ask you to speak to the people and tell them to go home for their own safety," Agrippa said. "They will listen to you. We will soon petition for your release through the efforts of influential men in Jerusalem and I hope you will be set free by the end of the summer."

Johanan was sceptical about the chances for his release. He knew that Antipas had a personal rather than a political reason to arrest him and keep him imprisoned, but he said he was willing to address the people outside the fortress. Agrippa suggested that he should first bathe and comb his hair and beard, and gave him his cloak to wear before he appeared in front of the crowd. The guards took him to the bathhouse and after he had washed and trimmed his hair and beard, he emerged from the gates of the fortress dressed in Agrippa's cloak. A shout of joy rang out in the distance and people came rushing forward to greet him. The guards prevented them from coming too near and Johanan raised his hands to stop their advance.

"I have come to tell you that these men will soon be working for my release and I hope to be with you again in a short while. I beg of you to return peacefully to your homes in Judaea and to avoid any clashes with the guards and soldiers of Antipas."

"We will wait for you here, Johanan," some of them cried, while others wept. "You are our saviour!"

"No, my friends," he told them. "I am not your saviour but only a messenger who came to bring you back to God, to return to the ways of goodness and righteousness, to tell you that the Kingdom of God is at hand. When the time comes, one who is greater than I will appear and lead you to it."

He went on speaking to them, his deep and powerful voice reaching far across the masses of people. It took a long time until they began to accept his pleas and turned back towards the west to retrace the long route they had come from the Jordan River. It was late in the afternoon when the guards led him back into the fortress and he said farewell to his visitors.

Agrippa parted from him with repeated assurances of every effort to secure his release. Before leaving, he instructed the guards to see that Johanan was better cared for and received enough food and drink. He must also be allowed to bathe daily, since he was a priest and they must let him go out into the courtyard in the mornings for some exercise and fresh air. The guards said that Johanan drank only water and ate dried fruits and nuts but refused to eat anything else.

James explained to Agrippa that the Zadokites believe that the body is the vessel of the soul and must be pure so that the soul will remain pure as well.

"I don't know about the purity of souls, James," Agrippa laughed. "But I believe the saying *mens sana in corpore sano*—a healthy mind in a healthy body—is almost the same thing."

James smiled at him and shook his head. "Souls and minds are totally different things," he said, but did not try to explain how they differed. They had to hurry back to Jericho before it became dark. As they all rode together, he heard his younger brothers discussing their impression of Johanan.

"Johanan looks just like one of the biblical prophets," Jude said. "He had such an intense look on his face when he spoke."

"I heard some of his followers saying he is Elijah the prophet come back to earth," Jose added. "It was more or less in this place that he went up to heaven in a fiery chariot."

Simon reminded them of the famous verse in the prophecies of Malachi:

Behold, I will send you Elijah the prophet before the coming of the great and dreadful day of the Lord.

"Do you really think these are messianic times, Simon?" James asked him.

"Since the death of Herod, so many 'messiahs' have appeared and were proved to be false," Simon complained. "Who can believe anyone who claims he is the true one."

Agrippa urged them to stop talking and to ride on faster before darkness fell. They crossed the Jordan at the place where it flowed into the Dead Sea and hurried on to Jericho.

After a good night's rest, James went up to Jerusalem and his brothers took the river road up north. Agrippa decided to stay one more day in Jericho. He did not tell the others why, but he wanted to visit the Zadokite settlement a few miles south of the city. Johanan had asked him to take a secret message to the overseer Amram who would transmit it to the head of the order. He had written it on a pottery shard and wrapped it in a piece of cloth.

Agrippa rode out and found the place easily, not far from the seashore. A young boy from the Levite settlement went to call Amram the overseer. Agrippa told Amram that he had just come from visiting Johanan at Machaerus, and related all that had happened there. He then gave him the wrapped pottery shard for the head of the Zadokite order.

"I shall do my best to have him released within two or three months' time," he said.

"God willing it will be so!" Amram said earnestly, and thanked him for coming.

Relieved at last to go home, he rode fast and reached Scythopolis by nightfall. Early next morning he was on his way to Tiberias, not stopping to rest until he dismounted at his villa and went inside. Cypros was delighted to hear of his successful mission and thought his uncle should feel greatly indebted to him. There would be no more talk of dismissal now! She said Antipas was waiting impatiently to know what had happened at Machaerus and that Agrippa should go up to the palace as soon as he had rested.

He was so tired after his journey that he fell asleep before he could even undress, so it was not until the afternoon that he went up to see his uncle. This time he was welcomed with warmth and eager interest to hear about the events at Machaerus. He recounted everything that had occurred there and assured

Antipas that there were no more people outside the fortress. Johanan had spoken to them and they had unwillingly obeyed him. He was not a revolutionary and had no interest in undermining the ruling powers. He was simply a religious preacher calling the people to repent of their sins.

"But what about this talk of the Kingdom of God and the approaching Day of Judgment? This is what made me think he was dangerous, prophesying doomsday and apocalypse. You know these Zadokites and their predictions of a war between the sons of light and the sons of darkness. A bunch of crazy fanatics they are, all of them, in my opinion!"

"As I understood it, this is a spiritual war that they foresee between the forces of evil and the forces of good. This is a religious movement, a reformation or a purification of the religious establishment and the Temple cult. It has nothing to do with political revolution."

"You are naïve, Agrippa. Revolution always starts through religious reformation. Look at what happened when your noble Hasmonean family began their religious reformation against the Hellenistic priests in the Temple. They could only do it by fighting against the Seleucid regime. It was a religious war at the start, but it brought them political domination. The irony is that in time you Hasmoneans became more Hellenised than those you had opposed so fiercely."

For once, Agrippa found he had nothing to say. His uncle may be right, and eventually the followers of Johanan might turn into a revolutionary mob even though this was not his intention.

"If you are still thinking I might release him, you can think again," said Antipas with determination. "I shall never release him."

Agrippa suddenly felt very saddened by the whole situation. He had come back filled with optimism at a mission successfully accomplished, and now felt it had all be in vain. Antipas went out with him into the plaza overlooking the city. He said he was going back to Sepphoris the next morning and they would meet again when the time came to go to Jerusalem.

As he walked down to his home on the lakeside, Agrippa felt tears coming into his eyes. His usual buoyant nature had deserted him, and he felt a deep sense of despair. Perhaps he was just getting older, although no wiser than he had been before. Better to put all his dark thoughts out of his mind and spend more time with Cypros to make up for his recent absences. The following month, when the weather in Tiberias became too hot for comfort, he could go with her to

Damascus and visit Marcus. He liked his company and his pleasant conversations with him. By the time he arrived home, his spirits had lifted and he was his old cheerful self again.

****

Jonathan rushed indoors and ran to Gorion's room, barely knocking before entering. He had just come back from the swimming pool near the Synagogue of the Freedmen in the Lower City. During this hot summer, he often spent his mornings there with his friends. When he saw the courier outside the house, he quickly took the packet of letters addressed to the Gorion family with the seal of the mailing house in Rome.

"Letters, Grandfather," he said excitedly. "Letters have come from Rome!"

Gorion looked up from the scroll he was reading and stretched out his hand for the packet. It was about time that Joseph had written. He was supposed to have been back a month ago, and it was now nearing the end of the summer. Nicodemus had been waiting impatiently to hear from Joseph before traveling to Rome with Jonathan for a brief visit.

There was a long letter to him, and an even longer one for Nicodemus. Inserted into it was another letter written by Jeshua for Jonathan. He could see how delighted the boy was to receive it. Jonathan swiftly snatched it up and ran up the stairs to his room to read it. It had a full account about the long sea voyage and the summer months in Britannia. He described Cornwall and said it was a beautiful place—hills, valley, cliffs overlooking the sea, tidal waves, burly fishermen, and big, handsome Britons. He and Arius had ridden out nearly every morning to the moors where they raced their horses across almost empty land, with the wind in their faces, and birds flying overhead. At the end of his letter, he wrote:

> *You know, Jon, the best thing here is the feeling of pure release from every care in the world. Arius has also been a good friend and companion, and I have learnt much from him about Roman life and customs. He will be happy in Cornwall with his new Roman friends who already have established a small community in Tintagel about a day's journey on horseback.*

He sent greetings to Jonathan's father, and said he was looking forward to meeting him soon in Rome. He also enclosed a drawing he had made of two Druids he had seen one day near a large stone circle called the Merry Maidens. They were performing some strange rite turning around with their wands. He found out about their religion from one of the Britons working in the mines. What strange people! He supposed that the priests of the Temple in Jerusalem would also seem strange to them as well. In fact, he thought there was even some similarity between them.

Jonathan meant to ask his father who had studied different religions in the world, to tell him about the Druids. He was always curious about people and their beliefs. Although his family were traditional Jews observing the commandments of the Bible they were not like those who kept themselves apart from non-Jews and made more and more restrictions to prevent close contact with them. His father on the contrary was always making new contacts with people of different backgrounds and beliefs, and the sessions in the upper chamber he and Jeshua had regularly attended were always so interesting.

When Nicodemus came home later that day and the family evening meal was over, Gorion gave him the letter from Joseph and then read out the one he had received which was clearly a letter meant for everyone else as well.

I hope this finds you well. We have at last returned to Rome, much later than expected due to the delay in the arrival of our ship, the Aurora. We had a large shipment of tin from our mines, and copper from the ones owned by another company in Tintagel, which will go to the foundries in Genoa where they make the bronze. Arius has done very well in learning all about the mining processes and the management of the company here. He has also been able to negotiate with the owners of the copper mines to have them ship their copper through us rather than through the expensive trading company in Gades.

Altogether, it was a very pleasant and interesting voyage and visit to Britannia, and both Arius and Jeshua have enjoyed it very much. We stopped at various places and stayed in some of them for a few days— Genoa, Massalia, Arelate, Narbo, Carthago Nova, Gades, and Hispalis. We also made some trips inland from the coast of Baetica along the river as far as Cordoba, traveling through the region known as the legendary Tartessos, which we believe is the biblical Tarshish.

I am glad to say that Jeshua has become almost thoroughly a Roman in his comportment and manners, mostly due to his close friendship with Arius. They spent many hours together riding out into the countryside, talking to every person they met, discovering all they could about the people here, and both of them have grown into strong, broad-shouldered young men, with healthy appetites and boundless energy. They often rode to Tintagel and made friends with many of the Roman families living there.

I left Arius there in very good hands and among friends. The company has ten men as overseers at the mines and the miners live with their families in cottages built nearby. The man in charge, Arturius, is a Romanised Briton who has proved his ability to manage both the miners and the trading post, and to supervise the dockworkers. Arius will be living with him, his wife and young daughter at the house I built on the island just off the coast. Arius has his suite of rooms on the upper floor and is very comfortable there with a few servants to attend to his needs. In time, I expect he will marry one of the young women he met in Tintagel and raise a family.

It was very hard, for me and even more so for Jeshua, to part from him. I told him that he could stay on with Arius for a few years if he wished. But he said he wanted to go home to his own family and his own people. We sailed on the Aurora down the coasts of Gaul and Iberia with good winds and a calm sea, and did not stop until we were through the Pillars of Hercules and had put in for water and supplies at Carthago Nova. From there, we sailed directly to Genoa to unload our cargo of tin and copper. By then, we had had enough of sailing and decided to leave the ship and travel comfortably along the coastal road to Rome in a carriage with two stops on the way. First at Lucca and then at Piombino. We both enjoyed the beautiful weather and lovely views of the countryside all the way down.

We arrived in Rome to find it very hot and that Aurelia was away at her seaside villa. Arianna was in the city because her husband became the urban praetor during the recent elections and was in charge of maintaining law and order in the city. Many of the wealthy and patrician families had gone away on holiday but Antonia was still there and so was Berenice with her children and grandchildren. Herodias had also

come to Rome with her young daughter to be with her mother and the
family after the death of her grandmother, Salome.

I hope this letter and the others ones to Nikki and Jon will arrive soon.
and that they can be on their way now to meet us here. Sorry for the
delay, but we will all be back in time for the autumn festivals in
Jerusalem.

With my best wishes, and greetings from Jeshua to you all,
Joseph

"Well, Jonny my boy," said Gorion heartily. "You can now go and pack for your journey to Rome."

"Can we hear your letter first?" Jon asked his father, curious to know what was in it.

Nicodemus shook his head. "It has mainly to do with administrative matters which I doubt will interest you."

After everyone had left, Nicodemus followed his father into his room. Gorion had noticed the words "Highly confidential" at the top of the letter, and knew at once that it was not one for family reading.

Joseph wrote that he had a heart-to-heart talk with Jeshua soon after they arrived at his house on the Aventine. He told him something about his Hasmonean relatives living in Rome. He wanted Jeshua to meet them although they must not know who he really was. He intended to introduce him as his ward, or even as his adopted son, but Jeshua had refused to meet them.

I thought he was ready by now to face his heritage and welcome it, to
see where he belonged among the Hasmoneans still recognised as
royalty even if they were in exile, and that one day he might be able to
take his rightful place as a Prince of Israel. I also want to adopt him
formally as my son and heir, which will provide him with the wealth and
status due to him. My family are more than well provided for and do not
need anything from me.

Nicodemus noted the frustration in these words as he read them out to his father after Jon went up to his room. He felt sorry for Joseph but he was not surprised at his failure to change Jeshua into what he wanted him to become. Gorion also thought Joseph was deceiving himself if he thought Rome would ever allow a Hasmonean to rule this country again. It would give the people illusions about gaining their independence by some miraculous replay of the Maccabee story and tempt them to revolt.

The letter ended with a request not to delay his departure for Rome. He had hired a fast ship through his contacts in Caesarea that would bring him and his son to Ostia within five days. Next morning Nicodemus was on his way to Caesarea with Jon, and a few days later, they boarded the ship with two decks of oarsmen to keep rowing round the clock. Nicodemus spent most of his time in his cabin writing, but Jonathan was up nearly all day looking out to sea or talking with the captain while the seamen hauled up the sails and turned them to catch the wind. This was his first experience of a sea voyage and it thrilled him. One day he would have his own ship and travel with a few companions to all the places he had read about in his history books. Now he would see Rome and then Alexandria, but he wished he could also see Greece and the Aegean islands. There were so many other unknown worlds waiting for him to explore.

At Ostia, a carriage was waiting for them to bring them to Rome as quickly as possible. It was a warm and happy reunion for the four of them, Joseph, Jeshua, Nicodemus and Jonathan. They sat and talked until late into the night on the terrace of the Aventine house, and made plans for the coming week. Most important was a visit to the heads of the Roman Jewish community in the Transtiberim quarter, which lay outside the city walls and on the western side of the Tiber River.

Nicodemus sent a message to Theodosius, the archsynagogus, who presided over the Synagogue of the Hebrews and was the spiritual leader of the community. He told him he had letters of introduction from the head of the Sanhedrin and from the City Council of Jerusalem to discuss certain matters of mutual interest and concern, and would like to arrange a meeting with him. The messenger had orders not to leave until he had received a reply and to bring it back immediately.

While Nicodemus waited for the messenger to return, Joseph decided to take Jeshua and Jon for a walk through the Forum Romanum. Jeshua had already been there before with Arius but they had just strolled through the Via Sacra to admire the buildings and see what people were doing there. This time Joseph intended to tell them something about this place, the very heart of Rome and of the Roman Empire.

As they stood on the terrace of the Aventine house, he swept his hand over the city from the banks of the Tiber and around the walls that encompassed it.

"Rome is built on a circle of hills around a sacred centre, the Forum Romanum, with its many temples and shrines."

Descending the slopes of the Aventine Hill they could see the huge and elongated Circus Maximus stretching across the valley dividing the Aventine from the Palatine Hill. It could seat more than 150,000 thousand spectators at the chariot races and other events held there. Passing the western end of it, they entered the Forum Boarium, the cattle market of Rome. In the centre, stood the Temple of Hercules and his bronze gilded statue facing the Ara Maxima, the altar dedicated to him. From there they entered the Velabrum, a busy industrial and commercial area for the sale of oil and wine. At the northern end was a short passageway that led to the base of the Capitoline Hill and into the Via Sacra, the Sacred Way, the broad central road that ran through the Forum Romanum.

"On the left, along the base of the hill, is the Temple of Saturn where the festivities of the Saturnalia are held for seven days every year during the month of December. It is a time of general rejoicing when people exchange gifts and there are no social restrictions. North of it stands the Temple of Concord, frequently used to hold meetings and official functions, and it has a large collection of Greek sculptures and paintings. On the right, you can see the large Basilica Julia that houses the civil law courts, government offices and banks. It is also a popular meeting place for the general public and contains shops and recreation areas."

At the entrance to the Via Sacra there was the Rostra, a high platform used for orators to address the crowds below on public issues. Joseph pointed out the six *rostra*, the warship rams of enemy ships captured during the naval battle at Antium nearly four centuries earlier, which now decorated the front of the platform.

"This was where all those famous speeches were given by Cato, Catilene, Cicero, Caesar, Brutus, and Antony. Public speaking was, and still is, an art, the *Ars Oratoria*. It faces the Comitium, the place where public assemblies were held to vote on laws proposed by the tribunes and the Senate House, the Curia, to the north of it."

Since it was still the summer season there were no sessions at the Curia, but many people were milling around the Rostra and the square of the Comitium, and others were going down the Via Sacra. Jon noticed a black marble paving on one side of the square and asked Joseph what it was.

"This is the Niger Lapis, the black stone which is said to mark the grave of Romulus, the founder of Rome more than seven centuries ago."

Jeshua was lagging behind them, staring up at a gilded marble column. Joseph went back to him, and said that this column was the *miliarum aureum*, the golden milestone on which the distance between Rome and the main cities in Italy and the Empire is marked. He looked for Jerusalem and was amazed to find it was nearly 1500 miles away.

Moving onward, Joseph pointed out the street going up along the right side of the Curia, called the Argilentum. They passed the large Basilica Aemilia on the left, which housed the city bankers. Standing almost directly opposite it, on the right, was the Basilica Julia where legal hearings were held mainly on civil matters and inheritance disputes. It was crowded at that time with people going in and out, and they decided to enter the Basilica Julia and look around it. It had a large central hall with a double row of pillars faced with marble to form vaulted aisles and upper galleries. A portico supported on piers ran along the side facing the Via Sacra. Numerous sculptures stood on the marble paving all around the vast interior. They remained there for a while, enjoying the coolness after their hot walk from the Aventine.

When they resumed their tour, they stopped at a railing that surrounded some altars and a puteal, a wellhead, where a small marshy lake had once existed. This was the Lacus Curtius, built in memory of Marcus Curtius, a young warrior, who fought in the wars between the Romans and the Sabines. According to Roman legend, he hurled himself into a chasm that a thunderbolt had opened at that spot in order to placate the anger of the gods by his self-sacrifice. This was now the place for the citizens of Rome to make offerings of money to the gods for the health of the emperor.

From there, they went on past the Temple of Caesar built over the place where they laid his murdered body and burned it on a pyre. Joseph halted there for a while, recalling what his father had told him about this great man. How beloved he had been by the Jews of Rome, and how they had wept at the site of his funeral pyre. Pompey had desecrated the Temple and slaughtered thousands of Jews during his conquest of the country and the city of Jerusalem. When Caesar came to power, he ordered a new administration of Judaea, reconstructed the walls of the city, restored the port of Joppa to Judaean control, and withheld taxation during sabbatical years.

Jeshua and Jonathan could see Joseph was deep in thought and retrospection so they moved aside to look at the two arches on the right that were erected in honour of Augustus. From the inscriptions on the arches, they discovered that one of them was to celebrate his victory over Antony and Cleopatra at the Battle of Actium nearly 60 years ago. The other one, set up ten years later, was in honour of the standards lost to the Parthians during the Battle of Carrhae and recovered later through diplomatic negotiations. Carrhae, as Jeshua soon learnt from Joseph, was the biblical Haran, a city on the upper reaches of the Tigris River in Mesopotamia, the place where Abraham had lived for a while after leaving Ur of the Chaldeans, and from where he had journeyed to Canaan.

Further to the right, and beyond the arches of Augustus, stood the Temple of Castor and Pollux with its tall Corinthian columns and podium that fronted it. Because of its large interior space the Senate often used it for those meetings that drew a large attendance of senators, with the podium serving as the speaker's platform.

Joseph told them the legendary story about Castor and Pollux in relation to Roman history. When the last king of Rome, Tarquin the Proud, waged war on the infant Roman Republic, the twin sons of Zeus, Castor and Pollux, miraculously appeared on the battlefield as two able horse riders in aid of the Republic. Later, they appeared in the Forum to water their horses at the Spring of Juturna and to announce the victory to the people of Rome. Fifteen years later, on the ides of July, this temple was consecrated to them, and every year on this day Roman cavalry riders parade in front of it in honour of Castor and Pollux. He pointed out the sacred shrine of Juturna, patron goddess of fountains, wells and springs, on one side of the temple, and the square basin, the Lacus Juturnae, fed by the spring that was supposed to have healing properties. The priests used it for their religious sacrifices. A pedestal in the centre of the basin supported the statues of the twins, known as the Gemini, holding their horses.

"We now come to the most important sacred area of the Forum," Joseph said pointing at the circular structure just ahead, surrounded by fluted marble columns. "Here is the Temple of Vesta, the virgin goddess of the hearth, home and family. The fire on her altar inside has to be kept burning at all times by the Vestal virgins who live in the large house you see beyond it on the left which is also the home of the Pontifex Maximus, the high priest of Rome."

As Jeshua and Jonathan went around the temple to look at the entire structure, Joseph stood again in thought, wondering at the comparison between the Vestal Virgins and the Temple virgins in Jerusalem. They were far from comparable, in spite of the similarity in terms. Jeshua's mother, Maryam, had been a Temple virgin who had spent a year or two before her marriage in service at the Temple. Here the Vestal Virgins lived in isolation from early childhood until they were nearly middle aged in years of service to the goddess, to preserve her cult of sanctity.

To the left of this temple and almost in front of it was the Regia, the official residence of the Pontifex Maximus, the supreme religious authority of the state. This trapezoidal building seemed skewed towards the north and stood at an angle to the other buildings in the forum.

"This is where the all priests in Rome assemble for their meetings with the Pontifex Maximus," Joseph explained. "This is also where all the most important records of historical events, legislations, and religious documents are kept."

"Why is it built in such a strange way?" Jon asked.

"It seems that is how the early kings of Rome built their royal palace, which is why it is called the Regia. The Romans like to maintain what they call the *mos maiorum*, their ancestral customs and traditions, even if they are now outdated, a kind of national pride in their history and heritage."

Joseph said that it was forbidden for the public to enter the Regia, but he told them that it held the shrine of Mars, the Roman god of war, where they stored the shields and lances consecrated to the god. According to legend, when the lances were seen to tremble it meant that some disaster was about to happen. On the night before the Ides of March in the year of Caesar's death, when he was the Pontifex Maximus, they began to vibrate, but he ignored this warning and went to the Senate meeting place where he was assassinated.

The road was now rising up towards the southeast and the Velian ridge below the Palatine Hill, the highest point of the Via Sacra. They were all tired by now, and the sun was already high overhead, so they circled to the left and took the street that skirted the western side of the Mons Palatinus and turned in the direction of the Forum Boarium. By the time they reached the house on the Aventine, they were eager for a cool bath and a good meal.

Joseph was surprised that Nicodemus was not in the house. The steward told him he had gone out about two hours ago without saying where he was going. It was now late in the afternoon and already time that a message should have come back from Theodosius at the synagogue. The poor messenger must still be waiting there to bring them his answer.

After a brief nap, Joseph went out to the terrace to watch for both Nicodemus and the messenger. A few minutes later he saw both of them coming up the Aventine at the same time, the messenger from the Forum Boarium in the north and Nicodemus from the east. Both arrived breathless with their efforts. The messenger was carrying a letter and Nicodemus was carrying a sketch of the city with some markings on it.

Joseph paid off the man with thanks and told him to go inside have a drink before going back with a return message. Nicodemus then opened the letter addressed to him and told Joseph what it said.

"He sends his compliments and says we can come to the synagogue an hour before the evening prayers held at sunset. He will be glad to receive us and hopes we will remain to have supper with him."

"Good, we will go there together and stay for supper," said Joseph. "Jon and Jeshua can go to the Circus Maximus and see what sports are being held there this evening."

They went in to send a message back with the messenger, and then retired to the quiet study at the back of the house overlooking the gardens.

"Where have you been, Nikki?" Joseph asked with curiosity. "And what is that sketch you have in your hand?"

"I was getting restless waiting for the reply from Theodosius, so I decided to take a walk up the route of the Appia aqueduct, the first one that was built in Rome. I sketched it from its end in the Forum Boarium and up through a tunnel under the Aventine. It then runs along the wall to the Porta Capena and drops over it. That is as far as I went, but it continues through another tunnel under the Caelian hill until it reaches the Via Praenestina and its source is somewhere further down beneath that road as far as I can gather from the maps I have seen."

Joseph smiled at his enthusiasm, and said he was becoming obsessed with the problem of the proposed aqueduct for Jerusalem. Nicodemus told him that Rome now had six aqueducts, the longest being the Anio which brought water from the springs in the valley of the Anio River nearly 50 miles away. Even more aqueducts were in stages of planning for future construction, one of them to follow the same route as the Appia.

"I envy the way Rome is so plentifully supplied with water, all the many fountains and water courses that lead throughout the city and supply all their needs. Jerusalem should have the same benefits of a steady water supply."

"Well, I promise you all my support in persuading the new prefect, Pontius Pilate, when we return to Jerusalem, although I understand he is a hard man to deal with."

"Yes, I could see that when I was in Caesarea about the military standards, but he must realise how essential the aqueduct is for the city and its growing population."

They spent the rest of the afternoon going over the matters they would discuss with Theodosius regarding the Jewish community in Rome. Although it had shrunk in size, it was still vibrant with life, but all the wealthier Jews had gone to Alexandria and left their business enterprises to the management of their proxies in Rome. The trouble was that, because of Sejanus, it was no longer possible to send funds to foreign countries, including the annual Temple dues that was always sent faithfully every year by the Jews of Rome to Jerusalem.

In the evening, they walked down towards banks of the Tiber, went outside the walls of the city through the triple gate, Porta Trigemina, and crossed the river over the stone bridge of Pons Aemilius. This area, the Transtiberim, had once belonged to the Etruscans until Rome conquered it, but there was no interest at that time in building developments there. Rivermen and barge sailors bringing goods from the port in Ostia inhabited it until immigrants from Eastern countries began to settle there, mainly Jews and Syrians. The only connection with the city at that time was a bridge built on wooden piles, the Pons Sublicius, constructed about seven centuries earlier, which still stood at a little distance below the Pons Aemilius. Joseph pointed it out and began telling Nicodemus the famous story of Horatio who had defended this bridge against the army of Lars Porsena during the wars between the Romans and the Etruscans.

"Yes, I read this story a long time ago at school during my Latin courses. We also read about the Janiculum Hill up there with the red flag flying over it to warn Rome of attacking armies. You should take Jon and Jeshua up there on your next walk, to have a view over the entire city."

They walked through the narrow, winding streets to find their way to the synagogue. The letter the messenger had brought contained a rough sketch of the route. Passing along the crowded buildings near the river, they emerged into a larger space where the streets were wider with well-built houses lining them. The synagogue, finely built with marble pillars at the entrance, was impressive. In all his years in Rome, Joseph had never ventured into this quarter and liked its dignified appearance.

As they entered the vestibule of the synagogue, they found Theodosius waiting to greet them with great warmth. He was a tall, broad-shouldered man of about fifty, with a trimmed black beard and elegantly dressed in a long silken robe and an embroidered cap on his head.

"Blessed be those who have come," he said first in Hebrew, and then went on speaking in fluent Latin. "I am always glad to welcome those who come to us from our Holy City of Jerusalem."

Nicodemus responded with the Hebrew greeting "Blessed be those who are here."

The archsynagogus took them inside to see the interior of the synagogue richly designed and with decorative lamps hung from the ceiling. They sat down on one of the many padded couches facing the central dais and the ark for the Torah scrolls beyond it.

"As one of the councillors of Jerusalem, we have been anxious to renew contact with you and your community in Rome. You have been unable to send the annual Temple tax or contributions to the poor of the city. But I understand that the restrictions will be less severe now after strong appeals to the emperor were made by the Jews of Alexandria, and he has promised to ease them."

"Yes," said Theodosius. "So I have been told, but it may take some time before they are lifted. So long as Sejanus holds power, the emperor's orders given in Capri do not always find their way quickly to the authorities in Rome."

"Fortunately," Joseph told him. "Some members of your congregation who moved to Alexandria have generously sent donations to us for our various charitable projects in Jerusalem."

Theodosius seemed gratified to hear that his congregants were still loyal to their ancestral homeland. He told them that this was what he constantly preached to his congregants on the Sabbath and on festival days. Many of them were no longer very observant of the commandments but they participated faithfully in all the religious ceremonies and rites of the Jewish faith.

"As you of course know," he told them, "we have been here for over two centuries, ever since the first contacts between Rome and Jerusalem were made by Judas the Maccabeus and a mutual defence treaty was signed between him and the Roman Republic against the Seleucids."

Nicodemus smiled inwardly at this, thinking it was more like a treaty between a lion and a mouse. Rome was a rising power in those days after the defeat of Hannibal by Scipio Africanus at the Battle of Zama when Roman dominance extended over the entire Carthaginian Empire. All this treaty did was to bring Rome into the sphere of the East and its subsequent conquest of all the lands as far as the Euphrates.

He recalled what Gamaliel the Elder had said at one of their meetings in the upper chamber: "Heaven has ordained this Roman nation to reign." He preached submission to the will of God, unlike the Zealots who constantly tried to inflame the people and cause them to revolt. "When a strong wind comes, the tree that stands stiff and upright will break, but the one that is supple and bends will survive the storm."

They retired to a small reception room and a servant placed some baked pastries and wine on the table before them. After the evening service, they went with Theodosius to his house nearby for supper. Nicodemus then broached the other matter about providing some good Roman engineers to undertake the building of the Jerusalem aqueduct. He realised what excellent work the Roman engineers did in building the city aqueducts and those that they built for Herod in Judaea. It would be another way for the Jews in Rome to assist the people in Jerusalem by bypassing the restrictions against money transfers, and he felt sure Theodosius would gladly comply with this request.

****

It was midsummer, and it was getting too hot for comfort in Tiberias, so Agrippa began preparations to leave for Damascus with Cypros. She was now at the end of her third month of pregnancy so it was safe for her to travel. He would make sure that the carriage was comfortable and the horses go at a slow and steady pace for the first half of the way over the uplands of Gaulanitis. Marcus had sent an armed escort to accompany them in case of attacks by bandits or marauders that plagued caravans and wealthy travellers on the highway. The carriage followed the western bank of the lake to Bethsaida and then went up northwards to Caesarea Philippi.

Arriving at his uncle's palace, they found that Philip had gone to Rome to attend the funeral of his great-aunt Salome. Agrippa and Cypros had decided not to go there when they heard of her death, even though Salome was his maternal

258

grandmother and the great-aunt of Cypros on her father's side, through Phasael, Salome's brother. Both of them disliked their Herodian relatives. Like him, Cypros identified herself with her Hasmonean heritage through her mother Shlomzion, Mariamne's daughter and Agrippa's aunt.

They spent a few days at the palace and in the cool and beautiful area surrounding it. He took Cypros to see the white marble temple Herod had built there and the waterfalls nearby. The steward at the palace told them that the tetrarch had sent him a letter to say he did not expect to be back for some time. Agrippa suspected that his sister Herodias may have persuaded him to extend his stay in Rome, and that she was planning to arrange a marriage between Philip and her daughter Salome in spite of the great difference in their ages. If they had a son, Agrippa assumed they could combine two tetrarchies for their mutual benefit.

When he mentioned this assumption to Cypros, she said she had always been sure Antipas would never consider him as his heir and he should no longer think of being the next tetrarch of Galilee and Peraea. She thought that when he could finally go back to Rome to face his debtors he could renew his former ties with the emperor and the imperial family. It was not beyond the realms of the possible that one day he might even find himself ruling the province of Judaea.

Putting all these speculations aside, they both set out from Caesarea Philippi early one morning with their escort for the journey to Damascus. It was easy going along an almost level plain, part desert and part cultivated areas wherever water flowed through tributaries of the river that ran through it. Midway along that route, they bridged the Pharpar River that streamed down from Mount Hermon and flowed southwards across the plains of Damascus, continuing as far as the borders of the Arabian Peninsula, but it did not pass through Damascus. The Abana River, fed by streams descending from the mountain range between Syria and the Lebanon, was the one that flowed through the city and supplied all the water it needed.

This was now all part of Provincia Syria, but most of the Romans in Syria lived mainly in the capital city of Antioch, in the far north of the province and in cities along the coastal area. He had visited Antioch more than once and was highly impressed with that city. It was almost like an eastern Rome, with a forum laid out in the Roman style and a long colonnaded avenue crossing through it. There was also the great temple of Jupiter on Mount Silpius. The city now had more than half a million inhabitants and they had all the forms of entertainment enjoyed in Rome, including a hippodrome modelled on the Circus Maximus although this one could hold only 80,000 spectators.

Damascus would be different, he felt sure. It was much older, founded more than three thousand years ago during the time of the early Pharaohs in Egypt, and settled later by the Aramean tribes about the time when the Hebrew monarchy was established. It was then the capital city of Aram-Damascus, a powerful kingdom extending its reach as far south as the Sea of Galilee. Over the centuries, it had become the crossroads between the major trade routes: the north-south one from Asia Minor to Egypt, and the east-west one from the Mediterranean to the Euphrates. Marcus was right to base himself in this city, the very centre of the entire network of converging roads and trade routes in the Roman East.

Their carriage arrived outside the walls of Damascus soon after dawn when they had just opened the western gate, and they drove along the colonnaded street that bisected the city, stopping at the entrance of a two-storied house just before the theatre on the left. It was an attractive edifice with a marble pillared front and an ornamented balustrade above it. Although it was still early in the morning, people were moving about busily on the ground floor. Coming up the garden path to greet them was Marcus with a wave of his hand and a smile of welcome.

"I saw your carriage from my balcony upstairs," he told Agrippa who had quickly descended to meet him. "I hope you and Cypros have had an easy journey."

He ushered them into an elegantly furnished office where he received his clients, while servants unloaded their travelling bags from the carriage.

"It was very easy, and we stopped at Caesarea Philippi to break our journey," Agrippa said. "I want to thank you for the armed escort you sent us. It made both of us feel secure."

They sat comfortably, exchanging news of each other since their last meeting in Tiberias. Marcus told him that when he returned to Damascus he found a Jewish merchant from Babylon waiting to see him about a profitable trade agreement. He had come by the caravan route that followed the line of the Euphrates River and then circled round towards Palmyra and down to Damascus, the ancient route of the Fertile Crescent. He took this opportunity to travel back with him and visit Babylonia and the Jewish community there, and was amazed at what he found there.

"You know, ever since Augustus wisely came to terms with the Parthian Empire through diplomacy and recovered the standards lost to them, it has become easier for Romans to trade with the people there. The Nabataeans have enjoyed a monopoly on trade with Babylonia for a long time, but we have many things to offer besides their merchandise. They have their long established network centre in Palmyra about 150 miles northeast of here."

Agrippa admired his friend's enterprise and business acumen and told him so. He said that he himself had no head for commercial or financial matters. Since he grew up in luxury, he had spent money without caring for how it came or how much debt he incurred. This was the reason why he was stuck here in Tiberias instead of being in Rome, where he had always lived.

"I am sure you will be back there in time, Agrippa. Although I lived in Rome for many years, I do not feel I should like to return to that city. I sense a deep antagonism towards Jews has been developing there even though we were thoroughly Romanised and loyal citizens. You escaped this since your family has been long associated with the imperial family."

Marcus took Agrippa and Cypros to their suite, a large bedroom with a bath, and a smaller living room where servants had laid out a meal out for them. They found silken robes and soft slippers near the beds for their comfort. The stone floor had woven mats covering it and the rooms were cool and airy. Marcus advised them to get some rest after their journey. In the afternoon, they could go out together to see the city and some of its interesting sites.

He returned at noon to invite them to his quarters for the midday meal. His dining room was in the Arab style of low cushioned couches and tables, and the food had the spicy flavour and taste of oriental cooking. Instead of wine, they received a cup of grape juice followed at the end of the meal by sweetmeats of various kinds. Marcus then ordered the servant to bring in a tray with small cups of a hot and slightly sweetened liquid called tea. He told them that the traders brought it from China and it the Arabs called it 'chai'.

"It is very refreshing and it is good for the digestion. Try it and see," he urged them.

After the meal, they sat for a while and listened to what Marcus told them about life in Damascus and the diversity of the population. Most of the inhabitants in the city were Native Aramean Syrians. They had originally moved from their tribal lands in the eastern deserts to settle in cities and towns in the more fertile west, much like the Arab Nabataeans had done in moving from the deserts of Arabia in the south to found cities and an empire in the north.

"There is a long central colonnaded street, the Via Recta, which bisects the city from east to west with narrow and winding streets in the older western part of the city branching off from it. In the eastern part, mainly inhabited by wealthier people, the streets are more widely spaced and laid out in parallel lines. The Jews in Damascus have clustered mostly near the western gate and engage mainly in small industries and the retail trade around a large marketplace in the southwestern quarter of the city. They have a synagogue there and Torah scrolls, but not many of them attend the services. Some of them travel to Judaea for the festivals, and they still keep to their religious customs and practices."

They all retired for the customary nap after the midday meal. Agrippa felt pleasantly relaxed. It was a long time since he had felt so much at ease, unlike the restless disquiet and tension he usually experienced in Tiberias. Marcus was a man at peace with himself and the world. He was just as ambitious and enterprising as he, Agrippa, had always been, but it did not prevent him from being open and friendly with everyone and with everything.

A few hours later, as the sun was declining in the west, they were in a carriage driving eastward along the colonnaded street. They passed the theatre a little way further on the right till they reached an archway just before the palace building on the same side, and continued until they came to the east gate of the city. It was massive and magnificent with three arches—a large central archway and two side ones. Their carriage then turned up one of the streets to the left and around towards the agora, the broad public square and market where people met and mingled for business or pleasure. From there a long straight road lined with columns, the processional way, led towards the monumental temple and sanctuary of Jupiter.

"What an immense sanctuary!" Agrippa exclaimed as he entered it.

"But not larger than the one in Jerusalem your grandfather built," said Marcus with a laugh. "He certainly outdid all those in the entire Roman Empire."

He told them that this had once been a temple dedicated to the Canaanite god Baal-Hadad whose cult was adopted by the Arameans. The Damascus architect, Apollodorus, who renovated and redesigned it as a Roman temple, decided to keep the same concentric plan of a temple within outer and inner courtyards, as in the Jerusalem temple, the plan commonly used in the temples and sanctuaries erected in Nabataea.

Agrippa said he had visited the great temple of Jupiter Capitolinus on Mount Silpius in Antioch built more than a century ago by Antiochus IV Epiphanes. But this one looked as if it would rival it in grandeur.

"There are many other beautifully designed sanctuaries and temples in Syria," Marcus said. "I especially admire the very lovely one in Palmyra dedicated to Bel and a most impressive one to Jupiter in Baalbek."

Cypros looked around with amazement and admiration, but then shook her head.

"I really cannot understand this craze for building all these magnificent temples in nearly every city. Supposedly for the glory of the gods, but it is really for the greater glorification of the rulers who want to impress their people and win their admiration and loyalty."

Marcus said he understood her feelings, but these temples were the expression of the highest and most intense desire of the human soul to show reverence to the gods and to gain their benevolent protection. Of course, kings and emperors satisfied the religious aspirations of the people in order to please and placate them, but this does not detract from the beauty and grandeur of these temples and sanctuaries.

Agrippa had a wry look on his face: "Grandfather Herod built his wonderful temple and sanctuary thinking to gain the hearts of the people and their loyalty to him, but they never gave it to him. He was always that Idumean usurper."

They returned through one of the streets on the left that led straight down towards the house on the Via Recta. After a light supper, Marcus said that in the morning he would take them to visit a famous philosopher and historian, someone whom Agrippa had known as a child in Herod's palace. At his questioning look, Marcus laughed in merriment.

"Nicholaus, your old tutor, Agrippa!" he said. "He was born in Damascus and has returned here in his old age to write his memoirs and historical works. Do you remember him?"

"What, that kind and gentle man who taught me and my brother Herod? Is he still alive? I remember him well. I was only five and my brother seven when they took my father away and executed him. He sat for days with us listening to our sobs and cries and comforting us as best he could. I can never forget him."

"He is now in his late eighties, but is still strong and active," Marcus told him. "He has spent the last thirty years since Herod died in producing more than a hundred books on the history of the peoples living in the East. He wrote a biography of Augustus and another for Herod. I met him at one of the conferences held at the theatre here by philosophers from the Decapolis cities since they consider Damascus as one of their group of autonomous cities. Philo of Alexandria was also here to discuss the philosophical work *On the Psyche* which Nicholaus had just published."

"I also remember that Nicholaus was in Rome a few years after I and my brother were sent there," Agrippa recalled. "He came with my uncle Archelaus after my grandfather died to support his claim as his heir. I was about eight or nine years old at that time."

"I was also there at that time with my father," Marcus said. "He came to see what Augustus would decide about the succession and whom he would appoint among the sons of Herod claiming their rights."

"So Augustus cleverly carved up the country amongst them," Agrippa said bitterly. "I wonder if it will ever be put together again."

"That will happen only under a Hasmonean king or prince," Marcus said. "At least that is what my father, Joseph, has always told me. The people will only accept a descendant of the Maccabees as their ruler."

Retiring for the night, Agrippa lay awake for a while thinking about what Marcus had said. Perhaps one day he or his son might regain the kingdom that had been lost. They were Hasmoneans although they bore the taint of their Idumean descent and many Jews might therefore deem them unworthy. It was all idle speculation at present, even though Cypros believed this was a possibility. Both of them were the grandchildren of Mariamne, the last of the Hasmonean line. But he was also the grandson of Herod and Cypros was the granddaughter of Phasael, Herod's brother.

The next morning Marcus said he had arranged with his Greek partner, Alcimus, to attend to the trading business while he took a few days off to be with them. Agrippa was eager to visit Nicholaus, and they drove out before noon towards his house on the eastern side of the city. The old man received them with tears of joy and addressed him as 'your royal highness'. Agrippa embraced him warmly, and introduced him to his wife Cypros. He stooped his grey head to kiss her hand and drew them both to the couch. They sat close to him to listen to what he would say.

"Marcus told me you were coming to Damascus and I made him promise to bring you to see me," said Nicholaus, looking at Agrippa with his face alight with love and his eyes bright with pleasure. "You and your brother Herod were so young when I last saw you both. Your sad faces in those dreadful times were imprinted on my memory."

Agrippa asked him to tell them what he remembered of all the many years he had spent as Herod's friend and advisor. Nicholaus leaned his head back against the couch for a moment to collect his thoughts.

"I was in Alexandria at the time where I had gone to study philosophy and history at the library and the museum. This was shortly after Gaius Octavius formed a triumvirate with Antony and Lepidus in Rome, and Mark Antony received Egypt and the eastern provinces to rule as a military dictator. Although he had married Octavia, the sister of Octavius, to strengthen their ties, he fell in love with Cleopatra, queen of Egypt, and they had twin children, a boy and a girl, Alexander Helios and Cleopatra Selene. When the children were about four years old, they hired me to be their tutor. Cleopatra had just given birth to another child, a boy she named Ptolemy Philadelphus for one of her famous ancestors. But sadly, six years later both parents were dead, committing suicide after their defeat by Octavian at the Battle of Actium."

"What happened to the children?" Cypros asked. "I know that Caesarion, her son born to Julius Caesar, was executed by order of Octavius."

"I took the other three children of Antony back to Rome and Octavia was noble and generous enough to take them in and bring them up."

"So what did you do afterwards?" Agrippa wanted to know. "How did you come to know my grandfather?"

"Well, I met him in Rome at the time. Herod was a close political ally of Marcus Antony but after the Battle of Actium and Antony's defeat, Herod sailed to Rhodes with bags of gold to meet Octavian and swear loyalty to him. When he came to Rome to be confirmed in his position as a client king, we chanced to meet at the home of Octavia where he had gone to pay his respects."

Nicholaus went on to say that when Herod heard he had been the tutor of Antony's children, he invited him to come to Jerusalem to tutor the two young sons of his wife Mariamne. He liked the energetic and ambitious Herod, and accepted the position. In time, they had grown closer in friendship and once the children had grown up Herod appointed him as his chief advisor and palace historian.

"It is not generally known that I was actually born a Jew, but my parents had long since become so Hellenised that I have always identified myself as being Greek. Although I can read Hebrew and Aramaic, I was completely ignorant of

Judaism or Jewish customs at the time, and still find them not to my liking. Like Philo, I am aligned in thought with the Pythagoreans and the Platonists and like him have tried to find a link between Judaic monotheism and the concept of the Pythagorean monad, the totality of all beings."

He invited them into the garden behind the house where they could sit in the shade of the wide-branched oak trees. A wooden table spanning two of these massive oaks served as his writing desk and this was where he usually sat and wrote his works. An hour later, they took their leave, promising to visit him again before they left Damascus.

Agrippa and Cypros went with Marcus on many trips outside the city and along the Abana River. On the last day of their stay in Damascus, Marcus took them to say goodbye to Nicholaus. They found him seated at his garden desk poring intently over a thick scroll. He started as they approached, but then smiled brightly at them.

"We have come to say farewell, Nicholaus," Agrippa said, grasping the arms of his former tutor. The heavy scroll fell on the desk and rolled down onto the grass beneath it. Marcus bent down to retrieve it and noticed it contained Hebrew characters. He handed it back to Nicholaus, and they all sat down on the bench on the opposite side.

"What were you reading, Nicholaus?" Marcus asked. "It does not look like one of the philosophical treatises you have in your library."

"No, this is something I received this morning from a friend of mine who was passing near the compound of that secret priestly sect in the Jewish quarter. One of the black garbed priests came hurrying out of the gate carrying a bucket full of scrolls like this, and dropped one of them in the roadway. Since the man had disappeared by the time my friend reached the gate and picked it up, he was curious enough to take it home first to read it before returning it. But since he could not read Hebrew he brought it to me to find out what it was about."

"What is written there?" Agrippa asked with curiosity.

"It is some kind of rule book to instruct the members of the sect. It contains exhortations and a series of laws or rather regulations of how to conduct themselves. It also talks about a 'new covenant' of some kind."

Marcus was very interested to know about this and asked Nicholaus to read them something that seemed significant. After looking through it, rolling the scroll open along the desk from one end to the other as far as he could, he translated some of the lines:

Children of light—avoid the ways of evil until the time of punishment is past. Israel has abandoned God and he turned away from them and from his sanctuary. He raised for them a teacher of righteousness to guide them in the proper way. We are the members of the Yahad, the new covenant in the land of Damascus who now await the coming of the Messiah of Aaron and of Israel. Each of us must love his brother as himself, support the poor and needy, and conduct our lives in perfect holiness.

"This is followed by a long series of rules and regulations for the Yahad community," Nicholaus added. "It ends with a blessing on those who stand firm during all the times of wrath. It all seems like one of those pietistic groups like the Essenes who have withdrawn from society to keep themselves untouched by the evils of this world. But it does not sound like the writings of the Essenes who are peace loving and go about among the people to care for the poor and the sick. These seem to be words of people who have angrily separated themselves from society and look forward to messianic times."

"Well, I hope they will not prove to be violent and a threat to anyone," said Marcus. "We all want to live in peace with each other in spite of our differences."

They parted from Nicholaus with their earnest good wishes for a long life and good health, and he thanked them for coming to see him. He hoped Marcus would keep him informed about them from time to time. As they travelled back to the house, Agrippa found himself thinking why the words of the scroll reminded him of something he had recently heard.

He suddenly remembered. It was what James had told him in Jerusalem about the Zadokite sect in the settlement near Jericho and the preaching of Johanan. Yes, that was it! They were of the same sect he was sure. He would be in Jerusalem again very soon for the festival period and would tell James what he had discovered today.

That evening, as they were having their last supper together, he told Marcus about his attempts to help Johanan and his plans release him from imprisonment. He also told him what he thought about the scroll that Nicholaus had received.

"This sect in Damascus must be a branch of the Zadokite sect in the Judaean Desert, and they must have arrived here later, perhaps as a group of younger members who wanted to create their own community in a better and more comfortable place than the Judaean Desert."

Marcus agreed with him and said that they were probably much more educated and more intellectually advanced than the Zadokites in Judaea.

Before he and Cypros left at the end of the summer, Agrippa gave Marcus a small gift, a carved ivory jewellery box he had bought during the years he had spent in Rome. It had been a very enjoyable visit, and he hoped they would keep in touch with each other from now onwards.

Agrippa and Cypros travelled back to Tiberias with the same armed escort that Marcus had given them, and without stopping along the way. Agrippa was glad to find that Antipas had gone to Rome. He would have a good month of quiet without him at the palace to annoy him. Standing once again in the evening on the shores of the lake, he breathed a sigh of relief and happiness to be home again.

****

Nicodemus felt satisfied that their visit to Rome was successful. Theodosius had introduced them to many of the well-to-do Roman Jews in his community and found three excellent engineers who agreed to come to Jerusalem to make an initial survey of the planned aqueduct. The Jewish community in Rome was willing to cover the cost of the survey, but he still had to convince both the Roman authorities in Judaea and the High Priest of the need to advance the funds to build it.

He was now preparing to go to Alexandria and meet the wealthy Roman Jews who had moved there temporarily because of the restrictions imposed by Sejanus. He needed support from them for the necessary improvements in the Lower City. Joseph was concentrating on the building projects in Bezetha and had left the Lower City problems to him and the Jerusalem Councillors. James was doing an excellent job in sanitation and general maintenance of the buildings, but he had much more do if he wanted to better the conditions of life there.

The original plan was for Joseph and Jeshua to accompany him and Jonathan to Alexandria, but James had sent a letter urging Joseph to return as soon as possible because of serious difficulties between him and Caiaphas. Joseph left immediately with Jeshua for Ostia to board a ship to Joppa, which was closer to Jerusalem than Caesarea, and Nicodemus decided to travel with Jonathan down the Via Appia to Brindisium and take a ship from there to Alexandria. He would stay in the city only for a few days to visit Philo and to see some of the Roman Jews there about financial support for the Jerusalem renovation projects.

As soon as Joseph and Jeshua arrived in Joppa, they hired a carriage to take them as quickly as possible to Jerusalem. When they entered the house, they could hear James arguing angrily in the vestibule with two priests from the Temple, and then came his cry of joy when he saw Joseph with Jeshua just behind him.

"You have come at last, Joseph," he said in relief. "I cannot handle this affair by myself any longer."

The priests turned and bowed briefly when they saw Joseph, and then strode out of the house indignantly without saying a word. Jeshua rushed forward to embrace his brother and then James held out a hand in welcome to Joseph. They both looked so well, especially Jeshua, who seemed to have filled out and become more muscular. His face was sunburnt and his fair hair seemed burnished like bronze. The boy was now a man fully grown.

They went to the living room and found that the steward had already set out food and drink for the travellers. They sat down together, and after some moments of silence, Joseph looked up with an inquiring look.

"What is all this about, James? Why have these priests come here?"

"It is Caiaphas again with his demands. This is not the first time he has summoned me to the Temple. That was just after you left for Britannia. He accused me then of influencing the people against him. Now he threatens to place a *herem*, a ban on those who are not willing to pay the Temple tax, and those who do not attend the ceremonies and rites held there because they prefer to offer prayers in the synagogue instead of sacrifices in the Temples."

"What does this ban mean, James?" Jeshua asked anxiously.

"It means that no one will be allowed to have any dealings with them, to speak to them, to visit their homes …"

"Why do these people not want to take part in Temple rites and ceremonies and offer sacrifices there as everyone does."

"They are not really against this, Jeshua" James explained. "But they accuse the priests of arrogance and rude behaviour and even extortion. When I suggested to them that prayers were as good as sacrifices, someone told Caiaphas what I had said and he considers me a troublemaker and accuses me of preaching against him."

Joseph was suddenly incensed, and stood up. "This threat of a ban must be stopped immediately," he said. "Only the Sanhedrin can impose a *herem*. The High Priest no longer has the authority to place a ban. Caiaphas wants to restore the former position of the High Priest as the supreme religious and judicial authority in the country superior to the Sanhedrin. This is not the case now that the Roman prefect appoints the High Priest and not the Sanhedrin."

He promised to consult with Nicodemus as soon as he returned from Alexandria, and was sure that together they could settle the matter. James felt reassured and suggested that the tired travellers should go up to their rooms. A few hours later, rested from their journey, Joseph and Jeshua came down to join him for supper. Afterwards James asked about their experiences. Gorion had told him some of it from the letter that Joseph had sent him, but he wanted to hear it from them, and enjoyed listening to the interesting stories about Britannia and about their stay in Rome.

"Jeshua liked Cornwall so much that I nearly left him there with Arius," said Joseph with a laugh.

"It was wonderful to be there, James," Jeshua told him. "But as the Shunammite said to the prophet Elisha: *I dwell amongst my own people.*"

"A very troubled and divided people, Jeshua," Joseph told him. "They need someone to rule them. At the very end of the Book of Judges, it is said: *In those days there was no king in Israel; every man did what was right in his own eyes.*"

"You may be right, Joseph," James said. "But in my view, the ruler should not be a king but someone like the prophet Samuel, your own ancestor from Ramatayim Zophim, whose authority kept the people united throughout his long life. When he became old, the people wanted him to appoint a king to reign over them and fight all their battles, like all the other nations. He warned them that a king would take their sons for his army, their daughters as his cooks and bakers, the best of their fields, vineyards, and olive groves for his officers, and make all the people his servants."

"What is the alternative, James?" Joseph protested. "Do you want political chaos, constant upheavals and conflicts, or warring parties and rebellion against authority? However cruel and bad Herod was, he kept the people in order and safe from foreign occupation."

"I do not know what the alternative could be," James said in response. "I envision a people united in brotherly love and harmony, following the moral precepts given in the Bible, living in peace under whatever authority is in power, as Hillel the Elder has always preached."

"Those are the dreams of messianic times which will never come to pass in our lifetime," Joseph told him. "I remember seeing Hillel at the funeral of Herod in Jericho thirty years ago. He was already past his hundredth year and still going strong. For all his talk of loving one's neighbour as one's self, he knew that this was not how people behaved. He was more realistic when he said 'If I am not for myself, who is for me!' He was a Babylonian Jew, a descendant of the royal house of David, who tried to live by the nobler ideals of the old world while facing the harsh realities of the new world of today."

Jeshua listened intently to their discussion and thought Joseph was probably right. In his mind, he understood his reasoning, but his heart felt drawn to what James was saying. Would the restoration of the Hasmonean monarchy really unite the people and bring peace with Rome, as Joseph believed? Or, on the contrary, should the answer to these troubled times be the emergence of a spiritual leader such as the prophets in the Bible to bring the message of love and brotherhood to the people, to rule them from within instead of from above?

Something that James was telling Joseph interrupted his thoughts. It was about Johanan and the petition for his release that Agrippa had written to Pilate, the new prefect. He had not known before that his cousin was in prison.

"When did this happen, James?" he asked with growing anger. "Why didn't you tell me about this, Joseph? You must have heard about it from Nicodemus when he came to Rome."

"He asked me not to tell you," Joseph said quietly. "He knew you would be very upset and it would ruin your stay in Rome with Jonathan."

"There is a good chance of his release very soon," said James in an effort to calm him. "Your brothers from Capernaum were here with Agrippa, the nephew of Herod Antipas, and left a letter signed by Agrippa to the new prefect claiming that Johanan was a Judaean and was therefore not under the jurisdiction of the Tetrarch of Galilee."

Joseph promised that during the festival period, Agrippa and a delegation of the Jerusalem councillors headed by Nicodemus would present the written petition to Pilate. As soon as Johanan was returned to Judaea, he would face trial by Pilate for insurrection, but they could provide a very strong defence against this accusation by proving that nothing was ever said by him against the rule of

Antipas or the Roman authorities, and that he was only preaching against transgressions of the religious laws of Judaism.

"We will go tomorrow to visit Elizabeth," Joseph told Jeshua. "She is now a widow and in mourning for both Zacharias and Johanan, and we must tell her of the plans for her son's release."

Joseph felt tired and dispirited. So many problems had cropped up in his absence. He left James to stay with Jeshua and retired to his study. Several letters were piled up on his writing table, as well as a detailed report from the builders in the Bezetha quarter on their progress, and requests for his comments and instructions. He decided to lie down for a few hours before dealing with all this, but he could not fall sleep and turned restlessly on the couch in his study.

Uppermost in his mind was seeing Maryam again the next day. It was time to ask her to let him adopt Jeshua as his son and heir. It was also time to tell her what he had always known about her parentage. Her mother, Anna, and Elizabeth's mother were sisters, and both of them were of Davidic descent through the maternal line. Maryam's father, Joachim, was the younger brother of Zacharias. As Zacharias put it, the house of Zadok and the house of David were once more united as they had been a thousand years before.

Strange that the old man had always believed the messiah would be born of this unity. He himself had discarded all such foolish speculation after the emergence of such claimants to the title and their rapid repression by the Roman authorities and by Herod as well. In fact, this was Herod's greatest fear, that the people would find someone who could undermine his rule over them. He had executed his own sons, Aristobulus and Alexander in the belief that they were plotting to kill him and reinstate the Hasmonean monarchy.

What would he have done if he had discovered that Alexander had married Maryam and that a son had been born to him after his death? Jeshua and his mother were saved from this danger, and all he wanted now was to see the young man regain the throne that had rightfully belonged to his father. He and Zacharias had previously intended to have Maryam betrothed to Marcus when the time came for her to be married, but destiny had intervened and decided otherwise. Yet he still regarded her as a daughter and felt responsible for her son whom he had come to love as his own. He was only waiting for the right moment to reveal the identity of Jeshua as the true Hasmonean heir to the Jews and to Rome.

Unable to sleep, he went to his writing desk and looked at the letters that had come during his absence. One was from Marcus telling him about his recent activities, his meeting with Agrippa and his wife in Tiberias and their visit to his home in Damascus. Another was from Philo eagerly expecting the visit by Nicodemus and his son Jonathan. The third one had the seal of the High Priest on it and was from Caiaphas. He already knew what it would contain, but when he read it, he was astonished at the hostility and almost rudeness of the tone. He thought of replying immediately, but decided to contain his anger and wait for Nicodemus to return. They must confront the man once for all and put him in his place. He was merely a functionary of the Temple and had no jurisdiction over what took place outside it.

When it was time for supper, he went down to join James and Jeshua. He told James about the letter from Caiaphas and that he decided to wait until Nicodemus was back in Jerusalem before going to see him. They would all three of them go to the Temple together.

"I will go with you as well, Joseph," said Jeshua. "I have not been to the Temple since I was a young boy when I had to present myself before the scholars and priests."

After the meal, they decided to walk over to Gorion's house and visit the old man. He must be already eighty or more by now Joseph thought. He had always admired him for his learning, his administrative skills, his diplomatic talents, and especially his love for all humanity whatever their race or creed might be. Joseph and Gorion were cousins by marriage and their families had always been close.

They found the Gorion family still assembled in the dining room after a late supper. Ruhama and Joanna rose to greet them, happy to see them safely returned from their long voyage. Gorion was amazed to see how Jeshua had changed and said he could hardly recognise him. The talk was lively with Joseph and Jeshua doing their best to answer all their questions. Mary came in from the kitchen to listen to the interesting stories, with her eyes fixed on Jeshua's animated face.

"I am home at last," said Jeshua finally. "I never want to leave my country and my people again."

"My traveling days are also over," Joseph added, smiling at him. "I doubt I shall leave Jerusalem again."

In the morning, they set out for Ein Karem to visit Maryam and Elizabeth and found them out in the garden watering the plants and flowers. Looking up at the sound of the carriage, Maryam froze in terror when she saw Jeshua. It was like seeing Alexander approaching her, a look of love and joy on his bronzed face and the gleam of early sunshine on his hair. Could this be the same pale, fair-haired boy she knew as her son? With his strong arms around her and his lips pressed upon her forehead, she nearly wept with happiness at his return. He turned then to embrace Elizabeth, looking so frail and worn, but smiling to see him again.

It was a long time before they could speak. Joseph led them to the garden bench and they sat together for a while until he broke the silence.

"I have brought your son back safe and sound as I promised you, Maryam."

"You have been more than a loving father would have been to him," she replied with a look of warmth and gratitude.

"I have not forgotten your son as well, Elizabeth," Joseph told her. "We will soon be making our strongest efforts to bring him out of the prison in Machaerus."

All he saw in her face was doubt and despair. She had long given up hope of seeing Johanan again. He was lost to her even before he was imprisoned, completely devoted to a cause she thought as futile. Her tired eyes filled with tears when Jeshua turned to clasp her hands in his for comfort and reassurance.

"James and I decided last night to go once again to the Zadokite settlement to see if there is any news of him," Jeshua said. "Perhaps they found some way to communicate with him."

"There is no point in doing so, Jeshua," Joseph protested. "Wait till we approach Pilate during the coming festival season and try to release him."

"I feel I must go, Joseph. I want to find out how he is. He may even have sent a message for us through one of the guards returning to Jericho. James said they take turns once a month to keep watch over the fortress."

Joseph shrugged his shoulders and said he doubted it was worth the effort. It was a hot journey down in this season with the usual fierce desert winds from the east, and the roads were dangerous as well. He argued with him all the way back to Jerusalem, but Jeshua was determined.

"He is my cousin, Joseph. We were born in this same house and were together during our infant years. I was only two years old when we left for Egypt and vaguely remember him from that time. Whenever I sit in the garden here, the scent of the flowers and the plants brings back flashes of memory of how I used to roll and tumble with him on the grass."

Joseph recalled the two children he saw that day in Ein Karem. One was so black-haired and dark-eyed and the other so fair-haired and with eyes as blue as the sky. One was so bold and daring and the other so soft and gentle. It was thirty years since then, but he could not forget the sight. The child had become a boy and the boy was now a man, with a man's determination of his future course. He had not spoken to Maryam about his wish to adopt Jeshua as his son. It did not seem the right time to do so. He would have to wait until it became an unspoken wish on both sides.

On their return, they found that James was already making preparations for the journey into the desert early the next morning. Long linen robes, turbans, strong sandals, back pouches for food and water, and a donkey with side panniers to carry a change of clothes, a tent, and bedrolls, since they had to sleep outside the settlement. They promised Joseph to spend no more than one night there.

It took most of a day to walk down the road from Jerusalem to Jericho, and then to turn south to the settlement. It was late in the evening when they encamped outside it, and decided to approach it in the morning. Although the weather was hot during the day, it was cold at night in the desert. They built a fire with some of the dried branches and bushes around and put up the tent, but instead of sleeping in it, they lay down on the sandy ground outside it, gazing up at the starry skies above.

"What do you know about the Zadokites in this settlement, James?"

"Only what Nicodemus told me," James said. "They have their own mystical interpretations of the Bible and they follow a different calendar than ours and so the festivals fall on different dates. So they live separately from everyone else."

Jeshua was puzzled. "What kind of calendar do they have?"

"They claim that in the time of the First Temple we originally followed the solar year of 365 days a year. The lunar calendar, which is only 355 days a year, was adopted during our period of exile in Babylon. But we insert an extra month, a second Adar, every four years to catch up with the solar year. If not, we might soon have the Passover festival celebrated in the autumn instead of in the spring."

"So how is their year divided according to the solar system?"

"They follow a calendar system of four periods in a year of 91 days each, or 13 weeks in each period. Altogether 364 days in a year, but they have to add an extra week at the end of every six years because the solar year is 365 days."

"It all sounds very strange," Jeshua said. "It seems as if they want to regulate time, to have everything ordered in some fixed pattern."

"They base their calendar on what is written in the Book of Enoch," James told him. "They also have all kinds of mystical beliefs derived from their astrological speculations. The last time I was here, I saw they had a sundial to regulate the different times of the day. Everything they do is arranged beforehand with the strictest discipline."

A hard life in harsh surroundings, Jeshua thought, wondering how Johanan had borne it. No wonder he had wanted to go out and preach to the people instead of living in this confined place.

The skies darkened and the stars seemed to blaze more brightly. There was no moon since it was nearing the end of its monthly phase, and would only appear in the early morning sky. Sleep came suddenly to the tired travellers, and they woke only when the first rays of the sun touched their tent.

Loud and clear voices could be heard coming from the walled compound. Through the gates they could see white-robed figures standing in rows facing the rising sun and singing what sounded like one of the thanksgiving psalms sung in the Temple.

> *Your holy spirit illuminates the dark places of the heart of your servant with the light of the sun. Only your truth shines and those who love it are wise and walk in the glow of your light. From darkness you raise our hearts. Let light shine on your servant for your light is everlasting.*

This was followed by some prayers recited by a young boy and an elderly man pronounced a blessing on all the assembly. They then filed into the main building where they would probably be having their first meal of the day.

James approached the gate and rang the bell hung over it. The gatekeeper came out from a side chamber and asked them what they wanted. Jeshua spoke first, saying that he was a cousin of Johanan the preacher and wished to know of any news about him.

"We have not heard anything from him directly since his last message," the man replied.

"What was his last message?" James asked.

"The one that some horse rider brought from Machaerus about a month or more ago," was the reply. "He gave it to the overseer, Amram."

James was astonished at this and then recalled what had happened after the visit to Johanan by his brothers and Agrippa. He had returned to Jerusalem and his brothers had gone up north to Capernaum, while Agrippa had remained in Jericho for the night. Could he have brought a secret message from Johanan to the settlement?

James asked the gatekeeper if he could speak to the overseer and a few minutes later he saw him coming to the gate. He remembered Amram from the time he had come there with Nicodemus. He greeted both of them and then asked which one of them was Jeshua, the cousin of Johanan. Wondering how he knew his name, Jeshua told him that he was Johanan's cousin and that this was James his brother.

"You are welcome to enter the settlement, Jeshua," Amram said, opening the gate. "And your brother James may also come in."

They entered the compound feeling a little bewildered but hoping to learn something more about Johanan and the message he had sent. Amram led them to room where the head of the order, Elimelech, received them and invited them to be seated.

"I have been awaiting your coming, Jeshua," he said, "so that the prophecies may be fulfilled."

"What prophecies?" Jeshua asked astounded.

"As the prophet Zechariah has said: *Rejoice greatly, Daughter Zion! Shout, Daughter Jerusalem! See, your king comes to you, righteous and victorious, lowly and riding on a donkey, on a colt, the foal of an ass.*"

He then said that Johanan had told him about the son born to his mother's cousin Maryam. He was not only Hasmonean through his father, but was both a Zadokite and of Davidic descent through his mother.

"I had always thought that Johanan was destined to be a future ruler of Israel, but he believes you are the one who will one day be our messiah and king. This is the message that he sent me from his prison in Machaerus inscribed on a piece of broken pottery. It was brought here by Herod Agrippa who is also your cousin, although he did not know what was written there in Aramaic."

Jeshua was dumbfounded and looked at James for help, but his brother sat silent, rapt in fearful thoughts that Johanan wanted Jeshua to take his place, to wear his mantle of preacher and prophet among the people. This would put him in the same danger of arrest and imprisonment. He had to take Jeshua away as quickly as possible from this place.

"It is useless to try and release Johanan," Elimelech continued. "Although that is what Agrippa said he would try to do. He is lost to us and he knows it. Your time has not yet come, Jeshua. It will be in seven years from now, according to our calculations."

James stood up and motioned to Jeshua to get up as well. He bowed and thanked the Zadokite leader and said that they wished to leave now before the day became too hot to travel. He could see that the old man was trying to delay them a little longer, so he hurried Jeshua out as fast as he could. He did not explain why he was in such a hurry, and it was only when they were folding up the tent and loading the donkey that he finally spoke to Jeshua.

"Don't listen to all this talk of prophecies, Jeshua," he warned him. "These people are only waiting for a chance to regain their place in the Temple as in the old days. Zacharias was wise enough not to join them here even though he also wished for a return of the rightful priesthood. He decided to remain in the Temple and wait patiently for the priestly messiah to appear. But Johanan did not want to wait and tried to force matters before their time."

Jeshua agreed that this was a dangerous idea and he did not want to have anything to do with it. Joseph had already said that it would take many years before the possibility of independence and renewed royalty could come about. He believed that some change in the political situation would occur that might provide the opportunity to renew Hasmonean rule over the people. It must be done gradually with the full consent of Rome and with her support. But in his view, it would not be by him but by Agrippa or one of his brothers, Herod and Aristobulus.

They took the road back to Jerusalem. It was uphill work for most of the way, and it was almost dark by the time they arrived. Joseph was waiting up for them and glad they had returned safely. James told him that there was no news of Johanan and none expected by the people in the settlement. They decided not to tell Joseph what the Zadokite leader had said, but wait for Nicodemus to return from Alexandria and for the petition for Johanan's release to be submitted. Antipas and Agrippa would soon arrive at the Hasmonean Palace in Jerusalem for the festival season and Pilate was due to arrive shortly afterwards. They hoped the appeal for Johanan's release would be successful.

****

Alexandria was even more beautiful than Nicodemus remembered. It was twenty years since he had last seen it. He came this time with his son Jonathan to visit his former tutor, Philo, now in his late fifties and esteemed for his philosophical publications. He also wanted Jon to see the many splendours of the city, the harbour, the famous lighthouse called the Pharos, the Musaeum, the Serapeum, the tomb of Alexander the Great. He had often felt that Alexandria should have been the capital of the world and not Rome, and said as much soon after they arrived at Philo's house.

Philo agreed with him and said he could not bear to live in a city like Rome. For all its grandeur, he found the city cramped together, overbuilt, and overpopulated. Here the streets were widely spaced and laid out in a regular pattern on level ground open to the sky and sun reflecting the typical Greek clarity and open assimilation of ideas and beliefs, while Rome, centred round its magnificent Forum, reflected concentrated strength and physical power. It was brute force over intellectual and spiritual insight. Not that Rome had any lack of great writers and poets as well as powerful orators and excellent historians, but it did not have that certain subtlety of mind, a finesse of perception that was uniquely Greek.

Philo had invited his younger brother, Alexander, and his two children Mark and Tiberius, to have dinner with them. Tiberius was about the same age as Jonathan and Mark was a year older. The two boys were proud to be Roman citizens and had undergone a Roman style of education and physical training in the gymnasium. Tiberius, well-built and strong, said he wanted to have a military career, while Mark was thinner and paler, and was more refined. Jon liked them both but realised how different his own education had been. Neither of them knew Hebrew so they spoke in Greek with Jonathan and seemed friendly enough towards him.

After the meal, Philo retired to his study, and Jon went out with his new friends to explore the city. Nicodemus took the opportunity to speak to Alexander. As the Alabarch, the magistrate in charge of taxation and customs duties in the city for the Roman government, he held a strong position in the Jewish community and was a generous contributor to its institutions. He was also appointed as the assayer for the gold sent from Egypt to Rome and became so wealthy that he once sent a gift of massive gold and silver plates to overlay the gates of the Temple in Jerusalem.

Alexander agreed to go out for an evening stroll in the gardens that led down towards the shore and listened as Nicodemus told him about the financial problems he was facing in Jerusalem.

"Besides visiting my old tutor and bringing my son to see Alexandria, I also came here to arrange a meeting with the exiled Roman Jews now living in this city."

"There is a large group of them living temporarily in some of the guest houses near the synagogue for official delegates from abroad, usually from our community in Jerusalem."

"I understood from Theodosius that they hired non-Jewish agents to handle their property in Rome and to continue with their business dealings."

"Yes, and they wisely kept part of their wealth invested in Alexandria which enables them to live well enough. But they cannot withdraw funds or receive any money from Rome. It also pains them that they no longer can afford to send their annual contributions to the Temple in Jerusalem."

"I have a solution, Alexander, which I will propose to them. There is a drastic need for more water in Jerusalem, both for the people and for Temple requirements. We are planning the construction of an aqueduct to bring more water from the southern hills and wish to employ Roman engineers to do the initial survey and then supervise the work."

"I think I already understand what your proposal is, Nicodemus," Alexander said with a smile. "They can instruct their agents to pay for the employment of the engineers, the cost of the equipment, their passage back and forth, and all the other expenses involved."

"Exactly, Alexander, and this will circumvent the contribution problem for them and also for the Jewish community still residing in Rome."

Alexander promised to arrange the meeting within the next few days and went back to the house to take leave of Philo. Nicodemus was sure that it would be a long time before Jon came back from his excursion into the city and decided to stay up until he did. Philo soon joined him in the living room and they sat talking together, enjoying the cool evening breezes coming through the open garden doorway. The conversation soon turned round to Philo's writings.

"I have a new publication to give you, Nikki. I called it *De Vita Contemplativa*."

"The contemplative life, Philo, like the kind of life you desire most?"

"The kind I admire most, but not the one I wish to live. I believe in the golden mean, both action and thought, work and study, social involvement and personal occupation."

He went on to say that the book describes the mode of life and the religious festivals of a Jewish society of ascetics he called the Therapeutae, very much like the Essenes, living in a colony settled on Lake Mareotis, south of Alexandria. They spent their days in pious contemplation, chiefly in connection with scriptural texts. On the Sabbath, both men and women assemble in a hall to hear a discourse on an allegorical interpretation of a biblical passage since they regard the literal meanings as symbols of an inner and hidden meaning. They live chastely with utter simplicity and consider temperance as a sort of foundation for other virtues.

"What I do not approve is their separatism, their isolation from society. The Essenes in Judaea and the Galilee live apart but they involve themselves with the people, with caring for the sick, assisting those in need, and showing love towards all men."

"We have a small community of Essenes living very close to us in the Upper City," Nicodemus told him, "right next to the southwestern gate which we call the Gate of the Essenes. My wife visits them frequently to learn their healing methods and their use of herbs to cure illnesses. And there are also two scholars amongst them who attend the meetings I hold once a week at my home."

He told Philo that he had visited their colony with one of these scholars and spoke to some of the learned elders of the community. They were very secretive about their doctrines but he had persuaded them to tell him about their beliefs. For them, the body is like a prison in which their immortal souls must live for a while, but find joyful release after death. The souls of good men go to a region that lies beyond the oceans where there are no storms or intense heat, where the air is freshened by a west wind blowing perpetually from the sea.

"What a lovely belief," Philo said. "It reminds me of the Greek belief in the islands of the blessed where the souls of heroes and brave men are rewarded after death and are given immortality."

"I prefer this idea to the Pharisee belief in a future resurrection of the dead at the end of time, although both ideas seem merely mystical speculations to me."

"Ever the rational mind, Nikki," Philo laughed. "You could never agree with my own mystical speculations in all the years I spent as your tutor."

"In this world of such conflicting beliefs, superstitions, messianic dreams, and sheer stupidity, I have to hold onto all my rational mind to remain sane."

Their discussions ended with Jon bursting into the room followed by Mark and Tiberius. He said he had driven with them through the central street as far as the Canopian Gate and then turned up towards the shore and driven back along the seafront and was thrilled by everything he saw, the harbour, the ships, and the lighthouse across the bay.

"I want to live here, Father," he told Nicodemus excitedly. "Please let me stay in Alexandria. I could finish my schooling here instead of in Jerusalem and will then find some interesting occupation to support myself."

"I thought you loved Jerusalem, my son. It has been the heart and soul of the Gorion family for many generations," Nicodemus said sadly. "How can you leave it?"

"I do love it, or rather I did, but Jerusalem bores me now, Father," Jon protested. "It has closed in on itself, absorbed with its past, with all its former glories, not the future which I feel is here."

"Your mother will never forgive me for leaving you here."

"She already knows what I feel and I am sure she will understand."

Nicodemus lifted his arms in defeat and then opened them wide to embrace his son. They stood together for a long time and then held each other apart. He found it strange that they were almost the same height. He had not noticed this before.

"I will leave you in the care of my former tutor and his brother," he said, turning towards Philo, and receiving a confirming nod from him. Mark and Tiberius patted Jon on the back and suggested that he return with them to their home to tell their father.

"Do not worry about him, Nikki," Philo assured him. "The boy is restless. He is not a scholar like you, but his eyes are bright with intelligence and curiosity about everything. Alexandria will be good for him."

"See that he comes home to Jerusalem at least once a year, Philo," Nicodemus said with a sigh. "We will miss him very much, especially my father."

Several days later, he was on his way back to Joppa and Jerusalem. The meeting with the Roman Jews had gone well and they had promised to provide generous funds for the aqueduct survey. He had also received a substantial contribution from Alexander and the Jewish community in Alexandria after making an appeal in the synagogue.

When he arrived home, Ruhama was not surprised to hear that Jon had remained in Alexandria. She knew he had not been happy in Jerusalem in recent months. Gorion was downcast at first, but admitted it was better for the boy in

Alexandria than in Jerusalem. The city had no outlet for young people, nothing that provided for youthful enjoyment and enterprise. There was too much tension in the city, too much controversy among the various sections of the population. He could feel the frustration in Jon, in spite of his strong attachment to his family and country.

"There is a lot of anxiety among the people now," Ruhama told him. "Pontius Pilate arrived last night from Caesarea with a large retinue and a company of soldiers."

"Antipas and his nephew are also here at the Hasmonean palace," Gorion added.

"Then I must go to Joseph now to get the delegation of Jerusalem councillors and notables ready for a ceremonial welcome tomorrow."

Still in his traveling clothes, but with the dust hastily brushed off and a quick wash of face and hands, he left hurriedly for Joseph's house a few streets away. He found James in agitated discussion with Joseph who was striding up and down the large reception room. At his entry, both of them rushed towards him in relief.

"I am glad to see you back, my good friend," Joseph said, grasping his arms in warm affection. James also came forward to greet him, but his face showed his deep concern.

"What has happened," Nicodemus asked anxiously, as they sat down together.

James then told him about the visit to the Zadokite settlement and that Jeshua had returned with a fever from the journey and distress over the failure to glean any information about Johanan. He did not tell him what Elimelech had said to Jeshua.

"Tell him we are going to do our best to release Johanan," Nicodemus said.

"Although Agrippa has not yet arrived, we will attend the ceremonial reception for Pilate tomorrow and submit his petition. Pilate will remember me from our encounter in Caesarea about two months ago, and will listen to reason again I hope."

Preparations for the grand reception of the new Prefect of Rome began at the Herodian palace. Guards and soldiers stationed themselves along the entry route into the city through the Joppa Gate. The hall was filled with Roman officers and administrators, as well as delegations from the various communities in Jerusalem.

Nicodemus stood among them with the other two councillors, and noticed the prominent position taken by Caiaphas with some of the Temple priests at the forefront of the crowd. Royally dressed, Pilate sat in a gilded chair on a high podium facing his audience.

"I bring you greetings from the divine emperor Tiberius Caesar who has given me full administrative, financial and judicial authority over Provincia Judaea. Let us hope we will receive your loyal cooperation in all matters concerning the proper administration of this province."

One by one, various groups of people approached to introduce themselves and to congratulate him. Caiaphas was the first to offer loud and elaborate words of welcome and to make the traditional blessings for kings and rulers. Two Sanhedrin elders also greeted him and made their polite salutations. Then Nicodemus and the two councillors came forward and introduced themselves.

Pilate immediately recognised him and gave a gracious nod to their bows and the traditional Hebrew greeting: "Peace be upon you." He waved his hand to all the assembled people, thanking them for their attendance and promising to receive any of them who wished to meet and talk to him. As the hall slowly emptied, he called Nicodemus and the councillors back and led them into a side chamber.

"I wish to receive your assurances that you will do everything to keep the peace during the coming festival period," Pilate warned them severely. "Any disturbances will be immediately suppressed and the instigators punished with death."

The councillor, Ben Zizit, affirmed that they had stationed men to keep order among the pilgrims to Jerusalem and that no rioting need occur now that he had the military standards removed.

"I consider their removal an insult to my emperor," Pilate said haughtily. "But in the interests of peace I conceded to the wishes of the people."

"We thank you once again," Nicodemus said in tones of conciliation. "You have acted with clemency and wisdom and we hope you will continue to do so. We bring you now, on this festive occasion, a special petition on behalf of a religious preacher who has been unjustly imprisoned by Herod Antipas for incitement."

"Herod Antipas of Galilee and Peraea has full jurisdiction over his tetrarchy," Pilate said firmly. "I cannot interfere with his decisions."

"The preacher, Johanan, is a Judaean and he has preached only within the territory of Judaea," Nicodemus protested.

Pilate's face darkened with anger and annoyance. He could see his ten-year appointment filled with repeated irritations. Jews were notorious for their constant petitions and complaints. Still, confronted by the calm and steady gaze of the chief councillor he agreed to accept the petition and to speak to Antipas.

"I already sent my regards to him through his nephew Agrippa, and I have his invitation to a reception in my honour at the Hasmonean palace tomorrow. I will speak to him then."

After expressing their gratitude, the councillors left the chamber. Nicodemus wondered what Antipas would say when he saw that it was Agrippa who wrote petition with the added signatures of the councillors.

The next evening, the Palace of the Hasmoneans was lit up with flaring torches and the walls strung with garlands. The sound of harps playing soft melodies greeted the guests entering the banquet hall, most of them from the wealthy families in the Upper City, but also including the High Priest, the Sanhedrin leadership, and other notables. Antipas had tried to outdo his father's flamboyant extravagance with a lavish spread on tables laden with gold and silver dishes and glass goblets.

Agrippa was at the other end of the hall, conversing quietly with Nicodemus and the Jerusalem councillors. He apologised for his delay in arriving, but in his view, there did not seem much hope in obtaining a favourable response to their petition.

"Pilate and my uncle seem to be likeminded about political rule. Quick and instant repression of dissent or opposition is their policy whatever the result may be."

Joseph and Jeshua soon joined them, both dressed in elegant robes. Jeshua was pale but held his head high, determined not to show his anxiety at being in such surroundings. Agrippa looked at him for a long moment, trying to recall where he had seen him before. Then shook his head, smiled at them, made his excuses, and joined his uncle in greeting the new prefect and his wife.

"What royal pomp and circumstance Antipas has prepared to impress Pilate," Joseph remarked. "All these lordly airs he puts on!"

"He regards himself as the real ruler of Judaea after his brother Archelaus was banished," Nicodemus said with scorn. "He expects Rome will someday allow him to regain the kingdom that Herod once ruled."

Joseph nodded in agreement. "He is even trying to get hold of the tetrarchy of his brother Philip through marriage with Salome, Herodias' daughter."

"She is barely twelve and he must be nearly four times her age!"

"When did that stop any of the Herodians from their schemes?"

They sat through the meal and the liberal servings of wine. At the end, Antipas stood up, lifted his goblet, and gave a rousing tribute to Tiberius Caesar and to the new Prefect of Judaea, to which Pilate responded graciously. This presumably signified the conclusion of the banquet, and one by one all the guests began taking leave of their host.

As the hall emptied, Antipas invited Pilate and his retinue to come out to the terrace overlooking the Temple. The evening had not yet darkened and the Temple shrine and courtyards were clearly visible. They stood along the balustrade while Antipas pointed to the various areas below, the magnificent Royal Portico along the southern wall overlooking the Court of the Gentiles. Beyond the eastern wall, they could see Solomon's Porch and the entrance into the Women's Court. Fifteen steps mounted up from that court towards the Gate of Nicanor and into the Court of the Priests, with the Holy Shrine in the centre.

Pilate admired the beauty and grandeur of the Temple sanctuary laid out before him and looking tranquil in the fading light of day.

"It seems so peaceful now," Antipas said with asperity. "But just wait until the crowds come during the festivals and you will see how noisy and even riotous they can be."

"Yes, I saw in Caesarea how headstrong and unruly the people are in this country. I shall have a hard time to keep the peace as Caesar has charged me to do."

"All you need is a firm hand and a quick response to any sign of opposition. I have the same problem with my Galilean subjects, who are even more unruly than the Judaeans."

They went inside and Antipas led Pilate to the vestibule where a military guard waited to accompany him back to the Palace of Herod. While exchanging friendly words and good wishes, Pilate mentioned by the way that he had received a petition concerning a certain prisoner held at Machaerus.

"A petition sent by whom?"

"It was written and signed by your nephew Agrippa with the signatures of the Jerusalem councillors. They claim that the man, Johanan, is a Judaean and not subject to your jurisdiction."

"It's that damnable nephew of mine again with his foolish notions! I have every right to arrest this fellow for stirring up so many of my Galileans against me."

"I wash my hands of all this, Antipas," Pilate told him. "I have no intention of interfering with internal matters of this kind, barring execution of course, which will require my assent."

"Oh, I and have no intention of executing him. Let him rot in the dungeons. Execution would only turn him into a martyr and become a cause for rebellion."

"Wisely said, my friend," Pilate said, as he turned to depart.

As soon as he had left, Antipas burst into a frenzied rage, calling down upon Agrippa's head every curse he knew. It was time that Hasmonean upstart was shown the door, whether Herodias objected or not. He looked around for him, but Agrippa had already gone, leaving a note to say that a message had come from Tiberias and he had to leave immediately for home.

****

The New Year and festival period had come and gone with much less trouble than anticipated. As Nicodemus predicted, the people were waiting to see how the new Roman governor would rule. The only thing that worried him was the serious depletion of the water reserves by the thousands of pilgrims and visitors to Jerusalem and the requirements of Temple sacrificial rites and especially the water-drawing ceremony at the end of the Feast of Tabernacles. In all the synagogues, they recited the prayer for bountiful rain in the coming winter season with fervour.

At the next meeting of the study group held in the upper chamber, Nicodemus read out the reply that Pilate had sent to the Jerusalem councillors concerning their petition.

To the Honourable Councillors of Jerusalem

I regret to say that I am unable to assist you with regard to the arrest and imprisonment of Johanan the Zadokite. I consider this an internal and personal issue between the parties concerned and not subject to my decision. My jurisdiction applies only to matters relating to public order and peaceful submission to Roman rule.

With all due respect

Pontius Pilatus, Prefect of Provincia Judaea

There was dead silence for a while and then the sound of a chair scraping at the other end of the table. Everyone turned around to see Jeshua standing up, his face pale and drawn, and walking out of the room. James immediately rose and followed him. Matthias was the first to speak.

"I would have tried to get Caiaphas to intervene since he has some influence on Antipas, but in this case he will do nothing. For him the Zadokites are anathema."

One of the Greek philosophers looked inquiringly at Nicodemus and asked who were the Zadokites.

"They are members of the high priestly clan known as the Sons of Zadok who served in the Temple since the days of David and Solomon. When the Hasmoneans came to power nearly two centuries ago, they ousted this clan from their rightful position and took over the high priesthood from them."

Ben Zakkai said that it was necessary to go further back to understand the course of events. After the Jews returned to Zion from Babylonia, the first high priest to be appointed over the newly built Temple was Joshua ben Jehozadak of the illustrious Zadokite priestly line, and his descendants continued to serve as high priests for over three centuries. When the Seleucids came to power, Jason, the brother of the high priest Onias III, bribed Antiochus Epiphanes with Temple funds to gain this position. He also promised that he would Hellenise Judaea and turn Jerusalem into a polis renamed Antiochia. Onias had always opposed Hellenization, and took refuge in Antioch among the Jews in the wealthy suburb of Daphne, hoping they would be able to influence the Seleucid king to reverse his decision.

"And the usurper, Jason, was then usurped" Nicodemus added with an ironic smile.

"Yes, he was," Ben Zakkai said with a laugh. "Menelaus, his envoy to Antiochus, offered even greater bribes to the Seleucid king. Jason had to flee to the land of the Ammonites in the East while Menelaus took over the high priesthood and had the support of the wealthy Hellenised families who had built their grand homes here in the Upper City."

He then related that the Zadokites called Onias the Teacher of Righteousness, and called Menelaus the Wicked Priest because he forced the people to adopt Hellenistic culture and the worship of Greek gods and placed a statue of Zeus in the Temple. Menelaus had Onias assassinated in Antioch, and his son, Onias IV, fled to Egypt. Under the protection of the Ptolemies Onias constructed another Jewish temple in Leontopolis where Jewish colonists had settled, and he continued to perform the traditional Temple services and sacrifices.

"But not all the Zadokites had followed Onias to Egypt," Nicodemus told the study group. "A large group of them went out into the Judaean desert to await their return to power. A few of them, like Zacharias, the father of Johanan, remained in Jerusalem and continued to serve as best they could under the Hellenised priesthood, the Sadducees, the Grecian term for Zadok, who claimed descent from him. It now appears that many years later, some of the younger Zadokites moved up north to Damascus."

Turning to the Essenes in the group, the Greek philosopher asked why they had also gone away into the desert.

"We were originally a sect of pious Jews called the Hasidim who decided to break away from the general population and live purer and monastic lives. Our intellectual beliefs and philosophy of life soon began to differ in many ways from the more orthodox Pharisaic communities in this country. Most of us settled in the region of Ein Gedi on the shores of the Dead Sea, but many groups were sent out from there to minister to the poor and the sick in the towns and cities of Judaea and the Galilee."

The discussions continued for a while until the sun began to set and the room slowly darkened. After the others departed, Nicodemus remained behind with Ben Zakkai to recite the evening prayers and then to go down to supper with the family. Jon, who had come from Alexandria to spend the festival with them, was already at the table, telling stories about the shipping company he wanted to found with some Greek partners and the voyages they had taken along the coast of North Africa. He had decided to stay on in Jerusalem for another week to attend the marriage of his sister Joanna to Ben Zakkai.

At first, Nicodemus had been opposed to the marriage since the rabbi was even older than he was. But his daughter, who was now eighteen, seemed determined to marry Ben Zakkai and no one else, so he finally yielded to her wishes, and the wedding would take place on the eve of the new moon, the month of Marheshvan.

****

Jeshua had been very happy to see Jon again, and they spent many days together before the festival helping James to set up booths for the residents of the Lower City and for the pilgrim families that were crowded into it. Palm fronds and greenery strewed the streets, and for lack of space many families had to set up tents outside the walls and in the Kidron valley among the many tombs and monuments. During the festival week, the whole family went up to Ramatayim to spend time together Joseph on his beautiful estate. Maryam and Elizabeth had also come to stay with them.

But once the holiday period was over, Jeshua began to relapse into a state of deep depression and shut himself up in his room for most of the day. Joseph and James tried to talk to him and draw him away from his sad thoughts about his imprisoned cousin Johanan, but had little success. They sent a message to Nicodemus to come over and see what he could do, and he went out immediately accompanied by Jon who was also anxious about Jeshua.

They found the house lit up and Joseph sitting on a couch with his head in his hands. James was near the door while Jeshua was pacing up and down the long reception room flinging his arms up in the air and speaking with intense passion.

"I am no Hasmonean prince, Joseph, just a plain carpenter's son from Nazareth in the Galilee. I am grateful for all you have done for me but in my heart I know I can never be what you want me to be."

Joseph stood up and faced him with fiery eyes, and his face streaked with tears.

"Your mother is the daughter of a Zadokite priest and his wife was of Davidic descent. Your father was a Hasmonean prince, the eldest in line to be heir to the throne of Israel. You are of noble blood and are the best qualified to restore this country to its former glory."

Jeshua threw his arms down in frustration. Then, turning towards the door, he saw Nicodemus with Jonathan and noticed how shocked his young friend seemed.

"It's alright Jon," he said gently coming towards him and holding out his hand. "I am sorry I did not tell you before."

He led Jonathan out into the hallway and into his own suite of rooms so that they could talk quietly together. James followed them out and retired to his own quarters.

"Make him see sense, Nikki," Joseph begged him. "I can do nothing with him."

"He was very distressed about Johanan and Pilate's letter as he must have told you," Nicodemus said with concern. "But I did not think it would cause this outburst."

"You should have heard what he said to me earlier" Joseph told him in a horrified voice. "I have never seen him in such a state of fury. He was completely unlike his usual gentle, gracious self, ranting about his bestial Herodian heritage and his corrupt Hasmonean one. I told him this was his chance to redeem his heritage, to renew the days of Simon the Just, the beloved priest and last member of the Great Assembly, to restore the rightful priesthood to the Temple and cleanse it of corruption."

"And if I am not wrong, he said power always corrupts," Nicodemus said. "And he still cannot see himself as the future king of Israel. The task seems beyond his abilities."

"I am not asking him to do this now, but only in another five or six years, after Tiberius dies and we have a more rational emperor to succeed him, who may restore the Hasmonean monarchy in Israel and its position as a client kingdom of Rome. It would be welcomed with joy by the people and prevent what will inevitably be an uprising against Roman rule under these cruel and rapacious prefects."

"He is just reacting now to Johanan's imprisonment, to its injustice. Give him a little time to see if Johanan's release can be obtained in some other way, by an appeal to the emperor over the head of the Pilate through the Alabarch Alexander. As you know, as the guardian of her property in Egypt, he has close connections with Antonia, the widow of his beloved brother Drusus and the mother-in-law of his lately deceased son, Drusus. He holds her in great affection and trusts her loyalty to him entirely, while being suspicious of many other members of the imperial family."

"You are right. I will travel to Alexandria as soon as possible and hope this will calm Jeshua for the present. But do speak to him yourself, since I know you have a very good and strong influence over him."

"I will do so," Nicodemus promised him. "And I would like to go with you to Alexandria and accompany Jon back to his new home there."

By the time Jon and Jeshua had reappeared, they could see that that the two young men were calmer and had come to some new understanding between them. Joseph then told them of the plans he and Nicodemus had agreed upon, and that they should not lose hope for releasing Johanan. He suggested that in the meantime, Jeshua and James should take a trip northwards to visit their brothers in Galilee and on the way there to see what the situation was with the followers of Johanan at Bethabara.

****

The wedding of Joanna to Rabbi Ben Zakkai, held within the circle of family and friends, was a joyful occasion for the Gorion family. Rabban Gamaliel conducted the ceremony and in his own hand wrote out the *ketuba*, the scroll that specifically records the obligations of the husband towards his wife and the dowry she brought him that would return to her if they divorced. Joseph offered the newlyweds a home in the caretaker's lodge at the entrance to the new garden villa and groves he had built for himself beyond the northern wall of the city.

A few days later, Nicodemus and Jonathan prepared to leave with Joseph for Alexandria. Before their departure, a letter arrived from Agrippa to the Jerusalem councillors saying that he regretted the petition to Pilate had not been successful. He had faced a severe tirade from his uncle and could do nothing further in this matter without endangering his position. His wife was expecting their first child during the coming winter season and he wished to devote himself to her and her welfare. But he had made sure that Johanan would be well treated in prison and hoped he would eventually be released after his uncle felt less threatened by the preacher's followers.

"I can well understand his position," Joseph remarked after reading the letter. "He is deeply in debt to creditors in Rome and entirely dependent on his uncle for his livelihood. All he can hope for is to succeed him as tetrarch if Antipas dies without an heir."

"I liked him very much," Nicodemus said reflectively. "He has a manly bearing and courtly manners that made him such a favourite with the imperial family, especially with Tiberius and his son Drusus."

"The rumour is that Drusus was murdered by an agent of Sejanus. And that Drusus' wife Livilla, Antonia's daughter, is complicit in the murder. She and Sejanus are known to have been lovers for years and he may be plotting to gain the imperial throne through her after Tiberius dies."

The five-day sea voyage to Alexandria went smoothly and when they arrived on a clear sunny morning, they were warmly welcomed at the dock by the Alabarch and his two sons. A carriage took them all to the palatial residence for a late breakfast, after which the young men went off to their own quarters leaving their elders comfortably seated in the reception room.

"You will be glad, Nicodemus, to hear that a large amount of money has already been collected for the Temple in Jerusalem earmarked for your aqueduct."

"I am sincerely grateful for your fundraising efforts, Alexander. The Roman engineers completed the plans for its construction and are ready to commence with the work. All that remains is for Caiaphas to pay up his share to complete it."

Joseph looked at him sceptically and then said he doubted the wily priest would part with a zuz unless forced to do so by the Roman administrators in the city. Then, of course, he would blame them for despoiling the Temple of its treasures. We must inform Pilate about the serious water problem and let him deal with Caiaphas.

When he told Alexander about Johanan's imprisonment and Pilate's letter rejecting intervention with Antipas, the Alabarch was greatly concerned and asked what he could do.

"The only thing that can be done is to appeal to the emperor," Joseph said. "We thought that perhaps you could write to Antonia and ask her to make the appeal. What should be stressed is that this situation might lead to an uprising by the people, initially against Antipas but spreading into general rebellion against Roman rule."

Alexander slowly shook his head and said the emperor had become a complete recluse in the island of Capri since the death of his son.

"He has withdrawn almost completely from administrative matters and has left everything to Sejanus whom he calls his *socius laborum*, the partner of his labours. Sejanus chose Pilate to be Prefect of Judaea. I will of course write to her about it, but I do not think she will be able to do anything to help you in this matter."

He saw the gloomy look on Joseph's face and asked what the reason was for his special concern about Johanan. There had been and perhaps always would be such preachers of doom and castigators against bad rulers.

"He is the cousin of Jeshua, whom I have taken under my care. His mother and the mother of Johanan are cousins. He was deeply distressed over the imprisonment."

"Jeshua, you mean Maryam's child, the boy that grew up here in Alexandria?"

"Yes, I sent them here nearly thirty years ago to avoid a dangerous threat to their lives. Philo was kind enough then to take care of them for me until they could safely return to Jerusalem."

Alexander gazed at him perplexed, and asked him what that danger could have been. Nicodemus nodded at Joseph and said they should tell their friend the truth about Jeshua. He then recounted all that had happened while Alexander listened in amazed silence to the long story. Joseph also added that during a visit to Rome, Antonia herself had seen the resemblance between Jeshua and his father. Philo must also have guessed at the reason for concealment although he never said a word about it to his brother.

They decided to visit Philo later in the afternoon and discuss the matter further. Alexander promised that he would lend them all his support whenever there was a chance for the restitution of a Hasmonean ruler over Judaea. However, he thought the time had not yet come because of the present situation in Rome, and estimated that it would take at least ten years before this was possible.

It was much later in the day when they arrived at Philo's house. The old philosopher was delighted to see them and invited them to join him at the supper table.

"It is good to see you again, Philo," Nicodemus told him. "It is a long time since you last visited the Temple in Jerusalem for the festivals."

"I no longer enjoy being there, Nikki. It does not have the same atmosphere of purity and tranquillity I used to experience in my earlier days. Its true purpose has been lost. The priests have become corrupt and mercenary."

Philo then mentioned the treatise he had recently composed on the special laws of Judaism in which he discusses the Temple and the sacrificial rites held there. In his view, the Temple in Jerusalem symbolises the entire cosmos and the high priest mediates between God in heaven and man on earth. The high priest offers sacrifices, prayers and thanksgiving not only for the Jews but for all people and for the world of nature in order to achieve perfect unity and harmony.

"Remember what Solomon said in his prayer to God when he dedicated the First Temple: *Does God really dwell upon earth? The heavens cannot contain you, how much less this temple that I have built!* It should be regarded only as a symbol of God's presence in the world, not literally, as most of the common people believe. And not as a commercial enterprise as the Sadducee priesthood is treating it."

Nicodemus reminded him of the book they had studied together, the Wisdom of Jesus Ben Sirach, translated from Hebrew into Greek by the author's grandson. It was luckily included in the Septuagint among various other books excluded from the canon of the Hebrew Bible.

"There was that wonderful description of the Zadokite high priest, Simon the Just. If I remember rightly, the passage begins something like this: *Greatest of his brothers and beauty of his people was Simeon the son of Johanan the priest; in whose generation the Temple was visited, ...in whose days the wall was built ...the water pool was dug* ...I forget the rest, Philo. But you know it well."

Philo nodded and said that the best part was the description of Simeon when he comes out of the Holy of Holies on the Day of Atonement: *Like a star of light from among the clouds. Like the full moon in the days of festival.* Ben Sirach goes on to borrow words from the psalm in which the righteous man is compared to a cedar of Lebanon.

Joseph smiled and said he knew this psalm by heart, the one that the Levites in the Temple always sang before the altar on the Sabbath day. It ended with the lovely lines in praise of them:

> *The righteous will flourish like a palm tree,*
> *they will grow like a cedar of Lebanon;*
> *planted in the house of the Lord,*

they will flourish in the courts of our God.
They will still bear fruit in old age,
they will stay fresh and green,
proclaiming, The Lord is upright
He is my rock ...

Philo added that the description in Ben Sirach ends with the hope that God's eternal covenant with Phinehas the son of Aaron will continue to ensure the position of high priest for Simeon the Just and his descendants. Sadly, the days of Zadokite primacy was over, although they still believed in their future reinstatement as the true Temple priesthood.

The talk then turned to recent events in Jerusalem and the imprisonment of Johanan. Philo advised them to do nothing more, and that any attempt to circumvent Antipas and Pilate might actually lead to Johanan being tried and executed. If there were less agitation for his release and his followers stopped demonstrating, Antipas would eventually see that the man was no longer a danger to him.

"As for Jeshua," he added, turning to Joseph. "From what I recall of him as a boy, he was a dreamer, living purely a life of the spirit and not of worldly things. He could never be a political leader however much support you gave him."

They reluctantly said goodnight to Philo and returned with Alexander to the Alabarch's residence. They decided not to prolong their stay with him but to leave within the next day or two. Joseph suggested that they take the slower caravan route across the Sinai and through Beersheba. He felt he needed the time to think about what he should do next with regard to Jeshua.

Nicodemus agreed to this plan and they made the travel arrangements the following morning. Jon said that he would accompany them as far as Pelusium and return to Alexandria from there by ship. When they reached the border fortress, he parted from them with a promise to come to Jerusalem again for the Passover festival with the family, and to see Jeshua again.

Joseph watched him as he rode away towards the docks along the shoreline.

"I wonder sometimes at the warm and close friendship between Jon and Jeshua," he said with a bemused smile. "Jeshua does not confide much in me or in James even though I know he loves us both very much. Perhaps he needs a younger person he can talk to without reserve, to unburden himself to someone he knows well and trusts not to betray his inner feelings."

"Jon was his first pupil when he came to stay with you. There was always this mutual love and understanding between them. Not on any intellectual level, mind you. Neither of them cared much for scholarly study or for philosophical discussions."

As the caravan travelled along the seacoast highway and into the southern desert, they grew more and more silent with their thoughts. Both of them felt they had come to some impasse regarding Jeshua and their plans for his future. Nicodemus felt that they should leave him alone to work out his own path in life, while Joseph believed that he needed more restraint and discipline in accepting the role for which his heritage had destined him.

"Joseph, it could be a tragic role rather than a heroic one," Nicodemus warned him. "For over twenty years, I have been working on the history of our people, and the hundred years of Hasmonean rule is filled with violent events and fratricidal plots. The last Hasmonean king, Mattathias Antigonus, mutilated his old uncle Hyrcanus and exiled him to Babylon in order to gain the throne and the high priesthood. He reigned for only three years until Herod overpowered him and sent him to Mark Antony in Antioch who scourged with whips, crucified, and then beheaded him. There are still some of Herod's sons alive who might try to have Jeshua killed if claims kingship, Antipas most of all."

"I would never let him be placed in such danger," Joseph protested. "Everything will have to be done with the consent of Rome and under the protection of the emperor. He will only rule over Judaea, so Antipas can keep his tetrarchy, and Philip can keep his as well."

"Well, let us leave everything as it is for the next few years and see what course history will take. You must launch your boat only at full tide, as you well know from experience. But somehow I do not believe that tide will ever come in."

They travelled on without further discussion. This was a long and slow journey which took ten days to cross the southern desert to Beersheba and then northwards to Jerusalem. Thoroughly wearied and dispirited, they arrived at Joseph's house to find that Jeshua had left with James for the Galilee only the day before.

It was already dark by the time Nicodemus reached his own home, and although he tried to let himself in without disturbing his wife and father, Ruhama heard him enter and came down in a rush. They held each other for a long while, until she made him lie down to rest on a couch and brought him some warm broth. She listened quietly to all that he told her about the visit to Alexandria and their failure to resolve the question of Johanan.

"Jeshua was here yesterday with James to say goodbye," she told him. "He had the determined look of someone who has finally reached an important decision. I doubt he will return to Joseph's house. He said to tell you he was 'going home' and would not return here for a long time."

"This will break Joseph's spirit," Nicodemus said sadly. "All the hopes he has had for Jeshua will be crushed. Better not tell him what you just told me, Ruhama."

As they went up to bed, he asked her why it had taken them more than two weeks to leave for the Galilee.

"James told me that soon after you left with Jon and Joseph, he had an argument with Jeshua. The next morning he found a note from him that said he was going down to Bethlehem and would then continue on foot into the desert towards Herodion."

"He must have been distraught to do such a thing."

"He came back a week later, dusty, red-eyed and footsore, and it took several days before he was fit enough to travel to the north."

Weary as he was, Nicodemus found he was unable to sleep that night. He tried to imagine what had been going through Jeshua's mind during his journey into the desert. Perhaps he felt the need to repudiate his Herodian and Hasmonean heritage, to shout imprecations at Herod's tomb for the monstrous evil he had done to his family. All those grand building projects, the magnificent city and harbour of Caesarea, the temples he had erected to honour Augustus in Samaria and elsewhere, and the glorious splendour of the Temple in Jerusalem may have impressed the Romans, but could never bring his people to love or honour him.

He understood now what Jeshua wanted. It was not to rule a people with power but to rule their hearts with love. He had gone back to the Galilee to find his true place among his people. Joseph would have to accept this and give up his dreams of a Hasmonean restoration. If he truly loved Jeshua, he would have to let him go.

****

James and Jeshua set out for Jericho on an early autumn morning while the air was still fresh and crisp in the Judaean hills, dressed in simple traveling robes and turbans to protect their heads against the sun. James rode on a strong mule harnessed to a cart filled with their packed bedding and food supplies, while Jeshua walked alongside, but occasionally stepped up on the backboard when he felt tired. They travelled down towards the Jordan Valley along with the many family carts and wagons returning from their pilgrimage to Jerusalem, stopping to rest at various points along the way.

James had not questioned his brother when he returned from Herodion. He did his best to get him bathed and fed and then let him sleep on and off for a few days until he recovered his strength and spirits. Now, resting on a rock by the roadside to eat some food, he asked Jeshua about the days he had spent in the desert and why he had gone there.

"I don't know, James. I just wanted to get far away from everything and think."

He rose and gazed eastward where the waters of the Dead Sea glinted in the early morning sunlight, his eyes reflecting the glow, and began recalling his desert journey.

"I rode my mare down to Bethlehem and stabled her, then went on foot across the desert to Herodion. I just sat there for hours looking up at that magnificent fortress where my grandfather lies buried. I went there in hatred and anger at him and his cruel acts, his violent temper, but the hatred did not last for long. I began to understand the fear he must have felt, the constant threat of murder by his own wife and sons with the help of Hasmonean supporters. I resolved then to forgive him, to realise what it meant to hold on to power in the face of opposition."

James looked up at him with a smile. "They say that understanding is the first step towards forgiveness."

"And that is why I cannot put myself into the same situation, to be forced to do evil in order to protect myself from my enemies."

He sat down again and went on talking to James, trying to explain the struggle within him between the role Joseph wanted him to play and his longing to live a life of peace and tranquillity among the green hills of the Galilee, sailing around the beautiful lake, the Kinneret with the shape of a harp. He recalled those days he had spent as a youngster with his brothers at Capernaum and at various places along the shores of the lake, blissfully ignorant of his royal birth.

"I am a Galilean, James," he told him vehemently. "I feel it in my bones and body. Jerusalem, for all its beauty and its pine-scented mountain air, oppresses me. I am a captive there, caught in the tangled web of intrigue, of dissension, of clashes between contrary passions and beliefs. It will kill me if I do not escape from it."

James shook his head as if trying to dispel these dark thoughts. For him, there could be no other place to live but in Jerusalem, the very heart of the nation, the city which David had founded, which had once been lost, wept over, and won again. All he wanted was to have it ruled wisely as in the days of Solomon, or later in the time of Josiah, the last King of Judah to rule independently. When the good king fell in the Battle of Megiddo fighting bravely against Pharaoh Necho II of Egypt, the whole country mourned his death and the prophet Jeremiah lamented him. He recalled the passage his father, Josiah, had read to him in the Book of Chronicles:

> Then Jeremiah lamented over Josiah, and to this day all the choirs of men and women sing laments over Josiah. They established them as a statute for Israel, and indeed they are written in the Book of Laments.

Josiah was the king who had ordered the renovation of the Temple that had fallen into disrepair. During the renovation work, Hilkiah, the high priest, discovered the Book of Deuteronomy, the last book of the Pentateuch, in which Moses, at the end of his life, recalls the years of wandering in the desert and gives his final instructions to the Children of Israel. The discovery then led to a renewal of the covenant and the centralisation of Jerusalem as the only place of worship.

In his view, it was high time they renewed the covenant once more under a good ruler, one who would love his people, be faithful to its God, and preserve the code of laws handed down from the time of Moses. James believed that Jeshua needed only a few more years with Joseph to be ready for that task, and find the strength and will to carry it out. He could stay in the Galilee for a while, but eventually it would not satisfy him and he would return to Jerusalem.

****

Agrippa returned to Tiberias as soon as the reception his uncle gave for Pilate was ending. He did not want to face the fury of Antipas. The man would most likely want to cast him off without further hesitation, unless in the course of a week or two his anger simmered down. True enough, when he next saw his uncle, there was no more than a heavy scowl on his face and he said nothing about the petition. All he was interested in was how much revenue was coming in from the taxation of the farms and from the trade with the cities around the lake.

Most of the Galileans who had followed Johanan to Bethabara on the Jordan River had returned home to plough and sow their fields before the autumn rains. Antipas saw no signs of an imminent uprising, and all Johanan's fiery preaching about the approaching apocalypse and the Kingdom of God had come to nothing, so he had calmed down and everything went on as it had before.

Herodias was still in Rome, having her daughter Salome educated in the Roman manner. She was turning out to be a real beauty and was exceptionally gifted in music and dancing. Her mother intended to marry her to her uncle Philip, Tetrarch of Iturea and Trachonitis, despite the great difference in their ages. He was now in his late fifties, had never married, and was anxious to produce an heir before he was too old. The poor girl was a pawn in her mother's ambitious plan to annex his territory with that of Antipas, and in time, he would lay claim to Judaea as well.

Cypros began feeling anxious about the future and of their precarious situation.

"Our stay in Tiberias can only be a temporary one until the final rupture between you and your uncle. And we will have nowhere to go after that happens."

Agrippa tried to reassure her and calm her fears. He would always survive whatever fate might bring. Still, he would have to think of some plan to fall back upon in case the worst happened. There was a very large estate that still belonged to the Hasmonean family adjoining the town of Ginossar and lying between Magdala and Capernaum. The town was situated on a high mound, and was now an outpost held by the Romans. The estate of Ginossar, which means 'Garden of the Prince', bordered on the Kinneret, the Sea of Galilee, with thickly branched trees, orchards, flowering plants and trellised bowers. This was where the family used to spend the winter months to ride along the tree-canopied paths, breathe the fragrant air, swim in the lake, or go boating.

Neglected for more than twenty years, the trees and plants were overgrown, and the cabins, low, wooden structures for holiday residence, had fallen apart. He would send some workers there to clear it up and restore it to its former state and then stake his claim to it as royal Hasmonean property. He could settle himself and his family there and even offer part of it as a trading post to Marcus instead of the one Antipas had built in Tarichaea, or as another port for the fish-processing enterprise in the area. It would be a Garden of Eden for him, for Cypros, and for their children.

****

For James and Jeshua, it was a long, slow journey down to Jericho and then up along the river road northwards to the Galilee. James noticed that the further they went the more relaxed and happy Jeshua felt. They walked or drove in the cart, making frequent stops to enjoy resting along the lush green banks and to take occasional dips in the river. When they reached Bethabara, they found that the encampment set up by the followers of Johanan was no longer there and the small groups that had remained behind were now preparing to leave.

James questioned them and they told him that Johanan wanted them to return to their homes. He promised them that another and greater leader would soon come to show them the way to the Kingdom of God. They had to get back to ploughing their fields before the rains came. A few of his faithful disciples were still at Machaerus, permanently settled in tents outside the fortress, to keep in touch with him through the guards. They treated him well but Johanan had no illusions about his eventual release.

They pushed on northwards at a leisurely pace, taking pleasure in the quiet stillness of the valley, the warmth of the sun, the coolness of the river water. In the evenings sitting on low rocks over the small fire of twigs and branches, Jeshua told his brother what he would do in the Galilee after James returned to Jerusalem. He decided to remain only for a short while in Capernaum with Jose, Jude and Simon, and would then look for some kind of employment in one of the large estates in the area.

"You want to go from prince to pauper?" James asked him in astonishment.

"I want to live for a while among the people, to share their joys and sorrows, to help those who are poor and oppressed."

"What could you possibly do to help them without changing the present regime and a country under Roman occupation?"

Jeshua did not answer at first, but looked silently into the fire and stretched out his legs towards it. The days were warm but the nights were cold. It was time to unroll their bedding and go to sleep. He unhitched the mule and tethered it to a tree, added some more dead branches to the fire. He knew that James was hoping that after a short stay in the Galilee he would return to Jerusalem and Joseph.

"I do not feel I am the one who could change it or gain independence from Rome. It would take someone who has close ties with Rome, who is familiar with the political wheeling and dealing that will persuade them to appoint a Jewish king to rule Judaea and Jerusalem. Someone like Agrippa could do this."

"Not Agrippa," James said reflectively. "He is a fine, intelligent young man, but is too much of a Roman to be accepted as a Jewish king, even if he ruled well."

"He is Hasmonean enough for the Jews and Herodian enough for the Romans," Jeshua told him. "I liked him for his frankness and sincerity in helping with Johanan."

Tired out by now, they stopped talking and lay down to sleep. It would take them another two days to reach Beth Yerah where the river merged with the lake, and from there they would have to travel up through Tarichaea, Tiberias, Magdala, Ginossar, until they reached Capernaum.

When they finally arrived, they could hardly recognise the village that seemed to have expanded into a large town. The three brothers, Jose, Jude and Simon, were now well-to-do, respectable members of the community and their synagogue had worshippers filling it every Sabbath. James and Jeshua were heartily welcomed, lodged in guest rooms within the family compound and provided with new robes.

There was a festive family reunion the next evening with all the wives and children of their brothers seated around the table. Everyone wanted to hear all that had happened since they had last seen each other, and felt sad to hear that the efforts to free Johanan had failed. Most of his followers no longer expected him to be released, and were now waiting for the new leader he had promised would soon appear to save them. Simon said the time for waiting had passed, and was adamant about the immediate need for revolt. He admitted he supported the Zealots, the underground revolutionary party in the Galilee.

"We still remember Judas the Galilean, who rose up against the Romans when they ordered the census to be taken more than twenty years ago. His two sons, James and Simon, are carrying on their father's legacy and are leaders of the Zealot party now centred in Gamla out of reach of the Romans."

Jude said that he and many others in the Galilee wanted the new leader to call for a general uprising against Roman rule and against the wealthy elite in Jerusalem who collaborated with them. Instead of waiting for the Kingdom of God, they should bring it about by force and military might as the Maccabees had done against Greek rule.

James and Jeshua looked at each other in alarm at their passionate spirit. This was revolutionary talk, but Jose smiled and said it was an absurd idea and that Johanan had not meant a revolutionary leader like Judas, but a spiritual one who would bring the people back to their faith through purification from sin. He believed that the Kingdom of God was approaching and those who did not repent would be punished.

He turned to Jeshua and asked what he thought of Johanan and his beliefs.

"I love and admire Johanan for his faith and fervour," Jeshua said slowly, "and I also think we need a spiritual leader not a revolutionary one, but I do not like his dire warnings of fearful punishment against sinners. What they should be taught is the love of God not the fear of him."

"The only revolution Johanan wants," James added in a quiet voice, "is to expel the corrupt and illegitimate priests in the Temple and replace them with the sons of Zadok, the rightful priesthood."

"Yes, but the Temple priests function under the control and support of the Romans," Simon protested. "Any attempt to expel them will bring Roman opposition. The High Priest receives his appointment by the Roman governors of Judaea and they keep his Day of Atonement vestments in the Antonia Tower until a week before the fast day. In my view this is sacrilege."

The anger and frustration was palpable in his voice. Jose tried to calm him down but Jude said he thought Simon was right. Revolt was the only way.

"I am the only pacifist in this family," Jose told them with a laugh, putting an arm around each of his two younger brothers sitting on either side of him. "We have given Simon the nickname Zelotes, and Jude is called Taddai, which in Aramaic means 'courageous heart', because he saved a boatload of fishermen singlehandedly during a storm. But it will take more than zealotry and courage to change things in this country."

The meal ended with all the children rushing out to play while the adults gathered around the hearth to talk of other things. They wanted to know what James and Jeshua wished to do during their stay in Capernaum. James said he planned to return to Jerusalem very soon, but Jeshua wanted to remain with them and find some employment in the area. He no longer wanted to live the life of luxury with Joseph but to find his own way.

"I feel happier here in the Galilee," Jeshua explained. "This is where I belong, not Jerusalem."

"Good Jeshua, you are welcome to stay with us," Jose reassured him. "Actually, there is a new project we have taken up which you could join, the run-down estate of Ginossar just few miles to the south, a little below Tabgha. Agrippa decided to restore it to what it was under the Hasmoneans. The gardens will be replanted and three Roma pavilion-style houses built in them. He asked us to do the woodwork for them and also to build a pier on the shore for fishing boats."

"Sounds good to me, if you will let me take part in the work," Jeshua responded with relief. His brothers gladly agreed and they settled the matter amongst them. It would be like old times again, the band of brothers working together.

"We have recruited a few others into this large project," Jose added. "Philip from Bethsaida will be the main supplier of building materials and supervise the estate renovation. Philip is also bringing a good builder, Nathanael bar Talmai who is known as Bartholomew because he is originally from Ptolemais. They have worked together for a long time in building projects in Caesarea Philippi."

Jude told him that he was forgetting their second cousins James and Matthew, the sons of Alphaeus who could help with building the pier. Also the Greek, Thomas Didymus, from Scythopolis, who would be a good architect for the houses. They could all live there during the week and return here to Capernaum for the Sabbath.

After James left for Jerusalem, Jeshua and his brothers rode down towards Ginossar with cartloads of wooden boards, planks, nails, and all the implements of the carpenter's trade. The other five men arrived by boat a few days later, bringing all the necessary provisions for a lengthy stay. They had an enjoyable time settling into what had once been the caretaker's lodge just outside the gates of the estate and set up a large workshop near the shore. A feeling of warm camaraderie quickly spread amongst them during those early days, with much laughter and friendly banter. After a hard day's work, it was good to sit around a fire in the open air, eat a hearty meal, and tell each other about themselves. Each had a different story to tell of their lives and experiences.

They were all most curious and interested in what Jeshua had to say about himself, his childhood in Egypt, his growing up in Galilee, and his adoption by a rich Jew in Jerusalem who took him to Rome and Britannia. They wanted to hear all about his travels, his descriptions of life in Rome, the sea voyage and his adventures in Cornwall. They sensed that he had acquired a higher level of education than theirs, but he still felt and behaved himself as one of them in every way.

Although he was the youngest of the group, they soon began to regard him with the kind of respect given to someone more knowledgeable and educated. During the Sabbath weekends in Capernaum, the brothers invited all their fellow workers to stay with them, and treated them as family members. They sat in places of honour at table and took part in singing the Sabbath eve psalms and hymns. In the morning, they all went to the synagogue to hear the weekly portion of the law and a selection from the prophets read out by an elderly scribe.

Jeshua realised that although most of the congregants there knew how to read the Hebrew verses, they barely understood their meaning. It was customary in every synagogue to have a learned scholar standing beside the reader to translate each verse into Aramaic, the common language of the people. He told Jose that he could volunteer to do this for their synagogue, and on the following Sabbath he stood up on the dais and translated the verses line by line for those attending the services.

"It seems the years I spent studying with Nicodemus were worthwhile after all," he said to his brothers, after the enthusiastic acclaim given him by the congregants. "Although I am not the scholar he wanted me to be."

"You have all the learning and skill in interpretation as any of the Pharisee rabbis in the Galilee," Jude said with pride. "We used to have a rabbi coming to give sermons on the Sabbath but he recently passed away."

"Perhaps Jeshua could give sermons on the Sabbath," Simon suggested. "It would bring many more congregants to our services."

"You will be our rabbi, Jeshua," Jose said with a smile. "You will be famous as the youngest rabbi in the Galilee!"

Jeshua's eyes lit up at the idea. He could be a preacher like Johanan, and pass his own thoughts and beliefs to the people in Capernaum. It might even fill the empty gap that his cousin had left among his followers who had returned here.

The sermons he began giving at the synagogue drew a large audience hungry for spiritual guidance and comfort, for the hope of salvation. The first sermon was on the words of Hosea, his favourite prophet, and the verse he chose was of the wonderful love of God for his people:

> *And I will betroth you to me forever; yea, I will betroth you to me in righteousness, and in judgment, and in loving kindness, and in mercies. I will betroth you to me in faithfulness, and thou shalt know the Lord.*

He told them that Hosea had spent about sixty years as a prophet in Northern Kingdom of Israel, warning of the approaching doom from Assyria, and died just before the conquest and exile of the ten tribes. In his words: *They had sown the wind and reaped the whirlwind*, but God would one day bring them back and make a new covenant with them. He would say to them: You are my people, and they shall say: 'You are our God.'

The following week he gave a sermon from the same prophet:

> *Come and let us return unto the Lord; for he has torn and he will heal us; he has smitten and he will bind us up. After two days he will revive us; in the third day he will raise us up and we shall live in his sight.*

One of the congregants asked him about the 'two days' and wanted to know what the 'third day' meant. He said that, according to one interpretation, the two days were the two temples built in Jerusalem, the First and Second Temples. One day a third temple would rise that would stand forever. The new temple would be open to all mankind, Jews and non-Jews alike.

"The prophet Isaiah spoke about the 'sons of strangers' in connection with God's promise that all those who wished to worship him would be welcome to enter the temple:

Also the sons of strangers that join themselves to the Lord, to serve him, and to love the name of the Lord, to be his servants, every one that keeps the Sabbath from polluting it, and takes hold of my covenant. I will bring them to my holy mountain and make them joyful in my house of prayer their burnt offerings and their sacrifices shall be accepted upon my altar, for my house shall be called a house of prayer for all people.

Some of the people who heard this were astounded at his interpretation and reported his words to the Pharisees in the nearby towns and villages. This caused an outcry against him by the leading rabbis who had gained authority among most of the people. The Pharisees preached a strict observance of the law according to their interpretations of it, and imposed additional ritual customs which they considered as a 'fence around the Torah' to create stronger barriers between Jew and Gentile. They also tried to keep those who were non-observant away from the community as outcasts and ritually impure.

The brothers were afraid the Pharisee rabbis would place a ban on their synagogue, and decided to stop Jeshua from giving any more sermons. Instead, they would organise a small group to meet at home and study biblical texts with him, especially the Prophets. The first one Jeshua decided on was Nahum, who had been born seven centuries ago in Kefar Nahum, the Hebrew name for Capernaum. When he was still a child, he and his family were among those who exiled by the Assyrians, but he lived long enough to see the approaching collapse of this great empire with its capital city Nineveh, and its conquest by the Babylonians.

"Nahum's tomb is located inside a synagogue in Alqosh, in northern Mesopotamia, not far from the ruins of Nineveh," Jeshua said. "Ruhama told me that the Babylonian Jews visit it every year to recite his book of prophecies."

The book had only three short chapters, but it contained magnificent diatribes against Assyria, calling down upon it all the anger and vehemence of a soul eager for the vengeance of God against them, and foretelling that they would suffer the same fate they had caused the people of Israel.

> *Woe to the city of blood ...Nineveh is laid waste: who will bemoan her? ...O king of Assyria, thy nobles shall dwell in the dust; thy people is scattered upon the mountains, and no man gathereth them.*

"Wasn't it Jonah who predicted the fall of Nineveh?" his brother Simon asked. "I remember we used to read it with Father on the Day of Atonement."

"You are right, Simon," Jeshua told him. "But Jonah lived about a century before the Assyrian conquest of Israel. God spared Nineveh at that time because the king and the city repented of their sins. Jonah knew this would happen if he obeyed God's command to warn them of their imminent destruction. He tried to run away and not go to warn them because he foresaw the conquest of Israel by the Assyrians and wanted Nineveh to fall."

For the next three months, they continued with their work at Ginossar and returned every weekend to Capernaum. After the years of living in comfort and ease, but almost in seclusion, Jeshua enjoyed working in the open air and in good company. He also enjoyed sharing his love and knowledge of the Bible with his brothers and their friends. He felt stronger and more purposeful in life, and surer that his decision to return to the Galilee was the right one.

****

Returning home at noon from the palace of Antipas overlooking Tiberias, Agrippa saw Jose of Capernaum waiting for him outside his house and received the welcome news that the renovation work in Ginossar was completed. After their meal and an hour's rest, they set out northwards on horseback. Two hours riding brought them to the estate, and Jose led Agrippa on a tour of the low-roofed houses. He was more than satisfied at the excellent renovation work, the polished stone floors, the panelled walls, and the furniture, and the thick wooden beams of the roof that overhung the walls and left an opening at the top of each wall to let in light and air. It would be a wonderful residence for him and Cypros during the summertime. The gardens around were also cleared and replanted and the orchards were already bearing fruit.

"And where are your companions, Jose?" he asked.

"They decided to take a day's trip around the lake to celebrate the end of their work. Come down to the shore and see the sturdy dock that we built there."

They strolled around the garden paths and then went down towards the lake. The sun was already low over the water and its rays danced over the rippling surface. In the distance, they could see a long boat coming towards them and could barely make out the figures. They stood there near the dock watching the boat approach and could hear the noise and laughter of the men. Four of them were rowing and three were hauling in a fishing net with their catch. Standing in the prow was a tall figure, stretching out an arm towards the shore and declaiming in a loud clear voice the opening lines of Homer's Odyssey to the amusement of the rowers.

309

SPEAK, MEMORY— Of the cunning hero,
The wanderer, blown off course time and again
After he plundered Troy's sacred heights.
Speak
Of all the cities he saw, the minds he grasped,
The suffering deep in his heart at sea
As he struggled to survive and bring his men home …
Speak, Immortal One,
And tell the tale once more in our time.

Agrippa stood in silent amazement, looking at the figure in the boat, his mind going back to his childhood in the palace of Herod. Running through the corridors and coming out into a large hall, he saw his uncle, Alexander, standing by the window and speaking to someone. He felt afraid at first, thinking he would be punished for entering without permission. Instead, his uncle turned around, his golden hair shining in the sunlight and his blue eyes smiling at him, his warm voice welcoming him, as he came forward and lifted him up in his arms. This was the same clear voice, the same face, the same hair and eyes with the sun casting a halo of light around him.

"That crazy Jeshua," Jose laughed going forward to the dock, "our little brother, always showing off his Greek learning."

The boat soon reached the shore and Jeshua was the first to spring up onto the dock. While some of the men moored the boat, Simon carried the fish up in a basket and called out to Jose to say that they had caught a big haul for supper. Then they all stood still in surprise when they saw Agrippa dressed in his elegant riding clothes and boots standing just behind Jose.

"Our noble patron has come personally to give us our wages and to thank you for your work," Jose told them. "Let us invite him to a good meal with your fresh fish before he leaves."

They all made their bows of welcome and followed Jose into the caretaker's lodge. Agrippa hung back and took Jeshua by the arm, drawing him aside into a grove of trees nearby.

"Didn't I see you before in Jerusalem at the reception for Pilate?" he asked. "You were with Joseph of Arimathea and the Jerusalem councillors at the time. What are you doing here as a common worker? Are these really your brothers?"

"Yes, they are my brothers, but from my father's first wife," Jeshua said with hesitation. "After my father died, my mother returned to her family near Jerusalem. Joseph is a close friend of the family and took me under his care, gave me good tutors, took me to visit Rome and Britannia."

Agrippa now recalled something that James had said about his brother traveling abroad with Joseph. He could not understand why Jeshua had left his luxurious life in Jerusalem to live in Galilee with his brothers. He also could not explain his amazing resemblance to Alexander. His mother may have been from some noble family in Jerusalem, perhaps distantly related to the Hasmoneans. If so, what could have been the reason for her marriage to a simple Galilean carpenter?

As the evening began to fall, they all crowded around the fire in the central room to feast on the fish roasted over it. Philip produced a jug of wine and several loaves of freshly baked bread. Agrippa could not remember having enjoyed a meal as much as this, and he listened attentively to the talk that Jeshua gave on some passages of the Bible relating to the sea.

Jeshua began with the first verses of Genesis and the Spirit of God moving over the face of the waters. He said that this means the seas were there even before the creation of the world, and everything emerged from the sea in natural sequence—first the earth and the plants and trees, then the living creatures, then those living in the water and later those on land, and finally man. This shows that creation was all for the sake of man. We are all the sons of man, Adam who is made from the earth—*adama*. When man sinned, then the earth submerged again under the seas, in the great flood.

Agrippa left them while they were still talking. Warmed by the food and the fire, he set out for home before it became too dark. He did not want to leave Cypros alone since she was due to give birth very soon. During his ride, his mind kept returning to the mystery of Jeshua and his amazing resemblance to Alexander. But all his speculations ended when he came home and was delighted to find that Marcus had arrived from Damascus bringing cartloads of rich merchandise—spices, perfumes, silks and beautifully woven tapestries. They were ordered by Antipas and Herodias who had decided to spend the winter in Tiberias rather than in Machaerus, and planned to entertain lavishly and on a grand scale.

"Marcus, I am very glad to see you again," Agrippa said as he grasped his arms in friendly welcome.

"I am also glad to be here again, Agrippa. It is certainly warmer in Tiberias than in Damascus."

Cypros had prepared a late supper and they sat together for a long talk about trade and politics. After she retired to bed, Agrippa told Marcus about the renovated estate in Ginossar and the dock he had built on the shore. He intended to install a caretaker and two men in the lodge to guard the estate since he had given up the idea of a trading post as impractical.

"I will take you to see the estate before you leave" Agrippa told him. "It is on your way back to Damascus up through Bethsaida and along the river valleys."

"Yes, and you will be accompanying me nearly all the way, Agrippa," Marcus said, smiling at him astonishment. "Your uncle arrived in the palace this afternoon and was angry when he did not find you were at home. He asked me to bring you a letter you must take personally to your uncle Philip, an invitation to visit Tiberias for the winter season and to enjoy the hot springs nearby."

"I know what he and my sister Herodias are planning" Agrippa said angrily. "They want him to marry Salome and unite the tetrarchies. So after Philip dies he will control all the northern territories."

"Well, it is better than having Philip's area under Roman Syrian control like the Decapolis," Marcus said. "Galilee will have Syrians too close to its borders."

"My uncle also wants to rule Judaea and regain his father's kingdom."

"And I can see you one day as the heir to this reunified kingdom. Since Antipas has no heir, you would be his most natural successor."

"But if Philip has a son with Salome, he would be the heir, not me," Agrippa said bitterly. "He has no affection for me and I am here only on sufferance for the sake of my sister."

"Then you must return to Rome, Agrippa," Marcus told him. "Renew your warm relations with Tiberius who still holds you in great affection. Borrow the money you owe from the Alabarch in Alexandria who thinks very highly of Cypros. I will write to my father in Jerusalem who is in constant touch with him and ask him to intercede for you. Once you are in Rome, you can regain your status at the imperial court and among your former Senator friends. My wife, Aurelia, is in Rome and can assist you, and my daughter Arianna is now married to a senator who is highly influential."

"Marcus, your advice is good but it is not yet the right time. Sejanus still holds controlling power over Rome and Tiberius is content to let him do as he pleases. The man will overreach himself one day and when he falls I will consider returning, if and when, of course, I can cover my enormous debts."

Marcus nodded and they stood up together, both too tired out by now to converse any further. Agrippa was anxious about going away now and did not want to leave Cypros so near her time to give birth. He decided to go immediately with Marcus the next day and return as hastily as he could.

They rode out in the early morning, leaving the drivers and their carts to follow at a slower pace, stopping only for a rest at Ginossar and the midday meal they had brought with them. The caretaker's lodge was empty and Jose and his working companions were no longer there. Continuing on to Capernaum, they decided not to stop but to reach Bethsaida before dark. Marcus knew an inn where they could get a good meal and a clean bed.

****

The workers at Ginossar had packed their meagre belongings, tidied the caretaker's lodge, and left in their large fishing boat for Capernaum. When they arrived, Jose and his brothers, Jude and Simon, went ashore, but Jeshua decided to accept the invitation of Philip and Nathanael to work in their building company and went with them to Bethsaida. The two sons of Alphaeus, James and Matthew had already gone ashore at Tabgha just below Capernaum, while Thomas found a large horse-wagon that was taking supplies down the lakeshore road to Scythopolis and paid the wagoner for a seat on it. All of them had agreed that they would continue to meet on festival days or on other occasions.

Jose knew that with three carpenters in Capernaum there was little employment for Jeshua as well, so he had suggested that Philip take him into his company at Bethsaida. The town was growing larger, and the tetrarch in Caesarea Philippi was intending to raise its status to that of a polis and rename it Julias in honour of Livia, the mother of Tiberius, who received the title of Julia Augusta when she married Augustus. There was a lot of carpentry work there, especially in furniture carving for which Jeshua was highly gifted.

As their boat entered the fishing port, Philip and Nathanael were hailed loudly by a large, burly man standing on the docks, and by two other sturdy looking men heaving panniers of fish onto a cart. Philip waved at them and they bellowed friendly curses at him, which sent everyone nearby into laughter.

"Simon, you old dog," Philip shouted at the burly man, as he leapt out from the boat. "What a haul you have had with the fish today!"

They clapped each other on the shoulder, and Simon gave a hand up to Nathanael and then to Jeshua.

"And who is this fair young lad you have brought us, Philip? No fisherman of course, as anyone can tell. Another of your fancy house painter artists I presume."

"This is Jeshua, the youngest of the Capernaum brothers. Came a few months ago from Jerusalem where he was living with his eldest brother. We were working together at the old Hasmonean estate in Ginossar and have just come back from there."

The two men working with Simon approached, and he introduced them as his partners James and John, sons of Zebedee.

"You know, Jeshua," Philip told him "these two are popularly known among the Greeks as the Boanerges, *bene rogez*, 'sons of rage' or 'sons of thunder' because of their short temper."

"Shut up, Philip," one of them growled. "Or you'll get some of our short temper," said the other.

"You see, just as I said," Philip laughed. "Simon bar Jonah here does not mind being called 'Petros' by the fishermen. Large and solid like a rock!"

Simon nodded in agreement and flexed his right arm to show off his muscles, and then put it around Philip's shoulders.

"Well, it is near dinner time, Philip, so before you go to your fancy house in town, come home with us and have a good meal after your tiring journey. And your friends are invited as well."

They went along with him, grateful for the offer of food, rest, and good company. His house was not far from the shore, and as they entered, the savoury smell of fried fish and spicy cooked food greeted them. Laying the table was a slender, slight young man who smiled shyly at them and quickly set three more places around it.

"This is my brother Andrew," Simon told them, putting a strong arm around him. "Not a fisherman but an excellent cook as you can see."

During the meal, Philip told him about the many weeks they had spent in Ginossar and about Agrippa. He was full of admiration for that noble Hasmonean forced to work for the despicable Herodian Antipas.

"Herods, Hasmoneans, Romans, whatever," Simon snorted in derision. "They can all go to hell for all I care. All rulers are the same, greedy, vicious, immoral ..."

"You sound like an anarchist," Nathanael said with a laugh. "I met some people in Ptolemais who are of the same opinion. What do you think, Jeshua? You have been living for the past ten years or more in Jerusalem where all kinds of rulers have held power."

Everyone turned to him expectantly. He looked around at their faces and wondered whether they would understand what he wanted to tell them.

"I have read and admired the book written by the Greek philosopher Plato, about the ideal city-state or republic as he calls it which he says should be ruled by a philosopher-king, someone who has a love of knowledge, wisdom, intelligence, who is ready to live a simple life while working for the benefit of his people. In other words, he is talking about the messiah that our own prophets have spoken about and which we hope will come one day to rule us, a just man, a man who will follow the laws of God and love his people."

The others around the table sat in silent wonderment, trying and failing to find words in response to this. Finally, Simon stood up and said in a loud, hearty voice.

"Jeshua, I appoint you as our philosopher-king and our messiah!"

There was general laughter all around as he placed a large hand on Jeshua's head in mock blessing. Across the table, Andrew gazed at Jeshua with shining eyes of comprehension and lifted his cup of wine to him in silent tribute to his words.

Simon pointed proudly at Andrew and said he was the only one in the entire fishing community who read and spoke Greek as well as Philip here.

"Besides keeping house for me, like a good brother, he spends a lot of his time reading whatever he can get hold of from the Greeks living here. But it's a waste of time as I see it and a lot of pagan ideas in my opinion for good Jews like us."

"What you good Jews need, Simon, is a synagogue or at least a prayer centre," Philip told him. "It is a long six miles to walk to the one in Capernaum where you go every Sabbath morning. Why not build one here?"

"We don't have anyone here who can read the scrolls of the law, Philip. Nor will any of the Galilee rabbis agree to come to Bethsaida to preach since it is prohibited for them to cross over the border of Galilee on the Sabbath."

"You have a large courtyard behind this house which could be used as a prayer hall. And Jeshua here, who is going to work for me in Bethsaida, can be your reader of scrolls and preach better than any rabbi."

Simon slapped his hands on the table and said it was a grand idea. He turned to Jeshua and lifted his eyebrows in mute inquiry. With all eyes on him, Jeshua blushed at first and then went pale.

"I would be honoured, Simon," he said in a low voice and looked around to see everyone else nodding in agreement. "We will need three more men to form a quorum of ten for community prayer."

"We'll have much more than that I can assure you, Jeshua, dozens more."

When the meal ended, Simon suggested that they should both go out and meet some of the people he knew and were living nearby. They walked along the shore road, stopping to speak to a few groups of fishermen on their way home, and then turning into the main street of the town. As they were passing an inn, they saw two men in the lighted doorway dismounting from their horses. As the stable boy led the horses away, the light fell on their faces.

Jeshua gave a startled exclamation, and hearing the sound, one of the two men turned towards them.

"Is that you, Jeshua," Agrippa called out in surprise. "I thought you went back to Capernaum. What are you doing in Bethsaida?"

"I found some work here, instead," Jeshua said in a low voice.

He saw Marcus standing close behind, recognised him immediately, and tried to move away with Simon, but Agrippa grasped his arm and drew him into the inn with them leaving a puzzled Simon outside.

They requested some refreshments and sat down at a table near the entrance. Looking at Jeshua who was gazing angrily at Agrippa, Marcus found him completely changed from the young boy he remembered seeing a long time ago.

"What do you want with me, Agrippa," Jeshua said, trying to wrench his arm away.

"I want to know more about you," Agrippa said firmly. "Marcus, you remember Jeshua, your father's ward or his adopted son?"

"Yes, of course I do," Marcus admitted. "But I have not seen him for over fifteen years."

"Who was his mother, Marcus?" Agrippa demanded. "She must have been of noble birth for Joseph to have taken him under his care."

"That is for him to say, not me," Marcus said, looking at Jeshua. "My father never told me why he took an interest him. All I know is that when I was a young man Maryam, Jeshua's mother, was to be married to me but the betrothal never took place."

"And then she married a common Galilean carpenter?" Agrippa said sarcastically.

Jeshua stood up and said fiercely that this was an insult. His father was a good, kind man who loved his mother dearly and had taken good care of both of them. Better than the way Herod had taken of him and his father.

He turned to leave, but Agrippa held on to his arm and forced him to sit down again.

"There is another mystery that I want to solve, Jeshua. Although I was still a young child, I remember my father and my uncle very clearly, and how much my older brother Herod and I cried when they took them away and executed them. You are the very image of my uncle Alexander, and there must be some connection or other between you and him."

Jeshua sighed deeply and decided to tell him and Marcus the secret of his birth. He first made them promise to keep it to themselves. It was a long story, and after he finished the two men sat back in stunned silence trying to find some words to express their amazement.

"You are my cousin, then, Jeshua," Agrippa said, finally finding his voice. "My father, Aristobulus, was the younger son of Herod and Mariamne. Alexander was the eldest, so you are the actual Hasmonean heir. Alexander had two sons, Tigranes and Alexander, from his first wife Glaphyra, a Cappadocian princess, but they had to disown their Jewish descent and revert to the faith of their mother, which means that they can never be accepted by the people here as their rulers."

Marcus nodded, and said he knew what had happened to these boys.

"After Herod's death Archelaus sent Tigranes to be educated at Rome, and ten years later he was appointed King of Armenia by Augustus. Both sons of Alexander have renounced their Hasmonean birthright."

"I am also, hereby, renouncing my Hasmonean birthright, Agrippa," Jeshua said firmly. "If a Hasmonean restoration ever occurs, you or your brother Herod will be the rightful heirs. Joseph holds the marriage contract, the *ketuba*, signed by a Temple priest who performed the hasty, secret marriage between Alexander and my mother. If ever this story became known, this document might not be

317

recognised as valid, perhaps even as a forgery, and I would most probably be considered a bastard by the Sanhedrin."

"My father would have contested that," Marcus assured him. "He has close friends among the influential members in the Sanhedrin and the Jerusalem Council, and also with the Roman authorities here and in Rome."

"But I do not wish to rule," Jeshua insisted. "I want to live among the people, to share their sorrows and their joys, to be free to come and go as I please amongst them."

He looked towards the entrance and saw Simon standing there arguing with the innkeeper and pointing towards the table where he was sitting.

"You see that fisherman there," Jeshua told them. "He is worth more than all the wealthy nobility in Jerusalem. I have spent one afternoon with him and already regard him with real respect and affection."

He walked across to the doorway, waving the innkeeper away and apologising to Simon for making him wait so long.

"I just wanted to see if you were in need of any help," Simon told him. "Who are these men and what do they want of you?"

"One is Agrippa, the nephew of Antipas who employed us at Ginossar, and the other is Marcus, the son of the rich man I lived with in Jerusalem. They just wanted to ask me some questions."

Simon looked at him doubtfully, but led the way outside. By the time they returned, Philip was anxious to take Nathanael to his home and family and to return to his own house. He saw that Jeshua was looking upset and spoke gently to him.

"You can stay with me for a while until you find a place to live, Jeshua."

"But choose a place not too far from here, Jeshua," Simon said warmly. "You must come and eat with us in the evenings and meet some more of the people in this neighbourhood."

The small group of friends and neighbours in Bethsaida soon became a close band that met frequently at Simon's house to eat together and to listen to the teachings of Jeshua. Andrew carefully wrote down as much of this as he could, especially the parables and maxims. Philip once met two Greek philosophers from Gadara, who were traveling northwards to Antioch, and had stopped at the inn in Bethsaida. He brought them to meet Jeshua at Simon's house and they had a long, interesting discussion together on the comparative merits of Greek and Jewish culture and philosophy.

***

The next morning dawned cold but clear. Agrippa wanted to return as quickly as possible to Tiberias, hoping that the winter rains would wait until he arrived home. He parted from Marcus near Dan in the Huleh Valley, going eastward to Caesarea Philippi while Marcus went northeast to Damascus.

He and Marcus had talked far into the night over Jeshua and the need for secrecy over his birth. He felt responsible for his safety and welfare, and decided to keep watch over him through his agents in Galilee. Marcus also told him he would write to his father about meeting Jeshua, promising to keep him informed about his doings through his many contacts in the north.

The tetrarch, Philip, welcomed his nephew, agreed to visit his brother Antipas in the near future, and allowed him to depart immediately when he heard that Cypros was due to give birth very soon. Agrippa arrived home to find her already in the early stages of labour and within a day was overjoyed with his first-born son who was given his own name, Agrippa.

"One day you and I will rule over the Kingdom of Israel and restore the Hasmonean dynasty," he whispered to the new-born child.

Cypros heard him, and said she was sure this would happen in the near future, however dark the prospects seemed at present. A year later, a daughter was born and named Berenice after Agrippa's mother. They lived quietly and were happy with their children, and ignored the plots and schemes being hatched by Antipas and Herodias. The aging Philip had consented to a betrothal with Salome and they would be married in three or four years' time when she was sixteen or seventeen.

Marcus kept in touch with Jeshua through his many agents in Galilee and notified Agrippa regularly about him. The houses in the Ginossar estate were now ready for occupancy after the winter months. Chuza, the steward at the palace in Tiberias, would send regular supplies of food and wine to the Ginossar estate and arranged for his wife Johanna to go there once a week to keep the newly built houses clean and in good order.

Agrippa then sent a message to Jeshua to say that he was welcome to stay in the guest house of the estate whenever he wished. The caretaker would admit him when he gave his name at the gate. He also sent a large sum of money and promised to send more funds through her at his request. Jeshua used much of this money to help Simon build the prayer hall behind his house and to pay for all the necessary furnishings and two Torah scrolls for the ark.

During the weekdays, Jeshua worked for Philip in the new houses being built in Bethsaida, but he occasionally travelled to different parts of Galilee, preaching in the village synagogues or in front of large gatherings, and gaining more and more fame among the people for his wise teachings and memorable sayings. Over the next three years, he managed to cover many of the towns and villages in the Galilee, teaching mainly by simple parables so that everyone could understand his meaning.

Andrew faithfully recorded these sayings and parables, and collected a large number of them from Simon who always went with Jeshua on his weekend travels to assist and protect him. Simon had decided to retire and give up his fishing business to his partners, the Zebedee brothers, and to accompany Jesus wherever he went.

Some of these sayings were memorable:

> *Whatever you ask for in prayer, believe that you have received it, and it will be yours. When you stand praying, if you hold anything against anyone you must forgive them so that your Father in heaven may forgive you your sins.*

> *So do not worry, saying, 'What shall we eat?' or 'What shall we drink?' or 'What shall we wear? The pagans run after all these things, and your heavenly Father knows that you need them. If you seek first his kingdom and his righteousness, all these things will be yours as well. Therefore, do not worry about tomorrow, for tomorrow will worry about itself. Each day has enough trouble of its own.'*

One of his more memorable sermons was preached on a mountaintop overlooking the Sea of Galilee.

> *Blessed are the poor in spirit, for theirs is the kingdom of heaven*
> *Blessed are the pure in heart, for they shall see God*
> *Blessed are the peacemakers, for they will be called the children of God*

> *Think not that I am come to destroy the law, or the prophets.*

I am not come to destroy it but to fulfil it.
Until heaven and earth pass, not one jot or tittle shall pass from the law,
till all be fulfilled.

Jeshua attended the Sabbath day services in different synagogues and the wardens usually invited Jeshua to sit in Moses seat and give the sermon on the *haftara*, the traditional selection from the biblical prophets that corresponded in its theme to the weekly portion of the Torah.

He came one Sabbath to his hometown, Nazareth, and when invited to give the sermon, he chose a few sentences in the selection for that week which happened to be from Isaiah the prophet.

A spirit of prophecy from the Lord is upon me, because the Lord has appointed me to proclaim joy to the meek, to bind up the broken-hearted, to proclaim liberty to the captives, and the opening of the prison to them that are bound ...For the Lord has clothed me with the garments of salvation, and covered me with the robe of righteousness.

Jeshua began by saying with a smile that today Isaiah's words seem to be fulfilled in him since he also felt he had received a mission from God to the people of Israel. Some of the congregants in the synagogue immediately interrupted his sermon to accuse him of presumption and self-glory and that his words were a blasphemy.

A clamour broke out among all the people there, some saying they had always wondered about young Jeshua being one of the carpenter's sons with his fair hair and blue eyes. Others suggested maliciously that his mother was a whore or that Panthera, the handsome blond centurion who once commanded the nearby camp, who had always ogled the girls in the town after getting drunk in the tavern, had raped her. A furious crowd gathered and drove him and his brothers out of the town and even threatened to throw Jeshua off a cliff. Simon managed to rescue him from the mob and bring him safely away.

All that Jeshua said afterwards was that a prophet could never find acceptance in his hometown and that never again would he return to Nazareth, that nest of vipers! .

****

At his palatial mansion in Sepphoris, Antipas stretched contentedly, sitting on his silken couch with one arm holding a wine cup and the other embracing Herodias. She had recently received the long awaited divorce from her husband Herod Philip, his half-brother and son of the second Mariamne when her priestly family, the House of Boethus, finally agreed to grant it. He and Herodias would be married soon, but not in Galilee where the people might riot. They would go to Machaerus in the next winter season and hold the wedding there. Herodias also wanted to hold the wedding of her daughter Salome, now past sixteen, to Philip the tetrarch soon afterwards.

Another reason for his contentment was that they had just heard the latest news from Rome. When Livia died two years ago, the most powerful man in Rome, Aelius Sejanus, boldly conspired with Livilla, the widow of Tiberius' son Drusus, to overthrow the emperor and seize the imperial throne. He had already eliminated the family of Germanicus by accusing his widow Agrippina of plotting against Tiberius and exiling her and her two eldest sons. Only the youngest son, Gaius, popularly known as Caligula, took refuge with Antonia who gave him her protection.

Antonia discovered the conspiracy and immediately informed Tiberius. She also hurriedly sent Caligula to Tiberius for his safety. The angry emperor ordered the Senate to bring Sejanus and his supporters to trial. Found guilty, and summarily executed by strangulation, his body was cast down the Gemonian Stairs and was abused by the Romans for three days before being thrown into the Tiber. The butcher of Rome was dead. As for Livilla, her mother locked her up in her room until she starved to death. She then sent the twelve-year old Tiberius Gemellus, son of Drusus and Livilla, to his grandfather in Capri where Tiberius announced that his grandson and Caligula would be his joint heirs.

Now was the time, Antipas thought, to make a few bolder moves towards his ambitious goal. Tiberius may be more open to those who showed him true loyalty and support. On the other hand, Pilate was no longer on friendly terms with him. The prefect had angered the people when he commandeered funds from the Temple treasury for building the aqueduct. When he tried to set up votive shields in honour of Tiberius in the Temple, Antipas had cleverly taken the side of the people by complaining to the emperor who sent a strong rebuke to Pilate and ordered him to remove them to Herod's palace.

The only thorn in the flesh was his nephew Agrippa. He had settled down more to his duties since the birth of his two children, but he seemed to be more secretive and was less forthcoming when questioned about administrative matters. Yet as long as matters in Tiberias were well run and trade with the cities and the surrounding region was flourishing, he left him to his own devices.

When summer came around, Agrippa prepared as usual to take his annual two-month summer vacation at the Ginossar resort with Cypros and the two children. It was now fully furnished and well stocked, and the gardens and orchards were a delight. He also liked to travel up to Damascus to spend a week or two with Marcus every summer. Whenever he did, he always passed through Bethsaida and find out how Jeshua was doing. He felt a certain responsibility towards him as his cousin, and liked him for himself as well.

He had heard of all kinds of stories about him, as a miracle worker, a healer, a gifted preacher, mixing with the lowest of the low to bring a message of comfort and hope for salvation from oppression to those outcasts of society, the beggars, the robber bands, the prostitutes. Some strange stories circulated about him, his turning water into wine at Cana, or feeding thousands of hungry followers gathered on a mountain slope above Tabgha with a feast of loaves and fishes.

No doubt all this was an exaggeration of what the resourceful Simon was doing to feed the crowds gathering to hear Jeshua and his sermons which he now gave outside in the open air instead of in synagogues. Jeshua used the funds he had been sending him every month to buy food supplies from neighbouring farmers and innkeepers for distribution among the poor. He heard other stories about his gift of healing which Marcus said he had learnt from his mother, Maryam, during her long stay in Egypt. Jeshua knew about the plants and herbs she had used to cure the poorer people in Alexandria of all kinds of illnesses, and to heal seizures that many thought was a possession of devils, by holding them down and staring into their eyes until they became unconscious. When they woke up, they were calm again and behaved normally. He also knew the cures that the Essenes used for leprosy and other diseases through Ruhama, who had learnt their healing methods, and applied them in the Galilee villages to the sick and ailing.

Once a centurion stationed near Capernaum sent a message to Jeshua through his brothers, asking for his help and advice to cure a young boy servant of his. When Jeshua heard what the symptoms were, he sent back a message telling him what he should do for him. After the boy recovered, the grateful centurion donated a generous sum of money for the Capernaum synagogue.

This time, when he arrived in Bethsaida, Agrippa found Jeshua on the seashore just back from a trip across the lake, his face full of laughter and joy from a refreshing swim and a race against a fishing boat rowed by the Zebedee brothers. He had changed so much in the meantime. Agrippa noticed that his features were more pronounced, and his mouth was firmer. This was a young man in his prime, strong muscled, bronzed by the sun, handsome and erect, with flashing blue eyes. When he saw Agrippa approaching, leading his horse, he strode eagerly towards him, and took his hand in a firm grasp.

"You are come just in time for a good meal at Simon's house, Agrippa."

"I cannot stay long, Jeshua. I have to reach the inn on the Syrian border by nightfall. But I would be glad of some food and drink, and so would my horse."

"We'll give it some oats and fresh corn in the stable, if it does not mind sharing it with our mule," Jeshua said, stroking its neck with a gentle hand.

They walked on together with John and James following behind. Simon greeted them at the door and Andrew hastily set another place for Agrippa, seating him in the place of honour at the head of the table where some men were eating. They ate in almost complete silence, a little overawed by the presence of the Hasmonean prince. After the meal, Jeshua took Agrippa to see the prayer hall behind the house that they had built with his funds, and also for a private conversation with him.

"Marcus wrote to say that his father is still grieving for you, Jeshua," Agrippa said accusingly. "On his visit to Jerusalem for the Passover holiday, he found him growing frail and that his hair has gone completely white."

Jeshua gazed at him sorrowfully, with tears in his eyes, and could not find the words to express what he felt.

"He also wrote that Nicodemus is asking anxiously about you," Agrippa added, "especially about reports of the constant tensions you are having with the scribes and Pharisees in Galilee."

"Only some of them," Jeshua said. "I have been telling my followers that the scribes and Pharisees sit in Moses' seat and that whatever they say should be observed. But they place too great a burden on the people with their strict interpretations of the law, and too much emphasis on the letter of the law instead of on the spirit of it."

"I heard you had serious trouble with the congregation in Nazareth and was nearly killed by some of the extremists there. What did you say to anger them?"

"I wanted them to feel that I was bringing them the gift of God's love and hope of salvation, but they thought I was glorifying myself by comparing myself to the prophet Isaiah. One of them shamed me by calling me a bastard, said that my mother was a whore or raped by a Roman soldier."

Agrippa was infuriated and said that this showed Joseph was right about wanting the truth about Jeshua's birth and identity revealed and confirmed by a Sanhedrin ruling. He was only waiting for the right moment to do so.

Jeshua gave him a wry smile and told him something that he had discovered while talking one day to old Gorion. He had asked him whether he remembered Alexander, and Gorion told him of his princely ways and how much the people loved him. He also told him about the appearance of a man shortly after the death of Herod who resembled Alexander so closely that everyone believed him to be the prince himself risen from the dead. The man claimed that he had escaped execution through bribery, and now demanded that Augustus should recognise him as the true heir.

"And what happened then?" Agrippa asked excitedly. "Was it really him?"

"You can't fool Augustus, Gorion told me," Jeshua said with a laugh. "The man looked exactly like my father, richly dressed and behaving with all the airs and graces of a nobleman. But when he approached the emperor and held out his hand in greeting, Augustus noticed the roughened palms and the dirty fingernails, and knew at once this was not Alexander but an imposter."

Agrippa slapped the arms of his chair in delighted amusement. What a story! Then more soberly, he looked at Jeshua and realised the point he was making.

"What you are saying is that people may remember this incident and think that you are an imposter if Joseph says you are Alexander's son."

Jeshua nodded slowly and said this was only one of the reasons for his decision to leave Joseph. The other one was that he was not suited to a life of wealth and luxury, or to the world of political intrigue and claims to royal power, a world that was continually in a state of strife and war.

"I want to be a prince of peace not a prince of war," he told Agrippa. "Let Caesar rule the people and I will be content to rule their hearts and minds."

Agrippa placed his hand on Jeshua's shoulder in silent appreciation, and stood up saying he was sorry he had to go so soon. Perhaps he would find him again in Bethsaida on his way back.

"Simon and I are going to Magdala tomorrow and will be staying there until the Sabbath. We hope to get a better reception there than at Nazareth."

"Well, come and visit me in Ginossar during the summer, Jeshua. I will be there for about two months and Marcus may come for a week or so. Let us try to time it so that you come when he is there."

They went back into the house and Agrippa thanked Simon and Andrew for their kind hospitality. When his horse was brought to the door, he mounted it swiftly, waved his farewells, and turned towards the road northwards.

"I do not understand what your connection is with Agrippa," Simon said bluntly. "It cannot be just because you met him once when you were staying with Joseph in Jerusalem, or because of his efforts to release your cousin, Johanan."

"You are right, Simon," Jeshua admitted quietly. "I cannot tell you yet what it is, because it may be dangerous now to do so for me and for you as well. When the time comes, I will tell you and you alone, because I trust you."

"I would protect you with my life, Jeshua."

"I know you would, Simon. I only hope you will not need to do so."

****

The decision to go and preach in Magdala came at the invitation of an eminent Pharisee rabbi who led the services at the synagogue there. The town was now a large and wealthy commercial emporium, and many rich families had settled there. The Pharisees were dominant in and around it, building four ritual baths, a splendid synagogue, and several Torah institutions to educate children and young men.

There had been conflicting accounts about Jeshua, and the sermons he was preaching in various synagogues and outdoor gatherings. He had said clearly that he supported the teachings of the Pharisees and their charitable work among the people who in turn faithfully observed the rulings of the rabbis. On the other hand, there were several reports of his unorthodox views, of reformist tendencies.

For example, while walking with his disciples across a field on the Sabbath, one of them plucked an ear of corn to eat. When someone reported this and the rabbis accused him of breaking the law, he said that the Sabbath was for the people and not the people for the Sabbath. There were still various interpretations as to what the 'day of rest' meant. For Jeshua, rest meant rest from work, from the daily toiling grind of the week. If someone was hungry, he could pluck an ear of corn to eat, and if someone was lame, he could ride on a donkey to the synagogue.

He asked who should determine what the Bible intended by the words 'day of rest'. The Sanhedrin was always at loggerheads on the interpretation of the laws, Pharisees against Sadducees, Hillelites against Shammaites. The rulings of the Sanhedrin, the halachot, were not always obeyed in practice by everyone, because 'halacha' did not mean 'law' but rather 'a rule or customary practice' to be adopted as the norm of religious behaviour. Such rules should always be subject change or modified by general consent and adapted to the perceptions and requirements of the day.

At Magdala, Jeshua and Simon received a cordial welcome. They joined the prayers and ceremonies of the Sabbath eve with the rabbi's family, and recited all the appropriate blessings on the bread and wine. After the meal, the rabbi inquired about the sermon that Jeshua intended to preach on the following morning.

"I thought of the theme of love," Jeshua said. "Every morning we recite the Shema, the most important prayer in our liturgy. It begins with the declaration of our faith: *Hear O Israel, the Lord your God, the Lord is One!* followed by the words: *And you shall love the Lord your God with all your heart, with all your soul, and with all your might*. In my opinion, this is the true relationship between man and God. And the love of God leads to the love of all that God has created in the world, the earth, the plants, the animals, and above all mankind, our fellow men."

"Well, these would be fine words for your sermon," the rabbi said with a subtle tone of warning in his voice. "We should all love our fellow men as long as they are good and faithful men who follow the laws of Moses."

"God also loves the sinners, rabbi," Jeshua replied earnestly. "All he wants is for the sinners to repent and be forgiven. Not to be cast out and vilified."

"Perhaps sinners may be forgiven if they repent," the rabbi said. "But what about evil men, robbers and murderers, and what about debauchery and adultery. Can we love people who do such things? You should hate them and anyone who was cruel to another, who hurt innocent people out of sheer malice. Suppose someone came up to you and for no reason slapped you on the cheek, what would you do, Jeshua?"

"Turn the other cheek," Jeshua said with a laugh. "Perhaps this would make him realise his wrongdoing. But Simon here would probably slap him back."

"And so he should," the rabbi responded, and received a vigorous nod from Simon.

"All I am trying to say," Jeshua persisted, "is that we should meet the forces of evil with the forces of good and try to change it, to avert it, to reform it, first by persuasion, and then by force if necessary, but not by death, by execution. The punishment of the first murderer, Cain, for killing his brother Abel, was not death but exile, as a fugitive and vagabond wandering through the world. If we keep on preaching the values of goodwill and charity to all, evil will one day disappear from the world and there will be no more robbery, murder, debauchery or adultery."

"You are a foolish idealist, Jeshua," the rabbi told him in scathing tones. "You will learn one day to your sorrow that, as the Bible says, man's heart is evil from his very youth. You cannot change the world. You can only control it as best you can by laws and heavy punishments."

While giving his sermon on the theme of love the next day, Jeshua looked around at the congregants filling the synagogue, searching around to see if anyone seemed to understand his message. The faces were all blank, expressionless. He quoted Hillel's dictum: *Love your neighbour as yourself, and do unto others as you would them to do to you.* There was still no response. He could see that these people were stolid, self-satisfied, and well-to-do, living in a town that was becoming wealthy through industry and trade. Not like the farmers and villagers who gathered around him eager to listen to his words, faces uplifted in gladness and gratitude.

When the service ended, no one came forward to speak to him. As they all filed out, he saw the rabbi in one corner talking quietly to some older men who were apparently the community elders and the synagogue patrons who had appointed the rabbi. Perhaps they were critical of his choice of preacher. He did not wait to speak to him because Simon was waiting for him outside. As he turned to the doorway he saw a young woman trying to enter the synagogue but being prevented violently by a crowd of angry, belligerent men.

"Get away, you whore," they shouted. "You cannot enter our synagogue with your filthy feet."

Simon shouldered his way through the crowd and managed to bring the woman over the threshold and into the entrance. He stood in the doorway with his arms stretched out to the jambs on either side and his burly form filling the space between them, so than no one could pass. He glared at the men until they retreated backwards into the street.

Jeshua rushed forward to lift the woman who had fallen on the entrance mat with her long reddish gold hair covering her face. She stood up and swept it back. Dark, violet eyes gazed into his, and he was stunned by her beauty, her graceful form, and by the lovely smile she gave him as she thanked him for his help.

The rabbi came up to them and looked sternly at her.

"You are Maria, the Jezebel from the inn!" the rabbi said pointing at her. "What are you doing here in our synagogue?"

The community elders came forward as well and ordered her out at once. She drew a sharp breath, turned and rushed out, nearly falling again in her haste. Simon immediately took her arm to support her and Jeshua quickly followed to take her other arm. They tried to take her through the mob still gathered on the street, but were faced by a phalanx of men with grim faces. Some of them held stones in their hands, cursing her as a harlot, strumpet, whore, and threatening to attack her.

Jeshua strode forward and called out to them in a loud, clear voice:

"He who is without sin let him cast the first stone."

Everyone stood still, and for a minute or two there was a frozen silence. Then, one by one, the men began to move away down the street.

"We'll accompany you and see you safely to the inn," Jeshua assured her.

She shook her head and said that she could not go back there now. She had left the inn without permission when she heard that he was going to preach at the synagogue. The innkeeper might beat her for doing so, especially when he heard reports of what had happened this morning at the synagogue.

She begged them to take her with them wherever they were going. Simon and Jeshua consulted together and decided not to return to the rabbi's house where that man would accuse him of aiding sinners and prostitutes. They had to wait until the Sabbath ended, find a place to sleep, and take a boat the next morning to Bethsaida.

"It is not very far from here to Ginossar, Simon," Jeshua suddenly said, recalling the open invitation Agrippa had given him. "It is only about two miles I think at the most. We can walk there and stay overnight. Maria can come with us since there are several rooms in the guesthouse and we can each have one for ourselves. And the caretaker will provide us with food and drink."

They followed the shoreline northwards, and during their walk, Jeshua told Maria she should have known that it would be dangerous for her to go to the synagogue. She tried to explain why she had done so.

"Yesterday, I was standing outside the inn which is close to the shore, and noticed you arriving by boat. Even after all these years, I recognised you as the young man who, many years ago, defended me against my rough handling by one of the rude customers. I was only twelve at the time, but I never forgot you. I wanted so much to hear your sermon, so I stood outside the synagogue by the open door to listen to it. You spoke so beautifully about the love of God. When the service was over I waited a while till the people began leaving and then wanted to enter and speak to you."

Jeshua tried to recall that incident at the inn until it all came back to him, the frightened young girl some rough fellow tried to embrace against her will. How furious it had made him! He wondered how she came to be living and working there, and whether she had now become what they called a 'fallen woman'.

"I am not a Jezebel as the rabbi said I was" Maria said bitterly, reading his thoughts. "My parents were Greeks who came here from Sidon and were employed in the inn as kitchen workers. When I was eight, both of them died of some disease and the innkeeper took care of me until I was old enough to work for him. I have never agreed to be a prostitute, although some people think that I am. There are some prostitutes who frequent the inn where they find willing clients for their favours."

They arrived at Ginossar two hours later, and the caretaker welcomed him, saying he had received instructions to provide him with all he wished. Tired but grateful for the meal provided by the caretaker's wife, they were then taken to the guesthouse. Maria recognised the woman as a Sidonian and spoke to her in the Greek Koine language she still remembered from her childhood. Jeshua also understood the language he knew from his own childhood days in Alexandria. He asked the woman if Maria could stay with them after he and Simon left, promising to arrange matters with Chuza and Johanna, and she gladly agreed.

They spent a comfortable night in the guesthouse, and in the morning, Jeshua and Simon borrowed the estate boat to return to Bethsaida. He said he would be back a week later when Agrippa arrived with his family for the summer vacation. He left a written message for Johanna about Maria and the possibility of finding her employment on the estate, perhaps as a nursemaid for the children of Agrippa and Cypros during the summer months.

Nicodemus heard through James that Elizabeth was failing in health. Maryam had done her best to strengthen her with nourishing broths and herbal remedies, and she wrote to James that the end was near. Joseph said that when this happened, Maryam should come and live in his home. Maryam's presence would be comforting after Jeshua had left.

Although he received weekly news of Jeshua through Marcus, Joseph was not happy to hear of his doings. All this teaching and preaching would lead nowhere, and salvation for Israel could never come through prayers and good deeds. Furthermore, he was antagonising the Pharisees who would be the main supporters of a Hasmonean revival. A political solution was the only option, and now his plans for this were completely frustrated. Still, he admired the young man's faith and will power, and had always loved him for his gentle ways and innate nobility. He was truly a prince in every respect and could make an ideal ruler if he only had the strength and desire to be king.

Three years of wandering around the Galilee was surely enough to convince him that it was impossible to change the social, economic and religious establishment in the country. There were too many power plays and vested political interests in it, and the people who loved and followed him today would desert him tomorrow when they found some other inspiring leader to capture their imaginations. If he really wished to change everything that was wrong, he had to do so from the top down, with ruling powers, and not from the bottom up, with the lower classes.

In his letter that week, Marcus said that Jeshua was continuing with his work in Bethsaida, and his itinerary preaching among the people in Galilee. He also took the weekly boat Philip sent from Bethsaida to Tiberias with building supplies so that he could see a young woman called Maria, whom he had saved from stoning by a mob accusing her of harlotry. Jeshua had persuaded Cypros to hire her as a nursemaid for the children during the summer months until he could find a safe place for her.

Maria was glad to be with Cypros and the children during the summer and when they returned to Tiberias she went back with them as their permanent governess. I think Jeshua has fallen in love with her, and may even decide to marry her. She is very beautiful, and seems to adore

Jeshua. Cypros is very pleased and satisfied with her care of the children, and they are happy with her. Little Agrippa is a year older than Berenice his sister, yet she takes the lead while he follows like a docile lamb.

Joseph felt certain that if Jeshua married this young woman, his fate would be with the lowborn and the outcasts instead of being with the high born. All his efforts had been in vain, and he now gave up any further hope of his return to Jerusalem and to him.

****

As summer turned into winter, the entire household of Antipas in Sepphoris began moving to Machaerus. He insisted that his nephew and future brother-in-law accompany them and attend the wedding, and Agrippa reluctantly agreed. As soon as he arrived at the fortress, he went to visit Johanan in his prison cell and was glad to find him still strong in mind and body.

"I know now about Jeshua and his Hasmonean parentage," Agrippa told him. "But he has renounced it and is now traveling among the people, teaching and preaching, and also healing the sick. I believe he will soon have as many followers as you have had."

Johanan's dark eyes came alive and he asked Agrippa to give Jeshua a personal and confidential message from him, which he hastily scratched on a pottery shard in Aramaic. Agrippa took it, wondering what it said. He did not know Aramaic, but he could not show it to anyone since it was confidential.

The wedding took place the next day with loud merriment and feasting that extended far into the evening. By midnight, wearied with it all, Agrippa retired to bed and fell asleep. But a few hours later, a frightened guard, the one who was in personal charge of Johanan, shook him awake. Shivering with cold and rising fury, he listened to a tale of horror.

Antipas had become increasingly drunk, and Herodias decided to go down to the prison cell in all her wedding finery to mock Johanan. When she returned, she saw Salome dancing in front of Antipas, while he was clapping and cheering her on, promising to give her all she desired for pleasing him so much.

In a trembling voice filled with pain and anguish, the guard told Agrippa what happened next.

"Herodias told her daughter to ask Antipas for Johanan's head, and although Antipas was hesitant, he felt he could not deny Salome after his promise to her. When Johanan was executed by order of the tetrarch, Herodias demanded that they bring his head to her on a platter. That woman is a she-devil!"

Agrippa pulled on his robe, rushed out towards the bedchamber of his uncle and shook the snoring Antipas until he awoke.

"You will be damned forever, you and my accursed sister," he shouted at him in frenzied anger. "This is the end of my service to you as well. I shall be leaving Tiberias tomorrow with my family and never return."

He arrived in Tiberias very late that day after having ridden at a devilish pace from Machaerus, and found Jeshua on the shore waiting to go back to Bethsaida. It was agonising for both of them when he told him about Johanan's execution. He held Jeshua in a tight embrace while he cried and sobbed loudly in despair. As they sat down together on the wooden dock, Agrippa said that Johanan had sent him a message, but it was in Aramaic so he did not know what it said.

On the pottery shard, it was written: *Are you the one who is to come, or shall we look for another?*

Printed in the USA
CPSIA information can be obtained
at www.ICGtesting.com
CBHW052109151023
1341CB00023B/83

9 781398 483514